IN THE BEDROOM

She reached the bed, and he stood, wrapping his arms around her. "You are sure?"

"Yes." She nodded and a smile grew on her beautiful face. "I am absolutely certain. I sincerely hope you know what to do."

He chuckled lightly. "Yes." Everything he'd ever learned would go into pleasing her. "I do." He took in the ties on her robe. His fingers itched to undo all of them. "May I?"

Alice nodded. "Yes. I am a little nervous."

That was understandable. "Tell me if I do anything you don't like, and I will stop. If you change your mind, I will stop."

She shook her head. "I do not want to change my mind. I want to be yours and for you to be mine forever . . ."

Books by Ella Quinn

The Marriage Game
THE SEDUCTION OF LADY PHOEBE
THE SECRET LIFE OF MISS ANNA MARSH
THE TEMPTATION OF LADY SERENA
DESIRING LADY CARO
ENTICING MISS EUGENIE VILLARET
A KISS FOR LADY MARY
LADY BERESFORD'S LOVER
MISS FEATHERTON'S CHRISTMAS PRINCE
THE MARQUIS SHE'S BEEN WAITING FOR

The Worthingtons
THREE WEEKS TO WED
WHEN A MARQUIS CHOOSES A BRIDE
IT STARTED WITH A KISS
THE MARQUIS AND I
YOU NEVER FORGET YOUR FIRST EARL
BELIEVE IN ME

The Worthington Brides
THE MARRIAGE LIST
THE HUSBAND LIST
THE GROOM LIST

The Lords of London
THE MOST ELIGIBLE LORD IN LONDON
THE MOST ELIGIBLE VISCOUNT IN LONDON
THE MOST ELIGIBLE BRIDE IN LONDON

Novellas
MADELEINE'S CHRISTMAS WISH
THE SECOND TIME AROUND
I'LL ALWAYS LOVE YOU
THE EARL'S CHRISTMAS BRIDE

Published by Kensington Publishing Corp.

The Groom List

ELLA QUINN

THE WORTHINGTON BRIDES

ZEBRA BOOKS
Kensington Publishing Corp.
www.kensingtonbooks.com

ZEBRA BOOKS are published by

Kensington Publishing Corp.
900 Third Avenue
New York, NY 10022

First Printing: July 2024
ISBN-13: 978-1-4201-5450-4
ISBN-13: 978-1-4201-5451-1 (eBook)

10 9 8 7 6 5 4 3 2 1

Printed in the United States of America

Chapter One

April 1821, Cleveland Castle

Gifford, Earl of St. Albans strode into his father's study. "You wanted to see me?"

The Duke of Cleveland had a rare sheepish look on his face. This usually occurred after Giff's mother had persuaded Papa that one of his long-held beliefs was wrong and needed to change. Had she convinced him to give Giff the heir's estate he wanted to control before he married? He couldn't think of another reason his father would send for him this close to departing to Town.

"Yes." Papa moved a small, wrapped package from one side of the massive oak desk to the middle of the desk between them. "You know I want you to look for a wife this Season?"

It wasn't the estate. Disappointment almost made Giff leave the room. "I agreed."

"Indeed." Papa focused on the package and nudged it closer to Giff. "You will need these. Your mother pointed out that it would be . . . ah . . . that you would be more eligible if you were the Marquis of St. Albans." He indicated the package. "Those are your new calling cards."

Giff stifled his disappointment. It wasn't the estate, but

it was something. Papa had been made to wait until he was married to be elevated to the courtesy title of marquis. Giff took the package. He'd like to know what argument his mother had made. "Thank you, sir."

"We will meet you in Town in a few days. Your mother is planning a ball and other activities."

Where eligible young ladies would be available for Giff to meet in the hope he'd like one of them enough to wed her. "Please thank Mamma for me. I'm sure the title will help."

"I still don't understand why it's so important. Earl or marquis, you're still the heir to the dukedom."

Giff shrugged. "Who can understand how ladies think."

Papa rose and held out his hand. "Have a good trip up to Town."

Giff took his father's hand and shook it. "I'll see you soon. And thank you. I'm sure Mamma is correct about the title."

"She usually is," Papa grumbled.

Giff nodded in sympathy. Once, several years ago, he'd decided to challenge his mother. He never did it again. "I'll see you in Town."

When he had gained the corridor, he grinned to himself, giving silent thanks to her, and headed to the hall. Gunn, his valet, had already left and would meet him at the George in Darlington where they'd spend the night before starting the almost week-long journey to Town.

Six days later, he entered Cleveland House on Park Lane. Not quite one hundred years old, the house was fancifully built in three sections with half-rounded facades that reminded him of towers. The front consisted of long windows with balconies on the upper floors. The inside had two wings. One built especially for the heir, his family, and servants. Due to some forethought on the part of his great-great-grandmother, the house had a circular drive in the front with gardens to the sides, and a large garden in the back. The stables were located on the other side of a high stone wall. The garden was so secluded one could almost forget one was in the metropolis. When Giff married, he and his family would live in the heir's wing whenever they were in Town. The rest of the year, they'd reside at Whippoorwill Manor near St. Albans. That was the property he would control after he wed. By the end of this Season if he found his bride.

Giff strolled into his parlor and glanced through the cards on his desk. Some were invitations. Others were personal cards left by friends who had already arrived in Town. One of them from a school chum he hadn't seen for a few years, John, Marquis of Montagu, caught Giff's attention. It would be good to see Montagu again. The last time had been at his father's funeral. Perhaps they could take a ride tomorrow morning before there were too many people in the Park. Giff pulled a piece of paper from the drawer and scribbled a note, then tugged the bell-pull.

A footman entered the room. "Yes, my lord."

Griff handed the man the message. "Have this taken to Montagu House."

"Straightaway, my lord."

After the servant left, he wandered into his bed chamber. His evening kit was already laid out. As was his custom, he would dine at home his first evening back. Aside from that, he needed to develop a strategy to find a wife. In addition to depending on his mother, that was. In the past he'd ridden his horse during the Grand Strut. But now he should consider taking his curricle. He glanced at the ormolu mantel clock. It was just after five o'clock. He had time to visit the stables before changing for dinner. And it was better to do it now than after he'd bathed.

Muffled noises from the dressing room informed him

his valet was there. "Gunn, I'm going to the stables. I'll be back within the hour."

"Very well, my lord. I'll have yer bath ready."

Giff grinned. All the household servants in London and most of them at Cleveland Castle might be English, but his mother had insisted his personal servants be good, reliable Scotsmen from the various parts of her family. Another battle his father had lost.

An hour later, after having been rebuffed by the stable-master, who insisted on having Giff's carriage sent around, he was dressed for an early dinner. He'd been pleased that his curricle had been newly painted, and the cushions had been replaced. He didn't even have to ask whose idea that was. Mamma was going to do her best to see him wed this Season.

The next morning, after having received confirmation of his invitation to Montagu, Giff rode to Montagu House and found his friend on the pavement next to his horse. "Good morning."

"Good morning to you." Montagu grinned. "Thank you for your note. It's been so many years since I've been to Town, I wasn't sure how to begin."

Giff studied his friend. "Wife hunting?"

"Exactly." Montagu grimaced.

"As am I. Perhaps we can help each other." Although Giff really didn't think he'd need much help convincing the lady he chose to marry him. He was, as his father had said, the heir to a dukedom, not bad looking, and had been told he made love charmingly.

Montagu mounted and gave Giff a dubious look. "How, if you've never searched for a wife before?"

"Ah." He turned Horace, his horse, toward the Park.

"This might be the first time I'm willing to be leg shackled, but it's not my first time enticing a female. Surely a young lady will be much the same. I imagine it will be even easier than with a more experienced woman. Not only that, but how many Mammas would want their daughter to reject the heir to a dukedom?"

"I suppose you're right." Montagu rode next to Giff. "Young ladies are disposed to do what their families wish."

At least English ladies were. His mother and older sisters hadn't had that attitude. But that was the Scot's side coming out. In a way, it was a pity. He'd like a lady more like his mother. Come to think of it, the lady he chose would have to show a strong strength of will in order to please his father. "We shall see."

Lady Alice Carpenter stared at the list she and her sisters had made.

Intelligent
Kind
Like house animals
Like children
Make us laugh, and think we are funny
Interested in the plight of the poor and unfortunate
Must support us in our charities and other ventures
Passable looking
Allow us to be ourselves
Be able to support a family
Must love us in return

Something was missing. Unfortunately, she could not think what it was. She put the list back in the drawer. It would come to her sooner or later. At the moment, she must meet her sisters for their ride in the Park. It was the first time they had been allowed to go with only a groom in attendance.

As usual, she was the first one to arrive. Robertson, her groom and a former soldier, cupped his hands to help her mount Galyna, her Cleveland Bay. True to her name, she calmly stood until Alice's sisters, Lady Eleanor Carpenter, Alice's twin, and Lady Madeline Vivers arrived a couple of minutes later.

Alice turned her mare toward the end of the square. "Shall we go?"

"Yes," her sisters said in unison.

Six years ago, Alice and Eleanor's eldest sister, Grace, who had fought for and won guardianship of them and their five brothers and sisters, had married Madeline's brother, Matheus, the Earl of Worthington, thereby combining all eleven of the brothers and sisters into one family. Before their marriage, because just seeing the way Grace and Matt looked at each other they all knew the two were going to wed, they had decided they would refer to each other as brothers and sisters without regard to last names or blood ties. One look at Madeline, and Alice and Eleanor silently agreed that the three of them would be triplets, and they included her in everything they did. Still, Eleanor's bond with her twin was as strong as ever. Shortly thereafter, Charlotte, their next eldest sister, Dotty, her closest friend, and Louisa, Madeline's eldest sister, wed. They were now the Marchioness of Kenilworth, the Marchioness of Merton, and the Duchess of Rothwell respectively. The next one to wed was Augusta. She was now Lady Phineas Carter-Woods. All of them were extremely happy in their marriages. Alice wanted the same for herself and her sisters. Fortunately, Matt had told them that as long as a gentleman was eligible, the decision would be up to them.

As they trotted to the Park, it was clear that spring had indeed sprung. Trees were green with small leaves, and the forsythias were already bright yellow. Even daffodils and crocuses were coming up.

Eleanor glanced around, smiling. "I cannot believe we are finally here."

Alice was not able to resist trying out the bored drawl she had been practicing. "We have been here for years."

"You know what she means." Madeline cast a glance at the sky. "We are finally making our come outs. It seems as if we have been waiting for years."

"We have been waiting for years." Eleanor grinned. "So have Matt and Grace."

Alice would not have described it as waiting. "You mean they have been dreading it for years."

Eleanor met Alice's gaze. As much as Grace had been preparing them for it, if they wed this Season their lives and Madeline's would be very different than before. It was strange to consider the changes.

"At least we will not be without assistance." Madeline smiled brightly. "For a very long time, Matt has been saying that it is "all hands on deck."

Alice laughed. Madeline had mimicked his stern command perfectly. What was interesting was Matt was the uncontested leader of the family that now included one duke and two marquises. All of whom had already arrived in Town. Only their sister Augusta, who had promised to return for their come out, her husband, and their eldest brother Charlie, Earl of Stanwood, had not yet appeared. They had been traveling on the Continent for several years. Alice hoped they arrived home soon. Augusta and Charlie had promised they would.

Alice and her sisters raced to a large oak tree then ambled around the Serpentine. Almost unconsciously, Alice followed her twin's lead and started Galyna back toward the gate.

"Why are we turning?" Madeline sounded surprised.

"I am hungry." Eleanor said. "By the time we are home, we will have just enough time to wash and change before going to breakfast, and . . ." She paused. "I wonder who they are."

"Who?" Madeline peered around Eleanor.

Alice leaned forward to be able to see around Madeline.

"Do not stare. They could see us." Eleanor's sharp tone caused Madeline and Alice to straighten. "There were two gentlemen riding just off to the side. They were galloping."

Madeline leaned forward again. "What did they look like?"

"They both had reddish hair, but of different hues. Well-dressed. One rode a black horse, and the other horse was gray."

Madeline's brows came together. "I wonder if they are the type of gentlemen who will be introduced to us."

"Only time will tell," Eleanor replied as they rode through the gate and trotted up Upper Grosvenor Street.

A boy running out into the street waving his hands startled Alice. Eleanor's horse shied, but she was able to bring her under control. What had the child been thinking, or had he? Whichever it was, it was a stupid trick.

Alice moved next to her twin. "Eleanor, are you all right?"

Her face was pale but determined. "I am fine."

Alice was about to suggest they question the boy, but Eleanor shook her head.

Jemmy, her groom, rode up. "That weren't no accident, my lady. He was standing quiet until he saw you."

"Thank you, Jemmy. You have confirmed my thoughts. Come, Adela, let's go home," Eleanor spoke to her horse.

Why would anyone want to scare Eleanor? They wasted no time getting home. As soon as they reached Worthington House, their grooms came to take the mares.

"Good morning."

Alice was glad to see Charlotte and Louisa strolling toward the house holding their older children's hands. Charlotte, Louisa, Dotty, and Grace all had children in the five-year-old range.

"You must be joining us for breakfast." Alice hugged the children.

"We're going to spend the day with Gideon and Elizabeth," Constance, Charlotte's daughter, named Matt and Grace's elder children.

Constance took Alice's hand. "We want to see Posy and Zeus too."

Posy and Zeus were Great Danes. Matt brought home Zeus after Duke had died and then Daisy died a year later, and Posy came to live with them. Yet, while Duke and Daisy had spent most of their time with Alice, Eleanor, and Madeline, Zeus and Posy belonged more to Elizabeth and Gideon. When they weren't trying to guard Edward and Gaia, Grace's eighteen-month-old twins, from bath time that was.

Alice made her way to her chamber. She, Eleanor, and Madeline had received separate bedchambers and shared a parlor that had been named The Young Ladies Parlor.

Bertram, Alice's maid, was supervising the filling of

the bathtub when Alice entered her bedroom. "Thank you. We have family joining us for breakfast."

"So I was told." Bertram tested the heat of the bathwater then turned toward the footman. "Thank you. This is perfect." Once they'd left, she helped Alice out of her riding habit. "It will only get busier from here."

Alice sank into the tub. "Very true." She considered telling her dresser about the gentlemen, but what was there to say? That they had different shades of red hair and looked to be gentlemen? She washed and stood to be rinsed. "I am looking forward to our first entertainments. Have you heard anything about our brothers or Lady Phinn arriving?"

"Master Walter and Master Phillip will be here for Easter. I'm sorry, my lady. I have been told nothing about Lord Stanwood or Lady Phineas."

Alice tried not to be disappointed. They had promised to be here, and they would be. She just wished she knew when they would arrive.

She gained in the corridor a second before her sisters. Suddenly, there were squeals of delight from the hall. It had to be them! And just in time! She exchanged quick looks with Eleanor and Madeline, and they rushed down the stairs.

Chapter Two

Alice stood back as the younger members of the family greeted Augusta, Phinn, and Charlie. Elizabeth had been a year old, and Gideon had been two when they left. But Grace and Alice's other brothers and sisters had read their letters to the children. Their sisters Theo, now fourteen, and Mary, eleven, were hugging the prodigals. Augusta's Great Dane waited patiently to be acknowledged. Alice vaguely remembered the dog being mentioned in one of her sister's letters.

Mary pointed at the Dane. "Whose dog is that and what is its name?"

"This is Minerva." Augusta indicated a box on the floor. "Etienne is in there. We found them in Vienna. Minerva's original owner died, and Phinn bought Etienne for me."

"It was one of my attempts to get her to marry me." Phinn smiled ruefully.

He had followed her to Europe when she went to travel with cousins.

"We are very happy to have you all back home." Grace exchanged a glance with Matt, who was smiling broadly.

"And in good time too," Matt said as he started walking

toward the breakfast room. "Will you stay with us, or have you made other arrangements?"

Augusta tucked her hand in the crook of her husband's arm. "Charlie has asked us to reside with him for the Season."

"How did you all manage to arrive at the same time?" Eleanor asked.

Charlie held Grace's chair then sat on her right. "I was in Spain when I ran into them on their way home. I decided it was time for me to return as well."

"What happened to your bear-leader?" Matt asked.

"He wanted to explore Europe for a while longer," Charlie said, accepting a cup of tea. "Since I was with family members, we agreed to part ways."

"I am glad everything worked out so well." Eleanor said. "Albeit, knowing Augusta, that does not surprise me at all."

"Oh, no. I cannot take credit." Augusta cut a piece of toast in half. "Cousin Prudence and Mr. Boman, Phinn's secretary, usually make the arrangements."

"They married not long after we did. They'll be visiting their families for a month or so," Phinn added.

Charlie took a slice of rare beef from a platter. "Speaking of secretaries, I must find one. I must also take my seat in the Lords."

"Well, then." Matt nodded. "I am happy to help you with both tasks."

Augusta glanced at Eleanor, Madeline, and Alice. "I suppose your first event is Lady Bellamny's soirée for young ladies."

"Almost," Eleanor said. "Lady Exeter's sister-in-law, Penelope, is coming out as well. We have been invited to tea with her and two of her friends."

"I would like to accompany you." Augusta's eyes

smiled. “I would love to see Dorie Exeter again. We have written to each other over the years, and she knows I’ll be here soon.”

“Or now,” Madeline commented.

Alice exchanged a glance at her twin. And they couldn’t stop from laughing. Charlotte and Louisa were silently laughing as well.

“Yes, now.” Augusta grinned. “While we have you all here, Phinn and I have an announcement. We are expecting a baby in September.”

“That is wonderful news,” Grace exclaimed.

“More cousins!” Elizabeth said.

As everyone congratulated their sister and brother-in-law. Alice caught Eleanor’s and Madeline’s eyes. If they married this Season, by this time next year they could be mothers. The only question was who would they wed?

Giff and Montagu arrived at the Park as three young ladies on varying colors of Cleveland Bay mares were departing. “We need to discover a way to meet them.”

“If they’re making their come outs, we will not be able to avoid it,” Montagu commented.

That was true. The question was at what level of Polite Society did they reside. Although, by the style of their riding habits and the quality of their horses, Giff surmised they were, like him, in the *haut ton*. If so, there would be no question of eligibility. “I need a lady who will be acceptable to my father.” Giff couldn’t help scowling. His father’s idiosyncrasies made his hunt more difficult. “Excellent bloodlines are important.” Yet, that wouldn’t be hard. “She must also be intelligent and not afraid to stand up to him.” Those weren’t qualities thick on the ground. In fact, he knew he'd have trouble finding a lady who would show her true self during the Season. "He detests cowards."

"I'm surprised he did not make a match for you." His friend had obviously not thought the matter through.

"Wouldn't have worked." Even if Giff's father had tried it, his mother would have been against it. "Any lady who would do what her father or mother said wouldn't have enough strength of character to be a daughter of his."

"I don't envy you your search," Montagu said.

Neither did Giff. "I'll find her. And when I do, I'll do everything in my power to make sure she marries me."

His friend raised his brows. "I daresay it will not be that hard for either of us. We're titled, not bad looking, and wealthy."

"Speak for yourself," Giff grumbled. "Until I wed, I have only what my father gives me. I just hope I meet someone who doesn't care about a love match. Messy things, those."

"I agree." Montagu practically shuddered. "My sister didn't care to have one, but they seem to get on well enough." They rode in silence for a minute or two, until he said. "Did you say your parents were in Town?"

"They arrive tomorrow." That reminded Giff that his time would no longer be his own. "Your mother and sister?"

"Got here yesterday. M'sister's at her town house, but Mamma is staying with me."

He was glad for Montagu that his mother had come to Town. "That will be helpful. If you decide you do like a lady, she will be able to arrange a party for the theater or some other event."

"I hadn't thought of that, but you're right." He sounded as if he hadn't realized that gentlemen could not host entertainments that included ladies.

"They can also tell you which events to attend." It

suddenly occurred to Giff that he was not in the habit of attending events with young ladies. "I don't have a clue which entertainments have the most eligible ladies."

"In that case, I will rely on her." Montagu appeared resigned. "As long as she doesn't try to matchmake."

Giff almost laughed out loud, but that wouldn't be helpful. "I'm not sure mothers know how not to matchmake. Mine certainly doesn't."

"This is going to be a long few months." Giff hoped not. He wanted this wife hunting to be over and done with. "I'm hungry," Montagu said. "Would you like to break your fast with me? I've instructed my cook I shall eat early, even in Town."

"Thank you." Giff could have kissed the man. The truly bad thing about living at his parents' house for the Season was that he was not yet allowed to occupy the heir's wing and had to adhere to his parent's breakfast schedule. "There won't be anything but toast to eat at my house for another two hours."

"In that case, you're welcome to take your potluck with me anytime you wish."

"Thank you." That was a relief. He'd been trying to work out a way to eat earlier on something more than toast and cheese. "I'll take you up on your offer."

They arrived at Montagu House and Giff followed his friend into the breakfast room. The aroma of food made his stomach grumble. Fortunately, no one seemed to notice. He followed Montagu to the sideboard and started filling his plate. This is what he'd order served in the mornings and at the appropriate hour. A pot of tea had been set on the table. They took their seats and began eating.

"My lord," a servant that could only be a butler handed Montagu a note. "This is from Lady Lytton."

"Thank you, Lumner." Montagu opened the seal and scanned the short missive. "I've been invited to m'sister's to join them for dinner. If you like, I'll ask if you can come as well."

Giff swallowed. All help was welcome. The more ladies he met, the more choices he'd have. "Do you think she'll know some eligible ladies?"

"Even if she doesn't, she'll be happy to help." Montagu sipped his tea. "I'll send a note around asking."

"Thank you." Giff resumed eating. He'd have to look at the invitations he'd received. But, quite frankly, he didn't think any of them would be worth his time. He needed young ladies looking to wed, not widows and high-flyers.

The next morning St. Albans met Montagu to go riding again. He'd like to get another look at the ladies he saw yesterday. The problem was gaining an introduction. No one else that could possibly know them and knew him as well was up and out that early.

"It is too bad you cannot attend Parliament," Montagu said, shocking Giff so much he almost spewed out his tea.

What the devil? "Why do you say that?"

"I was at a meeting at Worthington House yesterday. Several gentlemen I met have wives who will hold social events this Season. Of course, you know Turley. I believe even Littleton is supposed to be in Town this year. But I also met Exeter, who is also a friend of Turley's, and, of course, Worthington as well as some other peers. If you were a member, you would come to know the gentlemen more easily."

"Ah." St. Albans considered his friend's statement. It made a lot of sense. "For some reason, I hadn't thought of our friends' spouses holding entertainments. Silly of me really. Of course they would. They are part of the *ton,* and this is the Season after all." They rode to the Serpentine.

There was only one serious and insurmountable problem with what his friend had said. "I hope not to become a peer for a number of years yet. As much as m'father irritates me at times, I do not wish him dead."

"There is that." Montagu sounded sad, and Giff remembered that his father had died only a few years ago. "I hope you get your wish."

"As do I." Giff would be happier being the heir as long as he could have some real responsibility. "There they are again. The ladies. They're leaving." He was closer this time and could see that one had dark hair and the other two had blond hair. They looked almost exactly alike, but somehow different. The one on the far end caught his eye as a shaft of light shone on her. There was something about her. A quality he could not put into words. If he was a poet, he'd say that she had hair the color of the sun and a complexion like fine cream. But he wasn't, and that didn't capture what drew him to her. He was now certain he'd be introduced to her at some point. He was positive her family ran in the same circles as his. Or at least their mothers would.

"I wonder who they are," Montagu mused softly.

"We're bound to find out at some point." Giff hoped it was soon. He was thankful his mother arrived today. Montagu had been so serious about wanting a wife who hadn't a thought in her head that Giff decided to have some fun. "But it occurred to me late yesterday that if you want a lady who is a bit dim, you might want to appear the same yourself. Otherwise she could be wary of you."

At first Montagu appeared startled, then it was clear he was taking the bait. "That is exactly what I will do. Thank you for the hint."

"Anything to help a friend." Oh, good God! He was actually going to do it. This ought to be interesting.

Again, Giff joined Montagu for breakfast.

"Littleton was right. This ham is excellent." Montagu cut another piece.

"Did he tell you what he feeds them?" This was something Giff could do once he was given his estate.

Montagu swallowed. "Chestnuts."

"I'll have to suggest it to m'father." Maybe that would hurry the process along. "Have you visited Weston yet?"

"No. He has my measurements. My valet sent over my requirements. You?"

"I have an appointment later this morning. I like to go myself. It gives me something to do."

Montagu frowned. "Will your father not give you any responsibility at all?"

"Not until I'm wed." Giff drank the rest of his tea and rose. "I must be off. By the time I bathe and change, I will have to be at Weston's."

"Of course. I'll see you out."

As they strode to the door, Giff wondered if his mother might have some suggestions of things to keep him busy. In the meantime, he had his appointment at Weston's and would go through his invitations. After he'd been fitted for a few new suits, he strolled down Bond Street, then over to Bruton Street, and Piccadilly. When it occurred to him he was looking for ladies he could be introduced to, specifically one lady, he went home. It was a sad state of affairs when one was reduced to roaming the streets. After luncheon, he went to his desk and read through the cards. It was as he suspected, none of them were for events where young ladies would be. The rest of the afternoon was spent visiting Angelo's and Jackson's. But even they were thin of company. Fortunately, he arrived home as his mother's and father's personal servants along with the baggage were disembarking from the coach. That meant his parents would be here in an hour. Not for Mamma a hall filled with luggage. She wanted everything put away before she stepped into the house. Giff left a message to be notified as soon as their coach was sighted and was in the hall to greet them.

"Mamma, Papa, how was your journey?" He hugged his mother and shook his father's hand.

"Excellent," Mamma said as she removed her bonnet. "The roads were dry, and, of course, we only stay at the inns where we are known."

"What have you been doing since you arrived?" Papa asked.

"I had a card waiting from Montagu." Giff told them about their rides, but not the ladies.

"I had heard his father died," Mamma commented.

"Yes. He's here looking for a wife. He was never on the Town. We have decided to help one another."

Papa raised a brow. "That's the blind leading the blind."

Giff couldn't argue with that. Instead he gave his most ingratiating smile. "That is the reason our mothers are here as well."

Mamma graciously inclined her head. "Indeed it is. Come along with me. I expect to have received several invitations that should interest you." She glanced at their butler. "Ardley, I'd like tea in my parlor."

"Yes, your grace."

Giff followed his mother to her parlor and took a seat in front of her desk.

She donned a pair of spectacles and started going through a surprisingly large stack of cards. Tea arrived with sandwiches and biscuits. He helped himself and waited while she sorted the cards into three stacks.

Mamma placed her hand on one stack and glanced up. "These are invitation to entertainments where you will be able to meet eligible ladies."

"Excellent." Then his curiosity got the better of him. "What are the other two?"

Her hand moved to the stack on the right. "These are purely political events. Naturally, you may attend if you wish." She indicated the pile on the left. "These are from my friends. I will attend the events alone." She lifted one reddish brow. "Did you, by chance, receive any helpful invitations?"

Not unless she thought an orgy would be useful. "No. I have declined all the ones I received."

"I must say I am not surprised." She pulled the middle stack to her. "Most of these events will not take place until after Easter. However, there are a few balls, two Venetian Breakfasts, one musical evening, and a soirée." She took a breath. "Normally I do not approve of soirées for someone attempting to find a spouse, but this one is at Lady Thornhill's. It should be quite interesting."

"I will attend all of them." In fact, he'd go anywhere his mother suggested.

"In that case, I shall have my dresser provide a list to your valet." She pursed her lips. "It might be helpful if you were to attend a few morning visits as well. You will also want to invite any ladies in whom you are interested to ride in the Park."

Now was the time to acknowledge he had seen his carriage. "I thank you for refurbishing my curricle."

"It was my pleasure." Mamma smiled. "I enjoyed the process so much I decided to brighten up my landau." She glanced at the clock. "It is time to dress for dinner. I will see you in the drawing room."

"Until then." Giff rose. He'd have a wife sooner than later. He was sure of it.

Chapter Three

This evening was Lady Bellamny's soirée for young ladies coming out. Alice had heard about it from her older sisters. When Charlotte and Louisa had attended, Lady Bellamny had intimidated not only them, but the other ladies as well. But Alice had known her ladyship for so long she did not think she would be afraid of Lady Bellamny at all.

A knock sounded on her door, and it opened. "Are you ready?" Madeline asked.

"Yes." Alice took one last look in the pier looking-glass. This was their first adult event in Town, and she was happy to see she actually looked like an adult. Her hair was arranged simply in a high knot with curls framing her face. A yellow ribbon with seed pearls was wrapped around the knot and seed pearls were scattered across the bodice of her yellow silk gown. A Norwich shawl covered her shoulders. Nodding to herself, she picked up her reticule. "I am ready."

Grace was in the hall when they arrived and fixed each of them with a stern look. "I understand you have known Lady Bellamny for several years, but tonight is a bit different. You must act as if you are meeting her for the first time. Think of it as a test."

A test. That is what Charlotte had called Lady Bellamny's soirée. Louisa had said she felt as if she were a horse being inspected.

"It sounds daunting," Madeline said.

"It does," Eleanor replied.

They were both right, but Alice knew they had been prepared. "We will do well."

Her sisters nodded in agreement.

When they arrived at her ladyship's house, the line of carriages quickly discharged their passengers and moved away smartly. Footmen escorted the ladies to the door, not allowing anyone to linger on the pavement. From what Alice had heard about the long line of carriages at most events, this seemed like a very good idea. "That is efficient."

"What is?" Eleanor asked.

"Having servants to move the guests into the house."

Her twin glanced out just as they reached the front of the town house. "It is."

In no time at all they were greeting Lady Bellamny, who stared at them as if she had never met them before. One by one they made their curtseys. Alice gauged the depth of her curtsey to show respect and take into consideration their respective ranks.

When she rose, her ladyship's black eyes were twinkling. "Elegant, but I would expect nothing less from you, my dear. Mingle and meet some of the other ladies."

She joined Madeline and Eleanor off to the side to wait for Grace.

Lady Bellamny's lips curved as she greeted Grace. "Grace, once again you are to be commended. I suspect they will do exceptionally well this Season, and the gentlemen will think of something silly to call them. I suppose the entire family is here."

"They are indeed." She inclined her head. "Augusta arrived today as well."

Her ladyship's eyes widened. "Excellent. I cannot wait to talk to her about her adventures."

Grace left her ladyship and came to them. "You all did very well. Now you can relax a little. You already know the Lady Patronesses of Almack's. Most of them will be here this evening." She strolled with them into the first of a series of rooms connected by open pocket doors. "I will see you later."

Alice scanned the first drawing room. "I suppose we should go meet some of the other ladies."

"I am glad we have each other," Madeline said.

"As am I," Eleanor agreed. "But Alice is right. We should come to know other ladies too."

They passed one young lady who was dabbing her eyes with a handkerchief. The girl's mother or sponsor had an aggravated look on her face. "Melissa, stop tearing up. You did quite well."

"Thank you." Her voice was shaky. "I am terrified of Lady Bellamny."

"That is the point. The only thing more difficult will be meeting the Lady Patroness when you attend Almack's."

"Poor Melissa," Madeline whispered to Alice.

She nodded. "I am glad we already know most of the Grand Dames."

"That is probably the reason Grace has taken us out in her carriage during the Promenade," Eleanor said.

They found their other sisters and chatted with some ladies they had met before and introduced themselves to ladies they had not known. The time passed swiftly, and before Alice knew it supper was announced. Louisa found them and led them to a long table that had been set up. Before supper was over, Matt and their brothers-in-law joined them at the table.

As the meal was ending, a gentleman approached. "Good evening, my lords."

"And to you." Matt obviously knew the man. "Who are you fetching?"

"My mother." The gentleman glanced toward another table and inclined his head before turning back to Matt, obviously wanting to be introduced.

He appeared resigned. "I may as well make you known to those of my family you do not know. I believe you have met the gentlemen . . ." He motioned to Alice and her sisters. "Eleanor, Madeline, and Alice, may I present Lord Montagu? Montagu, my sisters, Lady Eleanor Carpenter, Lady Madeline Vivers, and Lady Alice Carpenter."

Lord Montagu bowed. "My ladies, it is a pleasure."

They inclined their heads. Eleanor stared at him for a long moment. "Are you the gentleman who rides a black horse in the Park most mornings?"

He smiled and bowed again. "I am."

"Perhaps you will join us some morning." Eleanor's brows drew together as if she had just thought of a problem. "If you get up earlier, that is."

"I am certain I can manage that, my lady." He turned as two ladies Alice had met earlier approached. "Mamma, Aurelia."

"Thank you for agreeing to come for me." His mother smiled politely.

"It was easily done."

Lady Montagu turned to Alice and her sisters. "I have enjoyed meeting all of you this evening."

"And we you," Eleanor said.

"Yes." Alice glanced at the lady next to Lady Montagu. "Lady Lytton, it was a pleasure speaking with you.

She inclined her head. "I enjoyed meeting and talking with you as well."

"I hope we shall see one another again," Madeline said.

"I hope to see you again soon." Lady Montagu glanced at her son. "We must not keep the horses waiting."

Alice was glad her twin had asked him if he was one of the gentlemen they had seen riding. He also seemed very interested in Eleanor. The only question now was the identity of the other man, and if they could rise early enough to meet them at the Park.

Madeline whispered something to Eleanor.

"What?" They left the supper room and were strolling to the front door.

Had she really not noticed how his gaze was focused on her? "The way Lord Montagu looked at you."

Eleanor frowned at Alice. "How did you hear her?"

"I did not." She lifted one shoulder in a shrug. "I knew what she was going to say because I thought the same thing."

"I will be very surprised if he can tell us apart." Eleanor snorted lightly. "A great many people will not be able to do so."

She had a point. Then again, if he was the right one, he would be able to see the difference. Even if they did look almost exactly alike, they were not identical twins. "It is a shame we are past the age of pretending to be each other."

"But if he can." Madeline looped her arm with Eleanor's. "It means that he sees you. That you are not just some young lady."

"Perhaps." Eleanor did not sound convinced. "We shall see. Remember neither Louisa nor Charlotte married the first gentlemen they met."

"Very true." Alice took her twin's other arm. "But simply because they did not, does not mean you will not."

"As I said, we shall see." Clearly Eleanor was not willing to be convinced.

"He must have the funds to support a family," Madeline mused. "Otherwise, Matt would not have introduced him."

That was a very good point. None of them had thought about that when they had made their list.

"I am not falling in love at first sight." Eleanor pressed her lips together. "He has many more qualities to meet."

"So it begins." Strolling in front of them, Matt groaned.

Grace patted his arm. "They have become shrewd ladies."

Alice grinned as she exchanged looks with her sisters. Grace seemed certain of them, but Matt needed more convincing.

He helped them all into the coach and took the seat next to Grace. "What did Lady Bellamny say? I remember Louisa telling us she thought she'd look at her teeth."

"Not much," Madeline began to tell him, and Alice and Eleanor added to what she said.

In the coach light, Grace's smile could be seen. "I think it was a matter of like recognizing like. I was very proud of the way the girls held their own under that gaze. Most of the young ladies would have started weeping."

"More than one of them did have tears in their eyes. One was weeping." Alice glanced at her twin. "What was her name?

"Melissa," Eleanor said.

"Yes, that was it. Then another one, she and her friend want to marry gentlemen who live close to each other so that they will not have to be apart, was dabbing away tears as well."

Grace took a breath and let it out. "Either Miss Tice or

Miss Martindale. Their older sisters wanted the same thing."

That was interesting. "Were they successful?"

"As it happens, yes, they were," Grace said. "You should ask Henrietta about them. One set of Martindale-Tices came out when she did."

It would be nice if they could ask her. "We haven't seen her since last summer."

"Dotty has invited us to Easter dinner." Grace said. "You will see her then."

Alice would be glad to see both of them. It would be almost like when they were children and lived in the same neighborhood.

"I shall look forward to it," Eleanor said. "It's nice to have so many people in Town we already know."

"It is," Madeline agreed. "Even if they are not coming out at the same time."

Eleanor yawned. "I do not know how I will stay awake during the entertainments."

Grace chuckled. "You will have so much to do during them that you will not be tired until you get home."

"Just remember we leave after supper," Matt added. "That worked well with your sisters, and now we have even younger children in the house to consider."

So far, everything was proceeding as she hoped it would. Then it occurred to Alice that Lord Montagu could now introduce them to the gentleman on the gray horse.

Alice rose early the next morning, excited that she might meet the gentleman who rode with Lord Montagu. She met her sisters in the corridor, and they went down to their mares.

She stopped short at seeing all three of their grooms

with horses as well. "I thought only one of you were to come with us?"

"We were all ordered to be here." Robertson helped her mount.

Matt must be worried about something. Once they were ready, they headed toward the Park, but Lord Montagu was not there. So much for him being able to rise early. Still, even though it was cloudy, the morning was lovely.

"What do you think happened to them?" Madeline asked.

There was only one reason for them not to be here. "Obviously, they could not get out of bed in time to ride with us."

Eleanor shrugged. "It does not matter. We will have a good ride on our own."

Alice supposed this was a lesson in fashionable gentlemen. Lord Montagu and his friend were not the only ones who could not get to the Park on time. She remembered a story about someone else. "Race to the oak tree?"

"Yes." Eleanor grinned.

They were well matched. Alice arrived just a nose before the others. They rode to the Serpentine then headed back to the gate.

"Do not look, but there they are," Madeline said.

Lord Montagu trotted toward them. "Good morning, my ladies."

Alice and her sisters greeted him. The gentleman on the gray horse had darker red hair mixed with brown, fair skin and green eyes that seemed to take in everything. Would Lord Montagu introduce his companion?

He grimaced. "I meant to awaken earlier, but I had a great deal of work to do last night."

Alice almost snorted. Madeline seemed not to believe him either.

Eleanor gave him a tight smile. Clearly, she was not convinced. "Sometime duties cannot be put off."

He motioned toward the other man. "Allow me to introduce my friend, Lord St. Albans. St. Albans, Lady Eleanor, Lady Madeline, and Lady Alice."

Lord St. Albans bowed from his horse, and Alice did not think anyone could have done it more gracefully. "Ladies, good morning." He smiled at them each in turn. "It is my absolute pleasure to finally be made known to you."

Eleanor raised a brow. "Indeed, my lord. We have wondered who was riding the gray. Now we know."

This was no time for her to act high in the in-step. Alice almost rolled her eyes "Good morning, sir. It is very nice to meet you as well."

Lady Madeline's lips twitched. "I shall add my greetings, my lord. It is a pleasure."

Lord St. Albans opened his mouth to continue when Lord Montagu said, "Must you return home now, or do you have time to ride some more?"

"I am afraid we are required to be back in time for breakfast with our family." Eleanor's tone was firm. "However, perhaps you will not have to work so late this evening and will be able to join us tomorrow morning."

"Yes. I will arrange that." He gave her a charming smile. "Until tomorrow."

Lord St. Albans glanced at Lord Montagu then to Alice. "The least we can do is to escort you to the gate."

"Yes, of course." This was her first encounter with a gentleman who was not related or whom she had not known for years, and it was exciting. The way his eyes twinkled when he looked at her was also exciting.

Lord St. Albans bowed. "We are at your command."

For some reason, Alice knew he must have said that

many times before, still . . . "How nice. I do not believe anyone has ever said that to me."

"I am certain I will not be the only one." The only gentleman she knew whose tone was as sophisticated as his was her brother-in-law Con Kenilworth.

Suddenly, Alice had a suspicion he might be a rake. "Have you spent a lot of time in Town?"

"My dear lady, I have been on the Town for years." As he spoke, a look came into his eyes that she did not understand. Prickles danced across her neck and shoulders before spreading to the rest of her body.

"You are the most beautiful woman I have ever seen." His horse sidled closer to hers. "And I've seen a great many of them." Alice didn't know what to say or even think. No one had ever been this bold before. "I would be happy to show you the sights."

He was not going to get the best of her. A change of subject was in order. "Although we have not been out, we have come to the metropolis during the Season for many years. Our brother and brothers-in-law are very active in the Lords."

"Fortunately, I have not yet ascended to my father's title." He gave her a look she could only describe as heavy or significant. "Are you interested in politics?"

"I am indeed. It is my belief we must all do what we are able."

"A very admirable view." It was an appropriate remark to make, but he did not seem to be referring to what she had said. It was almost as if he had not really heard her.

Alice waited for him to continue, but before he could speak Eleanor said, "Thank you for your escort. Perhaps I will see you tomorrow."

"I shall make it happen." Montagu bowed. "Until then, my lady."

Lady Eleanor inclined her head. "My lord."

"I will see you tomorrow as well, my ladies." Lord St. Albans included Madeline in his comment.

"Until then." Alice left with her sisters. Had Lord Montagu been flirting with her?

"Dear me," Madeline said jokingly as they reached Worthington House. "You two already have gentlemen interested in you, and there is no one for me."

"I am not sure about that." Alice dismounted. "I think Lord St. Albans is a bit too . . . too"—she frowned as she thought—"I cannot find the right word. Worldly? That might be it. He seems too experienced in capturing a lady's attention." She waited until her sisters were ready to enter the house. "I think I shall ask Matt about him."

CHAPTER FOUR

Giff watched Lady Alice ride down the street. Their meeting had gone extremely well. Physically she was the type of female that attracted him. Fair hair, eyes that reminded him of the sky on a cloudless summer day. Her close-fitting habit had given him a good idea of what lay beneath. He'd known he would find her enticing. Lady Alice's breeding was obviously unexceptionable. Of course, he'd have to test her character, and it was early days. He'd do well to meet a number of young ladies before making a decision. Marriage was for life. "Mind if I join you for breakfast again?"

Montagu glanced over as if he'd forgotten Giff was present. "Not at all."

When they strolled into the breakfast room in Montagu House, Montagu's mother and sister, Lady Lytton, were breaking their fast. He and Lytton set about filling their plates. Unfortunately, just as Montagu was about to take his seat, his sister reminded him about an early vote at the Lords and he departed, leaving Giff with the ladies.

"Good morning." He bowed to them and took a seat.

Lady Lytton gave him a calculated gaze over the rim of her cup. She obviously wanted information and had decided Giff was the one to give it to her. It was soon clear she was interested in Lady Alice's sister for her brother. Having been on the Town for several years, he knew exactly how much information to impart. Not only that, but he wanted to find out what they knew about Lady Alice. "He seems to want a lady of only moderate intelligence."

Lady Lytton looked as if she wanted to roll her eyes. "Did you tell him that was a mistake?"

"Not I. There is no point in telling a man something he must discover on his own." Giff smiled to himself. "I did suggest that if he wanted a stupid woman, he must make sure not to show his own intelligence or it might frighten her away."

Lady Montagu laughed. "Oh my." She waved her hand in front of her face. "This I cannot wait to see."

Lady Lytton's eyes widened, and her lips curved up. "Oh, dear. I have a feeling Lady Eleanor is not at all stupid, or of even moderate intelligence."

As the ladies began to plot ways to throw Montagu and Lady Eleanor together, Giff dug into his breakfast.

He'd not been paying much attention until he heard Lady Montagu mention an entertainment in which he would be interested. "A theater party? Or a party to Vauxhall."

Lady Lytton glanced at him. "And would you like to be included, my lord?"

"If you wouldn't mind, I would be delighted to be invited to make up your numbers." He was relying on his mother, but there was no sense in not taking advantage of the entertainment the ladies were planning. "I am looking for a wife, and she must be intelligent and have great strength of character. I get the feeling that you would be the one to help me find such a lady."

Lady Lytton inclined her head in assent. "That would give me a great deal of pleasure. Mamma and I are attending a meeting today that many ladies of that ilk will also attend. I would not be surprised to find a few young ladies there as well."

Lady Montagu gave Giff a narrow-eyed look. "Would this have anything to do with your father?"

Even though he'd mentioned the problem of his father to Montagu, Giff did not particularly want it to get out that Papa could be difficult. That might put off the type of woman in which Giff was interested. Still, these ladies were offering to help him, and that was something they should know. "Partially. I do want to spend my life with a lady of intelligence, but she must be able to stand up to my father. I will be able to aid her only so much."

Lady Montagu nodded thoughtfully. "As I thought."

Lady Lytton raised a brow. "Is he cruel?"

"Not in the sense you most likely mean." Giff shook his head. "He is not a brute. In fact, I can only remember him spanking me twice, and both times I had put my life in danger. He never allowed my tutor to physically punish me." Although a spanking or a rap on the knuckles might have been less painful than writing page after page of Latin declensions. He studied the ladies for a few short moments. "I have never heard him verbally attack anyone. He can be difficult. If he thinks that he can get the better of you, he will. When he tells someone to do something one ought not to do or really does not want to do, one fares much better to stand up to him and tell him no, than to meekly do what he wishes. It is hard to explain."

"Your mother's garden," Lady Montagu said abruptly.

Lady Lytton glanced at her mother. "You know them?"

"Of course I do. I came out the same year the duchess did. Now, let me tell you the story." Giff had heard the tale before. It was one of his favorites. In fact, he couldn't imagine Papa had been so reckless to try to interfere with

Mamma's garden. Other than her children, that was her pride and joy. "St. Albans's father told his mother he was going to tear out her garden and make a tennis court. She refused. When he pressed the issue, she had the gamekeeper arm his helpers and the gardeners with the hunting guns and refused to allow the men he had hired to enter her garden. She even held one of the muskets herself."

Giff would have loved to have seen that. "He gave up the scheme when she told him that he'd have a difficult time using a tennis court with a ball in his arm." Papa still grumbled about it every now and again. "She would have done it. M'mother doesn't make threats."

"Hmm, I see what you mean." Lady Lytton glanced at her watch. "I shall give it some thought. As for now, we should be going. I have things I must accomplish before this afternoon." She stood and bussed her mother's cheek.

Giff had stood when her ladyship rose. He should probably go home.

"Please finish eating." Lady Montagu motioned for him to retake his seat. "We can discuss any ideas you have for events to which young ladies will be invited."

He did as she asked. "My mother is planning a ball. You mentioned a theater party. Is Vauxhall a possibility? I know that it can be rather risqué."

Lady Montagu looked down her nose at him. "That depends entirely on the company one keeps. That said, the party must be small, one must keep an eye on the younger ladies." She requested more tea. "You might consider joining your mother for morning visits. You will be able to meet all the young ladies coming out and those for whom this is not their first Season."

An excellent point. "My mother mentioned I should escort her."

"Other than that, I am certain your mother will receive

the necessary invitations. Especially when it is made known that you are in search of a wife. And I shall send cards to her as well."

He finished his breakfast. "Indeed. I shall have no difficulty with choice." A faint smile hovered on Lady Montagu's lips. What was that about? "Thank you for your help."

"My pleasure. I expect I shall see you again soon."

Giff rose and bowed. "I bid you a good day. I will show myself out."

He was happy to see Horace waiting for him as he reached the pavement. He had to wash before speaking to his mother. Lady Lytton might not mind the smell of horse at the breakfast table, but his mother would. Not that he'd see her in the breakfast room. She broke her fast in her parlor. He'd never thought to ask why she did, but after seeing Lady Lytton in the breakfast room, he began to wonder. Giff shrugged his shoulders. It was no bread and butter of his where his mother wanted to break her fast. He did think he'd like his wife to join him for breakfast and early morning rides. He recalled Lady Alice's excellent seat. Yes, his wife must ride well.

Alice entered Dotty's house with her sisters, but they were soon separated. She threaded through the crowded rooms greeting ladies she knew and meeting other ladies until she finally found Georgie Turley. "Just the person I wanted to see."

She greeted Alice with a hug. "You are finally making your come out."

"I am. We are." She was glad she was not doing it alone. "I have a question to ask you."

"Very well. What is it about?"

"We, Eleanor, Madeline, and I, have been riding early. We met two gentlemen—" Georgie's brows rose—"It was entirely proper. Lord Montagu was introduced to us at Lady Bellamny's soirée."

"Very well. What has he done?"

"Him? Nothing. Although, he does seem interested in Eleanor. He had a friend with him, Lord St. Albans. Do you know anything about him?"

A slow smile grew on Georgie's face. "As a matter of fact, I do. Before Turley and I agreed to marry, I was visiting Adeline and Fitz Littleton at their estate. A neighbor decided to hold a house party, and Lord St. Albans was one of the guests. He was very witty and charming." She laughed lightly. "He was not at all interested in marriage at the time, but he did offer to make Turley jealous." She took two glasses of lemonade from a footman and handed one to Alice. "I really have not seen him since. But that isn't unusual. Many gentlemen who are not interested in marriage attend different sorts of events than I would." She took a sip of the lemonade. "However, I understand that this Season he is finally looking for a wife."

"How do you know that?"

"Oh, my mother and his are friends. The duchess is putting it around." Georgie smiled again. "She wants to make sure he is introduced to every eligible lady in Town. After all, it has taken him far longer than his mother wanted for him to decide to wed."

In that case, it was not surprising the duchess would do all she could to help him. Still, Alice needed to have her question satisfied. "Is he a rake?"

"Hmm." Georgie pressed her lips together and tapped them with one finger. "I do not think I would characterize him as a rake. He has never ruined a lady, and I would know if he had. He has been on the Town for several years, and he is known for being a favorite with many widows. I am certain he's had mistresses. Most gentlemen do. He apparently stays away from married ladies. Other than flirting with them that is."

He sounded rather shallow, although, Alice was glad he did not dally with married ladies. "Does he involve himself in anything important?"

Georgie frowned. "Such as?"

Alice had to think of the things Charlie did or even Phinn. "Estate business, or charitable endeavors, some other interest?"

"Not of which I am aware. He seems to be rather at loose ends. Turley mentioned to me that his father will not allow him to become involved in the estates until he is married."

If Lord St. Albans had put off wedding this long, he must not be interested in his future estates. "Thank you. I have a much better view of him now."

"My pleasure." Georgie linked arms with Alice. "Now, in what sort of charitable endeavors are you interested?"

That was a very good question. "I donate part of my pin money to Dotty's and Charlotte's causes, but I have not found my own yet. What are you doing?"

"Since Turley and I wed, I have been establishing schools and apprenticeship programs on our estates. That has taken up most of my energy. Between that and our son, I do not have much time left for anything else. Turley, of course, has the Lords and the estates to keep him busy."

Whereas Lord St. Albans had nothing demanding his time and no apparent interest in doing anything other than being a social being, Alice would allow him to entertain her, but that was all. She would look elsewhere for a husband.

* * *

The next morning, Alice and her sisters set out as soon as it was light enough to see. They were trotting toward the Park when Lord Montagu called out a greeting.

"Good morning," Alice and her sisters called at the same time.

Alice was interested to see he went straight to her twin. "As you see, I am able to rise earlier."

"When you are not working too late." Eleanor had a polite smile on her face.

"Yes." He glanced up at the sky. "It promises to be a lovely day."

"It does." They walked the horses through the gate. "The later spring flowers and shrubs are beginning to make an appearance."

If that was all the conversation he had, Alice could not see Eleanor being interested in the man.

"Good morning, my ladies." Lord St. Albans's tone was teasing and tempting at the same time.

How had she not seen him ride up?

"Alice," Madeline said. "Do you want to race to the oak?"

"I do." Racing was one of Alice's favorite things to do. "Ask Eleanor."

"Do you often race?" Lord St. Albans asked.

"Yes, indeed. But only early in the morning when no one else is here." She urged Galyna faster. "You may come with us."

"Yes, of course," Lord St. Albans said. "The restrictions."

If he said anything else, Alice did not hear him. She was galloping next to Madeline.

When they reached the tree, Lord St. Albans trotted up next to them. "Excellent. I must do this more often."

Alice laughed. He sounded as if he had never raced before, and that she did not believe. She glanced at Madeline. "To the Serpentine?"

Madeline nodded.

Alice might as well ask Lord St. Albans if he would like to come as well. "Are you up for another one, my lord?"

"I am." His eyes were warm as he smiled at her.

When they reached the Serpentine, Alice and Madeline dismounted and took out the bread they had brought for the ducks. St. Albans swung himself down from his horse in one fluid motion. It was not until he was standing that she noticed how tall both man and horse were. Being on the ground made his shoulders appear broader. His face seemed to have been chiseled. It was all lean planes; his nose was straight with a sight bump in it. He was exceedingly handsome. Madeline strolled off a little way, leaving Alice with his lordship.

"I do not think I have ever seen a horse quite like yours."

"He is a Lusitano. They were brought here originally as part of Queen Catherine's dowry."

She stroked the horse's nose. "What is his name?"

"Horace." He stroked the horse's neck. "And your mare?"

"Galyna." The mare sidled over demanding attention as well.

"And is she calm?"

Alice almost dropped her jaw. How had he known that? "Your Latin must be excellent."

Before he could answer, a group of ducks waddled up to them, and Alice quickly threw some of the breadcrumbs. One duck had been pushed out and decided St. Alban's boots looked like a good meal. She threw some crumbs directly at the duck, and he went after the bread.

"That was close." He stared down at his boots. "At least I wasn't wearing tassels."

Unable to help herself, Alice went into whoops as Lord St. Albans stared at her in confusion. "I am sorry." She started laughing again. "Our friend's husband used to wear tassels and a puppy got them."

Shaking his head, he chuckled. "Not something I would wear around a puppy or a duck."

"Alice, we should go. Eleanor did not follow us," Madeline said.

"Yes. Of course." The groom helped Madeline, and Lord St. Albans cupped his hand to help her mount.

It took very little time to reach Eleanor and Lord Montagu. She waved. "Has the Serpentine changed at all?"

"Nary a bit," Lord St. Albans said. "However, I am indebted to the ladies for bringing bread for the ducks. They are an avaricious group."

"We saved his boots." Alice felt slightly smug about it.

Eleanor looked at her watch. "We must be going."

The gentlemen fell in with them. Lord St. Albans rode next to Alice. "Now that the Season is begun, what do you have on your calendar?"

"I do not yet know. Grace, our eldest sister, makes all those decisions. I suppose we will find out soon." She wondered if he would be at some of the same events. Georgie was right. He was amusing. "And you?"

Lord St. Albans sighed. "As with you, I am not quite sure. My mother is in charge of my social schedule this Season."

He *was* looking for a wife. "We are attending Almack's on Wednesday."

He inclined his head. "I will be there as well and would be honored if you would stand up with me."

"Alice," Madeline said. "Lord Montagu has asked us all for a set."

"Oh." Alice had not been paying any attention at all to her sisters' conversation. How odd. "That would be nice. Lord St. Albans has just requested a dance."

He leaned forward and glanced at Eleanor and Madeline. "I would like to request sets from the two of you as well."

"Delighted." Eleanor inclined her head.

"A pleasure," Madeline said.

When they reached the gate, St. Albans bowed. "I look forward to seeing you again. If not tomorrow morning, then at Almack's."

That was two sets Alice and her sisters would dance. She was looking forward to meeting more gentlemen. Perhaps one of them would be approved to waltz with her.

Chapter Five

After breaking his fast with Montagu and Lady Montagu and Giff schooled his friend on what was needed to attend Almack's, he realized he had not informed his own mother that he wished to attend. He trusted she would have obtained vouchers, but it never hurt to ask. He hadn't gone in years. He prayed she was awake. He'd learned at a young age never to disrupt her sleep her unless it was an emergency.

Taking the stairs two at a time, he strode down the corridor and knocked on Mamma's parlor door.

"Enter."

He opened the door and stepped into the room. His mother was sitting at a round table with various breakfast items on it. Chief of which was a bowl of porridge. "We do have vouchers for Almack's, do we not?"

She covered her mouth as she yawned. "We do. I planned to attend even if you did not. However, I am pleased you have decided to take the bull by the horns."

Giff was strongly reminded of the shaggy highland bull at his grandfather's estate in Scotland. He'd thought it would be fun to see it up close and perhaps stroke it when it charged him. He'd barely made it over the fence. "That is an interesting way to put it."

"At least there are not hidden alcoves or other places

one can be compromised there." Her tone betrayed how serious she was.

But compromised? Him? "I hadn't thought of the possibility, but you are correct."

She made a shooing motion with her hands. "We will discuss it more later. Leave me to my breakfast."

"Yes, your grace." He bowed.

"Out! Now!" Mamma wrinkled her nose as she sniffed.

Giff backed out of the door and closed it. His mother had given him something unexpected to consider. Corridors, dark gardens, even terraces were all places he had taken widows before, but where one could be compromised and made to wed a person one did not wish to marry. While he'd been congratulating himself on his status and looks, making it easy to find a wife, he had not thought how that also made him a target. His temptation to flirt with a lady might also cause trouble by raising expectations. Lady Alice had not seemed susceptible—that he didn't understand at all—but some other young lady and her Mamma might decide he was about to make an offer. There was a fine line between merely social engagement and something more. He'd have to be careful. In fact, he'd have to change his conversation.

"My lord," his valet said. "Yer bath is ready."

"Thank you, Dunn." Years ago, Giff had stopped wondering how personal servants knew exactly what one wanted and when.

Shortly after he'd dressed, Dunn brought a stack of cards. He placed them in two groups, one in front of Giff and one off to the side. "These"—he touched the first stack—"are invitations her grace has accepted. Those"—he pointed at the others—"are ones she's nay seen. I'm to tell ye she expects ye to go with her on morning visits today."

"Thank you. When am I to be ready?" He hoped it was after luncheon.

"One o'clock," his valet answered.

Since neither of his parents partook of an early breakfast, luncheon was not served in the dining room. "I will eat at twelve."

"I'll tell Cook." Dunn bowed and left the room.

Giff glanced at the cards and decided they could wait until later. He'd ordered a book on new farming practices in order to be ready to take over the Whippoorwill estate once he'd married. Donning his hat and gloves, he picked up his cane, and went to the front door.

"My lord." His father's butler was holding a note. "This just came for you."

He placed the cane against a wall and opened the missive.

My dear Lord St. Albans,

I have been directed to inform you of the death of your great-uncle, the Honorable Angus Dewar.

No! How could that be? He'd just visited Uncle Angus two months ago. Granted he was old, but he seemed to be in good health.

You were mentioned in his last will and testament. Please inform me of a time I may call on you.

Yr. Servant,
Cecil Throckmorton
Solicitor
Throckmorton and Throckmorton

The address was near the Inns of Court. Giff could, and probably should, send a note back stating a time, but he'd rather not wait. "Call for my curricle. I'll want Fergus to accompany me as well."

"Straightaway, my lord."

Giff resolved to wait patiently. It wouldn't take that long, and the last time he'd ventured to go to the stables here, the stablemaster had told him to go wait in the house until he was informed that his carriage or horse, as the case may, be was ready. According to the stablemaster, it was unseemly for a future duke to go to the stables for either his horse or carriage while in Town. Although, it was perfectly respectable to do so in the country. He remembered his sisters complaining about rules. Apparently, he had to follow them as well. Albeit, probably not as many.

Ardley bowed and opened the door. "Your carriage awaits, my lord."

"Thank you, Ardley."

Fergus stood by the curricle. "Where we goin', sir?"

"To the City. My great-uncle Angus died." Giff climbed into the carriage.

"That's a loss." His groom climbed onto the back where a seat had been built. "He was a grand old mon."

"That he was." Since he'd been a boy, Giff had visited his uncle every year. He'd hoped his children would know his uncle as well.

Thirty minutes later he jumped down from the curricle and his groom ran to the horses. "I'll walk 'em."

Giff nodded, looked at the names on the building and made his way to the first floor. The office was decorated in dark wood paneling, but long narrow windows lit the area.

"May I help you?" a clerk asked.

"I'm Lord St. Albans." Giff handed the man a card. "I received a letter from Mr. Cecil Throckmorton this morning. I'd like to meet with him."

The clerk's jaw dropped. "I'll get him." And he dashed off.

A short time later, a tall, lean man dressed in a black jacket, knee breeches, and a starched cravat, modestly tied, bowed and greeted him. "My lord. I am Cecil Throckmorton. I would have been happy to attend you."

Giff inclined his head. "Thank you, but I have time this morning, and I'm busy the rest of the week."

Throckmorton waved his arm toward an open door. "I have had the file put in here. Would you like some tea?"

"Please." Giff wondered how long this would take. He took a seat at the head of a long table as another clerk set out the documents.

Throckmorton sat to his right. "There is a letter for you from Mr. Dewar. After you read it, I will explain your bequest."

"Thank you." Giff broke the seal and shook the paper open.

The hand that had written the letter seemed firm.

Giff, my boy,

If you're reading this, I'm dead. I've had a good life. That's as much as a man can ask for. None of that useless English mourning. When you can find a good bottle of whisky, have a dram or two and remember me life. More than any other of my nephews, you were the son of my heart despite you being half Sassenach. I never understood why your mother couldn't have found a good Scotsman to wed. But I'm taking too long to get to the point. Besides a few bequests, I'm leaving you everything. I trust you to take care of the house, land, and servants.

All the best,
Uncle Angus

Giff blinked back tears. "Do you know how he died?"

"He fell off his horse," Throckmorton said. "I must admit, I was slightly shocked to have been told he was over ninety. I'm sorry to tell you that the funeral has already been held."

Giff was sorry he'd missed the funeral but was glad his uncle had been doing something he loved. "He would have rather died riding then in his bed."

The solicitor cleared his throat and handed him several sheets of paper. "He last will and testament."

The first list was of bequests. He chuckled as he read the stipulation that every servant who wanted to retire had to replace themselves and train the replacement. "Have the servants been told of the requirement?"

"They have, my lord. According to the solicitor in Scotland, none of them were surprised."

Giff nodded. His uncle had probably informed them all beforehand. The only part that was surprising was the amount Uncle Angus had in funds and in the bank. "I had no idea he was that warm."

"According to the accounts I reviewed, he invested well. What will you do with the funds?"

"I'll not change any of the investments. I would like the direction of his man of business. If you agree to represent me, I'd like you to open an account in my name at Campbell & Coutts. The principle will remain with the Bank of Scotland"—Uncle Angus would haunt Giff if he moved it all to England—"An amount of five hundred pounds will be transferred immediately to the new account."

Throckmorton bowed. "I would be honored to represent you, my lord. Would you like me to write to the steward?"

"No, I'll do it. It's better he and the staff hear from me." Giff rose and held out his hand. "I look forward to doing business with you."

The solicitor looked surprised but took his hand and shook it. "The feeling is mutual. There will be documents to sign. Would you like me to bring them to you?"

Giff considered the question. His father would not be happy about Uncle Hector's bequest. They had never got along. His mother, on the other hand, would be thrilled after she got over her uncle's death. Giff decided to keep it to himself for the time being. "No. Send a messenger when the papers are ready."

"As you wish, my lord."

When he reached the street, he was torn between weeping for an uncle he loved dearly and smiling at his good fortune. It appeared weeping was going to win out. He waved to Fergus.

"Bad news, sir?"

"Just the opposite, but there was a letter in Uncle's hand." Giff couldn't finish the sentence.

Lips pressed together his groom nodded. "Take yer time. That's what my mam told me when Granny died."

He climbed into the carriage and started the pair. Had anyone written to his mother?

When he arrived home, he was greeted with the news that his mother wanted to see him. Giff went directly to her parlor. One look at her and he knew she had been informed.

"Oh, Giff." Her eyes filled with tears.

He went to her and kneeled next to her chair. Taking one cold hand, he rubbed it between his. "I know."

"I suppose I thought he would live forever." Her handkerchief was already wet, and he handed her his.

"I did as well." She sniffed and dabbed at her eyes. "My father told me he left everything to you."

"Yes. I've just come from the solicitor."

"That is good." Mamma removed her hand from his

and blew her nose. "I do not think I am up for morning visits today."

"Neither am I. There will be other days." A thought occurred to him. "You don't by chance have any whisky, do you?"

She gave him a watery smile. "How very good of you to remember. It's in my dressing room on top of the first wardrobe."

He brought it out and poured them each a glass. "To Uncle Angus. Long may he live in our hearts. *Fill to me the parting glass, and drink a health whate'er befalls, Then gently rise and softly call Goodnight and joy be to you all.*"

Three toasts later, he went to his room. The last time he saw Uncle Hector, a man who'd never married, Uncle Hector had sat him down and told him it was time for him to find a wife. He shuffled through the cards, separating them out by event. Balls, Venetian Breakfasts, a musical evening, and a soirée. The first event, though, was lmack's where he would ask one of the Lady Patronesses to recommend him for a waltz with Lady Alice.

Even though Alice had asked Georgie about Lord St. Albans, she still wanted Matt's opinion as well, but she did not know how to bring up the subject. She met her sisters in the corridor before they went down to the breakfast room. "What is the best way to go about asking Matt whether Lord St. Albans is a rake?"

Madeline just stared at Alice for a moment. Then Eleanor said, "I will do it. We all need to know."

They went down to breakfast and after the children had gone to their lessons, Eleanor glanced at Alice, then at Matt. "What do you know about Lord St. Albans?"

Madeline closed her eyes and huffed. "Is he a rake?"

His brows rose, and he frowned. "Not that I have heard, and I've made a point of discovering who should not be made known to you." He took another a sip of tea. "How did you meet him?"

Eleanor glanced at Madeline and Alice nodded. "Lord Montagu saw us in the Park, and Lord St. Albans was with him. He seems to be rather worldly."

"As he might." Matt took a piece of toast. "He's been on the Town for several years."

First Georgie now Matt. Alice did not understand why that was the first thing anyone said about the man. Now to discover if Matt had any concerns about Alice and the others dancing with him. "He has asked us all to stand up with him at Almack's."

"Lord Montagu has as well," Eleanor said and quickly turned to ask Augusta a question.

Alice wanted to know more. "Is that all right? I mean, is he a proper person to know?"

Matt looked at her for a long moment as if attempting to work out what she actually wanted to know. "I have no objection to him."

There had to be something more. "What does 'on the Town' actually mean?"

Her brother-in-law set down his cup. "It means that he has been a carefree bachelor who has taken time to sow his oats. That is all I'm going to say."

"Oh." Well, that was disappointing. She was going to have to find out for herself. She heard Grace say that Louisa and Charlotte had been nervous. "Other than you and Matt, who is attending Almack's with us?"

"Everyone who is in Town," Grace said.

"Walter and I will be there," Charlie gave them an encouraging look. "Remember. All hands on deck."

"That's right." Walter grinned. "You have nothing about which to be concerned."

Madeline's eyes filled with tears. "I am very glad you are my brothers."

Alice felt happy tears in her eyes as well. "I am too."

Phinn whispered something to Augusta. "Augusta and I will be there as well."

Everything would be fine. Alice and her sisters were the luckiest ladies to make a come out.

Chapter Six

The following day, Giff spent the afternoon accompanying his mother on morning visits. She'd been right that he would meet a great number of young ladies. Sadly, none of them were suitable for him. Several of them glanced at their mothers before being willing to utter a word beyond a greeting. Others were clearly only interested in being a duchess one day, and a few had nothing good to say about anything or anyone. He was able to speak with some ladies of sense, but they were all married.

Lady Turley gave him a skeptical look when they ended up at the same house. "Morning visits?"

He took a seat next to her. "My mother thought it would be the quickest way for me to meet the greatest number of eligible young ladies in one day."

Giggles broke out across the room causing Lady Turley to chuckle lightly. "You look as if you are in pain. That will not do."

Blast it all! He had let his mask slip. "This whole finding a wife business is more difficult than I thought."

"I am not sure I would call morning visits difficult. However, I can see how you might find it challenging. Have many caps been set at you?"

He stifled a sigh. "Yes. But I was expecting that. It is the ones who are bored by life that I do not understand."

"You know as well as anyone it is considered provincial to appear to be enjoying one's Season," she gently reminded him.

He knew that, but Lady Alice had not appeared bored. There was nothing false about her or her reaction to him. And that's what it was about the other ladies. "It is clearly an act."

"Oh, I agree wholeheartedly." Lady Turley nodded once. "Which is the reason I never tried it."

It was time to discuss something more interesting than young ladies. He remembered a bit of news he'd heard. "I've been told you and Turley have a son."

Her ladyship beamed. "We do. He is extremely handsome and intelligent."

She was clearly very happy about her acquisition. Giff would like a son as well. If he got married, he could have one. "I hope to have one within the year."

"I wish you luck." She lifted one brow. "Perhaps I can help. What are you searching for in a wife?"

"I'm not particularly demanding. Intelligence, a willingness to speak her mind, and the ability to stand up for herself." Beautiful hair of gold, blue eyes, and a lush figure.

"Hmmm." She tilted her head as she regarded him. A group of ladies made their farewells, and she stood. "I must go as well. I shall give it some thought. Shall I see you at Almack's?"

"Indeed. Will you save me a set?"

"Of course." A sly smile appeared. "If only to see Turley's expression. One must not allow a husband to become too comfortable."

Giff quietly laughed. Why couldn't the younger ladies

converse with such sense? Once her ladyship left, it occurred to him he'd not seen Lady Alice. Had he simply missed her and her sisters? How did one arrange to meet a lady during morning visits? The process seemed quite random. Ah, well. He'd see her at Almack's. And dance with her.

That evening, Giff dressed strategically. Most gentlemen would be wearing black jackets and breeches. In contrast, he wore deep blue. He affixed an emerald tie-pin, knowing it would enhance the green of his eyes. He'd been told that, although his hair was an unfortunate color, his eyes were his best feature. The first thing on the agenda was convincing one of the Patronesses to allow him to waltz with Lady Alice. He trusted she would be suitably impressed with him for making the effort. He knew the process but had only been tempted to do it once before, and that had been a disaster. The lady had been so afraid, she'd forgotten how to dance.

He met his mother in the hall. She wore a gold silk gown with a green trim, a red shawl with gold thread, and a turban with the same colors as well as the Cleveland diamonds. She inspected him as if he was still a boy.

"I can promise you I have no dirt on my face or frogs in my pockets. You look very fetching. I approve of that turban."

"I am glad to hear you have grown out of that stage at least. I like my turban as well." She straightened her shawl then took his arm. "Come, let us go."

Several minutes later they arrived at the assembly rooms. She handed the gatekeeper their vouchers, and they were admitted.

Mamma stood near the entrance and scanned the crowd. "I see some old friends. I will be with them."

Giff inclined his head. "Try not to get into too much trouble."

"Silly boy." She wiggled her fingers as she swanned off.

He glanced around, found Lady Jersey with one of the other Patronesses speaking with Montagu and his mother, and joined them. "My ladies." He bowed. "It is wonderful to see you again."

"St. Albans, I trust your parents are well," Lady Jersey said.

"They are. My mother has accompanied me this evening." He indicated the direction Mamma went.

One of Lady Cowper's mobile brows rose. "And is there someone who has interested you?"

"Yes. Lady Alice Carpenter. I would like to waltz with her."

Her ladyship's lips seemed to twitch. "And are you able to recognize the lady apart from her twin?"

What a strange question. Of course, he could recognize her. He hoped she and her party had arrived. He started to search the room, but he didn't have to. His gaze was immediately drawn to her. "Yes. She is wearing a butter-colored gown with purple on it. Why do you ask?"

"We would not wish to recommend you to the wrong lady," Lady Jersey said. "I will perform the duty. Find me at the end of the second set."

Suddenly, Montagu said, "Is it possible to be recommended earlier?"

Giff glanced at Lady Alice's group. Several gentlemen had either already joined the family or were headed in that direction. Damnation.

Lady Jersey sighed. "I do believe we are going to have one of those Seasons."

Lady Cowper nodded. "I think you are correct." She looked at Montagu. "Accompany me, my lord."

One of those Seasons indeed. Giff huffed.

Lady Jersey's lips twitched. "Very well, St. Albans, you may come with me."

"With pleasure, my lady." He held his arm out for her to take, and they followed Lady Cowper and Montagu. Alice was standing next to a young matron who looked very much like her.

"Lady Kenilworth, I am pleased to see you again," Lady Jersey said.

"And I you." The lady held out her hand and they touched fingers.

Lady Jersey smiled at Lady Alice. "My dear, Lady Alice, I would like to recommend Lord St. Albans to you as a suitable partner for the waltz."

Lady Alice's eyes sparkled as the corners of her lips tipped up. He hadn't noticed how rosy they were. "Thank you, my lady."

Lady Jersey left as Lady Sefton approached with that bounder Lord Lancelot. Giff almost stepped in front of Lady Alice, but another gentleman stepped forward first.

"Oh, dear." Lady Sefton didn't look at all sorry. "I fear you are too late, my lord."

Lord Lancelot made a rather theatrical bow. "Ah, my dear Lady Sefton, that only means that they may now waltz with the lady." The music for the first set started, and he bowed to Alice. It was all Giff could do not to take the man by his elaborate cravat and throw him out a window. "May I have this dance, my lady?"

Next to him, Alice stiffened slightly. There must be a way to stop his lordship.

Harry Stern, whom Giff knew from school, bowed. "I am sorry, my lord, but Lady Alice has done me the honor of promising her first set to me."

Stern always had been brilliant. Giff glanced at Lady Eleanor. "Lady Eleanor, I believe this is our set."

She gave him a polite smile. Then Montagu claimed a set with Lady Madeline, thus thoroughly routing the here-and-therein.

A dark-haired gentleman who was vaguely familiar to Giff fixed a hard look on Lancelot. "Their first three sets are taken. We will leave after supper."

The worthless fribble's bow was not nearly as showy as before, and he slinked away. By then the group around them had become larger. Giff recognized some of the other gentlemen.

"Good Lord," a gentleman with tanned skin standing with a lady who looked like Lady Madeline appeared as if he'd eaten a worm. "Not him again."

The lady's brows drew together. "He looks to be improved. At least he is not wearing a spotted kerchief as a neckcloth."

"But is he?" The gentleman who appeared familiar raised his quizzing glass at his lordship's retreating form. "I will make inquiries."

"It would be a shame not to be able to stand up with someone that gorgeous." Giff could have sworn Lady Alice had sighed.

"If you like peacocks." Giff tried not to show his ire. "He reminds me of a Gainsborough painting I once saw of a young boy in a light blue suit."

Lady Eleanor's eyes widened. "Do you know him?"

He couldn't very well tell them Lancelot's brother had caught Lord Lancelot attempting to importune a lady when Giff had been present. "Not so much know him as know of him. I went to school with one of his brothers. Lord Lancelot is said to be as spoiled as his name might suggest. He fancies himself a poet."

Stanwood's lips flattened. "I was in school with him. He was a dead bore. Perhaps it will be easier if I have a conversation with him to see if he has changed."

"I, for one, will stand up with him if he asks," Lady Madeline said. "Then we will soon know if he has improved or not."

The man who had spoken previously rubbed his forehead as if it ached. "He will not be allowed an introduction until I have determined he is the type of gentleman you should know."

Worthington. That's who he was. Ladies Alice, Eleanor, and Madeline were his wards.

Guests were taking their places for the dance. If they were going to dance this set, they must make haste. Giff held his arm out to Lady Eleanor and escorted her to the dance floor. The sisters and their partners along with one other couples joined them in circle. It was easy to carry on a conversation during the quadrille as two couples danced at the same time while the other two couples waited until it was their turn to dance.

Giff and Lady Eleanor took their places. She curtseyed, and he bowed. While they were awaiting their turn, he should attempt to discover more about Lady Alice. "Lady Alice said that the only thing different about being in Town this year was that she was finally making her come out."

Lady Eleanor shook her head slightly. "We have been coming to Town during the Season for several years. However, I do think she will change her mind about nothing being different. After all, we have never before been to balls and other entertainments. This is the first year we are allowed to go riding in the mornings without Matt or one of our brothers with us."

"I hope you are right. I would hate for her to be bored." He'd dislike it immensely if she faked enjoying herself.

"I am certain she will not be."

The other two couples returned to their places, and it was time for them to begin.

His next set was a country dance with Lady Madeline. "You have such a large group around you. Will you tell me who they are?"

"My sisters, brothers, and brothers-in-law." She grinned. "My brother, Worthington, married Alice and Eleanor's sister. Lady Grace Carpenter. They both had guardianship of their respective sisters and brothers. Ergo, we became one large family."

Giff could hardly imagine it. And they all seemed to get on with one another. He'd heard Kenilworth and Rothwell had wed. Giff hadn't known they'd married into the same family. He escorted her back to the group. The next set was the waltz. He looked forward to dancing with Lady Alice.

He led her out to the dance floor and took her in his arms, or as much in his arms as propriety would allow. Giff looked forward to learning to know her better, and this was one of the best ways to do it. Providing, of course, she did not forget how to perform the steps. The music started and within the first two movements it was clear she was extremely accomplished. She responded to his every move as if they had been dancing together for years. He spent a minute or so enjoying the set. Then he looked down into her summer blue eyes and something inside him happened. He wasn't quite sure what it was, but he was certain he needed to spend a great deal more time with her.

"What are you looking forward to most this Season?" The instant she raised her brow, he knew what a stupid question he'd asked. She was here to find a husband, just as he was here to find a wife. How could she even answer that question? And when had he become so inept? "I mean, your sister mentioned this was the first time you were allowed to ride with only a groom. Are there any other activities that have been denied to you that you may now do?"

"Driving our carriage when it arrives." She did not seem impressed by his conversation.

"What type is it?"

"A high-perched phaeton."

He knew many married ladies drove them, but a lady just out? "They can be dangerous. I'm surprised your guardian would allow it."

Her eyes narrowed slightly. "We have all been well-trained by a friend of our family who is a famous whip. Tell me, my lord. What interests you?"

Was that a bite in her tone? He did not dare tell her he wanted to marry to get his estate. That and a son. Then again, he did have his uncle's house now. "Naturally, to enjoy the Season."

"What do you do when you are not in Town?" Once more, there was something in the sound of her voice.

"I do the usual things. House parties, hunting." He almost cringed when he considered the house and hunting parties he'd attended. "I suppose you will be doing the same things now that you are out."

Lady Alice mumbled something that sounded like 'I doubt it.' "Do you do anything to help people?"

That hurt. He wanted to take care of dependents and contribute in some way to the unfortunate, but he had not had an estate, and his father kept him on a small allowance. He couldn't even afford rooms on Jermyn Street. Yet, he was not going to tell her that. "I generally leave that to others."

"I see." He'd never been at a loss in conversing with a lady. Why was this so much different? "Do you enjoy going to museums?"

She appeared interested. "Very much.

Finally, he'd found something that interested her. "I would like to take you to see the Elgin marbles if you like."

He twirled her. "I must have my eldest sister's permission. I do not think she will allow me to attend alone with you."

Naturally. How could he have forgotten? Young ladies weren't allowed to go anywhere but riding in an open carriage with a gentleman. "I will get up a party. Perhaps your sisters would enjoy the outing."

Lady Alice frowned slightly. "If you could arrange that, she will probably give her consent."

She waltzed better than any lady with whom he'd danced, yet Giff would be glad when this set ended. Lady Alice was the most disconcerting lady he had ever met. Still, he found her intriguing. And entrancing. His body tightened as he twirled her again. He wished he could be alone with her.

By the time supper, such as it was, was served, Giff had been introduced to the rest of her family and was able to join in some of the conversations. He escorted Lady Alice down to the supper room and found himself being almost herded toward a long table where the whole family was gathering. "Do you always sit together?"

She gave him a weary look. "This is our first event, but I assume we will have supper together at the others. That appears to be the habit."

After he helped her into her chair, he joined the other gentlemen in fetching supper. Somehow, Montagu appeared to have got lost. Giff made a plate for his friend to give to his lady as well. He found Montagu striding to the refreshment table and handed him the plate. "I thought you might not know."

"Thank you." He accompanied his friend back to the ladies. "Is this typical of an evening at Almack's?"

"Yes." His friend seemed focused on their table. "Albeit it is more interesting to be in the Worthingtons' group. They are all quite remarkable."

Giff had been alternately listening to Lord and Lady Phinn discuss their travels and trying to work out why he was having so much trouble conversing with Lady Alice.

Montagu said something to Lady Eleanor when Lady Worthington said, "She will do what her sisters have done before her. She will have toast and tea before riding, then join the family for breakfast." Lady Worthington gave him a considering look. "My lord, you are welcome to break your fast with us if you wish. It is no trouble at all."

That was the perfect way to spend more time with Lady Alice. "Early breakfast?"

Lady Worthington laughed lightly. "You may join us as well."

"Thank you, my lady." Giff was pleased his ploy had worked. By the time a date was set, he would have had a chance to adjust his approach to Lady Alice.

Then Montagu said, "I am happy to accept your invitation, my lady. Would tomorrow be too soon?"

She picked up her cup and looked at him over the rim. "Not at all."

That was much too soon. She glanced at Giff. "Excellent, my lady. If you will excuse me, I must go to my mother."

Lady Alice gave him a look he couldn't interpret. When had he become such a dullard? Perhaps he should go back to what he knew, flirting always seemed to work.

Chapter Seven

Alice heaved a sigh of relief when Lord St. Albans said he had to go back to his mother. When she had first seen him tonight, it struck her how handsome he was. His auburn hair curled perfectly. His eyes were so green they vied with the emerald he wore in his elegantly tied cravat. He danced better than any of the gentlemen she had stood up with at the entertainments they had attended in the country. All that male beauty and grace, and there was nothing inside. It was a shame his parents had not taught him to be more charitable to others. On the other hand, she had no idea what his family was like. The duchess could be the reason he did not appear to care about anything. Or it could be the duke. Or even his nurse.

She rode home with Matt, Grace, and her sisters. Both the inner and outer lanterns had been lit allowing them to see each other.

As soon as they were settled, Grace said, "What did you think of Almack's?"

"It was not as oppressive as I thought it would be," Madeline said. "Yet, that might have been because I was surrounded by my family and friends."

"I was happy to be able to waltz." Eleanor looked delighted.

Alice wished she had had as much fun. "It was fine." She was not looking forward to attending again. "I suppose we must go back next week."

Grace gave her a sympathetic look. "We will. But there are many other entertainments to which to look forward."

"We were supposed to attend Lady Castlereagh's, no, Lady Londonderry's ball tomorrow, but they are now in mourning," Eleanor said.

"Is there anything thing else to attend?" Madeline asked.

"Lady Markham has arranged a ball to take its place," Grace replied.

"The following night is Lady Harrington's ball," Eleanor added.

Hopefully, Alice would meet other gentlemen who had more to offer than Lord St. Albans.

"You will not have to worry about being well entertained." Matt's tone seemed almost unhappy.

Well, he need not worry about them. "We will not give you any trouble at all."

He raised both brows and pinned her with a stern look. "I've heard that before."

"It was not Dotty's fault those ladies mistook what she and Dom were doing." Madeline said. Although, that ended up well. "Or that Charlotte was kidnapped. Or that Louisa announced her marriage a bit too soon. Or that Augusta wanted to attend university." In fact, they all had happy endings.

Matt dragged a hand down his face. "Be that as it may, I would like to get through this Season without any of those things occurring again."

Her sisters, brothers-in-law, brothers, and cousins joined them for the supper Grace had planned. While everyone was getting settled, Alice decided to voice her opposition about St. Albans coming tomorrow morning. "Grace, did you have to invite St. Albans to breakfast?" Alice took a glass of wine from Thorton and was tempted to toss it down. "I am not at all certain I want him there."

"She did not have much of a choice," Matt pointed out. "He was rather like a hungry puppy."

"I suppose so." If one could call such an elegantly dressed and experienced gentleman a puppy. Alice sat down next to Charlotte and Con on one of the two large sofas in the drawing room.

"What has put your back up about St. Albans?" Con asked.

"He does not appear to care about anything. When I asked him about charitable works, he was not at all interested."

Con's eyes sparkled with mirth. "When Charlotte and I met, I was the same. I cared only for my own entertainment."

Alice had not known that. Then again, she had only been twelve years old. And he was nothing like that now. "But you changed."

"Very true. I did. Something happened that proved to me Charlotte was right about an argument we had been having. It caused me to step back and look at the life I was leading."

Were most gentlemen like that? Matt had not seemed to be, but he was responsible for his sisters. "Maybe I could talk to Lord St. Albans and make him understand how important it is to do even small acts of charity."

"You can always try. Although, I believe a gentleman must have something happen in order to effect lasting change." He glanced at Matt. "Take Worthington. He led much the same type of life I did until he decided to marry and found the lady he wanted to wed." Con's brows drew together. "I might even remember when it happened. We'd both been invited to a hunting party, and he suddenly left saying something about needing to go to Town." Con glanced at her and shrugged. "The next thing I knew he had wed."

Alice had not known that about Matt. And she did not know how she could create an event that would change someone. She should take Georgie's advice and simply enjoy Lord St. Albans's company. Yet something told Alice that it was not something she was likely to do. "Surely, he must do something other than have fun. How can one live like that? He must have some purpose in life."

Con raised a brow. "If he does, I don't know what it is. I do know he doesn't have any horrible habits."

Which habits was he thinking about? "Such as?"

He stared at her as if he did not know what he should tell her. "Gambling for instance. He hardly gambles at all, and I have only once seen him drink to excess."

Well, that was something. However, not wasting money on cards or drinking moderately did not seem such a great thing. Then again, the *ton* was full of people who ruined their families engaging in those habits. Alice nodded. "Thank you for telling me."

Con inclined his head. "It's my pleasure. Just ask if there is anything I can do to help."

Louisa suddenly broke out into laughter. "She is setting a test for him."

What was going on?

Charlotte leaned over Con. "Eleanor thinks we should bring the children to breakfast tomorrow."

Alice had to smile. That would give both her and her sister more insight into the gentlemen.

Rothwell groaned. "He's in for it now." He glanced at

Eleanor. "If you are sure that is what you want, we'll bring them."

"I for one think it is a very good idea," Dotty said. "After all, if he cannot deal with the whole family, then what good is he?"

"I agree." Charlie said. "We are an extremely close family. As evidenced"—he grinned—"by the extra trunk I had to purchase to hold all the letters I received from you."

"One does not marry the person, but the family." Rothwell appeared chagrinned. "As I have reason to know."

"It was not that bad." Louisa looked at him lovingly.

He glanced at Matt. "It did teach me to listen to more experienced heads."

"It's settled then." Con tossed off his glass of wine and stood. "Any potential spouse must get on with all of us." He helped Charlotte up and turned to Alice. "If we are going to participate in Morning Mayhem, we must be off."

"Not you too!" Eleanor sounded disapproving, but her lips were twitching. "Morning Mayhem indeed."

"You must admit"—Grace finally stopped laughing—"it does fit. Marquises picking egg from the table—"

"And dukes wiping eggs from faces," Dotty added. "The *ton* would be in shock."

"They would expect the footmen to run around cleaning up after the children, if"—Charlotte gave them an arch look— "they would even have children join them at breakfast."

Eleanor rose. "I'm for my bed as well. Morning comes earlier and earlier. Good night."

Alice was tired too. She stood and glanced at Madeline. "I'll join you."

"Yes, I am coming. It is past my bedtime."

The three of them followed Con and Charlotte out of the drawing room to the hall then to their rooms. Normally

Alice would have joined her sisters in their parlor, but this evening she wanted to keep her thoughts to herself. Even though she did not think she could fall in love and marry Lord St. Albans, he needed help. She could provide that while she was waiting for her eventual husband to appear. She still did not want him joining them to break his fast in the morning.

Giff went back to the ballroom and found his mother, who was speaking with a lady who had two young ladies both with brown hair and rather sallow complexions standing next to her.

"St. Albans." His mother took his arm and looked at the matron. "Susan, allow me to present my son, St. Albans. St. Albans this is Lady Woodville."

He bowed. "A pleasure, my lady."

The lady curtseyed. "I have heard so much about you."

Mamma glanced at one of the ladies. "Lady Ester, please allow me to present my son, Lord St. Albans." Mamma squeezed his arm. The only thing she could be suggesting is that he dance with the lady. "St. Albans, this is Lady Ester Powell."

Giff bowed and Lady Ester curtseyed gracefully, but not as gracefully as Lady Alice. "May I have the next set?"

Her lips trembled, and he didn't know if she was afraid of him or of smiling. "You may, my lord."

"Thank you. I will come for you when the prelude begins." He turned and stopped himself before he could tell his mother he wished to depart after the next set. He'd have to have a word with her when he brought Lady Ester back.

Giff circled the large room and was not pleased to see the Marquis of Normanby had been admitted. Giff hadn't liked him at school, and nothing had changed. He couldn't cut him, but he could pretend not to have seen the man.

"St. Albans," Normanby said.

So much for that idea. "Normanby. I trust you are well."

The man started to raise his quizzer, but the look in Giff's face must have made him change his mind. "Never better. I didn't think to see you here."

Giff was not at all happy with the idea that Normanby was wife hunting. "I suppose you are looking for a wife as well?"

"Indeed. It is time," the man confirmed.

It was time for Giff to have a life other than one of frivolity. But that was a subject he wouldn't mention.

Normanby sketched a shallow bow. "Good luck."

"To you as well. Please excuse me. There is someone with whom I must speak." Giff walked off. Fortunately, the prelude to the next set began. He circled around to where Lady Ester was still standing with her mother and led her to the dance floor for a country dance. She appeared more at ease than she had previously.

They took their places, and he bowed as she curtseyed. "Are you enjoying yourself this evening?"

"I am, my lord." She gave him a polite smile, and it occurred to him that she had the same expression most of the ladies had. Except for Lady Alice who had clearly showed her delight and her displeasure. "We are at Almack's, are we not?"

He gave the same smile back to Lady Ester. "We are." Complete with weak tea, sour lemonade, stale bread and butter, and dry cake. They moved forward with the movement of the set then turned to dance with the next partner.

She danced well though she was not as graceful as Lady Alice. When they came together again, she said, "Will you be at Lady Winter's ball?"

Lady Winter? He knew who she was but did not recall that being one of the events he was attending. "I am not certain. I will accompany my mother to whatever event she wishes to attend."

"I understand." The smile remained pasted on Lady Ester's face. "We have been having lovely weather."

The weather had been favorable lately. "Yes, it has been lovely." At this point he would have dropped a tidbit of gossip, but the gossip he normally discussed was not suitable for young ladies. What the devil was he to talk about? They had a new monarch. That might work. "Have you been reading about the coronation?"

Lady Ester's smile broadened a little. "Yes, indeed. How exciting it will be. Papa said we will attend. I suppose you will be there as well."

Not if he could avoid it. Giff hoped he would be on his honeymoon by then. "I imagine I will."

When they came back together again, Lady Ester said, "Did you hear that we will all be in Tudor costume?"

Giff had not and was very glad that the dance did not allow extensive conversation about the subject. It appeared being king would not halt Prinny's spending at all. He was looking forward to hearing what his mother would have to say. The set ended and he escorted Lady Ester to her mother, who had been edged out from his mother's circle. He bowed. "Enjoy the rest of your evening."

"I shall, my lord." She gave him a coquettish look.

Giff made his way to Mamma. "Are you ready to leave?"

"Yes, my dear." She made her farewells, took his arm, and they strolled to the stairs. "Who were the ladies you danced with earlier?"

"Lord Worthington's wards. Ladies Alice and Eleanor Carpenter and Lady Madeline Vivers."

"How interesting. Lord and Lady Worthington's love

story was all the rage several years ago. I hear the family is quite large."

"It is. I am joining them for breakfast after my ride tomorrow morning." They waited while their coach was being brought around.

She tilted her head as she gazed at him. "Where have you been breaking your fast?"

How did she even know he'd been dining elsewhere? "At Montagu's house. They breakfast early."

"You poor boy." Mamma patted his arm. "Soon you will have your own house, and you may eat as early as you wish."

"I trust you are correct." He noticed that she didn't offer to have Cook make him breakfast. Giff helped her into the town coach. "I have been having a problem making conversation with the young ladies."

Mamma went into a peel of laughter. "I did wonder. After all, your normal charming chatter is not suitable for them. Dear me. I suppose you should start reading some of the gossip sheets and pay more attention to court news."

He pulled a face and she laughed again. "I am glad to have amused you, ma'am."

Mamma rapped his arm with her fan. "It is your own fault. You must have known you would have to make some changes."

Giff leaned his head against the soft leather swabs and tried to form a list of suitable topics. The weather was always appropriate, as his mother had said, the royals, fashion. He knew a few gentlemen who attracted a lot of female attention because they could discuss gowns. Horses. Lady Alice had a very fine Cleveland Bay mare. Good works. She also seemed interested in those. On the other hand, he was the heir to a dukedom and what lady didn't want to be a duchess?

Chapter Eight

The next morning, Alice's sisters and brothers-in-law gathered in the breakfast room with their older children. Because they had been promised a trip to London Tower if they behaved, each one of her nieces and nephews were on their best behavior. Even Hugh, Charlotte and Con's son, was trying his best to behave. Unfortunately for him, it had not stopped a piece of egg from his fork from flying across the table, or his sister taking him to task for it.

She watched Lord St. Albans's interactions with her family, especially the children. Or rather his lack of interaction as he said very little. Yet, after Alice's talk with Con last night, she had decided to give him another opportunity to prove himself. It had not happened. He had not appeared to like having the children there at all. Of course, that did solve her problem of whether he could be made a suitable husband. In fact, she was glad he had failed the test. Every time she was around him she felt as if her skin no longer fit her properly. How or why that could be she had no idea. Alice tried to catch her twin's eye, but Eleanor was focused on Lord Montagu who had just risen from the table.

"I regret to say I must take my leave if I am not to be

late for the vote today." He bowed to Grace. "Thank you for inviting me."

"It was my pleasure." Her sister smiled.

"I must be going as well." St. Albans stood abruptly.

Alice was glad he had decided to leave.

Matt pushed back his chair and rose as well. "I'll walk you to the door."

Then the rest of her brothers-in-law departed as well.

Her sisters and Dotty remained for a while longer before going. As Alice started up the stairs, her twin gave her an odd look. "You are happy this morning."

"You obviously did not see how disgruntled Lord St. Albans was by having to share his breakfast with the children." It occurred to her she was almost gleeful about his behavior. "I do not believe he approved at all."

"You think this will convince him to look elsewhere for a lady?" Eleanor's tone was dubious.

"I certainly hope he does." Alice reached the landing and waited for her sister. "He must understand that he does not fit with the lives we have."

"We knew not many gentlemen would," her sister reminded her.

"Very true. I hope you discover Lord Montagu is one who does." Alice opened the door to her bedchamber. "I shall meet you in our parlor."

An hour later, they and their footmen made their way to the new Burlington Arcade. "It is a shame the Pantheon Bazaar has become so shabby. It used to be fun going there."

"And so inexpensive," Madeline said.

Eleanor nodded. "But the Burlington Arcade is much nicer now."

They entered a store with personal ornaments.

"I need a fan for this evening." Eleanor said, glancing

around the offerings. She picked up a fan with a scene painted in emerald green, deep pink, cream, and yellow. "What do you think?"

Alice tried to remember what her twin was wearing this evening. "You are wearing your yellow and cream gown?"

Eleanor nodded. "Yes."

That would go well. "It will brighten it up."

"Oooo. Look what I found." Madeline pointed to a pair of garnet combs displayed in a glass case.

"They are beautiful." Eleanor said. "They will sparkle in the candlelight."

Alice glanced at Eleanor. "I was going to have my maid use pearls, but now I think I would like the hairpins."

"I agree." She chose emerald glass-tipped pins and held them up.

"Yes." Alice imagined them with her sister's gown. "They would be perfect. I like the purple hairpins."

She could see her sister doing the same thing she had just done. Eleanor grinned. "I agree. The purple will go well with your gown."

Once they made their purchases, they went to Hatchards, then home for luncheon. Alice was thrilled Charlie was there as well.

"Can you give me time to speak with Matt and Charlie about my coal mine idea?" Eleanor asked.

"Of course." Alice wished she was as drawn to a cause like Eleanor was. It had been fortunate that she had inherited land that included a mine. "Try to be quick. I am quite puckish."

She smiled over her shoulder. "I will."

Alice waited with Madeline until her stomach started to growl. "I am going to have luncheon."

"I will go with you." Madeline looped her arm with Alice's. "I am a little envious of Eleanor. She has found her cause, and Lord Montagu seems to be coming along nicely."

Alice sighed. "I was just having the same thoughts. I wish I would meet a gentleman who meets the qualifications."

Giff had been rather shocked to see young children allowed at the breakfast table, especially when guests had been invited. His father would never have permitted it. Giff had even disapproved. But on his way to Cleveland House, he remembered the times he'd visited his mother's parents. Her eldest brother and his family lived in the castle along with the youngest brother and his family. As they'd been doing for centuries, everyone still broke their fast in the great hall, including the children. And his cousins had been no better behaved than the little boy whose eggs landed on the table at Worthington House. He could see his mother raise a brow at his initial reaction and question his reasons. He'd get a child, but not want it around? How, she would ask, could he possibly think such a thing was natural? The only answer, of course, was that it wasn't. Drat it all. What was it about Lady Alice that had him questioning himself? He gave himself a shake. Of course, he might question himself. He was about to change his whole life. He'd be stupid not to look at things a bit differently.

When he arrived home and dismounted, Fergus was there to take Horace. "I heard her grace wants to see ye."

"Thank you." If Fergus knew then Gunn knew and was probably getting Giff's bath ready. He wasn't going to his mother smelling of horse again. He reached his chamber and found he'd been right. Once he'd bathed, he went to Mamma's parlor and tapped on the door.

His mother's maid opened the door. "Oh, good. Her grace has been waiting for ye."

"Good morning." Mamma sat behind her desk. "I wanted to go over the next few days of entertainments with you."

He slid into the plush chair in front of her desk. "I'm all ears."

She gave him a doubtful look. "I will also give the list to Gunn." She picked up one card and put it in front of him. "Tomorrow afternoon we are going to Lady Thornhill's." Giff nodded. "The next evening, we will attend Lady Markham's ball." Giff nodded again. "Two days after that is Lady Brownly's musical evening. Do not forget and plan to be somewhere else. That is all for now."

He didn't know where the hell she thought he might go. He'd refused all the invitations he'd been sent. And he'd told her he'd do as she said. Something must have got under her skin. "Yes, ma'am."

The next day Giff accompanied his mother to Lady Thornhill's afternoon soirée. "Aren't these things usually held in the evening?"

"It will most likely continue to early evening," Mamma said. "A number of artists attend. I have always thought it was not just for the connections, but the food as well."

"A charitable venture then." Was this the type of thing to which Lady Alice had been referring?

Mamma's eyes twinkled as if she wanted to laugh. "Something of the sort. It is a way for artists to meet patrons. Although, I have never thought of it as charity. Merely a helping hand." She glanced at him as they entered the house. "Why do you ask?"

"Someone mentioned charitable activities to me the other day." He was damned if he'd tell his mother about

Lady Alice. She was perfectly capable of stirring the pot in the name of assisting.

Lady Thornhill greeted them as they entered her enormous drawing room. Giff was surprised when she bussed his mother's cheek. "Mairead, it is good to see you again. Is all well with your family?"

"In general." She drew him forward. "I'd like to present my son, the *Marquis* of St. Albans."

Her ladyship gave Mamma a look of approval. "Well done, my dear." Lady Thornhill offered her hand. "It is a pleasure to finally meet you, my lord."

No curtseying then. Taking her digits in his hand, he bowed. "The pleasure is mine, my lady."

By the sounds of it, another group came in behind them. "Your grace," Lady Thornhill smiled at Alice and her sisters. Why the devil were they here? From the little his mother had said, this wasn't a place for young ladies. At least that's what he'd thought. "Allow me to introduce to you Lady Eleanor Carpenter, Lady Alice Carpenter, and Lady Madeline Vivers." They curtseyed. "Ladies, the Duchess of Cleveland."

"It is very nice to meet you." His mother did not seem at all surprised they were here. "May I present my son, the Marquis of St. Albans?"

They curtseyed, and Lady Alice's eyes narrowed slightly. "We already know his lordship."

Mamma got a look in her eyes that did not bode well for him. "Indeed?"

"Yes, ma'am." He cleared his throat and bowed. "We were introduced by Montagu one morning when the ladies were riding and again at Almack's." When his mother didn't respond, he kept talking, "I waltzed with Lady Alice and danced with Ladies Eleanor and Madeline."

"I see." Mamma gave her attention back to the ladies. "I hope he entertained you."

Why in the bloody hell-hounds had she said that?!

"Yes, your grace," all three of them said at the same time.

At least he could take the opportunity to ask her for a set at the next ball. "Lady Alice, I'd like to ask you for the supper dance at Lady Markham's ball."

"I would be delighted, my lord." Her words were what he had expected, but she didn't sound as delighted as she should.

"Thank you." He glanced at her sisters. "I'd like to ask you for sets as well. Whichever ones you choose."

"The first country dance," Lady Eleanor said.

"The Quadrille," Lady Madeline replied.

"My pleasure." He offered his arm to Lady Alice. "Will you do me the honor of strolling with me around the room?"

Alice wanted to tell him she would not, but that would be not only churlish, but impolite, especially after she had accepted his offer of a set to be polite. "Of course."

"I've been told there are artists here."

That is what Grace had said. "I have been told that as well."

"There are also some politicians and philosophers. Lady Thornhill gathers a rather eclectic group." He sounded different than usual.

"Are you speaking with a Scottish accent?"

Lord St. Albans's reddish-brown brows shot up. "Am I?"

Well, that had surprised him. "You are."

"I've been with my mother a great deal lately. I'm probably getting it from her. She can be very Scottish when she's not in public."

That was interesting. "Have you spent much time in Scotland?"

He seemed uncomfortable for some reason. "Part of

every summer and almost every other Hogmanay. New Year's. It's what my maternal grandfather insisted upon in order for my father to marry my mother."

"I see." She glanced at a group and started in their direction.

"Who are they?"

"One of them is the artist that painted my sisters and me last year." The gathering was having a lively discussion. "I do not think I should interrupt them. The artist in the blue gown is Louisa Stuart Costello. She is extraordinarily talented."

"I shall mention her to my mother. She will know someone looking for a portraitist."

Alice was almost shocked. That was the first helpful thing he had said. "Thank you."

They had almost finished their stroll. "I wanted to tell you that your breakfast the other morning reminded me of my mother's family. Two of my uncles and their families reside with my grandparents. They all dine together as well."

Alice had been so sure he had not enjoyed the meal. She had to search for something to say to him. "I suppose they are better behaved."

He shook his head. "Not at all. I hope the little boy didn't get into too much trouble."

Poor Hugh. "He does try, but according to Worthington he takes after Kenilworth a great deal."

Lord St. Albans put a hand over his lips. "The poor child. I trust he will not inherit all of his father's bad habits."

There it was again. Con had not been funning when he said he had been different when he had met Charlotte.

They arrived near the door where Grace was speaking with Dotty. Harry Stern was standing next to Madeline, and Eleanor was with Lord Montagu. Grace had been right about these soirées being well attended. Alice was glad she had come. She was even pleasantly pleased with Lord St. Albans. Even if he had not said anything of note.

He bent his head to her and whispered, “Will you accompany me on a carriage ride tomorrow afternoon?”

“Thank you. I will.” Perhaps he would turn out to be better than she thought. Her skin started to prickle again. Maybe agreeing to a ride had not been a good idea.

Chapter Nine

Giff awoke to rain the next day, but it didn't matter. He would finally be able to have Lady Alice to himself this afternoon. His only problem was that he had nothing to do for the rest of the day. Perhaps he could find a book or visit a shop.

"Me lord, I laid out your kit," his valet said. "Cook agreed to make you breakfast. I'll fetch it when you're dressed."

"Thank you, Gunn." Had Mama given the order to Cook? Giff rose and completed his ablutions and just finished dressing when a knock came on the door.

His valet answered it and turned around with a tray of food and set it on the table. The scent of bacon filled the room. What else did he have? He lifted the lid. Eggs, porridge, bacon, and toast. The pot of tea had been set to the side. Next to it was a letter. Giff picked it up and opened it.

Dear Lord St. Albans,

The documents are ready to be signed. I will await your pleasure.

Yr. Servant,
C. Throckmorton

"Have the town coach brought around in about forty-five minutes." Giff dug into his meal.

Gunn cleared his throat. "If yer going to take the coach, you'd best be right back. His grace has need of it later this morning. It's stoating out there. If ye want to wait, the weather will clear by the afternoon."

It might be prudent to buy his own coach now that he had the funds to do it. "Thank you for telling me, but I must go immediately."

"That's what I'm here for, me lord." His valet disappeared into the dressing room.

Giff arrived in the hall just as the coach was being brought around. His father's butler handed him an umbrella and opened the door. It was coming down hard. He sprinted to the carriage where a footman wearing an oiled coat and hat waited to open the door. Fortunately, the coach had a cover over the coachman's seat. Even the horses had oil skin covers.

The traffic was heavy as they made their way into the City. He'd have to sign the documents and go directly back home. The footman had taken the umbrella and held it out as he opened the door. "We'll wait here, my lord."

"Thank you, Peters, isn't it?"

"Yes, my lord." Giff nodded and went inside.

The solicitor had anticipated his arrival. He bowed. "The documents are waiting, my lord."

"How long will this take?" Giff strode into the same room as before. "I must return soon."

"Signing them will not take long at all." Throckmorton handed Giff a pen. "However, the estate books for the past year have been sent as well along with the steward, Mr. William Kennedy." So much for not mentioning his inheritance to his father. The steward would expect to stay at the house. "He was instructed to stay at a hotel while he is here."

Giff let out a breath. "Please tell him to attend me in about two hours."

"As you wish, my lord." The solicitor signaled to one of the clerks, and the man donned a coat and departed. "I do not wish to appear forward, but do you have much experience with estate books?"

He leaned back in the chair. Giff didn't want to appear ignorant, but he was, and it wouldn't help him to pretend otherwise. "I do not."

"We have a young gentleman whose father sent him to us for legal training in preparation for him to take over his family's estate. His father is a client of ours, but lives in a remote area, and it is not always possible to quickly seek legal advice." Throckmorton studied Giff as if to assess his interest. "The gentleman, Mr. Quinney, does have significant experience running his father's estate. If you would like, he can attend your meeting with Mr. Kennedy." Throckmorton paused for a moment. "It is not that we do not trust Mr. Kennedy, but we are acting on behalf of the solicitor in Inverness who represented your late uncle's estate, and we do not know him."

The one thing Giff did not want was to appear ignorant in front of the steward. Having someone there who knew what he was doing might be helpful. At any rate, it couldn't hurt. "Yes please. I would appreciate Mr. Quinney's advice."

The solicitor seemed relieved. "Very good, my lord. I will ask him to arrive before Mr. Kennedy."

"About an hour earlier I would think. He can tell me what to expect, and I can ask him any questions I might have." Giff went back to the documents and finished signing them. "Here you are. I will expect to see Mr. Quinney in an hour." As he was a gentleman, no one would think twice about him visiting Giff.

Throckmorton picked up the documents. "The funds you requested will be in the bank by tomorrow."

Giff inclined his head. "Thank you."

It was still raining cats and dogs. He almost dashed to the coach, but not only would his valet be annoyed to have to deal with a wet jacket and boots, but his father would wonder why the seat was wet. Peters ran over to Giff and held the umbrella while he climbed into the coach. They arrived at Cleveland House none too soon. He'd just made the first landing of the staircase when he heard his father stride into the hall. He'd need to decide how long he wanted to keep his father unaware of his inheritance. But right now, he was having fun acting on his own. There was no doubt at all that Papa would try to take over once he found out, and that was something Giff could not allow. Everything had to be settled before then. He informed Gunn that he was expecting a friend.

The next several hours passed quickly. Young Mr. Quinney turned out to be only a year or two younger than Giff. The family was from Northumberland. By the time Kennedy arrived Quinney had given Giff an overview of how farming and animal husbandry worked. Kennedy arrived with his son, and Giff learned that the family had served as stewards for the Dewars for several generations. As they poured over the books, Giff was thankful for Quinney's earlier lesson.

Yet another book was set before him, and he began to read. "My uncle has a still?"

"No' just a still." William Kennedy shook his head slowly. "It's a legal venture. We make"—the man fixed Giff with a look—"ye make some of the finest whisky in the land. How much time do ye plan to spend at Dewar Hall?"

More than Giff originally thought he would. "As much time as I need to. I will also be responsible for an estate a few hours north of London that I'll receive when I wed. I hope to do that this Season."

"Yer uncle hoped ye'd be convinced to come up and marry some nice Scots girl, but I suppose yer da would have somewhat to say about that?"

Giff did not even want to imagine his father's response to him finding a local Inverness girl to wed. "That would be one way of putting it."

"That's what I told Angus." Kennedy went on to explain how the whisky business worked.

Then the discussion turned to sheep, Cheviot sheep in particular, that were raised for their wool. "Ye understand that the Dewar family did no' turn out their people. They moved some houses, but made it all work to benefit everyone," he said.

Giff had learned of the enclosures and the number of people who'd been made homeless as a result. He'd always felt that was the reason his maternal grandfather insisted he spend time with the family. He would, eventually, be in the Lords and responsible for governing the country. One thing had made him curious. "I would have expected you to stay here. What made you decide to get a hotel room?"

The older man rubbed his chin. "It's not so much a hotel as boarding house. It's run by a Scotswoman. Angus didn't want us bothering yer da."

"I understand." Someday that would change, Giff hoped.

They closed the books and put them in the bags. "What will be the protocol when I am in England?"

Kennedy slung the strap of a bag over his shoulder. "I'll send any correspondence ye need to sign or approve by express. I'd appreciate it if ye got it back as soon as ye can."

Giff nodded. "I'll keep you advised of where I am."

"Thank ye."

His son grabbed the rest of the bags and grinned. "It was a pleasure to meet ye."

"I'm glad to have met you too."

The father donned his hat. "Yer not nearly as ignorant as Angus thought ye'd be."

Before Giff followed the steward and his son out of his parlor, he glanced at Quinney, who grinned. It had been a very good idea to have him here. After the Kennedys left, Giff turned to Quinney. "Do you have any suggestions as to how I can acquire more information about the sheep and the whisky?"

"Other than speaking with other people involved in those businesses, there should be books about them. Hatchards will either have them or can order them for you."

"I'll stop by today. Thank you again for your help."

Quinney smiled. "It was my pleasure. I enjoyed seeing how other properties are run." He pulled a face. "Now back to the law."

Giff barked a laugh. "I take you're glad you didn't decide to be a barrister."

The other man's look changed to one of horror. "God forbid. Give me a horse and land to look after any day, even a cold and rainy one."

What would it have been like to have been able to learn about the estate instead of being left to his own devices? At least he'd never gone into debt or drank to excess. Well once each. That had been more than enough. His stomach growled. Gunn had kept them in sandwiches and tea, but Giff was still hungry. He'd have to eat something before he went to collect Alice. He supposed he should think of her as Lady Alice, but last night after a particularly erotic dream that involved her in his bed, he'd decided she'd be his wife, and he might as well get used to calling her by her name.

Gunn brought him more sandwiches, some apples, and a newssheet devoted to the royal family. Now he'd have something to talk about that would interest her. An hour and a half later, he pulled up in front of Worthington House. After hopping down, he threw the ribbons to a groom, and strode the short way to the front door that opened for him.

The butler bowed. "My lord. Lady Alice will be down shortly. Indeed, as he looked up the main staircase, she was descending. She wore a pale green gown embroidered with small flowers, and a spencer that hugged her form. On her head was a medium crowned bonnet decorated with flowers that had a modest brim and a wide ribbon. He was glad he could see her golden curls beneath it. God, she took his breath away. To think he'd be spending the rest of his life with her.

Giff moved to the stairs and held out his hand. "My lady."

Her lips curved into a smile. "My lord."

Alice said a short prayer that Lord St. Albans would be as pleasant as he'd been the day before. He was so handsome it would be a shame if he was not. He escorted her to his glossy black curricle with gold trim and two beautiful, perfectly matched white horses. "They are beautiful! What made you decide to choose white instead of black horses?"

When he lifted her up into the seat, she had trouble breathing. He must be holding her too tightly. "It was by chance. I was going to purchase a pair of blacks, but I couldn't find any that would do. Most of them were purely for show. Then I saw these fellows."

Lord St. Albans went around to the other side and

climbed in, took up the ribbons, and started the horses out of the square. "They are certainly a handsome pair."

He flashed her a smile that warmed her. "Did you hear the queen has decided to come to the coronation to be crowned? Word has it the king will not allow it, but she has a great deal of support from the people."

Alice had not heard about it, nor did she care. "I had not."

He appeared pleased and continued in the same vein. They reached the Park and fortunately, there were enough people they had to greet to stop his flow of royal information. He pulled up beside Lady Bellamny's carriage. "My lady." Alice smiled. "I am glad to see you."

Her ladyship gave her a wry look. "I am happy to see you as well, my dear. I trust your family is well."

"They are, thank you."

"St. Albans," her ladyship said. "I approve of your curricle. Shall I see you and the duchess at Lady Markham's ball this evening?"

"Indeed, my lady. We will be there."

"Excellent." Lady Bellamny waved them along, and he moved forward.

By the time they reached the gate, Lord St. Albans had finished with the royal family and started telling Alice about Lord Byron absconding with a young wife of an Italian count. Alice was fairly certain that was not proper conversation for a lady just making her come out. And she could not imagine running off with Lord Byron. The curricle finally came to a stop in front of Worthington House, and she almost jumped down by herself. But Lord St. Albans was there ready to help her. She held out her hand, but he wrapped his hands around her waist instead. *Drat*. There was that feeling again. The prickling. It must be because she was irritated with the man. And to think she had promised him the supper dance this evening.

Alice gave him a polite smile as he escorted her to the door, then curtseyed. “Thank you for the ride, my lord.”

He lifted her hand and kissed her fingers. Thank goodness for gloves. “The pleasure was all mine.”

The door opened, and she forced herself to keep a measured pace into the house. How could Georgie Turley have thought he was amusing? “Are either Eleanor or Madeline here?”

“No, my lady. They have not returned yet. And her ladyship is meeting with Mrs. Thorton.”

“Thank you.” Alice climbed the stairs to her room, took off her bonnet, and threw herself down on the bed. Between the ride and the dance this evening, this was going to be the longest day of her life.

CHAPTER TEN

Giff climbed back into his carriage. That had gone well. The only problem was that he now had nothing to discuss with Alice during their dance and at supper this evening. He wished she had been a little more talkative, but he now knew she was an excellent listener. He'd have to read some more news sheets. Try as he might, Giff could not work out why making conversation with her was so difficult. Words should flow easily from his lips as they always had before.

He'd planned to time his arrival at Lady Markham's ball to coincide with the set before the supper dance, thus avoiding having to stand up with another lady. But he wanted to see Alice and arrived with his mother. The moment he stepped into the ballroom his gaze was drawn to her. She seemed to glow. It could have been the gold in her cream-colored gown or the way the light made her hair shine. His first thought was to join her and remain by her side, but every time he stared toward her another gentleman claimed her attention. The fribble with whom she was now speaking said something and she laughed. She'd never laughed at anything Giff said. He started toward her when the sound of the next set started, and she went off with the other man. Who the devil was he, and what had he said to her? When the gentleman turned, Giff recognized Hereford and let out a relieved breath. As far as he knew, Hereford wasn't looking for a wife. Giff had finished his second circumference when he noticed Montagu holding onto one of the many potted trees decorating the room.

Giff lifted his quizzing glass. "Dancing with trees?

His friend dropped his hand as if it had been burnt. "I wanted to see how sturdy it was."

After scanning the room, he saw what he thought had distracted Montagu. "It had nothing at all to do with Lady Eleanor standing up with Bolingbrook, I suppose."

"Nothing at all." That was a lie.

"Of course not." Giff polished his quizzing glass with a handkerchief. "That would indicate some sort of jealousy. One doesn't experience that emotion unless one is falling in love." He caught a glimpse of Alice dancing with a gentleman he didn't recognize. His jaw tightened. It took an effort to loosen it again.

"I would think gazing at a lady standing up with another gentleman is the same thing." There was laughter in Montagu's tone.

Giff raised a brow and drawled, "I beg your pardon. Did you say something?"

"Nothing." The man's lips twitched. "Nothing at all."

It was time for a change of subject. "Your mother, sister, and Lytton arrived quite a while ago. What made you decide to come later?"

"I had some business to finish."

A large part of Giff was envious of his friend, but soon he'd have responsibilities with which to occupy himself.

"Lord St. Albans." Lady Markham strolled up to them. They were caught now. He knew better than to stop long enough to be noticed. "Please make your friend known to me."

Giff smiled and bowed. "With pleasure. My lady, allow me to present Lord Montagu. Montagu, Lady Markham."

His friend bowed. "Good evening, my lady. I trust my mother told you I would be a bit late."

"She did." Her ladyship's smile reminded him of a cat's that had caught her prey. "Now that you are here, I shall introduce you to a young lady who is in need of a dance partner." She raised a brow a Giff. "You may come along as well, my lord."

Damnation! Just what he'd hoped to avoid. Montagu was made known to a young lady, and Giff was introduced to Lady Prudence Lawler. Lady Prudence was very pretty with dark hair and brown eyes. Unfortunately, her complexion was sallow. He bowed as she curtseyed. "If your next set is free, may I claim it, my lady?"

Color rose in her cheeks and her lids lowered. "I would be delighted to stand up with you."

Giff had barely noticed the lull in the music until it started again. "Shall we?"

Smiling, she took his arm, and he led her out to form the line for a country dance. "Are you enjoying your Season?" He didn't know why he'd asked that when Lady Prudence had had to rely on their hostess to provide a partner for her.

"I am. We arrived just a few days ago, and I barely know anyone."

"I am certain you will soon make the acquaintance of a great many people." The steps separated them and brought them back together. Still, he didn't have much about which he could converse with a young lady. "Have you heard that the king is requiring those peers attending his coronation to dress in Elizabethan costume?"

"Is he indeed?" Her smile grew. "How droll. Then again, he is known for his opulence."

And spending money he didn't have. "He is."

"Will you attend?" she asked.

Not if he could find a way out of it. "I am as yet uncertain. My father will be there."

"I will not be at the coronation itself, but we are attending one of the balls afterward. I think wearing an Elizabethan gown will be a great deal of fun."

"It will certainly provide tailors the opportunity to find an inventive way to pad the hose."

She giggled lightly. "Oh dear. I had not thought of that."

Giff did not understand how the same conversation with Alice could have been so different. The set ended, and he made his way toward Alice's group. He reached them at the same time as Lady Markham and Normanby.

"Lady Madeline"—her ladyship gathered Alice and her sisters with a smile—"and Lady Alice, may I present Lord Normanby? My lord, Lady Madeline Vivers and her sister, Lady Alice Carpenter."

"My ladies, it is truly a pleasure to meet you." Normanby bowed. "Dare I ask if one of you has the supper dance available?"

Worthington looked put upon, and his lady stepped over to Lady Markham and Normanby. "I am sorry, my lord, but they both have partners. Perhaps, you could make arrangements for another time."

It was time for Giff to make his presence known. "Normanby."

"St. Albans."

He bowed to Alice and held out his arm. "Lady Alice, our set."

Her look was tight as she placed her hand in his. She must have taken a dislike to Normanby. "It is, my lord."

As he placed one hand on Alice's waist and took her hand with the other, she seemed to relax a little. He'd have to ensure that worthless here-and-therian didn't bother her.

"My father ordered his costume for the king's coronation. My mother said it was fortunate that the ladies didn't have to dress in Elizabethan gowns."

Was that all Lord St. Albans talked about? "I agree with her."

He beamed at her. "I cannot imagine the panic the modistes would be in if they had to make that many gowns."

That was actually a good point. Alice opened her mouth to respond when he continued, "I am glad I will not be present."

She would have told him that her brothers-in-law were not happy with attending, but it was their duty. While Lord St. Albans talked, she imagined the conversation she would have if she could get a word in. She would say that ladies presented to the queen were required to wear the strangest gowns. The bodice was the same as the modern fashion but the skirt was wide with the Georgian hoops. They would go on to discuss some of the reforms MPs and peers in the Lords were attempting to make. Alice made a mental note that Lord St. Albans was still talking, and for the first time she understood how Augusta had separated her thoughts from the words coming out of a gentleman's mouth. It gave Alice time to consider Lord Normanby. He was good-looking. Compared to Lord St. Albans and her brothers-in-law he could not be called handsome. But his features were pleasant and regular. She wished she had had a set to give him. With any luck, he would send a card or call on her to take her for a carriage ride. Perhaps he would meet all her requirements. He seemed nice. Lord St. Albans stopped for a breath. Separating her thoughts was an interesting process, but Alice did not think she would want to do it again. Sadly, the only good thing about standing up with his lordship was that he was an excellent dancer. She never had to think about where her feet were going, or his for that matter. The set ended. When he removed his hand from the small of her back a warmth she had not noticed left as well leaving her slightly chilled.

He bent his head and whispered. "I hope you enjoyed the dance."

At least she could tell the truth about that. "I did. Very much."

After leading her to the table that had been set up for her family, he went off to fetch their food without even asking what she liked. Alice had told her sisters she was not going to let him beat her, but it was time to give up. She considered Lord Normanby again. He was a possibility. The only thing about which she was certain was that she would no longer accept invitations from Lord St. Albans. No matter how handsome he was or how well he danced.

The next night Alice and her sisters arrived at Lady Brownly's musical evening. She had no sooner entered the drawing room when Lord St. Albans sauntered over to her, took her hand, and placed it on his arm. "Come, let us find a place to sit."

How dare he? What gall! It was all Alice could do to rein in her temper. The prickling affecting her hand and arm only increased her anger. It must be due to her dislike of him. She was tempted to remove her hand from his arm, but people were watching. "I am so sorry, my lord. I have promised my friends I will sit with them." She trusted her raised brow was sufficiently imperious. "Perhaps if you had asked earlier, I would have been able to join you."

His jaw went slack, and she turned so that no one could see her drop her hand. "I wish you a good evening."

Turning on her heel, she strode over to Penelope and Eloisa. Madeline and Harry came up to Alice. "Now what happened?" Madeline asked.

Alice pressed her lips together. "He assumed I would sit with him without even asking me ahead of time or at all."

"Not the brightest thing to do," Harry said.

The other two ladies nodded in agreement.

It was good to know that there were some reasonable gentlemen. "You see, even Harry agrees."

She tried to enjoy the singer who was indeed excellent, but Alice could feel St. Albans's gaze on the back of her neck. She would have to do something drastic to make him stop annoying her. She did not like hurting anyone's feelings, but it might be kinder to tell him she was not interested in his attentions. The problem was that one could not just go over to a gentleman and tell them to leave one alone. She could, however, avoid him and hope he got the hint. Fortunately, she would be busy with the preparations for her come out ball.

The following morning, St. Albans sent roses again. Well, at least she was not allergic to them.

"What did the roses do to offend you?" Grace asked.

"The flowers? Nothing. The gentleman is another matter." Perhaps Grace could help. "Have you ever known a gentleman who was all wrong for you, but he had the entirely different opinion?"

"No, but I only had half a Season. Augusta has had that experience. She solved it by leaving the country and marrying Phinn before she returned." Grace frowned. "Matt could tell him you are not interested."

That would be the easy way out. "No. This is something I must do myself."

"My lady." Thorton held out a note. "This just came for you."

"Thank you, Thorton." Grace took the letter, opened it, then handed it to Alice. "Lord Normanby would like you to go walking with him during the Promenade this afternoon."

Alice scanned the letter. "I wonder why a walk and not a carriage ride."

Her sister shrugged lightly. "You will take Williams with you."

"Of course." Matt always insisted a footman accompany them. "I shall write to accept." There was a request she had to make to Grace, and Alice did not know quite how to phrase it. She took a breath. Directly might be the best way. "Have you sent the invitations to the come out ball yet?" Alice, Madeline, and Eleanor had spent the better part of two days writing and addressing them.

"They are to go out today. Why do you ask?"

"I do not want Lord St. Albans there."

"Very well." Grace's eyes narrowed a little. "You do realize that I will have to make a note on his parents' card that he is not invited otherwise they might think he is included in their invitation."

"I am sorry." This was probably a huge breach of etiquette. "But I just cannot have him there."

Her sister let out a sigh. "I will think of some way to put it that will not be an insult."

"Thank you." She was not looking forward to facing the Duchess of Cleveland. Alice went to her writing table and penned her acceptance to Lord Normanby. Walking might give them more time to talk. That could be either good or horrible. Even Lord Bury, who was very entertaining, would drive her mad if there were not constant interruptions when he took her out in his curricle. She had only met Lord Normanby briefly, and her first thought was that she wished she could have exchanged partners, but it had nothing to do with Lord Normanby's looks. They were rather ordinary. He was tall, but not as tall as Lord St. Albans. Lord Normanby's hair was a dark blond that lacked the depth of Lord St. Albans's deep auburn hair, and Lord Normanby's eyes were blue gray. Nothing out of the usual. Not like Lord St. Albans's deep green ones. However, she knew that a handsome gentleman did not necessarily equate to a handsome person on the inside. This was an opportunity to get to know a new gentleman. Perhaps he was the one she would wed. Provided, of course, he was looking for a wife. Alice gave herself a shake. She was too concerned about finding someone to marry when no one was putting any pressure on her at all. Then again, Eleanor and Lord Montagu were becoming closer, and Madeline and Harry already seemed as if they belonged together. That left Alice alone. She gave herself a shake. She was worried over nothing.

His lordship arrived promptly at four o'clock. That was one mark in his favor. Almost immediately, Williams knocked on the parlor's open door. Never one to be late, Alice had already donned her hat and gloves. She picked up her reticule and stepped into the corridor. "I hope you're ready for chaperoning."

"My lady, I'm ready for anything." He patted the side of his jacket where she knew all the footmen had a thin holster pocket to carry a pistol.

"Hopefully, he has nothing nefarious on his mind." She had read a book not long ago where the heroine was strolling with a gentleman, and he had hidden a closed carriage near to the path they were taking. She had only had a young maid with her who had gone into strong hysterics. Which was no help at all. Alice took a deep breath. She was letting her imagination run away with her sense. It would be very hard to abduct someone in the Park.

As she reached the bottom tread, his lordship came forward and bowed over her hand. "Thank you for agreeing to a stroll with me."

She smiled as was expected. "It is my pleasure." Alice took his arm and Thorton opened the door. "Shall we?"

Lord Normanby glanced around. "Your maid?"

"My footman will accompany us." She was rather impressed that he had asked about a chaperon. It spoke well for him.

As if he had just noticed Williams, his lordship nodded. "In that case, we are ready." As they strolled down the street out of the square, his lordship looked down at her. "I suppose I should first ask how your Season has been going, but that seems rather trite. You would have to say that all is well. We can both see the weather is fine." So far, so good. "I must tell you that the purpose of my asking you for this walk was to secure the supper dance at Lady Turley's ball. I am only in Town for a short while. I leave for my home tomorrow."

Alice had not even been told when Georgie's ball was being held, but there was no reason she could not accept the supper dance. "Thank you. I accept your offer."

He smiled. "Thank you. Lady Markham said you are much in demand, and I am very late coming to Town."

That was odd. Why come to Town only to leave again? "How long have you been here?"

"I arrived two days ago." He gave her a rueful grin. "My mother is remarrying, and I am in charge of securing the special license. I will return after the wedding."

Alice remembered when Madeline's mother, Matt's

stepmother, although they were very close in age, remarried. There had been a great deal to do. "I hope you like her choice of husband."

"Oh, yes. He is a capital fellow. She is much happier with him than she was before." He flushed slightly. "I should not have said that."

She had thought his mother's happiness was because she was no longer a widow, but apparently not. "I wish her happy."

"Thank you. I think she will be." He sounded thoughtful. "They are going to the Continent for their honeymoon."

"Lady Markham said you and your sisters had come out together." He let the sentence hang.

"We did." She gave him a broad smile. No one would discover from her how quickly she was feeling. "Although, nothing has yet been decided, I expect them to be betrothed in the near future."

"Yes, of course." He grinned at her; his blue-gray eyes were a mix of sympathy and something else she could not place. "Very lucky. Are they love matches?"

"Yes. Everyone in the family has married for love." For some reason Alice could not explain, she needed him to believe she was not sad about her sisters marrying before her. "I am very much like one of my older sisters. She came out with another of my sisters and a dear friend and was the last to wed. In the end, it turned out to be fortunate. Her husband is perfect for her."

"That is good to know." Lord Normanby kept his head turned attentively toward Alice. "Your family is very large I take it."

She enjoyed his attention. And his interest in her and her family. "I know families who are much larger, however, our family continues to grow."

He gave her a curious look that indicated he did not know if he believed it. "That sounds wonderful."

"I think so." She glanced around and saw that they had circled the Park without speaking with anyone. How had that happened? Who had she ignored? "Tell me, do you like large dogs?"

"Of course. I have always been intrigued by them." Another mark in his favor.

"You will have to meet our Great Danes."

He briefly inclined his head. "I am sure I will like them immensely."

Alice would ask Grace to arrange a breakfast to see if Lord Normanby liked children as well. For their first engagement, it was going quite well.

CHAPTER ELEVEN

Lord Normanby departed, but fortunately the next few weeks flew by. Alice had dreaded seeing the Duchess of Cleveland again, but her grace's response to Lord St. Albans not being invited had been rather droll. She had been amused by it and blamed it on him. The next night, as they all expected, Montagu proposed to Eleanor and two weeks later they married.

Alice had come down with a bad cold and recovered just in time to attend the ceremony. Both Lord Normanby and Lord St. Albans as well as some other gentlemen had come by to leave small gifts for her ranging from bonbons to oranges and flowers. Unfortunately, just as she was feeling better, Lord St. Albans sent hyacinths that made her start sneezing again. Why could he not have asked someone which flowers she liked?

This evening was Georgie Turley's ball, and Lord Normanby had asked for the supper dance. Finally, Alice would have an opportunity to stand up with him.

They took their places on the dance floor, and he placed one hand on her waist and clasped one of her hands with his other. She had expected to feel something that would indicate he was the right gentleman for her, but there was nothing.

"I'm glad the supper set is a waltz," he said as he twirled her.

"I have noticed that they usually are." Alice wondered why that was.

"Interesting. I had not noticed."

She felt as if he was rather a stiff during the set and was a bit surprised that he was not as good a dancer as she supposed he would be. Technically, he was excellent, but there was something missing beyond his stiffness, and she could not put a name to it. She attempted to discover what it was as they went down to supper with her family.

"You must tell me what you like to eat," he said as she took her seat.

She was happy that he had actually asked her rather than assume she would like what he selected. "Almost everything but the lobster patties."

He gave her a startled look and placed a hand over his heart. "No lobster patties? What is the world coming to when people stop eating lobster patties? Hostesses will be stymied attempting to find something to replace them." He bowed. "But your wish is my command, my lady. No lobster patties it is."

Alice laughed and inclined her head. "Thank you, my lord."

She turned her head and caught the glare Lord St. Albans shot at Lord Normanby. Harry said something to Lord St. Albans, and he strolled off.

"What do you think that was about?" Madeline asked.

"I have no idea." And Alice did not care.

Harry arrived with ices in addition to with the food, and he and Madeline were soon lost in a discussion. Alice hoped she had found the person she wanted to wed in Lord Normanby. Time would tell.

His lordship did an excellent job of bringing a selection of what must have been everything but the patties. "I hope you enjoy the supper." He lowered himself into the chair next to hers. A footman came over and poured them glasses of champagne. "I brought you a few different types of ices to taste."

"Thank you." The offerings he set before her included sliced chicken, ham, poached salmon, haricot vert with thinly sliced almonds, asparagus, cheeses, fruit tartlets, and a trifle. "This is excellent."

He picked up one of the ices and tasted it. "This is wonderful. I think it is champagne." He gave her a spoon and she took a small bite. "This is lovely. It is very refreshing."

"Would you like to go walking with me again tomorrow?"

She would, but tomorrow was the party for her nieces and nephews, and she did not know how long it would last. "I am very sorry. We have a family event tomorrow that will probably last all afternoon."

"Perhaps the day after?"

"Yes. I would be delighted." Alice smiled. It was nice to have a gentleman be so solicitous instead of assuming she would like what he did.

The next day, Harry proposed to Madeline, or she proposed to him. The story Alice got from her nieces and nephews who witnessed the betrothal said both things. In any event, her sister and Harry were getting married. Alice was thrilled for them. They were perfect for each other. But again, there was only two weeks to plan the wedding. She exchanged a glance with Henrietta Fotherby, Harry's sister. Their grandmother, the Duchess of Bristol had been so certain the two would make a match she had bought a house, leaving Alice and Henrietta to decorate parts of it.

Henrietta joined Alice and said, "It is a good thing it is almost complete."

"Not that I think they will find a house they like better, but what will the duchess do if they do?"

Henrietta gave her head a little shake. "They will not. None of the other houses they will be shown are at all suitable."

Alice grinned. That sounded like something the duchess would do. "Leave it to your grandmother to be so sly."

"That is what I thought when she wrote to me."

She was certain Madeline would love the house. It also had the benefit of not being too far from Worthington House. "I cannot wait to hear what they think about it."

Henrietta leaned closer to Alice. "Nate thinks we'll be caught out. If not by Madeline, then by Harry."

At the end of the next day, that is exactly what happened. But they loved the house, and Madeline was glad not to have to do everything herself.

Lord Normanby once again arrived promptly at Worthington House for their walk. Alice tucked her hand in the crook of his arm. "It is not that I do not like strolling with you, but do you not like to drive a carriage?"

He smiled down at her, giving her a meaningful look. "I do, but then my attention would be on my horses and not on you."

That was true, she supposed. She must be careful to glance around from time to time today. "I had never thought of it in that light." This was the first time they had

had an opportunity to talk since he had returned to Town. "How was your mother's wedding?"

"Being her second marriage, it was small. One of my older sisters attended her. It was held at the chapel at our house."

"That sounds lovely. I have visited houses and castles with chapels and even small churches. Living in a house like that must be wonderful."

It was a devil of a lot of work and took a great deal of money. Money Normanby didn't have. Lady Alice smiled at him as if she was imagining experiencing the house. If there was one thing he'd learned about ladies it was to always agree with them. "It was a great deal of fun as a child. We even have priest holes."

She glanced up and looked around. "We must greet Lady Bellamny."

"How amazing." That old busybody. He escorted Lady Alice to her ladyship after she greeted Lady Bellamny. He bowed. "My lady."

She inclined her head. "Normanby. How is your mother? I have not seen her in Town this Season."

"She recently remarried and is off to France on her wedding trip."

"Coltrane?" she asked.

"Who else? He has been her faithful cicisbeo for years."

From the corner of his eyes, he could see Lady Alice watching the conversation. Would she even understand it? From what he'd heard and seen of her family, they were depressingly monogamous. Even Kenilworth had got rid of his mistress and not taken another.

"Lady Alice, I do not suppose you have heard from Lady Eleanor yet?"

"No, my lady. It has been too soon."

"You two be on your way." He was glad when her

ladyship waved them off. If anyone could discover his masquerade, it was her. All Normanby had to do was hold on for a few more weeks, and he would have everything he wanted in a wife. Good bloodlines, beauty, and wealth.

When they reached Worthington House, he bowed. “May I see you again tomorrow?”

“I have another engagement.” She lightly bit her bottom lip, and he could see himself bedding her. She would not compare with his mistress, Celeste, but he would be able to perform. “I will not be available for the next two weeks.”

“Are you going away?” That would scuttle all his plans.

“No. I simply have a great many engagements which I must attend.”

Normanby had hoped he’d have her betrothed by then, but that would have to be good enough. He’d wanted to be seen with her enough to cause some tongues to start to wag. “Until then.”

“I am looking forward to it.” She curtseyed. “In a few days you will hear about it.” With that cryptic remark, she entered the house.

As Alice had expected, the next two weeks were madness. To make things worse, just before the wedding, Lady Wolverton, Madeline’s mother, decided to object to Harry. Alice did not know how it was resolved, but it was. Harry’s grandmother, the duchess, and his parents came to Town. If it was not for the early morning rides in the Park, they would have all been ready for bedlam. The only thing that spoilt the rides was that Lord St. Albans continued to attend. Not that Alice had to speak with him much at all. Georgie Turley, Henrietta Fotherby, and Dorie Exeter were there as well.

Matt was able to contact Montagu and Eleanor, and

they arrived the day before the wedding. The ceremony itself was held in the garden. Harry and Madeline were surrounded by their family including the Great Danes. As Alice listened to the vows being said, she was at once overjoyed for her sister and at the same time felt alone. Her sisters were on their way to creating their own families, and she had been left behind. She gave herself a shake. Lord Normanby was waiting to take her walking again. This time she would find out if he met the requirements on her list.

Giff had stayed up late into the night going over the information Mr. Kennedy had sent trying to make sense of it all. He was probably going to have to send a note to Quinney asking for his help. As a consequence of Giff's late night, he arrived at the Park as Alice was departing. At least he'd have a chance to see her this afternoon at the Venetian Breakfast they were both attending at a riverside estate near Richmond. He just hoped Normanby wasn't there.

When he arrived, she was standing with Lady Turley and some other ladies. Giff made himself stroll in a circuitous manner to Alice's side and greeted the other ladies. "Lady Alice, would you do me the honor of strolling with me?"

"Of course, my lord." She glanced at the others. "Please excuse me."

The day was warm and as they neared the river the slight breeze was refreshing. He stopped and faced her. "I would like to discuss the possibility of you becoming my wife."

Alice sniffed and looked down her lovely nose at him. "You are not qualified to be my husband."

The devil I'm not! "What do you mean I'm not qualified?" This couldn't be happening. "I'm the heir to a dukedom."

She raised one imperious brow. "Be that as it may, I have a list, and you do not meet the qualifications."

"A list?" He'd thought things had been going well. He could have sworn he'd recovered from not being invited to her come out ball. Normanby must have something to do with this. Giff wanted to bash his head against a wall.

"Yes." She nodded sharply. "A list of qualifications a gentleman must have before I will marry him. You do not meet the qualifications, and marrying a duke or a future duke is not one of them."

"What are they then?" They could not be that difficult.

Her beautiful blue eyes hardened into an icy glare. "One of them is to listen. Do you realize that this is the first time I have been able to get a word in when you start talking?"

"I paused." He thought she hadn't wanted to speak.

"Only to take a breath and talk again. It is as if you are more enamored with the sound of your own voice than hearing what the person with whom you are conversing has to say."

That hurt. "What do you wish to discuss?"

"Almost anything but the royal family and gossip." She glanced around, and he followed her gaze. "We are going to attract attention." Without another word, she strolled off.

What in perdition was he going to do now? *Bloody hell-hounds!* Stern had been right. Giff knew next to nothing about Alice other than he wanted to marry her. Well, he was not going to give up. The problem was how was he to find out what she liked and discover the qualifications so that he could meet them. Once he had succeeded, she would change her mind and be happy to wed him.

"Send them flowers, waltz with them, compliment them. Being wealthy and having a title is all part of it. She will see that being a future duchess is in her best interest."

Giff couldn't believe he'd truly uttered those words. What a fool he'd been. One good thing was coming of this. At least he could stop reading the court pages and gossip rags.

He watched as she walked away, her spine stiff, her shoulders straight, and her hips swaying softly. God, she was magnificent. It occurred to him that he should immediately apply to Worthington for her hand. He made his way to his hostess and thanked her for a lovely event then drove back to Town.

Chapter Twelve

Giff was admitted to Worthington House by the butler. "Good day, my lord."

He wanted to run a finger under his cravat. For the first time, it occurred to him that if anyone knew Alice had summarily rejected him, he might not be allowed in. "I would like to see Lord Worthington."

"I shall see if he is available." The man left without showing Giff to a parlor. Could it be that Worthington meant to refuse to see Giff? Before his thoughts went any further, he was mugged by a young Great Dane with a lead trailing from her mouth.

"Miss Posy," a footman said as he hurried after her. "You must give me the lead."

Ignoring the servant as very young aristocratic ladies were wont to do, "Miss Posy" leaned against Giff and begged to be stroked. Unable to resist her beseeching brown eyes, he complied and managed to get the leash away from her and hand it to the beleaguered-looking footman.

"Thank you, sir." He attached the line to the dog's collar.

Other than at his mother's family house, he'd never

seen large dogs living inside a house. Especially a London town house. "Does this happen often?"

"Only when she decides to be naughty." The servant gave Miss Posy a hard look and Giff could have sworn she batted her eyes at the man. Although, she did switch her attentions to the servant for the desired pats.

"You're a fickle lass." She turned to Giff again.

"Miss Posy," the butler said as he entered the hall. "Be a good girl and go for your walk. Master Zeus is waiting for you." Once the footman had taken the dog away, the butler glanced at Giff. "My lord, if you will please wait in the parlor, his lordship will be with you in a few minutes."

"Thank you." He handed the butler his hat, followed him to a well-appointed room off the hall, and made himself as comfortable as he could while he awaited his audience with Worthington. He almost wished the man would just give his approval and tell Alice of his decision, but Giff knew that was not likely to happen. Montagu had already informed Giff that Worthington had said it was Lady Eleanor's choice. Harry Stern had been told the same thing when he'd asked to wed Lady Madeline. What Giff hoped he'd gain from this was Worthington's permission to ask Alice to dance twice in an evening. Mamma had been right when she'd said dancing was the best way to charm a lady. Then again, nothing he did seemed to charm Alice. Never one to back down from a challenge, he was determined to find out what was on the list and charm her right into their marriage bed. The door opened, but it was not the butler. He rose as Lady Mary, Alice's youngest sister, slipped into the room leaving the door partially opened.

Why the devil was she here? A sense of dread slithered down his back. "Has he sent you to come to get me?"

"No." Her long braids swung as she shook her head. "Matt is with someone else at the moment." She tilted her head and gave him a knowing look very much like her eldest sister, Lady Worthington's. "I am here to offer you assistance."

He was about to scoff. After all, she was still in the schoolroom, but who would know Alice better than her sisters? "About what?"

She perched on the chair, and he resumed his seat on the small sofa. "We do not like Lord Normanby. There is something smoky about him." Cant from a schoolroom lady? "Theo and I pray daily that Matt will discover something is wrong with him." Lady Mary narrowed her eyes. "We both have a bad feeling about him. Even Posy does not like him."

That *was* bad. He'd only just met her, but she seemed like a dog who would take to anyone. Suddenly, Giff knew with whom Worthington was meeting. "He's here with your brother."

"He is." The girl's dark blond brows rose. "Now, do you want to hear what I have to say, or am I wasting my time?"

Good Lord! She sounded like Lady Bellamny. How old was she? "Yes. I wish to listen."

"Good." Still keeping her back straight, she seemed to settle more deeply into the chair. "You need to become Alice's friend."

Giff had never had a female friend. "How do I do that?"

Lady Mary appeared as if she'd like to roll her eyes. "How does one become anyone's friend? You do things with her that you both enjoy. You are there to listen to her when she needs to talk. And you are there to help her when she requires it."

"I can't very well take her to Tats or meet her at a club or coffee house." Giff knew one thing he and Alice would enjoy, but it would involve getting her into his bed.

"No, of course not." Lady Mary let out what sounded like an exasperated breath.

He dragged his thoughts back to what she most likely meant. "Go shopping?"

"That is one activity. Many gentlemen do enjoy shopping with ladies. You *do* read?" The last part was said with a high degree of skepticism.

"I do. Naturally, I read." Although, he'd never read any of the romance novels of which the ladies were so fond. And currently he was wading through books on estate management.

"Have you read Anna Maria Porter? Alice enjoyed her latest book and is looking forward to reading *The Village of Mariendorpt* quite a lot. She has also read the American author James Fenimore Cooper's *Precaution*. It was interesting in that it tried to copy the works of more successful English female authors."

Giff had heard of the book. "I thought that was written by a woman?"

Lady Mary waved her hand as if it was of no importance. "It was originally published under a pseudonym. The point is that you could read it and discuss it with her. She also likes Miss Austen's books. Such a shame that she died."

He had the feeling she was not only mourning the woman, but the books that would no longer be forthcoming. As to Fenimore, Mamma had enjoyed *Precaution*. He could borrow her copy. "I could discover which other books she likes." They still rode together in the morning. "That's a start, I suppose."

"I assume you must know something about running an estate. Alice is very interested in the subject." Lady Mary turned her head sharply, and there was the sound of someone entering the hall. "And no hyacinths. She is allergic to them. I must go."

Damn him for an idiot. He didn't even know the flowers Alice liked. He hadn't ever bothered to find out.

Lady Mary left the parlor as quietly as she had entered it. From the hall he heard her say, "Good afternoon, my lord."

Giff went to the door to better listen to what was being said. Something told him the girl had a plan.

"Good afternoon." It was Normanby, and he grumbled at her. That was not well done of him.

She, on the other hand, sounded cheerful. "How did your meeting with my brother go?"

"As well as it could, I suppose. Although, why anyone would allow a lady to choose her own husband is beyond me."

Giff wished he could see Lady Mary's reaction to that.

"It is a family tradition." There was a bite in her tone. "Just as there is a tradition of keeping our family close even after one marries."

"I must suppose that would depend upon who one marries."

"Not at all. Have a good day."

The door closed, and the butler entered the room. "My lord, his lordship will see you now."

When Giff followed the butler into the hall, Lady Mary was gone. What she had said about the family maintaining close ties struck him. He'd seen it at the breakfast he'd attended. If he wanted Alice, he had to be prepared to accept the rest of her family as well. Even the children. Especially the children. Blast it all. He should have asked Lady Mary about the list.

CHAPTER THIRTEEN

Alice awoke to rain, meaning she would not be able to ride today. However, Lord Normanby had asked her to walk with him this afternoon. Throwing her legs over the side of the bed, she donned her robe, crossed the corridor into the parlor, and took out the list she and her sisters had written.

Intelligent
Kind
Like house animals
Like children
Make us laugh, and think we are funny
Interested in the plight of the poor and unfortunate
Must support us in our charities and other ventures
Passable looking
Allow us to be ourselves
Be able to support a family
Must love us in return

Taking out a pen, she dipped it in the standish and wrote, *Be a friend* at the bottom. Since Eleanor's wedding, it had struck Alice forcibly that as she would not have her sisters with her all the time, whoever she married must be a friend as well as a husband. Thus far, Lord Normanby seemed intelligent and kind. She would know more by the end of their walk today.

She went back to her bedchamber, washed, and dressed, then went down to the breakfast room.

Elizabeth yawned. "Posy is not happy. She tried to hide under my bed, but George found her and took her out."

Alice smiled as she pictured the Dane attempting to crawl under her niece's low bed. "I am surprised she did not come to my chamber."

"The door to the nursery was closed," Gideon said.

The footmen were most likely tired of hunting for Posy when it was raining.

Mary and Theo took their seats. The two of them had their heads together. Alice wondered if Mary would feel left behind after Theo wed. The three years between them had not kept them from being fast friends, but it would stop them from coming out together. A footman set a pot of tea on the table in front of her, and she poured a cup.

"What would you like this morning, my lady?"

"Shirred eggs, toast, and whatever fruit we have." She would have to find something to do until her walk this afternoon.

"The table looks empty," Gideon said.

Matt looked at him with slightly raised brows. "It won't when everyone visits."

"We will have to put another leaf in the table when the rest of the family is here," Grace added.

Looking at it from Gideon's point of view, Alice had to agree. When she married, there would be one more person gone. That is how it felt when her older sisters had wed.

But then he and Elizabeth were able to join them. "In no time at all Edward and Gaia will be sitting at the table."

"They're just babies." He stuck a fork in the eggs he'd been brought.

"So were you," Mary said.

His little face scrunched up. "I suppose you're right. I just never think about them growing up."

Matt covered his mouth with a serviette, and his shoulders shook.

Grace regarded her eldest son. "It is the way of things that children grow."

"And if things proceed as usual," Theo said, "you will have new cousins next year."

Well, that brough it full circle back to Alice. She was ready to be a wife and mother and have a house of her own. If only she could find a husband. Normanby had to be the one. He had already displayed most of the necessary traits. She did not want to be left behind.

"Alice," Grace said, "what do you plan to do this morning?"

That was an excellent question. She may as well keep to the regular schedule until she could think of something else. "I will do some shopping and go to Hatchards."

"While you are at Hatchards, would you mind collecting the books I ordered?"

"Not at all. Did you happen to order Miss Anna Maria Porter's latest book?"

Grace's eyes widened in surprise. "I did not know she had a new one."

That would give her more time to see what else the bookstore had. "I will look for it and place an order if they do not have it."

"Take the town coach if it is still raining," Matt said. "I'll have it sent back for you."

"Thank you." Alice finished her breakfast. "When do you depart?"

He glanced at the clock. "Shortly." Rising, he went to Grace and kissed her cheek. "I shall see you later."

Alice looked at Mary and Theo. "Is there anything you would like me to fetch for you?"

"Yes, please," Mary said. "I will write a list."

"I shall add what I want to her list," Theo rose and turned to Mary. "If you wish to get that done before classes, we had better go."

Mary glanced at Alice. "What time do you plan to leave?"

"Around nine-thirty. I will go to the Arcade first."

Giff sighed with relief when he heard rain hitting his window. When he'd returned home from the lecture Lady Mary had given to him, he had gone to the library and found copies of Miss Austen's books and a copy of Cooper's *Precaution*. He spent the rest of the day and most of the night reading. By the time he finally went to sleep, he understood exactly why Cooper's book had missed the mark, and why Lady Mary thought it could be a topic of discussion with Alice. He rose, and was pleased to see his breakfast was waiting in his parlor. Now that he had some idea of the tact he should take, he could imagine sitting across the table from Alice and discussing books. Of course, it was even easier to envision waking up with her next to him.

A knock came on his door.

"Enter."

A footman came in and handed him a note on a silver salver. "This just came for you, my lord."

Giff opened it, and his jaw almost dropped.

Dear Lord St. Albans,

You should be at Hatchards no later than ten-thirty and wait as long as you need to.

Yer friend,
M.C.

He was being managed by an eleven-year-old. Yet surely, she had not sent a footman. "Who brought this?"

"A boy who said to give it to you straightaway."

"A street urchin?"

"No, my lord. He was clean enough and looked well nourished."

Where had she found a lad to do her bidding? Giff gave himself a shake. He'd eventually have his questions answered. He pulled out his pocket watch. He only had an hour, and there were a few things he must do. Chief of which was to speak with his mother.

He knocked on the door of her parlor. Her maid let him in. "Good morning, Mamma."

She gave him her cheek to buss. "Good morning. What can I do for you?"

"I need to discover more about Normanby's family. There is something about him I do not trust, but I can't put my finger on it."

One dark russet brow rose. "Would this have anything to do with Lady Alice?"

"Yes. I think I know what I've been doing wrong in approaching her, but Normanby has been courting her. I don't want her to accept an offer from him before I have a chance to mend my mistakes with her."

"Hmm." Mamma picked up her teacup. "What could he be hiding, I wonder? His mother did not come for the Season, which is unusual. She also recently wed when she said she would never do so again. Let me see what I can discover."

"Thank you." Giff had learned that the older ladies, not that he thought his mother was that old, had avenues of information others did not possess. In the meantime, he would look around as well. "I will see you at dinner."

A line appeared between her eyes as if she was thinking, then she glanced at him. "Until then."

"Thank you." A thought occurred to him. "I'm going to Hatchards. Do you want me to bring you anything?"

Mamma's face brightened. "Please see if they have a new book by one of the Misses Porter. I believe one is releasing soon."

That was fortuitous. "My pleasure."

Giff arrived at the bookstore shortly before the appointed time and began to peruse the shelves. He'd been there on many occasions before but only to pick up books he'd ordered. This was the first time he'd taken the time to just browse. He found the section on estate management and discovered several books he'd not known about. As he started toward the area that housed novels, the outside door opened, and Alice greeted the clerk.

"Good morning." She sounded as if she was in a good mood. "I must fetch the books my sister, Lady Worthington, ordered after I search for something for myself. Can you tell me if you have received Porter's *The Village of Mariendorpt*?"

"Good morning to you, my lady. We have several copies. Shall I get one for you?"

"No, thank you. I would rather look for myself."

"As you wish. I will wrap up the books for Lady Worthington."

Giff glanced over the rail in time to see her flash a smile at the clerk, then ducked back. He was staring at the shelves when she entered the area. “Lord St. Albans. What are you doing here?”

He plucked a book by Miss Austen off the shelf. “Searching for books.”

“I did not know you read.” Alice sounded surprised.

What was it about him that made the ladies in her family doubt his reading skills? “I did attend university. It is a required skill.”

Chapter Fourteen

Alice was astounded to see Lord St. Albans in Hatchards. Well, not the bookstore precisely, but in the section with the novels. She had, of course, said the first thing that came to her tongue without passing through her brain first. Naturally, he had the skill to read. She strained to see which book he held. "I meant I did not know you read novels."

"I find Miss Austen extremely erudite and witty." He glanced at the books again and started to scan them. "Have you seen *The Village of Mariendorpt*?"

Now she was shocked. "That is the book for which I am searching."

He backed up, glanced again, and took two books from the shelf. He handed her one. "Here you are."

"Thank you." Alice had what she came for but was strangely reluctant to leave. "Are you here just for Miss Porter's book?"

A flush crept into his cheeks. "Ah, no. I need a book on estate practices and sheep husbandry if there is one." He focused on her as if trying to make a decision. "I am quite ignorant on the subjects."

"Indeed?" He was full of surprises today. "I thought all gentlemen were trained to run their estates."

"Yes, well, my father has some odd ideas, and he has not allowed me to learn." Lord St. Albans frowned. "I mean, I could have read about the subject, but I have not been given an opportunity to have any practical knowledge."

How curious. And aggravating. "I do not understand that at all. What possible reason could he have to keep you ignorant about a subject with which you must be conversant?" If nothing else, she could help him find the right tomes on estate management. "I shall help you."

Lord St. Albans gave her a relieved smile. "I would appreciate that a great deal."

Strange. He did not seem at all amazed that she knew about the subject. Then again, he was a friend of Montagu's, and he might have told Lord St. Albans about Eleanor's knowledge. "Come with me." She led him to the section on farming, estates, and animal husbandry. "Many of the books will essentially apply to all areas of the country. However, you will have to adapt some of the methods."

He nodded then glanced at her. "Would it help to know where the estates are located?"

Why could he not have discussed this with her before? "It might."

St. Albans's green gaze met hers. "The estate I will first have is only about three hours north of here. That is the one for which I will be responsible for the remainder of my father's life."

Alice interrupted him. "Will be?"

He gave her a look of long suffering. "Yes, I will tell you about it later." She nodded. "The dukedom's main estate is north of York near the sea. There are several others." He took a breath. "The one that is my current and main concern is in Scotland near Inverness. My great-great-uncle on my mother's side left it to me."

"And you know nothing." It was not at all good to be thrown into something as complicated as estate management. "Oh, dear."

He let out a breath. "I assure you my response was much stronger. I am immensely grateful he left it to me. He and I were close, and I spent a great deal of time there. However, I am totally unprepared for the responsibility."

Why did his uncle not train him? "Did he know that?"

St. Albans's gave a light shrug. "To be honest, it never came up. He refused to tell anyone who he had named his heir."

What a bunch of numskulls. "You seem to have a great many odd relatives."

He winced. "I can only suppose he expected my father to attend to it."

The less said about his father the better. At least until she knew the whole story. "We had better get started." Alice reached up but could not reach the book she wanted.

"May I help you?"

"Please. I want Grisenthwaite's *A New Theory of Agriculture*. It was published a few years ago, but it is an excellent place to begin." St. Albans—when had she stopped using "lord"? She shook her head. This was not the time to ponder the change. "I do not suppose you have heard of Coke of Norfolk or Holkham Hall?" St. Albans—*Lord* St. Albans shook his head. "I do not know why I asked." She took the volume. "Now we are looking for Davy's *Elements of Agricultural Chemistry*."

"I've got it here." He tugged a book out and gave it to her.

"Excellent." She put it on a table with chairs around it.

"We can go over these before you start reading on your own."

"I also require books on sheep and whisky."

He really did need a great deal of advice. "We will get there. Although, I must admit, I know very little about whisky."

A smile grew on his well-formed lips. "My uncle believed that in England it would one day rival brandy."

"Never having tasted either libation, I have no opinion." Which only meant she must remedy her lack of knowledge. "Be that as it may, I advise you begin with one subject first then move on to the others. Davy's book will touch on sheep and other animals." She took a seat. St. Albans lowered himself into the chair to the near side of the rectangular table. Alice turned the book so that they could both see it and began to explain what was in the different chapters. When she was done, he had a dazed look about him. "Are you well?"

"Yes." He gave himself a slight shake. "Yes. It is a great deal to take in."

She closed the book. "If you are going to do something, you should do it well."

"I agree." He inclined his head. "What about the next one?"

"It is very much the same but from a slightly different perspective. Davy's book was developed from a compilation of papers written by landowners"—she did not need to tell him they were Whig aristocrats—"discussing the results of thc different farming methods."

Understanding donned on his lean face. "Which is where I discover what worked in different areas."

"Exactly." It occurred to her that she was pleased he had immediately made the connection.

He gathered the books together. "If it was not raining,

I would ask you if you would like to go with me to Gunter's. If you like ices, that is?"

How very nice of him. "I do like them, and we can go today. The rain had cleared by the time I arrived here. I sent my groom back for my high-perched phaeton."

St. Albans grinned. "You mentioned it to me once. I would be delighted to ride in it."

He was the first gentleman who had not blanched when she mentioned taking them up. He had, apparently, also changed his perspective on her driving one. "In that case, let us pay for our purchases and go to Gunter's."

After gathering up their books, he offered her his arm, and they went to the clerk's desk where Grace's volumes were waiting. She handed the man the books she had decided to purchase. "Please wrap these as well."

Once that was done, the clerk attended to St. Albans's books. He took all the packages, and they strolled to the pavement where Robertson was walking her pair. Without asking what to do with them, St. Albans deposited the packages into the box built onto the back of the carriage as they passed it. He then helped her into the phaeton.

As she settled her skirts, St. Albans climbed into the other side. "I assumed you'd tell me if the books didn't go into the box."

Alice gifted him with a smile. One of the few he'd received from her. "You did well. We added it for that purpose."

"Thank you." This was the first time Giff had not had to worry about conversing with Alice. It occurred to him that if he had just treated her as a person he would have been much better off. Still, he took what her sister had said to heart. He would become her friend.

She turned toward her groom. "I will see you at home."

"Yes, my lady." The man bowed and strode off.

"I very much like your phaeton." It was painted the same color as the Dunnock bird's eggs. It had gold piping and seats in a tan color. A very practical convertible cover was matched to the blue of the carriage. Her dappled gray horses seemed designed to coordinate with the overall color scheme. "Your pair are beautiful. Are they Percherons?"

She smiled at him again. "They are. We looked at a few different breeds, but the Percherons are known for their steady temperament."

Thus, making them excellent carriage horses. Giff remembered the name she had given her hack also indicated a dependable temperament. That must be important to her. He was dependable. Giff must remember to show her that trait. "They are indeed."

Alice started the horses and expertly wove her way around the traffic to Berkeley Square and Gunter's.

She pulled up to the side of the street and a waiter ran out. "Would you like to hear our specials?"

"Yes, please," Alice immediately responded.

Giff just nodded, and the man rattled off several different types of ices. He glanced at her.

"I will have the raspberry ice."

"I will try the pineapple." It was a flavor he'd never tasted before.

Alice turned to him. "Harry said it was very good, but Madeline really only likes chocolate."

Giff hadn't known Stern took Lady Madeline to Gunter's. And on a fairly regular basis it would seem. "I don't know what I would have done without your help. How did you become so knowledgeable?"

"Grace taught us as she did our sisters before us." Alice's light laughter reminded him of tinkling bells. "Even Augusta had to learn, and she is really only interested in languages." Giff had no idea who Lady Augusta was, yet he suspected she was at the breakfast he attended and probably at one other event. As if Alice knew he was having trouble placing her sister, she said, "She was the lady next to Phinn Carter-Woods. They are married."

Giff had heard Carter-Woods had wed. "Ah, yes. Dark hair and looks very like Lady Madeline and your sister Rothwell."

Alice nodded as the waiter returned with their ices. She took a bite and closed her eyes. Just seeing her enjoyment made him hard. If only he could make her look like that. Hoping to cool himself down he quickly ate his ice. A highland loch would have worked better.

"Will you tell me why your father would not teach you how to care for your future estates?"

Her question ended his vision of her with him in a loch. "It is some sort of strange tradition. I'm not at all sure how far back it goes, but his father, my grandfather, did the same thing. The heir is only allowed to have the heir's house and learn by doing when he is married. I was not even allowed to ask our steward to teach me."

One brow rose. "The reason you wish to wed is so that you can have the estate?"

Of course, she would pick up on that. "Me? No. I mean, I do want the estate. It is my favorite of them all. But he has held it over my head since I came down from St. Andrew's. I refused to consider marriage until I was ready to have a wife and children."

Her concentration on him was so intent he wanted to run a finger under his collar. "Is that the reason your uncle left you his estate?"

"I don't know. It might be. He and my father didn't like one another." She was extremely shrewd. "My mother's father made my father agree that I would spend part of every year in Scotland. Usually over New Year's and in summer."

Alice nodded sharply. "That sounds like something Matt would do."

Once again, he noticed the similarities with her family and his mother's. "So I have heard."

She tilted her head at him and laughed. "I imagine Montagu told you about it."

"He did." Giff smiled remembering how put out his friend had initially been. "One of your brothers-in-law told him before he proposed to Lady Eleanor."

"I had no idea they had been so busy," Alice mused.

If she only knew it was not just the gentlemen who were involving themselves. "I think it must be done out of caring for your sister."

"Yes, of course." She appeared to think about that as she sucked the last of the ice from the spoon. An image of her lips on him caused Giff to suppress a groan.

The waiter came for the cups, and he paid for their ices, but she didn't start the horses. "What is the estate like that you will receive when you wed?"

It occurred to him that this was the only place they could continue to talk. She could not take him home unless she stopped at Worthington House and picked up a groom. That was something else Montagu had let drop. They were always accompanied by male servants. "It's called Whippoorwill Manor."

The interest in her beautiful blue eyes increased. "What is a whippoorwill?"

"It is a bird native to North America. Apparently. Well, the story is that one of my great-great-grandmothers lived in Canada for several years, and she had fallen in love with the song of the whippoorwill. When they moved into the manor, she renamed it."

"I am surprised her father-in-law allowed her to change the name."

He was too. "I asked about that as well. The change was not official until he died, and she became the duchess."

She opened her brooch watch, looked at it, and closed it. "I had no idea how long I have been gone." She pulled a face. "I must go home."

Alice mustn't feel badly about not being able to take him to his house. "I will walk from Worthington House. I'll enjoy the stroll."

"If you are certain." She obviously was not convinced.

"Very. I would have walked to Hatchards if it hadn't been raining when I left."

She started the carriage, and when they arrived at Worthington House he jumped down and went to her side of the phaeton. The carriage was too high for him to have lifted her into it, but he could lift her down. Giff clasped his hands around her waist and didn't ever want to let go. Her breathing quickened. She sucked in a breath when her feet reached the pavement and he had to pry his fingers from her one by one. "May I call on you if I have any questions?"

"Yes, of course you may." She smiled at him again.

"Thank you." He would have a great many inquiries, of that he was certain. In fact, he should make a list.

"It was my pleasure." Alice took his arm as they walked to the door. "It is always nice to converse with a gentleman who listens."

He had been a total idiot. "I apologize deeply for not attending to you before. To be honest. I didn't know what to say to you."

Her brow went up again. "Did it not occur to you to

speak to me as you did to other ladies? Quite frankly, I could not understand how they thought you were so interesting."

That was blunt. "I was afraid of offending you by flirting. You cannot imagine my relief at not having to read the court and scandal sheets."

She let out a peel of laughter. "At least I now know that it was as painful for you as it was for me."

He bent over her hand and kissed the back, wishing she wasn't wearing gloves. "I hope we will be friends."

Her eyes widened and the corners of her rosy lips tipped up. "I do as well."

The door opened revealing the butler. Straightening, Giff reluctantly gave her back her hand. "Let me know how you like *The Village of Mariendorpt*. I will have to wait until my mother finishes the book before I am able read it."

"I shall. Then, after you have had a chance to read it, we may discuss the story."

"I'd like that." He'd like any time he could spend with her. "Until we meet again."

Alice started to turn and stopped. "I have a country dance open at Lady Millsworth's ball."

His heart almost stopped beating. After what had happened yesterday, he never thought she would offer him a dance so soon. "May I have the set?"

"You may, my lord."

"Thank you." All he had to do was find out when the ball was.

Chapter Fifteen

Normanby was escorted into Mr. Greenway's office for the purpose of discussing the settlement agreements Normanby was now almost certain he wouldn't require. Miss Greenway's name had been given to him by his man of business as a way to alleviate his financial situation. The Greenways had only been told that Normanby had seen Miss Greenway and was smitten by her. They were grasping enough to believe it. Subsequently, an introduction was arranged. She was quite beautiful and practical and was willing to do as her parents wished. Ergo, marry into the peerage. Her manners and speech were acceptable. She could pass as gentry. If it were not for the fact that her father was a Cit, she would have done. However, her father *was* a *Cit*. Her mother was a daughter of a Cit, and a chill snaked down his spine every time he thought of sullying his bloodline. God only knew what kind of mongrel blood would run through his children's veins. Normanby repressed a shudder. Thankfully, he would only have to play this game for a little longer. Soon Lady Alice Carpenter would agree to wed him. Yet for the present, his creditors knew he was betrothed to the daughter of the very wealthy

Mr. Greenfield of the City and that would keep them at bay until he secured Lady Alice.

The man rose, bowed, and came forward as Normanby entered the faintly ostentatious office. "My lord. Thank you for meeting me here."

Normanby inclined his head. What he did not want was for the man to see his reduced circumstances. He could probably explain it, but why go to the bother when he could bestow such a boon on his so-called future father-in-law. "It is my pleasure."

"Please have a seat." Greenway indicated a chair situated at a round table. "Tea will arrive shortly."

"Thank you." Normanby settled himself into the plush, dark, leather chair. At least the tea and biscuits would be of good quality. One clerk entered the room with a tea tray and another with a sheaf of papers. Once the tray was placed on the table, he poured and handed Greenway a cup.

"Thank you." The man waited while he added sugar and milk to his tea before fixing his own. "I have a draft of the settlement agreements for you to review. Of course, you will want your solicitor to look at them as well."

He bit into a ginger biscuit and savored the sharp taste. "Naturally."

Greenway nodded nervously. "There is one, ah, issue that has come up. Your mother is still living. Naturally, we all want her to continue to a long life. However, in the event of your untimely death, we wish to know that Miss Greenway would have a place of her liking in which to live."

Normanby could not imagine a circumstance under which his mother would tolerate the daughter of a Cit living under the same roof as she. "I see your point."

"Good, good. Mrs. Greenway suggested that our daughter and you, of course, might find a property that would be acceptable as a dower property."

"Mrs. Greenway is extremely astute." As long as he wasn't expected to pay for said property, he didn't care. "How would that be arranged?"

"I would put forth the funds for payment. I see that as only fair considering it is my daughter's desire."

Perfect. "A very satisfactory arrangement. Might I suggest that, as it will be Miss Greenway's house in the event of my passing, she and Mrs. Greenway will wish to choose it?"

The man ventured a small smile. "I am sure they would like that, my lord." He stared at the papers and frowned. "My wife would like to ensure that our daughter will be presented at court."

With any luck at all that would never occur. "I will see to it."

"Thank you."

As the meeting was coming to an end, he finished his tea and biscuits. When Greenway stood, Normanby did as well. He took the sheaf of documents. "I will have my solicitor look at these and get back to you as soon as possible."

"At your convenience, my lord." Greenway took a breath. "My wife would like to know if you have a particular date for the wedding in mind."

"I shall leave that to the ladies." It occurred to Normanby that he did not want banns called at St. Georges. "Do you have a parish church?"

"Oh, yes. Yes. St. Mary-le-Bow. Our families have been attending for years."

"As I said, leave it to the ladies." Not that they were "ladies." Yet it appeared to make Greenway happy. "I shall see you soon." Normanby donned his hat and took his cane from a clerk. It was a long walk back to Mayfair, but he didn't want to spend the price of a hackney. He should probably stop in at White's on the way home. If only to be seen. It would give him something to do until his appointment with Lady Alice.

The afternoon had turned out warm and sunny, causing Alice to choose her light-yellow walking gown for her stroll with Lord Normanby. By the end of their outing, she would not know the answers to all her questions, but she would have more of them answered. And the sooner the better. She stared at her image in the pier-glass. The pale-yellow did look good, but she wanted brighter colors from which to choose. It was silly to wish to wed for more colorful gowns, and she would not do it only for that. But the colors denoted a change in status in her life she wanted almost desperately.

Bertram strode into the room. "Lord Normanby is here."

Something about the dresser's tone made Alice take notice. "Do you not like him?"

"Not me, my lady. I've not met him. Posy wouldn't go to him the other day." Her maid shrugged. "They say dogs know."

Alice also knew of dogs that were devoted to cruel masters. "When was that?"

"When you were in Richmond at the breakfast. He came to see his lordship."

He must have come to ask permission to marry her. "I see." Perhaps Posy was merely not up to meeting anyone new. "I must be off." Alice left the room before her dresser could say anything else. When she reached the main landing, Lord Normanby glanced up and the corners of his lips rose. She descended the remaining stairs. "Good afternoon, my lord."

"A good day to you, my lady." He held out his hand. "I trust you have been well."

She placed her hand in his. "Yes. Very well. Thank you for asking."

They turned and walked out of the house. She smiled at him. "Do you like dogs?"

"I do, very much." He returned her smile. "I thought I was going to meet one of your Great Danes, but she changed her mind."

Ah, so it was Posy and not him. "I wonder what got into her?"

"Who can tell with dogs and other animals."

He did not seem to be surprised the Danes were in the house. "How do you feel about charitable endeavors?"

Looking slightly amused, he said, "That they are necessary. I must suppose you are interested in them."

"Yes, indeed." This would be a good time to let Lord Normanby know that she intended to continue her work. "I give part of my pin money to a few charities. Although, I plan to become more involved in them."

They entered the Park, and as usual it was full. She thought he had a moue of distaste on his mien, but it disappeared so quickly, she might have been wrong. "I would be interested in hearing about them."

"My sister Worthington and my brother-in-law as well as other members of my family help war veterans, their children, and widows by providing training and positions. The children attend school. My sister Kenilworth is involved in aiding poor children as is my sister Rothwell and our cousin Merton."

"All worthy efforts," Lord Normanby said.

She was happy he agreed. That made three stipulations

on the list he met. One more, and she would stop for the day. "You mentioned an older sister to Lady Bellamny; is your family close?"

He barked a laugh. "Not at all. But I have seen that your family is."

"We are." This was going very well. "We even have yearly gatherings."

"That must be delightful." He smiled at her again.

"We all enjoy them very much." She returned his smile.

Lord Bury stopped his curricle next to them. "I say, is this a new fashion?"

A growl seemed to emanate from Lord Normanby, and Alice hid a grin. "Bury." Lord Normanby raised his quizzing glass. "Do you mean to tell me you have not discovered the joys of walking?"

Lord Bury glanced at her. "My lady, it would be my pleasure to stroll with you."

Now what was she to say? They had an appointment for a ride tomorrow afternoon. "I think a carriage ride is also enjoyable."

He inclined his head. "As you wish, my lady. I shall see you then."

As he rode away, Lord Normanby said, "Do you prefer a carriage?"

Alice glanced at him, then lowered her lashes. "With Lord Bury I do."

"That is good to know." They spent the next several minutes greeting others they knew. "Would you be available to stroll with me the day after tomorrow?"

She wanted to say yes, but Lord Hereford had asked her to ride with him. "I cannot, but I am free the day after that."

"Excellent." His tone was rather dry, but he did not appear upset. "I will look forward to strolling with you again."

"As will I." They reached the gate as Lord St. Albans was about to drive in. He stopped outside. "My lord, good afternoon."

He smiled at her and ignored her companion. "My lady."

She had almost forgotten he and Lord Normanby did not get on. "There are a great many people here. I hope you enjoy your ride."

The look in his eyes reminded her of a sad puppy. "It will be poorer without your presence, Lady Alice."

So, this was what the other ladies were talking about. "But you must survive."

He put his hand over his heart. "Only if you insist."

She grinned and waved as she and Lord Normanby strolled through the gate. "Until the next time."

"I shall live for the moment." Lord St. Albans drove through the gate.

"Popinjay," Lord Normanby muttered.

Recalling her conversation with Lord St. Albans about his estate, she turned to Lord Normanby. "I know you have priest-holes in your house, but how is the rest of your estate?"

His eyes widened in surprise. "There are four in total. I want to look into modernizing all of them, beginning with my main estate."

It was good that he wanted to improve his holdings. "Are you conversant with Holkham Hall?"

He nodded. "I have heard something about it. I suppose I should write for an appointment to visit. It is no more than two days ride from Normanby."

"You can also ask my brothers-in-law. They have all visited and come away with excellent ideas."

They reached Worthington House, and he bowed. "I look forward to our dance at Lady Millsworth's ball tomorrow evening."

Alice had almost forgotten about her dance with him. "I shall see you then."

He bowed over her hand. As he left, he was almost run into by a young boy running to the servants' entrance. Lord Normanby stiffened. For a second, Alice thought he might lash out at the lad, but he continued down the pavement. Why would she think he could abuse servants? She gave herself a shake. Then chuckled as she remembered Lord St. Albans's flirtatiousness. He was much more entertaining than he had been before.

She went to her bedchamber, removed her bonnet and gloves, then ambled to her parlor. This was when she missed her twin and Madeline the most. They used to gather together and talk about the gentlemen with whom they had ridden. Alice supposed she could imagine the conversations. She knew them well enough to know what they would say. Still, it was not the same.

Just as she sighed, a knock came on the door. "Yes?"

Theo entered the parlor. "How have you been? It must be lonely for you not to have Eleanor and Madeline here."

What a sweetheart. "It is rather. Do you miss them as well?"

"I ordered tea." Theo sat on one of the sofas. "I do miss them. But I was thinking how Mary would feel when I wed. If I marry before she does."

Theo was three years older than Mary. "Why do you think you would not?"

The girl lifted a shoulder in a light shrug. "I might wait until she is eighteen. We could come out together."

Oh, dear. Alice wondered what Matt and Grace would think about that idea. "I came out with Eleanor and Madeline, and I am the last one to wed."

Theo's forehead wrinkled. "That is true. I must think on

it some more." The tea arrived, and they fixed their plates and cups. She ate two biscuits. "How was your walk?"

Alice might as well tell her sister. "It was nice. You probably know we made a list of qualities a gentleman must have. I asked him questions today. He has met four of them so far."

Theo nodded. "Making a list was a good idea. Could I borrow it when the time comes?"

"Certainly." Alice might as well show it to her. She rose, went to the desk, and took it out. "You may read it if you wish."

Her sister's eyes widened as if she was astonished. "Really? That would be wonderful!"

Alice kept her smile to herself and handed the paper to Theo. "It is not a secret."

"Thank you." Drinking her tea, she perused the list. "These are all extremely excellent attributes."

"I am glad you agree with them. You can see at the bottom I added being a friend. It occurred to me that since I will be going off to live with someone else, he should be a friend as well as a husband."

"Yes, indeed." Theo's dark brows drew together reminding Alice of Louisa. "I do not believe anyone else has considered that." Theo handed the paper back to Alice and set down her cup. "It was nice talking to you."

As short as the conversation had been. "I appreciate you coming by."

Her sister rose from the sofa. "I shall see you in the drawing room."

"Until then." She started to put the list away but decided to read through it again.

Intelligent. Lord Normanby seemed intelligent.

Kind. She had not seen that he was not kind. Was there a way she could test this?

Like house animals. Well, he said he did. Perhaps she could give Posy another chance.

Like children. Still an open question.

Make us laugh, and think we are funny. Hmmm. He had laughed today, but he had not made her laugh.

Interested in the plight of the poor and unfortunate. He agreed that charities were necessary.

Must support us in our charities and other ventures. Would he allow her to support her charities? He indicated that they were necessary, and he had not said he did not want his wife involved in them. But would he tell her before he asked to wed her?

Passable looking. He was not the most handsome gentleman she had met, but he was quite good looking.

Allow us to be ourselves. Unknown.

Be able to support a family. Matt would know more about that, but he had allowed Lord Normanby to dance with her and walk with her.

Must love us in return. Did she love him? Could he love her? Time would tell.

Alice slipped the list back into the drawer. It was important she get this right.

Chapter Sixteen

Giff arrived home to another note from Lady Mary.

Dear Lord St. Albans,

I would greatly appreciate it if you would have someone watch the mews behind Normanby House just after six in the morning and follow the female who leaves through the back gate and has a hackney waiting.

Yr. friend,
M.C.

Bloody-hell hounds! Was she referring to a mistress? If so, how would she know about such a thing? And what in perdition was Normanby doing with a mistress when he was courting Alice? Giff ran a hand down his face. He should probably tell either Worthington or his lady, but he didn't want Lady Mary to get into trouble for trying to help him. Still, he had to do what she asked. As much as he didn't want that bounder Normanby around Alice, for her sake Giff had to know what was going on. The problem was if the man did have a ladybird, how could he tell her? Would she even believe him? He held the note to a candle and lit it on fire, placed it in his cold fireplace, went to the stables and found Fergus. Giff handed the groom a small sack of coins. "I have something I want you to do."

Always up for a lark, the man's pale blue eyes were bright. "What is it?"

He told him what was in Lady Mary's note, but not how he came about the information. Fergus nodded. "I'll get one of the other grooms to take care of Horace tomorrow."

"When she arrives to where she is going, make note of the address, and I'll talk to her myself if need be."

"I think I can find out about her another way." He tapped his nose. "If it's what yer thinkin', one of the maids will talk."

"Good man." Giff really did not want to have a conversation with Normanby's mistress. That could cause all sorts of trouble. "I wish I could be there myself."

"Better you go riding with the lady, me lord."

The man was a sage. "You're right."

The next morning Giff awoke to rain. There'd be no riding with Alice today, but he could go with Fergus.

Gunn entered the room. "What are yer plans for the day, my lord?"

Giff flung back the covers. "A little spying is in order. I'll need something nondescript."

His valet went into the dressing room and came out with a set of older garments he wore in the country. "I'll notify Fergus."

It wasn't until he was halfway through dressing that Giff realized that his valet must know what his groom was up to today. Not that he was concerned it would go any further. His Scots servants treated the English ones as if they were still at war. In the politest way possible, of course. Several minutes later he'd donned a waxed coat, hat, and had arrived at the stables. A small, unmarked town coach he hadn't seen in years stood ready, with Fergus sitting on the covered box. Giff climbed in and it rolled forward without him having to knock on the ceiling. Soon they came to a stop, and he got out. The carriage was in the middle of a small alley down two stables from one that was open.

One of the servants from the open stable strode up the street to them. "Ye can't stay there. A hackney's comin' soon, and I don't want to be the one she screams at if she can't get right in."

Giff had moved toward one of the gates and pretended to look at it, giving Fergus the lead.

"Wouldn't want ye to get into trouble. Me employer is just looking at this property. We won't be a second." Silence fell while Giff tried to look as if he had a purpose there.

"How much longer?" the servant asked.

"She must be a real bitch," Fergus said.

"That's bein' kind. Ain't happy she's to come here, but his lordship can't be caught seeing her."

"If he's a laird, what does it matter?" Fergus said innocently.

"He needs a leg-shackle, or we're all lookin' for new places. How much longer?"

"Almost done," he said.

Giff took the hint, strolled back to the coach, got in, and it started forward. Behind him came a hackney. They drove around the corner, stopped, and waited until the hackney drove out of the mews then followed it to an area of row houses known to be home to several high-flyers. A woman got down from the hackney and ran to the house.

Giff's coach came to a halt, and Fergus appeared at the carriage door window. "I'll be a few minutes. She'll be in a temper at the weather. Someone's bound to come in or out for somethin'." The groom strolled down the street as if he enjoyed being out in the rain. "Here now, let me help ye with that."

Giff glanced out and saw Fergus with a woman.

"Oh, thank you." The servant handed him the basket. "My mistress is going to be upset that her breakfast is late. Especially in this weather."

"That's a might heavy for someone as slight as ye."

"It will all be over soon, and we can get back to normal," the woman said. "None of this running back and forth at night and early morning."

"I'm glad for ye," Fergus said sympathetically.

That was the same thing the other servant had told them.

"What's going to make the change?" he asked.

"Her protector is getting married. Once that happens it will all go back to the way it was."

"Didn't know a gentleman gettin' married kept his mistress."

"It's not a love match." They passed by the coach window, but all Giff could see was her bonnet. "Here we are. I'll take the basket now. Thank you for your help."

"Not at'all. I'll carry it to the door fer ye."

"That would be lovely. Thank you."

Giff's hands curled into fists. That blackguard. He'd kill Normanby if it would solve anything. Somehow Giff had to stop Alice from marrying the cad. The question was how to do it. He forced his hands to relax and focus on the two pieces of information he had discovered. First, Normanby was under the hatches, and second, he had no intention of giving up his mistress after he married, and he was taking great pains to continue to be with her. Giff had always known the man was a runagate. He could tell Worthington and leave it in his hands. But young ladies weren't always capable of seeing the truth about a gentleman. Even a lady as astute as Alice might do something stupid like elope with the rogue. No. It would be better for Giff to continue to befriend her and be there when Normanby's true nature was revealed, either by chance or because Giff engineered it. And it would be better for her to discover the cur's infamy that way. Her anger would soon end any feelings she had for him. He glanced out the window and noticed they were almost home. Another visit to Hatchards was in order. He had a feeling she was often at the bookstore.

Rain.

Alice rolled over and pulled up the covers. She really could not complain. They had not had much rain at all this Season. It was England, and one needed rain for all sorts of things. A longish nose appeared in the opening between the bed hangings. "You can come."

Posy's nose and head poked through, followed by one paw placed on the embroidered counterpane. The other paw joined it. Eventually, the rest of her body made it onto the bed, and she snuggled next to Alice with a soft moan.

"Someone is going to be looking for you soon." How had the Dane escaped? It did not matter. Alice had no reason to rise immediately. The door opened and the muffled sounds of the fireplace being cleaned, then a fire being built could be heard. It really was early.

Suddenly the hangings were drawn back. "My lady. There you are!"

Where else would she be but in her bed? Something heavy landed on her stomach. She glanced down. Posy's head. Alice rubbed her eyes. "I must have gone back to sleep."

"It's time to get up now," her dresser said. "Come, Miss Posy. As much as you detest the rain, you must go out."

"Someone should build a covered area for them." Alice would mention it to Matt. She pushed the dog. "I cannot rise with your head on my stomach. Up." Posy looked at Alice as if she had betrayed the Dane. It was time to be firmer. "Up." Reluctantly the dog climbed out of the bed. She swung her legs over the side and almost stepped on Posy resting on the floor. Alice carefully arched her back to miss the dog as she left the bed. By the time she had dressed, a footman had taken the Dane to go for a walk.

When Alice reached the stairs, Theo and Mary had their heads together, speaking in hushed voices.

What were they up to? "Good morning."

The girls broke apart and greeted her.

"Are you going to Hatchards today?" Theo asked.

"Probably." There was not very much else to do in the mornings.

"Oh, good." She smiled. "Will you pick me up a book on sheep? The kind whose wool is used for carpet making?"

Why in God's name would she be interested in . . . "Sheep?"

"Yes." Theo nodded. "For making rugs. From the wool. They are very useful animals."

Alice had not thought she meant the animal itself. "I will take a look."

"Thank you." Her sister flashed her a smile. "I am starving."

"I am peckish as well," Mary said, and they both dashed down the stairs.

Alice followed at a much more sedate pace. It would take her some time to find the right tome for her sister. Still, there really was nothing else to do this morning.

Well, that sounded like moping. It was time to find something to occupy her time. It occurred to her that she had still not found her purpose. Perhaps this was opportunity to do just that.

She took her place at the table and was glad to see it had been shortened, making it feel not so empty. Alice heaved a sigh. She really was feeling sorry for herself. It had to stop.

By ten o'clock the rain had ceased and the sun, although not fully shining, was peeping out from the remaining clouds. She went to Grace's office, found it empty, and strolled to the hall. "Thorton, do you know where her ladyship is?"

"She is visiting Lady Evesham."

Alice remembered hearing that Phoebe Evesham was finally in Town. "I am going to Hatchards."

"I shall call for Williams."

Drat. Alice had forgotten to inform her footman. Fortunately, he came immediately. "Are we walking, my lady?"

"Yes." A good stroll was the best way to shake herself out of this mood. "I will attempt to limit the number of books I purchase."

Williams's lips twitched, but he did not respond. They strode out of the square and turned toward Piccadilly. She arrived shortly before ten-thirty. By now she was thoroughly familiar with where the books she wanted were located and went directly to the section dealing with land and animal husbandry.

Seated at the table was St. Albans. "Good morning."

He raised his head and gave her a distracted smile. "Good morn to you."

Alice scanned the shelves for volumes on sheep. "Do you happen to know which sheep are used for making carpets?"

"Scottish Black-face, Welsh Mountain Sheep, and Piebald. Which breed you want depends on where you are."

She almost dropped her jaw. Just a day ago, he said he knew almost nothing about them. "How did you learn so much in such a short time?"

He tapped the book. "Reading. I have a great deal of opportunity for it." He'd risen when she entered the space. "What brought on your interest?"

"My sister Theo wanted me to bring her some information on sheep for rug making."

He frowned. Did he not like ladies involving themselves in the subject? But that did not make any sense. He had asked Alice for help. "How old is she?"

Laughter burbled up inside. "Fourteen. Mary is eleven. They surprise me as well. Sometimes they remind me of older people in young bodies."

"I understand what you mean." He took two books down from the shelves and placed them on the table. "This will get you started."

Alice took the chair opposite St. Albans. "Thank you."

His green eyes danced with mirth. "It is my pleasure. After all, where would we be without sheep?"

She chuckled lightly. He really was fun to be with. "A most erudite topic of conversation. I wonder how it would be received during morning visits."

"You would no doubt have the other ladies wishing they had thought of the subject. Gentlemen would hang on your lips waiting for pearls of wisdom to drop."

The burble of laughter threatened to become a peal, and she covered her mouth to hide the sound. Tears blurred her vision by the time she got herself under control. "Oh, dear. You should not make me laugh so hard."

His eyes widened as he assumed an innocent look. "I? Why, my lady. I would never do such a thing. I of all people know one is only supposed to laugh with closed lips."

That set her off again. He handed her his handkerchief to dab her eyes. "Stop. Show me the sheep."

For some reason, that caused him to start laughing. If anyone came by they would think they were ready for Bedlam. Alice handed St. Albans her lace-trimmed handkerchief. Accepting it, he bowed. "As you wish. Sheep it is."

They spent the next hour comparing not only sheep, but the crop differences between the Highlands and England.

Was he preparing to take over Whippoorwill Manor? Had he a lady in mind to wed? Could she ask him? If they were truly friends the answer was yes. She had rejected him after all. "I take it you have found a lady you are thinking of marrying."

"I have." He gazed into her eyes, and her awareness of him grew. Alice did not understand what was happening. "Although, it is early days."

"I see." Yet, for some reason, it did not make her happy. She should want him to gain the estate he should have already been given. "I suppose having inherited your uncle's estate has obviated the need you felt before."

St. Albans leaned back in his chair and seemed to consider her. "Yes. I still want it, but I now have an estate of my own to see to. In effect, I no longer feel as if I have a sword hanging over my head. Or that my life has little meaning."

He understood. Did he know she felt the same? "That is it exactly. A lady's life does not begin until she is wed. Unless, of course, she has a cause. In that case, marriage is needed for having children and a life partner, but it is no longer needed to find meaning."

He studied her for a few moments. "Have you found your purpose?"

Alice blew out a breath. "Not yet. My sisters have."

"You mean particularly Lady Montagu and Lady Madeline?"

Alice nodded. "Yes. Eleanor has her coal mine, and Madeline focuses on helping people any way she can." She told him about the changes at the mine and the boy and girl Madeline and Harry found and saved. About the charities of their older sisters and what her brothers-in-law do. "I do not seem to be able to focus on just one thing."

St. Albans leaned forward, closing the distance between them, enabling her to breathe a scent that was all him. Clean and masculine. Not to mention the tingles. Why were they still affecting her when she now liked him? "Is there a reason you must you pick one endeavor. Can you not do bits of everything?"

What an interesting idea. "What do you mean?"

"Start schools on the estates of whomever you wed or improve them. Help train and hire people in need. And help those you find. The boy has a unique story, but the girl selling flowers does not. There are hundreds if not thousands of children like that all over the country."

"Sort of a jack-of-all-trades." He inclined his head. "I like your idea."

St. Albans seemed to move closer. Alice had to stop herself from reaching out and touching him. "It would give you more flexibility and scope, if you will."

He was right. "I agree. I think you have solved my problem." She glanced at her watch. "I should go. I am glad you were here this morning."

His well-molded lips tilted up at the ends. "As am I. Allow me the pleasure of escorting you out."

He took the books, and she placed her hand on his arm. It was a shame she had not got to know him before he had met the other lady, and she had met Lord Normanby. Still they were becoming friends.

Chapter Seventeen

Giff had escorted Alice to her home from Hatchards. He now understood why Normanby wanted to stroll with her in lieu of riding. Even when one stopped to greet acquaintances, one had a great deal more time to converse. He tied his cravat and fixed it with an emerald pin. The ball tonight was going to be excruciating. He'd have one set with Alice, but Normanby would have the supper dance. Giff hoped the blackguard would trip up somehow, but hope was not a strategy. He had to do something to snatch Alice from the cur's clutches. Yet it must be in a way that caused the least harm to her. What was it Lady Mary had said?

"Theo and I pray daily that Matt will discover something is wrong with him."

Ah, yes. Theo of the sheep.

Giff had a feeling he'd need more than a mistress to show Normanby for the scoundrel he was. The servant said they'd all be out on the street without a marriage. How could Giff find proof of the cad's financial difficulties? There was, of course, the time-honored method of starting a rumor. But he wanted solid proof. Perhaps Mamma could help. Gunn helped Giff into his jacket and fixed his pocket watch and quizzing glass to his vest.

He made his way to the small drawing room and was surprised to find only his mother. "Where is Father?"

"He had a committee meeting. He will dine out." She handed Giff a glass of sherry. "Have you made any progress with Lady Alice? I hear Lord Normanby is hopeful of a match."

Giff decided to keep his conversation with Lady Mary and her notes to himself. "A bit. We've met at Hatchards twice now. I had been approaching her in the wrong way. We're getting on much better now. About Normanby, I discovered he is still keeping a mistress."

His mother raised one brow. "That is not something a lady like Lady Alice would appreciate. I heard a whisper that his mother married and is on the Continent because her gambling was out of control."

That might be the reason Normanby was seeking to marry money. "I have reason to believe he might be on the rocks."

Mamma fixed him with a disgusted look. "Can you please not use cant around me?"

Giff bowed. "My apologies. It means—"

"I know very well what it means." Her lips pressed into a thin line, and she gave him the look. "He has little to no funds." She took a sip of her wine. "If that is true, he is hiding it quite well." And that was the problem. His father's butler entered the parlor and announced dinner. Mamma placed her hand on Giff's arm, and they strolled to the family dining room. "Rumors are all well and good, but I think you had better focus on charming her away from his lordship."

"You might be right." Now that he knew where he'd

gone wrong, there was a chance he could cut Normanby out. “I have a dance with her this evening.”

Mamma looked at him in surprise. “Well done. Considering the set down she gave you the other day, I am impressed.”

“I was as well.” The servants had been steadily offering them dishes, and he took several pieces of asparagus sautéed with mushrooms. He had to make the most of that dance and be seen standing up with other ladies. He wasn’t ready to let her know that the lady upon which he was focused and hoped to wed was her.

Mamma swallowed. “How are you doing with the Scottish estate?”

“I am reading everything I can find. Mr. Quinney has been very thorough in answering my questions. I want to travel to Inverness as soon as I am able.”

“Perhaps on a wedding trip?” she said archly.

“If that wedding trip includes Lady Alice, I rather think she would like to visit Paris. Both her sisters are there on their honeymoons.” Yet, she might be willing to travel to Scotland. “It’s too soon to make plans. I must first secure the lady’s hand.”

Mamma rose. “Speaking of that, we should be going.”

They entered the ballroom before the first set. Alice was standing with her family. Normanby was nowhere in sight. Then again, he had the supper set and had no reason to attend earlier. Giff accompanied his mother to a group of her friends and made his way toward Alice’s circle. Bolingbrook led her out for the first dance.

Almost immediately, Lady Millsworth approached him. “My lord, please come with me. There is a lady in need of a partner.”

Giff inclined his head. “It would be my pleasure.”

He was made known to a Miss Butterworth. The next

set went to Lady Amelia Grant. Then it was time to dance with Alice. If she had been taking note of his previous partners, she did not give herself away. They took their places opposite each other, bowed and curtseyed, and the music began. He took her hand as they came together. "You look exceptionally lovely this evening."

"You are very handsome." The color of her cheeks deepened as they danced apart.

The next time he offered an invitation he thought she might like. "There is a balloon ascension in the Park on Thursday. Would you like to accompany me to it?"

"I would indeed," she managed to say before the dance separated them again.

He'd conversed in snatches of conversation before, but they had never been important. This was. "I imagine some of the younger children would like to attend it they are allowed."

"I am sure they would. I will have to ask if they may."

Alice was amazed he had invited the children to the balloon ascension. At the breakfast he'd attended, she had the distinct impression he did not like children. However, perhaps that had been because he did not know how to approach her. She enjoyed his company much more now.

He escorted her back to her family and immediately led her to Matt. "My lord," he greeted her brother-in-law. "I have asked Lady Alice to attend the balloon ascension with me. If it is possible, I would like to extend the invitation to the children."

"Perhaps not all the children, but certainly Mary and Theo would like to accompany you."

Alice thought how hurt her niece and nephew would be to be left out. "Gideon and Elizabeth would like it as well."

Matt looked at her. "That would entail nursemaids. I doubt you'd have much fun trying to keep track of them in what I imagine will be a huge crowd." He seemed to gather her other brothers-in-law and Merton with a look, and they made their way to him. "What would you think of taking the children to the balloon ascension on Thursday?"

Con grimaced. "The girls might be well-behaved, but I'd have to keep Hugh on a leash. The first thing he'd do would be to try to climb into the basket just to get a better look."

Matt gave him a sympathetic look. "I hadn't thought of that. Even Gideon would be tempted." He glanced at St. Albans. "It's better if you just take Theo and Mary with you."

He seemed a little disappointed but nodded. "I bow to your knowledge of the other children." He turned to Alice. "If I do not see you before then, I shall collect you at one o'clock."

"I shall be ready." This was the most exciting thing she would have done while in Town.

"That was exceedingly kind of him," Rothwell said. "If we could have limited it to the girls it would have been fine."

Con gave him an exasperated look. "We'd have a mutiny on our hands."

"Who would munity?" Grace asked.

"St. Albans invited Alice and the younger children to the balloon ascension on Thursday. I told him he could take Mary and Theo, but not the younger ones."

Grace heaved a sigh. "Mary and Theo have already been invited to attend with Phoebe Evesham."

"It looks like you will have to go with just St. Albans," Matt said.

"It is not a problem. He simply wanted to ask the children as well." It might actually be better being alone. Then they would not be responsible for anyone else in what was certain to be an enormous gathering.

Lord Normanby joined them. "Are you discussing the balloon ascension?"

"Yes." Alice turned to him. "I have been invited to attend, and we were discussing taking some of the other children as they were asked as well."

"How very nice of the person. However, I was going to ask you to accompany me." His tone was glib, and, suddenly, she had the feeling he had not even heard of the event before then. Very odd. "Our set is next," he said.

"It is." She glanced around and saw St. Albans speaking with a matron and her daughter. Was that the lady in whom he was interested?

As it happened, the next morning was fair, and she saw St. Albans riding in the Park. For once, he was before her. She rode up next to him. "Good morning."

"And to you." He smiled and motioned his head in the direction of the large oak tree. "Do you care for a race?"

"I do." Her mare stamped a foot. She was ready for a run as well. "On the count of three."

A wicked grin appeared on his face just as he said, "Three."

Galyna was ready for him and dashed forward, catching up with his gelding in a few short seconds. They reached the tree at the same time.

"Excellent race," he said, eyes bright with excitement.

Alice narrowed her eyes at him. "You cheated."

"Me? I wouldn't dare. I merely counted one and two to myself." He glanced at her mare. "Aside from that, I could see she was ready to go."

They trotted to the Serpentine. "Why did you name your horse Horace?"

"I am addicted to the poems of Quintus Horatius Flaccus, a Roman poet who lived in sixty-five BC. He had a famous quote: '*Seize the day and put the least possible trust in tomorrow. Begin, be bold and venture to be wise. Remember when life's path is steep to keep your mind even.*' Horace is derived from his name. How did you pick Galyna?"

Eleanor and I decided to use Latin names. Galyna means a girl who remains calm." Alice glanced at her mare. "She usually is."

St. Albans chuckled. "We all have our moments."

"Very true." They meandered around alternatively trotting, walking, cantering, and talking.

"I'm sorry to see the hyacinths have gone," he said.

"I am not."

He gave her a shocked look. "They are so pretty."

"They are, but they make me sneeze."

A look of horror passed over his countenance. "I sent them to you."

"The servants enjoyed them."

"I'm terribly sorry. Our housekeeper had suggested lavender, but they were not quite in bloom, and I thought hyacinths would do just as well."

He appeared so distraught. "I think your housekeeper might have recommended lavender for the plant's healing properties."

"I made a mull of that." He shook his head in disgust. "The next time I will send fruit." His brows drew together in concern. "You are not allergic to any of them, are you?"

"Not that I am aware." Why could he not have been like this before? She should ask about his lady, but Alice would rather not know. "Hopefully, I will not be ill again for a long while. I caught my cold from one of my nieces or nephews. They all had it."

"Small children tend to be generous with their germs. The nursery at my maternal grandparents' house came down with a stomach disorder, and soon the whole keep had it."

What had he said? "Keep?"

"Yes, you know. The castle and its grounds."

"Your grandfather's estate in Scotland?"

His eyes were sparkling, and his lips twitched. "The very one. Mine is not nearly as large, although, it is quite old."

Everyone seemed to live in an interesting house but her. "Do you have priest holes?"

St. Albans barked a laugh. "I can do better than that. I have secret tunnels and corridors. Cleveland Castle does as well."

She would have loved playing in those as a child. "I wonder why none of our homes have them."

His eyes sparkled with laughter. "Most likely because your houses were not built before the fifteenth century and are further south?"

He was right. "Ours are quite modern comparatively." How depressing. Although, there were benefits of living in a newer house. "Are they cold and uncomfortable?"

"They would be if the men had anything to say about it, but, at least in the past two hundred years or so, the ladies have taken charge and made them very comfortable."

It was a shame she would never be able to see them.

"My lady," Robertson said. "We should be getting back for breakfast."

"I had not realized how late it was getting." A thought occurred to her, and she glanced at St. Albans. "Would you like to break your fast with us?"

"It would be my great pleasure." They galloped to the gate, and he came to a stop. "I would like to change. When should I arrive?"

She took out her watch. "Forty-five minutes."

"Until then." He headed toward the end of the Park.

Where did he live, and why did she not know? Well, that lack of knowledge would be remedied this morning.

She and her groom rode back to Worthington House. As soon as she had informed Thorton of the guest joining them for the morning meal, bathed, and dressed, Alice went to the library and took out a copy of Debrett's. She flipped to the page where the Dukes of Cumberland were listed and ran her finger down the page until it mentioned a house on Park Lane. The clock chimed the hour, and she closed and reshelved the book. Alice headed toward the breakfast room at the same time the knocker was plied on the front door. She glanced at her watch. St. Albans must be early, but instead of a deep melodious tone, she heard high-pitched squeals. Who was here?

Quickly striding to the hall, she stopped short to see most of her family there. Had she forgotten they were gathering this morning, or had she not been told? A small body almost knocked her over.

"We came to cheer you up," Hugh said, hugging her.

Charlotte laughed and bussed Alice's cheek. "Not to cheer her up, to keep her company."

"Well, I want to make her happy." Hugh had a stern look on his childish mien.

She hugged him. "You are cheering me. Would you like to escort me into the breakfast room?"

He held out his arm as he had probably seen his father do. "I'd like to." She placed her hand on it. "Besides," he whispered. "Gideon's not here so I'm the oldest boy."

He was the only boy, but she would never tell him that.

His sister and cousins were chatting as they strolled to the large breakfast room, while her sisters and brothers-in-law were greeting Matt and Grace.

The door closed and opened again. *St. Albans*. He strode in smiling and greeted the others, then looked at her. "I see a gentleman was before me."

Hugh straightened. "Yes, you are correct."

St. Albans gave one nod acknowledging his defeat. "May I walk on your other side, my lady?"

Alice met his gaze and her heart sped up. "Yes, my lord."

He bowed to Hugh. "If his lordship has no objection, that is."

His chin rose. "I do not."

"Oh dear," Constance said in a perfect imitation of her mother. "There will be no living with him now."

Alice exchanged a glance with St. Albans. His lips twitched, and she almost went into whoops. How mistaken she had been about him.

Chapter Eighteen

Giff was surprised, but not overly so, to see the same members of Alice's family as he had the first time he'd been invited to breakfast. She flashed him an apologetic smile while everyone said their greetings. Apparently, this gathering hadn't been planned. Still, he was happy they were all present. It would give him an opportunity to do what he had not done the last time. Come to know her better and her family. He might also have a chance to show her he deserved her notice as more than a friend.

The little boy—was his name Hugh?—who was always getting into trouble proudly escorted Alice into the breakfast room. However, he not being tall enough to pull out the chair ran into a bit of a problem in helping her take her seat.

"Allow me to assist you, if I may." Giff pitched his tone to be appropriately sober.

"Thank you, sir." The child inclined his head. "I will have to grow taller."

"I have no doubt that in a few years you will be as tall as your father."

Hugh's grave demeanor slipped as he grinned. "I will leave you to it."

The adults at the table as well as Ladies Mary and Theo were doing a credible job of not laughing.

"I had no idea everyone would be here this morning. I do not even know why they are here," Alice whispered as Giff held Alice's chair and he pushed her toward the table.

Worthington helped his lady take her seat, and said, "In my study after we break our fast."

"What will you be discussing?" Alice asked.

"The Enclosure Acts. Another one has been introduced," Worthington said. "There is a vote in the Lords this afternoon. We have been assembling supporters to defeat the bill."

Interesting. Naturally, Giff knew they took their positions in the Lords seriously, but he hadn't really understood how politically active they were and how they worked together gathering votes for their causes. He recalled Montagu telling Giff that it was a shame he was not a member of the Lords. He finally understood what his friend had meant. From some of the things Alice had said, Giff surmised she and her sisters were active in not only charities but politics as well.

As before, footmen came around with pots of tea for each of them, various types of eggs, meats, cheeses, fruits, and racks of toast. Alice selected a baked egg, ham, and a bowl of berries. He took a dish of buttered eggs, rare beef, and berries as well.

"Lord St. Albans," Lady Merton said. "I am having a political soirée next week. Would you be interested in attending?"

He swallowed a piece of toast. "I would. Although, I don't know what I can contribute."

She gave him a sly look. "You would be surprised. Lord Hawksworth, another duke-in-waiting, has become extremely politically active. He and his wife are attending. I will introduce you." She raised one black brow. "After all, you need not wait for your father to die to contribute to society."

"Dotty is known for plain speaking," Alice whispered.

Her ladyship looked like the type of person who would be straightforward. "That is good to know. Will you be at her soirée?"

"I do not know yet. Balls and other more social events are being given priority."

"These Enclosure Acts have got out of hand," Lady Kenilworth said. "There are thousands of them."

Giff knew how badly the laws had affected small farmers in Scotland, but he'd had no idea it was the same in England.

"You are correct, my lady." Giff was glad he could contribute. "The new farming methods have made them profitable for landowners and their tenants. The larger problem is that they are supposed to have been publicly debated and agreed to at the local level. I understand that requirement is being bypassed."

"Indeed, it is," Worthington said. "That is the case with this bill."

At the same time the adults were discussing politics, the children were holding their own conversation apart from the adults. But, somehow, neither discussion interfered nor interrupted the other. Occasionally, one of the adults would drop into the children's conversation to explain something or correct a misapprehension.

Alice pressed her lips together. "Forcing families to leave their homes because of these acts ought not to be allowed. There must be a way to pass a bill requiring landlords and even villages and small towns to take into account the harm the enclosure would cause and require them to ensure a family does not lose their home."

"That would certainly alleviate the hardship many of these acts are causing," Merton said.

"An excellent idea." Kenilworth lifted his cup to her. "Draft something, and we will see what can be done."

Giff was dumbstruck. He knew Alice had opinions on a number of subjects, but it never occurred to him her points would be taken so seriously by the gentlemen in her family. And to expect her to write up a proposal was a complete surprise.

"No, Wellington was the younger brother," Lady Mary said quietly correcting an assertion one of the children had made. She glanced up. "I find it shocking that such requirements can be disregarded."

"I agree," Lady Theo said.

Apparently, they had been following both discussions at the same time. Then again, nothing they did should surprise him.

Giff felt as if he'd entered a different world. At one point, Kenilworth caught Giff's eye and gave him a look that seemed to say he knew what Giff was feeling. It was no wonder Alice had not been interested in his attempts at gossip when she was engaged in much more serious subjects at the breakfast table. If all families did this, society would be in much better shape. He glanced around the table. If he could convince Alice to marry him, this is what their breakfast table would look like.

Ladies Mary and Theo were the first to rise. "Gideon, Elizabeth, and the rest of you must get ready for your lessons."

The children rose and started wishing their parents a good day. Lady Mary passed by Giff and Alice and under the guise of hugging her sister, slipped him a folded piece of paper. He'd like to know how she learned that trick.

Worthington stood. "It is time for our meeting."

The rest of the gentlemen kissed their wives, stood, and headed for the door.

"Do we have anything we need to discuss?" Lady Worthington asked.

The ladies shook their heads.

"Not at present," the Duchess of Rothwell said.

Lady Worthington rose. "In that case, we should be about our days."

Giff stood at the same time as Alice and held out his arm. She escorted him to the front door. "If you are going to Hatchards later this morning, I will see you there."

"I will be. I must become knowledgeable about the selling of produce and other things."

She grinned. "As long as you are not concerned with whisky, I have some expertise."

He bowed and took her hand. "Excellent. I'll see you there."

Having sent his carriage home, Giff decided to walk back to Cleveland House.

As soon as he entered his chamber, he opened the note Lady Mary had given to him and unfolded it.

Intelligent

Kind

Like house animals

Like children

Make us laugh, and think we are funny

Interested in the plight of the poor and unfortunate

Must support us in our charities and other ventures

Passable looking

Allow us to be ourselves

Be able to support a family

Must love us in return

Be a friend

Alice's list!

She'd been telling the truth when she said being a duchess or marrying a duke, or any peer for that matter, was not important to her. Giff fancied he met all the qualifications but one. Was he in love with her? He'd been in lust for a while, but even he knew that was not the same thing as love. How would he know? And could she love him? The only person he could talk to about it was his mother. Even though they didn't always agree, his parents did have a love match. That gave him pause. Why had he not wanted one when everyone in his family had married for love? He folded the paper and put it in a secret drawer in his desk, then went to his mother's parlor and knocked.

"Enter."

"*Madainn mhath*, Mamma."

"I see you are practicing your Gallic." She grinned. *"Madainn mhath, bhobain."*

He never knew if she was calling him her darling or her rascal. Both could apply at different times. "I need to know how I'll know if I'm in love."

She raised her brows. "Could we start at the beginning?"

He told her about being invited to breakfast and the conversations. "It was unusual, but right at the same time."

"Well, I am not surprised. If you were paying attention, you would have noticed the same thing going on at meals at your grandparents' table. Although, the voices were probably a great deal louder."

That was true. Everyone had their say at the tables. "You're right. I just took it for granted there. It seemed so different here."

She pressed her lips together. "I apologize for not setting the example. It was one of the subjects your father and I did not agree upon."

Although Scotland and England were supposed to be one country, it really was mixing two different cultures. "How did you decide whose traditions to use?"

"We sorted it out as we went along. For example, there is no point in trying to keep much of Hogmanay in England when one is doing it by oneself."

But they opened windows and burned herbs in the fireplaces. "We do chase out the evil spirits."

"Aye, that we do, but there's no dark-haired man to come to the door at midnight to give us luck."

Giff grinned. He usually remained home for Christmas and went to his grandparents for New Year's, and as a redhead, he was kept far away from the front door until the dark-haired man appeared. "We celebrate Christmas more than they do at my grandparents."

"I must confess, I did not mind adding the Christmas celebrations," she mused. "Enough of this for the moment. Tell me what has been going on?"

"We see each other at Hatchards a great deal and have been talking and helping one another. She knows a lot about estate management. Yesterday, she had questions about sheep I could answer."

His mother fixed him with a look. "This is a very strange courtship. You should send her flowers."

He returned her look. "I did. She was allergic to them." Thankfully her sister had told him. "I think I made it up to her by explaining how they came about."

With a wave of her hand, she asked, "What else do you do?"

"When it's not raining, we ride in the Park early in the morning. We both like to race."

"Do ye let her win?" Mamma's brogue became more pronounced indicating she was taking more interest.

"I don't have to. Her mare is equal to Hector." As Alice was equal to Giff.

"Ye have nay mentioned feelings. You have them, aye? The sort a mon has for a lass?"

They were going to be speaking in Gallic if this kept up. "Most definitely."

She nodded. "Here's the most important question. Do ye want to see her every day even when yer angry at her?"

He'd never thought of that. His parents could have massive arguments and later he'd see them kissing. One time his father had searched the house until he found her just to ensure she was well. Giff knew he wanted to see Alice at the breakfast table. Each morning when they rode, he felt as if the day would be better. Even when she'd given him that set down, he wanted to see her again. "Yes. Yes, I do."

Mamma nodded sharply. "Then it seems to me you're in love with the lass."

"Thank you." He just needed to discover if she could love him in return. "I'll be at Hatchards."

Charlotte caught up to Alice as she reached the hall. "Lord St. Albans seemed to enjoy himself. I was rather shocked to see him here."

Considering the way she had felt about him before, that was not surprising. "He is much different than I thought he was."

Her sister linked arms with Alice, and they started toward the morning room. "What happened?"

That was a good question. "I am not quite sure. One day I told him he was not qualified to be my husband. The next day, he was in Hatchards. He was looking for a book, and we started talking. For the first time, he was not trying to tell me all the gossip he'd learned." He had, in short, been himself. "He told me he was glad I gave him a set-down. He had not liked reading the gossip either. We've started to become friends."

They entered the morning room and stood at the window watching Zeus and Posy play. "Do you see him frequently at Hatchards?"

Alice turned around and leaned against the window. "Yes. He recently inherited an estate from an uncle, and he needs to understand how to run it."

Her sister smiled. "And, naturally, you helped him."

Alice returned the smile. "It was the least I could do."

Con strolled into the parlor. "I thought I'd find you here." He kissed Charlotte on the cheek. "Take the carriage home if you wish. This meeting will take a while."

She nodded. "I will. We were discussing St. Albans."

"He made several good points on how we could combine the new farming methods without running off small farmers." Con rubbed his jaw. "We might not get them repealed. In fact, the Tories want to pass more enclosure laws. But at least we can limit the damage by talking with other landowners." Con glanced at Alice. "He was much more relaxed than the last time he was here."

"He was trying to find his way forward." Charlotte's attention was fixed on her husband.

"I know that feeling." Con raised her hand to his lips. "Sometimes it takes a while to get the lay of the land with this family." He turned to Alice. "Speaking of this family. Did you know that Mary and Theo are taking pickpocketing lessons?"

They had decided it might be a useful skill and one of the boys the family had taken in had made his living that way. "Yes. How did you know?"

He raised a brow and, in a tone as dry as sand, said, "She gave me back my watch."

"Oh, dear." Charlotte started to laugh. "I taught her how to pick locks as well."

"Good Lord." Con dropped his head into his palm. "There will be no stopping her."

"That is what you said about us," Alice reminded him.

"It is indeed." He headed for the door. "I will see you later, my love."

A marriage like theirs was what Alice wanted. Which reminded her she had to test Lord Normanby on the rest of the list. Unfortunately, she would not see him until tomorrow.

Chapter Nineteen

Normanby had woken to his mistress swearing as she dressed. She must have sensed he was awake. "When are you going to ask her to marry you?" Celeste's tone was tense. She detested not being allowed to entertain him in her house. The one he'd given to her after telling his father's mistress she had to leave the residence. Celeste hated even more dressing like a servant to travel to and from her home.

"Soon." He would have already done it, but he wasn't quite sure of Lady Alice yet. If only her guardian would have immediately agreed to the wedding. "I must ensure she will accept me."

Her lips formed a moue, and she lifted one shoulder in a dismissive shrug. "You make love so charmingly. How could a young lady resist your kisses?"

"I haven't kissed her." He hadn't even come close to touching more than her arm.

"You English. Always so correct. Send her letters declaring your love. I will tell you what you must say."

Celeste knew nothing of young ladies of the *ton*. "And how would I explain the letter when her guardian read it?"

Her eyes widened in confusion. "But why would he?"

"All correspondence addressed to a young unmarried lady is read by her parents or guardian."

"*Bah*. In France it would not happen. I received *les lettres d'amour* all the time before we had to flee."

The only thing he knew to be true about her was that she came from a titled family in France. That had been proudly confided to him by the Austrian diplomat he'd stolen her from. Normanby didn't know, and doubted he ever would know, what had caused her to become a courtesan. Perhaps it had something to do with the love letters.

"*Bah*! Kiss her where everyone can see you. Then she will have to agree."

"I would if we were ever alone. She's more closely guarded than the crown jewels."

She stamped her dainty foot now covered in a poorly made shoe. "*Mon Dieu,* Normanby! Can you not bribe her maid?"

"Footman." The damned footman. "Her guardian does not allow her out with a maid. She has a footman who's large enough to stop anything I might try." He pulled Celeste into his arms. "It won't be long. I promise. I am walking with her again today, and tomorrow evening I will ask her."

Celeste pressed against him as sinuously as a cat. He wished she didn't have to leave. "I shall wait. *Mais,* if this lady does not wed you, you must take *la bourgeoise, oui*? I am serious when I tell you this cannot last."

It was better to compromise Lady Alice than marry Miss Greenway. But he was not going to argue about it with Celeste, and it would be a last resort. "I understand."

"Bon." She glared at the plain, straw bonnet before donning it. "I shall see you tonight."

"I'll be waiting." As he always was.

She threw a playful smile over her shoulder. "I know, *mon cher*. I know."

He'd have to marry Lady Alice quickly. Mr. Greenway had already had the first of the banns read. Normanby felt as if a noose was tightening around his neck. Damn his parents for putting him in this position. He watched the gentle sway of Celeste's hips as she strolled through the door. If she had money, he'd marry her. She wouldn't be the first Frenchwoman in the family.

Giff arrived at Hatchards before Alice. He was happy to see the table and the area where the estate books were kept was empty. Fortunately, he didn't have long to wait. One of the many things he'd recently noticed about her was how prompt she was.

She smiled at him. "Shall we get to work?"

"Yes." As he had earlier, he held her chair, then took one across from her. "I am more concerned about the changes I might have to make to Whippoorwill Manor than the estate in Scotland. There is a family who has been the stewards for at least a century. The position is passed from father to son."

"Really? How interesting." Alice tilted her head as she leaned forward. "I have read about that, but I had no idea it still occurred."

"Um. I do need to know how things are done, but I'm concerned that Whippoorwill has been left alone for too long. There might be problems there."

She nodded. "It is never good to ignore an estate or leave the management completely up to someone else. What would you like to know first?"

Giff groaned. "Everything. How the prices are set, who does the selling, and everything else."

She pulled at her bottom lip with her straight, white teeth, and he almost groaned again. But for an entirely different reason. His desire to kiss her, to touch her, was constant. "You will need to consult with other large landowners."

"Such as your brothers-in-law?"

"Yes." She appeared pleased he'd caught on so quickly. "All the crops you are selling are sold to a middleman. He will want to buy as cheaply as possible, and you will want to sell as high as possible. You will end up settling on a price somewhere in the middle. Therefore, you need to know what the going rate is for, oh, say apples."

This wasn't as difficult as he thought it might be. "That way I'll know what is a good price and what is too low."

"Exactly." Her smile almost blinded him. "The other thing you should do is gather together as many of the local farmers and possibly other larger landowners so that you have more negotiating power."

He was tempted to reach across the table and take her into his arms. "For some reason I thought it would be more complicated."

Her finely arched brows drew slightly together. "The important part is to find a middleman who is trustworthy. Where is Whippoorwill Manor?"

"About three hours north of Town."

Her forehead cleared. "If there is a problem, I might be able to help you. It is a long story, but we know of a company in that area." She placed her elbow on the table and cradled her cheek in the palm of her hand. "If you are interested, I could introduce you to the owner."

It was amazing the things she knew. "I wonder if the estate is already a client."

"There is only one way to find out. We will go speak to him."

"Now?"

"Yes. Why wait? It will probably take a few days for him to find out if they do work with Whippoorwill Manor."

"Do we need to go into the City? I did not bring my carriage; do you have yours?" Giff had already stood and was helping Alice rise.

"No, it's not far. I will tell you some of the story on our way." She tucked her hand into the crook of his arm. "Before I forget, I am meant to inform you that Theo thanks you for the books. She is finding them quite interesting."

Did her family educate the girls by bringing them into their conversations and starting their educations early? "Were you interested in animal husbandry when you were her age?"

Alice stared off somewhere as her forehead puckered. "Not as much as Theo. Eleanor, Madeline, and I were still more interested in fashion, but we were being introduced to the management of an estate and other important matters. Augusta married when we were fifteen. Charlie was on his Grand Tour, and Grace decided it was time for us to learn. We were the eldest ones at home. Walter and Phillip were at school."

Giff had felt disconnected from his family when he'd been at school. "I remember returning from school and so much had changed. My sisters married when I was away and were no longer there. It was very strange. But your brothers were present."

"Yes." Alice nodded. "Matt sends a coach for them whenever there is a holiday or school break." She appeared thoughtful for a moment, then said, "Now, you are going to meet Bobby Fields. He's still quite young but has a good head. His father was a middleman. After his untimely death, Bobby inherited the business. He is being trained in it as well as in the end result of what happens to the produce. The whole story is rather long. I will tell you it some other time."

They made their way from the bookstore to Bond Street and a grocer's shop. A boy was speaking to customers as an older man looked on with approval.

"Mr. Robbins," Alice said. "We have a matter for Bobby when he has a moment."

"Yes, my lady. Let him finish with this customer, and he'll be right with you."

"Yes, of course." She smiled politely.

This child owned a business? At first Giff couldn't believe it, but in the peerage it happened all the time. A father would die, and a child would be the new peer. He really had to expand his way of thinking. He waited next to her while the customer completed the purchase.

"Lady Alice." He grinned. "How may I help you?"

"Good day." She indicated Giff. "My lord, this is Mr. Robert Fields who we call Bobby. Bobby, this is Lord St. Albans."

Bobby stuck out his hand. "Good day, my lord."

Giff took the smaller hand in his. This was the second time today he'd seen children acting like the adults they would be. "Good day, sir. Do you happen to know if your firm represents Whippoorwill Manor?"

Bobby flattened his lips and his forehead wrinkled. "The name doesn't sound familiar, and I'd remember a name like that." He looked at Giff. "Just to make sure I'll write to Crampton, my assistant, and ask him."

"Thank you," Alice and Giff said at the same time.

That was the very last time he would underestimate a child. "The property is near St. Albans if that helps."

"Yes, thank you. If we do not handle the manor, I shall find out who does."

"Thank you, Bobby. Mr. Robbins, have a good day," Alice said.

"Yes, thank you for your time." Giff strolled off with her. This had been an extremely informative day. "Do you have any shopping to do, or are you going home?"

She glanced at him and tilted her head slightly. "I think I would like to go to the Burlington Arcade."

He inclined his head. "It would be my pleasure to escort you."

Alice was happy to have someone with whom to go shopping. She really missed her sisters. "Do you know anything about ladies' accessories?"

St. Albans gave her an almost wicked look. "You might be surprised at what I know." They retraced their steps to Piccadilly. When they arrived at the arcade, he unerringly led her to the shop Alice and her sisters had gone to for their fans. "Now what are you looking for or are you browsing?"

"Hmm. I am not sure. If I find something that catches my eye, I might purchase it." She really did not need anything. But she had so little to do.

"This would look well with any of your evening gowns." He held up an exquisite fan with a Pomona green background painted with gold and trimmed with gold lace.

From experience, she knew it would cost most of the rest of her allowance. "It is beautiful, but a bit dear for me at the moment."

"At low ebb, I see. It is close to quarter day." He turned back to the fans. "What about this one?"

The fan was painted a pretty turquoise with people

wearing Georgian dress. It too would go well with most of her evening gowns, and it was not nearly as costly. "That is perfect."

St. Albans bowed. "I am at your service, my lady." He wandered around the shop and picked up a reticule of Pomona green silk with a silver frame. He and Lord Bury thought along the same lines when it came to a good color for her. "A few seed pearls, and this will be perfect."

He was right. It was too plain as it was. "What a good eye you have."

"Thank you." A smile lurked in his green eyes.

Williams coughed. "My lady. You will not wish to be late for luncheon."

"Is it that time already?" Alice took the reticule and the fan to the clerk. "I would like to purchase these."

"Very good, my lady."

After paying him, she glanced at St. Albans. "Would you like to join us for luncheon?"

He pouted sadly. "I would, but I am promised elsewhere. If it isn't raining, I will see you tomorrow."

"Yes, of course." She should have remembered he was courting another lady. "I will see you then." Alice took her package and left with her footman. "We must make haste. Her ladyship will leave directly after luncheon on morning visits."

"Yes, my lady." As if he did not know the schedule.

This had been an excellent, a perfect, morning. Why was she out of sorts, again?

That afternoon, Lord Normanby arrived as the clock struck the hour. Alice had stopped waiting to be told he was here, and when the front door opened, she went to the stairs.

He held out his hand as she reached the bottom tread. "How lovely you are."

She fought the blush rising to her cheeks. "Thank you."

He took her hand and tucked it into the crook of his arm. He had never done that before. "Shall we?"

"Yes, indeed." They strolled out the door and down the street. She had only a few more questions before she would know if he met all the qualifications on the list. "How do you like children?"

He glanced at her and chuckled. "I find them delightful. Why do you ask?"

This was very good. "In my family, the children are used to dining with us unless we have guests. I plan to do the same thing with my children."

He inclined his head, and his breath touched her ear. "Of course, if you wish it."

"I do." Alice wondered how bold she could be in her questioning. He had not, after all, offered for her. Then again, he had spoken to Matt. "I also want to continue to support and be involved in my charities."

"I do not know why that would change." Lord Normanby's tone had never been so low, so seductive.

A shiver raced down her back. This must be the feelings she had been told about. Not the prickles she had with St. Albans. Those had been strangely disconcerting.

Lord Normanby gazed down at her. "At the ball, would it be possible to have another set in addition to the supper dance?"

Oh, no! Alice did not have any sets left. "I am so sorry, but I have none."

"I waited too long." He pouted, but it was not the same as St. Albans's earlier pout. It seemed a bit calculated. She shook off the thought. "It is I who should beg your forgiveness."

"There is always the next ball." That should make him certain of her position.

Something, a look she did not recognize, lurked in his blue eyes. "In that case, I would like to ask for them now."

"Of course." If he proposed soon, he could have all her sets. She would like to ask him what he wanted from a marriage. He already met her requirements. Did he not have some of his own? Unfortunately, until he mentioned marriage, she could not ask.

"Then I think I shall look forward to that ball more than the one this evening." He bent his head again as if he did not want to miss anything she might have to say.

What should she say? "I will as well."

"I cannot tarry in Town much longer. I am needed at my estate."

What did that mean? Was he just going to go home? "I understand. Needs must."

They had reached the Park and entered. For a long time, it appeared as if all they would do was to greet friends and acquaintances. Finally, they were as alone as they could be during the Grand Strut. "I would like to settle some things before I leave."

Alice's heartbeat more rapidly. "What would that be?"

"As you must know, I am searching for a wife. Would you allow me to speak with you a bit later?"

He was going to propose! "Yes, I would."

Nothing more was said on the subject, but she knew it was settled. He would ask for her hand, and she would accept. Alice wanted to skip like a girl. Finally, she would be wed.

They finished their walk, and he returned her to Worthington House. She reviewed the list in her head, but hardly remembered what was on it. If he wanted to marry her, he must love her. That she could not forget. When he asked, she would tell him how she felt and wait for him to respond. She did love him. She must. Why else would she be excited that he was going to ask her to be his wife?

"I will see you this evening," Lord Normanby's tone was lower than usual causing butterflies to dash around in her stomach.

"I look forward to it." She entered the house, and he left, glancing back over his shoulder as he did.

When would he ask her to marry him? Would it be this evening at the ball? Alice practically floated up the stairs. Soon he would propose, and she would be married just like her sisters.

Chapter Twenty

Later that afternoon, Mamma summoned Giff to her parlor. He entered and bowed. "Mamma?"

She pointed at the chair across from her. "Come and sit. I have had some news."

His mother appeared both apprehensive and excited at the same time. "What is it?"

She poured him a dram of whisky from the bottle on the small table at her elbow. "You asked me to look into Normanby. I did, and I finally have an answer that is reliable."

Giff took a sip. "And."

"He is broke." His mother took a drink as well. "His father beggared the estates and mortgaged everything that he could. If he doesn't marry for money soon, the loans will be called in."

"Only on the property that is not part of the entail." That's the reason he was courting Alice. He knew the blackguard was up to no good.

"Which is most of the holdings. His father did not continue in entail on anything other than their main estate."

Her dowry would go a long way to paying off those loans. "I take it he has put it about that he will soon wed

Lady Alice. But how has he kept anyone from finding out?"

"He is betrothed to a young woman from the City. The daughter of a wealthy merchant," Mamma stated flatly.

Giff couldn't believe what he was hearing. "He's betrothed, *and* he's courting Alice?" He'd murder him. There was another question. "You do not have contacts in the City. How did you discover this?"

Mamma took another small sip. "I might not have contacts, but I have friends who do. The first of the banns was called at a church this past Sunday. My friend also told me about his finances."

Something wasn't making sense. "Why the deuce is he courting Alice?"

One of his mother's brows rose in an extremely haughty way. "Blood."

Bloody, Bloody hell-hounds. He had to get Alice away from the scoundrel. "Betrothed himself to a Cit's daughter to keep the banks happy but court a lady for her dowry and her bloodlines. He needs to be shot."

"I agree, but not by you." Mamma downed half of her glass. "If anyone is going to challenge him to a duel it must be someone from her family."

Giff would rather just run him through. That was much neater than shooting the scoundrel. "You're right, of course. But something must be done. I'll speak to Worthington this evening."

"That would be for the best." She finished the whisky. "I shall accompany you to the ball."

"I will be honored by your presence." Giff stood. "Thank you for the information."

His mother gave him a sly smile. "I admire Lady Alice a great deal and would be most pleased to call her daughter."

He inclined his head and strolled slowly back to his

parlor. He could write to Worthington, but even if he sent the letter by messenger, it might not be read until tomorrow. No. The best thing to do was to inform him what Normanby was up to and let Worthington take care of it. He would tell Alice, who would be hurt and furious. Yet, she would have her family and Giff for comfort. He would not be able to ask her to marry him as soon as he would like. But propose he would, and hopefully she'd have him. But what if the devil was going to ask her tonight? He'd have to find a way to keep her away from the cur. The only way to do that was to remain close to her all evening. Giff grinned to himself. That would be no hardship at all.

A few hours later, he and his mother entered the ballroom, and he immediately found Alice and her family. Fortunately, Normanby was not with them. Giff scanned the room until he saw the worm standing with a few of his friends across the large assembly room space from the Worthington family.

He made his way to Alice's circle intending to speak with her guardian when she noticed him. "Good evening."

"Good eve, my lady. That fan goes quite well with your gown." That was the tone to keep. Light as if nothing was wrong. Giff tried to catch her brother-in-law's eye, but he was speaking with someone else. Aside from what he had to tell Worthington, Giff wondered how the vote went today.

"Thank you." Her smile was merely polite, but her eyes danced.

The music started, and a gentleman came over to claim her for the set. Giff positioned himself where he could watch Normanby. There was no way he was going to catch Alice alone.

* * *

Alice finished her set with St. Albans and glanced around for Lord Normanby. She was certain he was going to propose. She just wished he would do it soon. He met all the requirements on the list she and her sisters had written and even exceeded some of them. He was certainly the most attentive gentleman she had ever met—well, almost. Alice glanced across the ballroom. Normanby was standing with two of his friends in front of a grouping of plants. Not that he could have avoided the trees and shrubs. There were a profusion of them. The theme was a tropical garden. The three men looked to be in close conversation, and she would like to know what they were discussing. Perhaps St. Albans's friends were giving him advice on when to propose. It would not be at all difficult to slip behind the shrubbery and listen to what he was saying. Alice started weaving her way through groups of people and behind the plants. A few minutes later, she was directly behind the gentlemen. She felt, rather than saw, someone come up next to her. A tingling sensation and a light scent that reminded her of the woods reached her. *St. Albans*. She put her finger to her lips, and he nodded.

"When are you going to ask her?" one of the gentlemen said.

"It has to be damn soon," Normanby replied. "I need to get out of Greenway's grip. Him and his daughter's. I will not be wed to a female who is not a lady or one related to a Cit."

"It's a deemed shame your father mortgaged the estates and your mother gambled away the rest."

"My mother's a fool." He spat the words. "Thankfully, I was able to make her understand that she was better off married to her cicisbeo. She and her gambling are his problem now. He took her to the Continent."

"Leaving you with her debt," the other gentleman commented drily.

"As soon as I wed Lady Alice, the debt and the mortgages will be settled. And I'll be free of my betrothal to Miss Greenway."

"You actually proposed to her?" The first man sounded shocked.

"I didn't have a choice if I wanted to keep the creditors away. However, Greenway's mistake in agreeing to the betrothal was that he thinks the rules for people like him are the same as for us, and that I won't jilt her. She's not a lady and doesn't need to be treated like one."

Alice's jaw dropped. She shut it. How could he? *He is planning to use my dowry to pay his debts!* And he's going to jilt some poor woman. The bounder. The blackguard. She wished she had stronger language to use. It was all she could do to remain quiet. St. Albans must have felt her rage, for he gently touched her arm.

"It's a shame you have to marry to afford to pay them," the first man said.

"I have to wed at some point, it might as well be now," Normanby said. "Once I get my bride with child, I can leave her in the country. It shouldn't take long, her family breeds like rabbits."

Alice's jaw was starting to hurt from being clinched so hard. There was no way on earth she would have him now.

"Will her family let you do that?" The second gentleman sounded concerned, and he should be. Matt would never allow her to be treated shabbily. First of all, he would never allow her to wed a man who would not agree to her keeping her property with him as the trustee. What would Normanby do then? Jilt her?

"What can he do? She'll be my wife. My property." The superiority in Normanby's voice caused her hands to form fists. "Aside from that, I have no intention of giving my beauteous Celeste her congé."

A mistress? He was going to keep a *mistress*? Alice should not be surprised. After all, he was going to jilt another woman and marry her for her money. The cad was thoroughly rotten. To think she had thought he was kind. She was going to hit him hard enough that he fell down.

St. Albans touched her arm again, shook his head, and whispered, "Allow me. You do not want to bloody either your gown or gloves."

Alice did not know how St. Albans knew what she planned to do, but he did have a point. She inclined her head, and he removed one of his gloves. The next thing she knew there was a crunching sound. St. Albans grabbed her hand, and they ran behind the plants to the terrace doors before they stopped. He then donned the glove, and she tucked her hand in the crook of his arm as they strolled onto the terrace.

As soon as they reached a part of the terrace that was not crowded, Alice covered her mouth with her hand as she started to laugh. It was a while before she could speak. "Thank you for defending me. What did you break?"

"You're a bloodthirsty minx." He grinned like a boy. "His nose. I was tempted to go for his jaw, but his nose was easier and faster."

"I'm very glad he does not know it was you. He is exactly the type of person to call you out." Just the thought of St. Albans in a duel gave her chills and not the good kind.

"Hence the reason we didn't stay around." He pulled a face. "It was a rather sneaky thing to do. Not very honorable."

"He did not deserve to be confronted with honor." Anger surged into her again. "Not after what he was planning."

She had an idea. "I can put it around that I hit him and did not wish to cause a scene."

St. Alban's lips twitched.

"What?" He should know by now that she had many skills. "I know how to punch a man."

"I am quite sure you do. The only question is if anyone saw the hand that perpetrated the deed, they would know it was not yours."

She glanced at his hands and hers. How had she not realized how much larger they were? "Oh. I see your point. I suppose it will have to be our secret."

His shoulders shook as he tried to stop from going into whoops. She would have hit Normanby if St. Albans hadn't stopped her. That would have caused a scene. Alice doubted she would have stopped there. She probably would have given him a set-down as well. "That would be a much better idea."

"There you are." Charlie strolled up to them. "I've been looking for you."

Thank God he had not been out here earlier. "Lord St. Albans and I decided to get some fresh air."

Her brother glanced from St. Albans to her. "You missed the excitement."

Her partner in crime assumed the most innocent look she had ever seen on a gentleman. "I hate to miss anything thrilling. What happened?"

Charlie glanced from Alice to St. Albans again. Her brother's eyes narrowed slightly as if he suspected something. "Someone punched Normanby."

Alice raised her brows as if she was surprised. "Really? Who?"

Her brother shook his head. "No one knows. He was

with some chums and suddenly a fist came out from the foliage."

"That's odd." St. Albans frowned. "Who would do such a thing?"

"Maybe it was a lady he wronged." Alice knew she had to tread carefully if they were not to be found out. "Lately, I have been getting the impression he is not all he appears to be."

"It happened so quickly, no one knows who it could have been." Charlie gave them another look. Naturally, he would know that not many females were taught to fight. "I suppose a lady would be more apt to hit a man and want to remain hidden."

"If she did not wish to cause a scene." Alice couldn't look at St. Albans because she was sure her guilt would be apparent to her brother, and she could not glance at Charlie for the same reason. "We had better go in. St. Albans owes me a dance."

Her brother shook his head and frowned again. "I'll accompany you."

Giff tried hard not to allow his chest to puff out. He not only had a second dance with Alice, but it was the supper set. He still had to speak with Worthington. But at least she did not seem to be as upset as he thought she would be. At any rate, she wasn't now. Who knew what would happen later this evening. For the present, he would do his best to keep her entertained.

By the time they arrived at Alice's family circle, Normanby had departed, and the set was forming. It had seemed like years since Giff had waltzed with her. He took her into his arms, and she suddenly stared at him. Damn, was she missing that rogue's touch? "What is it?"

"Nothing." She shook her head slightly and smiled. "Nothing at all. I am glad you are here."

"I am too." The music started, and he twirled her. No other lady danced as gracefully as she did. He wanted to ask her how she felt, but this was not the place. This, however, was the place to begin courting her in earnest. He caught her gaze and smile. "No other lady dances as well as you."

A blush rose into her cheeks. "I might say the same about you. I never have to think when I'm dancing with you."

It occurred to him she had never been happy with what he had brought to her for supper. "You must tell me what you like at supper."

Alice chuckled lightly. "Not lobster patties."

"Duly noted." They twirled again. "But what do you like?"

"I enjoy asparagus, ices, almost everything else. And champagne."

An image of her naked as he poured champagne into her belly button caused him to tighten. "I shall ensure you are well supplied."

"I would appreciate that," she said in a heartfelt tone.

"Is there anything else you like to eat? Poached chicken, salmon?"

"I enjoy both dishes." Giff wished he could pull her into his arms.

He grinned. "I still like lobster patties. I'll bring one for myself if you do not mind."

"Not at all. You may enjoy them all you wish." The moves of the dance placed her back at his chest. She had such a smooth neck. He wondered how she would taste. "I used to like them. However, when one can eat them most evenings, they lose their desirability."

"I never thought of it in that manner." He was very sure he would not lose his desire for her even if he had her every evening. He bent his head and almost touched the shell of her ear with his tongue before remembering where he was. Then the music stopped. "Come. Let us find your family, and we can all go to supper."

When they approached her circle, Mamma was speaking with Worthington. His visage darkened, and he glanced at Giff. He hoped Alice's brother-in-law was not angry at him for not telling him about Normanby first. Giff escorted her to the table and made his way to where supper was laid out.

Worthington caught up with him. "Is there a reason you did not tell me?"

"Yes. I tried to catch your eye, but you were in conversation with someone else and obviously didn't see me. I was more concerned about keeping Lady Alice away from the scoundrel. I did not want him to get her alone."

"I see." Worthington seemed to relax. "Was that the reason you and she were on the terrace?"

They had kept the knowledge from her brother, but Giff did not think he could keep it from her guardian. "Partly. I found her slipping around the edge of the room to where Normanby was standing with friends. I got to her just as she arrived, hidden behind a plant." They made their way along the line speaking quietly. "She heard him tell his friends what he'd done and what he had planned. Including keeping his mistress."

"Who punched him?" You had to respect a gentleman who knew his family.

"She was about to, but I did it." He grinned at Worthington. "Then we ran to the terrace."

Her brother-in-law bit his lip as he tried not to laugh. "Thank you for looking out for her."

Giff inclined his head. "The pleasure was mine. I'm just glad that I was able to be there for her."

Worthington gave Giff a searching look. “You seem to be getting on better than you did in the beginning.”

“Yes, well, it turns out I can be a fool at times.” He wanted to cringe.

“Cannot we all.” Worthington had a wry look. “It never occurred to me to ask one of the ladies to see what they could learn about Normanby. I had a feeling, but nothing solid.”

Giff often thought it was amazing how one’s senses attempted to warn one. “I felt the same. That was the reason I asked my mother.”

Worthington signaled to two footmen to help them, and Giff slipped them vails. “It was an excellent idea.”

“And just in time.” A chill struck him. What would have happened if Mamma had not received the information when she did?

“Indubitably. I take it you’re still interested in marrying her.”

“I am.” Absolutely and entirely. “Even more so now than before if that’s possible. At first, I was dazed by her beauty and grace. Now that I’ve got to know her, I’m dazed by her mind.”

Worthington smiled. “I think that’s the way it is with all the ladies in my family.”

Giff wondered what Worthington meant, but they had reached the table, and their conversation ended as they attended to their ladies. The footmen set down the plates and another servant brought champagne. Perhaps Giff would ask later. “I brought you everything except lobster patties.”

“This is wonderful.” Once again Giff was blinded by her smile. Good Lord! Was he in love?

Chapter Twenty-One

Alice was happy and thankful St. Albans had been by her side when she heard Lord Normanby speaking to his friends. Despite all her lessons in deportment, she probably would have caused a scene. She still wanted to hit the scoundrel. And it was better to have found out what he was up to now and not after they had wed. Alice could not believe she had been so stupid, so blind. She had been so intent on finding a husband she matched him to her list without being certain he was qualified. When she looked back on their conversations, she realized she had attributed the requirements to him when he had not objected to anything she had said. And why would he? All he wanted was her dowry. What would he have done when he discovered that he would not have control over it? It did not bear thinking about.

"It might help if you had a good cry," Grace said.

They were in her parlor with a glass of wine each. "I am more disgusted with myself than sad."

Her sister narrowed her eyes. "Did you not love him?"

"I thought I did." Alice tried to be analytical in thinking how she could have allowed herself to be "in love" with him. “I think I was more in love with the idea of being in love and having a husband.”

Grace nodded. “I understand. I do not think any of us considered how alone you would feel if Eleanor and Madeline wed first.” She moved over to Alice and hugged her. “I should not have left you so much on your own.”

Tears pricked Alice’s eyes as she hugged her sister. “I have been lonely and feeling left behind. I can see now how much I rushed into wishing to wed him.” Not wanting Grace to see her tears, Alice blinked her eyes. “I am glad St. Albans was with me.”

“Matt told me what he did by watching over you.”

Alice had been told that just before the ball, St. Albans had found out what the cur was up to. “He is a good friend.”

Grace reached for her glass of wine. “He appears to be.”

“I want to write a letter to tell that blackguard I never want to see him again.” If Alice couldn’t hit him or run him through with her parasol sword, she had to do something to take control of the situation. “Even though Matt is writing to him warning him not to approach me again, I think I should say it as well.”

Her sister nodded. “That is wise. He might, after all, believe you are still interested in him if he does not hear it directly from you.”

“I agree.” The clock chimed the hour, and she slumped. “I am very tired.”

The worried look appeared in Grace’s face again. “I shall wish you a good night.”

Alice finished her wine and rose. “I will see you in the morning.”

Tears began to roll down her cheeks as she left the parlor. She did not want to cry. Especially over such a horrible, deceitful excuse for a person. People married for money all the time, but to hide his circumstances and to plan to break his vows before they were even made was inexcusable. It was more than that, it was cruel and unforgiveable. She swiped at her cheeks.

I will not cry over him!

When she got to her chamber, Bertram was waiting. "Let's get you ready for bed. Miss Posy is already there."

"How?" Alice shook her head. "Thank you."

"What's a dog for if it can't provide a bit of companionship." Her maid began unlacing Alice's gown. "Let's get you to bed. You'll feel better after a good sleep."

She did not think she would sleep well at all, but after the Dane snuggled in, the next thing Alice knew was the sky was beginning to lighten. First, she would have a ride, and then she would write a letter. Swinging her legs to the floor she padded to the screen to brush her teeth. She hoped St. Albans was at the Park. Once dressed, she started down the stairs and stopped. He was standing in the hall petting Zeus.

St. Albans glanced up. "Good morning. I'd met Miss Posy, but I didn't know you had Master Zeus as well."

Alice was stunned that St. Albans was behaving as if it was the most normal thing in the world to be greeted by a Great Dane. "Yes. Ever since Grace and Matt wed, we have had two. He had one before they married, and we had one as well."

"That makes perfect sense." St. Albans glanced at the dog. "I must be on my way." He gave the Dane one last stroke and held out his arm. "Shall we? Galyna was being brought around just as I arrived."

"Yes, of course." Alice could not believe he was here to escort her riding. "Thank you for coming to fetch me."

He shrugged quickly. "I rode past the Park and didn't see you."

"You came to see how I was?" She had not realized how truly kind he was.

"Oh, no." St. Albans grinned. "I knew you would be fine. I merely wished to honor myself by escorting you."

She did not even try to cover her laughter. It felt so good. "Thank you, in any event."

"You are quite welcome."

He lifted her onto her mare and swung gracefully onto his gelding, and they rode out of the square. A few minutes later, they were racing to the oak tree. Then they walked the horses to the Serpentine. "I have decided to write to him and tell him I want nothing to do with him again. Matt is writing to him as well."

Interesting. Apparently, Normanby would no longer have a name. "Wise." Giff was pleased Alice had made the decision, but he was concerned the scoundrel would not give up. That, though, would not be a problem. He planned to remain close enough to her that nothing could happen. "What are your plans for the morning? Hatchards?"

"I suppose so." That was uttered without much enthusiasm.

"Is there something else you would rather do?"

Alice gazed across the Serpentine. "I would dearly like to hit something."

He didn't blame her at all. He studied her profile. She said she knew how to fight. He could box with her and let her hit him. "I can help you with that."

Her head jerked around to him, anticipation in her eyes. "Would you? When?"

"Whenever you wish." Giff wondered if he ought to ask her brother-in-law first, then dismissed the idea. He had to have countenanced the activity before in order for Alice to have learned.

She nodded. "Yes. I would like that."

"I am at your service, my lady." For the rest of our lives.

They trotted back to the gate, and as they were about to go through, she said, "Would you like to break your fast with my family again?"

Just the thought of spending more time with her made his heart beat harder. "I would, indeed. Yesterday, I found the conversations fascinating. I still don't know how the children manage to hold their own discussion without interrupting the adults."

Alice laughed. "I do not know how it happens either. Somehow it just works."

"I will change and meet you shortly."

"I shall see you soon." She rode away, and he waved to her before riding up Park Lane to Cleveland House.

Giff quickly washed, dressed, and grabbed a bag with boxing gloves in it in the event he needed them. Hitting Normanby had felt damn good. It was no wonder Alice wanted to experience the same pleasure. She might not be able to hit the object of her ire, but she could hit someone. There was, after all, a reason some gentlemen frequented Jackson's Boxing Salon. Giff was beginning to think it was a pity ladies did not have the same sort of outlet for anger. Then again, most men would shake in their boots if their women could knock them down. But could a female gain the advantage of a gentleman if he knew what was coming? Or would it have to be a surprise?

His carriage came to a stop outside of Worthington House. He jumped down and strode to the door. Williams, Alice's footman, opened it and bowed. "The family are gathering in the breakfast room. If you will follow me."

"Lead on."

They went not to the same room Giff was in the day before, but to a much smaller, cozier one. The family had not yet taken their seats.

"St. Albans." Alice glided to him. "I am glad you are here."

"Come, it is time to eat," Lady Worthington said.

He helped Alice take her chair, then sat himself. A pot of tea, then a rack of toast arrived. The other foods were much the same as before.

"What are your plans today, my dear?" Worthington asked his lady.

"I am catching up on some of the accounts this morning."

"Do not forget the balloon ascension is tomorrow afternoon." Lady Mary's tone was matter-of-fact. Almost too prosaic. What was she up to? "Are you going to attend?"

Lady Worthington gave her youngest sister a narrow-eyed look. "I had not planned on it."

Gideon and Elizabeth's eyes had flown wide at the mention of the balloon. Giff was about to invite them, but Alice put a staying hand on his arm.

The little boy sat straighter. "Mamma, Elizabeth and I would like to see the balloon."

"Will you take us, pleeease?" The pleading look in little Elizabeth's eyes made Giff want to say yes.

Her ladyship exchanged a glance with her husband, who winced. She glanced back at the children. "I have stipulations."

Elizabeth nodded her head so hard Giff was afraid she'd do damage. "Anything, Mamma."

"Very well. We will take the landau, two nursemaids and two footmen. You may move in the carriage to get a better view. You may not leave the landau for any reason whatsoever." She looked from one child to the other. Both nodded.

"I want verbal ascents."

"I will not leave the carriage no matter how much I want to," Gideon said, making the sign of a cross over his heart.

"I will not leave the carriage even if I wish to," Elizabeth said. "I promise."

"Very well. We will attend." Her ladyship did not appear happy. Yet, for some reason, Giff didn't think she would mention it to Lady Mary.

She exchanged an almost covert glance with Lady Theo, and the two of them continued eating.

Alice removed her grip on his arm and continued her meal as well. When she'd swallowed her last piece of toast, she said, "St. Albans and I are going to practice boxing this morning. Which room should we use?"

He almost barked a laugh when Lady Worthington smirked at her husband.

Worthington looked as if he wanted to roll his eyes and addressed Alice. "The back parlor. I'll have the servants roll up the carpet and push back the furniture. Will you use gloves?"

That wasn't a question Alice had been expected to be asked. "I do not know." She turned to Giff. "Will we?"

"I would like to have them in the event we wish to use them." He'd let her get her anger out of her system hitting him. If they wanted to actually spar, they could use the gloves.

"Well then," Worthington said. "It appears as if all of our next two days have been planned."

His wife gave him a wide-eyed look. "What will you be doing tomorrow, my dear?"

The corners of his eyes crinkled. "I shall accompany you to the ascension. If you do not mind."

The corner of her lips tilted up slightly. "Not at all. We will enjoy your company."

The children smiled happily but remembered to finish their breakfast.

And that was how it was done. What could have been a

disaster or at least an argument was calmly settled. He could imagine he and Alice having discussions like that. In fact, many of her expressions were much like her older sister's.

As soon as the meal had ended, Worthington stood. "Alice, I will need your letter. You may write it while the parlor is being prepared."

"Straightaway." She rose.

Giff got to his feet. "I can help you if you'd like. Just to ensure it is worded in a way he must accept."

Her forehead wrinkled, and Lady Worthington said, "I think that is a wonderful suggestion. The males of the species frequently do not understand when a lady is serious."

Alice placed her hand on Giff's arm. "We will use the morning room."

Her ladyship motioned to one of the servants. Giff tucked Alice's hand into the crook of his arm. "You can refer to him as a maggoty runagate, a rubbishing commoner who is from the gutter." Behind them someone barked a laugh. "A curst rum touch who is not worthy to look upon you."

She glanced up at him. Sorrow filled her lovely blue eyes. "Or I could just tell him he is a black-hearted scoundrel that I never want to set my eyes on again. And if he does not stay away from me, he will wish he was never born."

"You can write that as well." Giff wished he could hold her in his arms.

She raised her head. "We will think of something appropriate that he cannot mistake."

"We shall." She led him to the morning room. It was painted an almost yellow cream. The curtains had a light yellow background and were decorated with a profusion of colorful flowers. Paintings, some excellent, some not, filled the walls. Two large sofas stood across from each other with a long table between them. Other chairs, some wooden, some covered in chintz were arranged in disparate seating areas. Small tables of various woods and colors stood next to the chairs and at the end of the sofas. He'd never been in such a comfortable room. At Cleveland House, even the morning room was more formally arranged. Only his mother's parlor could be called casual. Long windows and a set of French windows covered one wall, which led to the garden. The other outside wall was also lined with windows. Light flowed into the parlor. A small cherry desk and a large dark ash rectangular table were also in the room. He could imagine games being played on the larger table.

Alice took a piece of foolscap, the standish, and a pen, and set it on the large table, then lowered herself into a chair.

Giff sat next to her. "The first thing to do is decide how to address him."

Her lips formed a thin line. "I had thought to start by writing Lord Blackguard."

"That would make you feel better, but it would also allow him to believe you were merely angry and could forgive him."

"Harrumph." She pulled a face.

Giff suppressed his grin. "Allow me to suggest merely writing Lord Normanby."

"Very well." She wrote the name. "Now what."

"You need to let him know that you are aware of his plans." Giff caught her gaze with his. "Remember, as far as anyone realizes, you did not hear him."

She took a breath and let it out. "True. We were supposed to have been on the terrace the whole time. Matt would have told me."

"Yes." Giff watched the emotions cross her mien as she

thought. Anger combined with calculation. He was very glad he was not on the receiving end of that letter.

"I will say my guardian has informed me that you intended to wed me merely for my dowry."

"He will of course deny it."

"He would." She was quiet for a minute or so. "I will say that I know for a fact he is betrothed to another woman. I am appalled he would court me when he is promised to another. Do not approach me again. I will have nothing to do with a person who would betray the trust of another no matter her status."

That was actually a very good way to put it. And it was something he couldn't explain away. "I think that might do it."

Alice stared at the paper on the table. "I would really like to send it on foolscap."

That might indicate to the cur how low she thought him. However, it would not set the tone that she was too good for him. "But you know you must send it on pressed paper."

"I know." She took a piece of pressed paper from a small stack.

"As soon as you're finished, we can get to fisticuffs." Giff hoped that would make her feel better. She was so brave. Still, at some point she would have to admit her pain. Hopefully, she would be able to do it while hitting him.

Chapter Twenty-Two

Alice led Giff to a back parlor where the servants were just finishing rolling up the carpet and pushing furniture against the wall. Her footman put his bag with the boxing gloves on a chair. A similar bag was on a small sofa.

How to begin? He raked a hand through his hair. "Right, then. Never having boxed with you before or seen you box, I would like to get an idea of your technique and strength."

Her finely arched brows were drawn together, but she nodded. "I understand. How do you want to start?"

"Well"—he grinned—"pretend I'm Normanby and you're hitting him." Palms facing out, Giff held up his hands. "Strike my hands as hard as you can." Alice appeared a bit uncertain, but made fists, keeping her thumb outside of her clenched hands and struck. The punch was harder than he'd thought it would be, but not as hard as he suspected she could hit. "You'll have to do better than that to break his nose." The next strike was more forceful. "You can do better than that. Picture his face." She punched so hard the force almost knocked Giff back a step. "That's better. Now punch his chin with the most powerful upper cut you have."

This time she did cause him to step back. Alice began hitting harder and faster. Soon he was wishing he'd worn his gloves. Her face was flushed with anger and hurt. Tears began running down her cheeks, and she started to sob. "How could he have done that to me?" The anguished words sounded torn out of her. Her arms dropped to her side. "Why me?"

The next thing Giff knew she was in his arms. He held her close, not wanting to let her go. "I do not know if it will make you feel better, but he didn't care who it was. He just wanted the money."

Alice gave a little hiccup and laid her head on his chest. The hairs at the back of her neck were damp. He wanted so much to kiss her, but that would have ramifications he was certain she was not ready for. "He was not honest about it."

She was correct. Many men needed to marry money, but a gentleman would be truthful, honorable about his needs and offer something in return. "No, he was not. If you ever do have the opportunity to strike him, don't let him know what you are going to do. You are quite strong, but he is larger."

"That is good advice." With her face against his coat, her voice was muffled.

Giff wondered how long it would be before someone came in and put a stop to him holding her. From the corner of his eye Worthington and his lady entered Giff's vision. "We can do this again if you would like." Placing his hands on her arms, he stepped back then held up one palm. "I think the next time I'll wear my gloves."

Alice glanced at his hand and up at him. Her blue eyes were still watery. "I did not mean to hurt you."

Giff was glad she'd had the strength to redden his

hands. "I encouraged it." More than ever, he wanted to murder Normanby. "Do you feel better now?"

Although her cheeks were tear streaked, she smiled. "I do. It is rather amazing that hitting something can make one happier."

Again, there was a reason, other than exercise, for Jackson's salon. Giff took one of her hands. Her knuckles were red and chaffed and starting to swell. "You had better get some ice on these."

She winced. "They do hurt a little."

"Alice," Lady Worthington said. "St. Albans is correct. We should take care of your hands."

"Of course. I would not want them to swell." Alice glanced up at Giff. "Would you like to accompany me for a carriage ride this afternoon?"

He made a short bow. "I would indeed. Shall I meet you here?"

She nodded slowly. "Perhaps you would like to join us for tea at three o'clock as well."

More than almost anything in the world. "I will see you then."

Worthington's steady gaze met Giff's before the man left the parlor.

As Alice joined her sister, Giff realized how much her family loved and protected her. Lady Alice Carpenter had been no match for Normanby's deceit. Worthington could have kept the rogue at bay but hadn't had the information he needed to understand the danger. Other than knowing about the blackguard's mistress, Giff had only had intuition to go on until last night. The same as Ladies Mary and Theo. He pulled his jacket sleeves down. He'd make sure Alice was even more protected than before. He'd be damned if he'd allow anything to happen to her.

Williams, Alice's footman, walked Giff to the front door and bowed. "Thank you, sir."

"It was my pleasure." He donned his gloves and took his hat and cane. "Have an excellent day."

"I will, my lord. You as well."

The door closed behind him, and he headed home. Even the servants were protective of Alice. Still, it behooved him to find a way to keep track of Normanby. The man would soon be desperate, and desperate men were not to be trusted to behave in a reasonable manner.

By the time Alice reached her bedchamber, her dresser had a bowl of ice water ready. She placed her hands in it and jerked them out again.

"I know it is uncomfortable, but you will feel better later." Grace gently pushed Alice's hands back into the water. "I trust you have expended some of your hurt and anger."

Thanks to St. Albans, she had. "I did. Although, I am surprised Lord St. Albans allowed me to pummel him."

"He seemed to know just what you needed to do." Her sister's tone was thoughtful.

"He did." Alice had said she would like to hit Normanby. Yet, she had not thought St. Albans would allow her to vent her anger hitting him. "He is a very good friend."

"Hmm." Grace's tone indicated she did not believe he was merely a friend.

"He is interested in another lady." Alice wished he was not. She wished she had been able to get to know him before she sent him on his way. Before she had met Normanby.

"Oh?" Her sister met her eyes in the toilet table mirror. "Who would that be?

"I do not know. He has not confided in me, and I did not ask." Truth be told, she did not want to know.

Grace turned and looked at Alice directly. "Has he said anything about her?"

"Only that he had met her, and he seemed to be making progress." Whatever that meant.

"I see." Her sister glanced around the room. "Soak your hands for at least fifteen minutes. After that, I shall apply a cream." Grace left the room.

Why? She cut a glance at her maid. "I could apply the cream. Or you could do it."

"I suspect her ladyship has her reasons," Bertram said. "You will want to freshen yourself. I will get out a clean gown."

Alice looked in the mirror. Her hair was a mess, as was her face. She was also a little sticky. And hungry. Alice could not see the clock from where she was. "How long is it until luncheon."

"A good two hours. I'll have Cook send up something."

"Thank you." Alice's hands were numb, but the rest of her felt better than it had since the start of the Season. She hoped it was not because of St. Albans. She did not want to be hurt again. This time she feared her heart really would be broken.

After her hands had been well soaked and dried, she went to her sister's upstairs parlor and was waved to a chair. Grace held a jar of something green. "This will heal your hands in very little time."

She opened the container and an acrid smell wafted out. Alice wrinkled her nose. It had been years since she had needed it. "What is it exactly?"

"Horse liniment." Grace glanced at the jar and shrugged. "I do not know what is in it. My groom makes it."

"I am going to smell of it all day." Alice wondered if St. Albans would think it strange that she wore such a disgusting scent.

Grace grinned. "It is not that bad. The worst of the smell will dissipate within in a few hours." She worked the cream into Alice's hands. "You will be able to go with me on morning visits."

She wondered what, if anything, would be said about Normanby. She had to admit it was a little exciting knowing something only a few others did and most never would.

After luncheon, they arrived at Lady Brownly's house first and found a group of ladies already in attendance.

"Lady Worthington, Lady Alice, how good to see you," her ladyship greeted them. "Please have a seat."

After Alice had been served a cup of tea, Miss Connors said, "Do you know how Lord Normanby is doing? He appeared quite battered."

"No." Alice raised one brow. "How should I?"

The color in the other lady's cheeks deepened. "Excuse me. I thought you had been spending . . . I mean, you have been seen with him lately."

"Indeed?" Thank Heavens for Grace's insistence that Alice not show any partiality until she was certain of herself and him. "I dare say I have not been seen in his company any more than any other gentleman's."

The lady's mother glanced at them. "There, Susan. Did I not say there was nothing to your supposition?"

"Yes, Mamma." Miss Connors looked at her folded hands. "My lady, I apologize for my mistake."

"It is no matter." Alice breathed a sigh of relief. "Anyone can make an error." She hoped the lady would not throw her cap at the cad.

"Are you speaking of Lord Normanby?" another lady

asked, her voice dripping with insincerity. "I think his nose was broken. Such a shame. He will not be quite so handsome as before." She popped a small biscuit into her mouth.

Alice wondered what he had done to the lady and was more than glad she was finished with him. She and Grace left when more guests arrived and went on to the next house where one lady expressed displeasure that some gentlemen were so ill-mannered as to fight in a ballroom. Alice was pleased the incident had been, for the most part, dismissed by the *ton*. And that she had been present to depress any thoughts that she cared about Normanby. She did not want her name linked with his.

Normanby touched the plaster over his swollen nose. Thank God his stablemaster had been able to set it. What he wanted to know was who the hell had hit him and why.

A knock came on the door and his valet entered. "My lord, a note came for you from Worthington House."

He held out his hand. It was probably Lady Alice worried about his health. He hadn't seen her in the ballroom as he'd been carried out, but she would have heard about it. As soon as he could rise, he'd ask her to marry him. He broke the seal and a second letter fell to the bed. Shaking out the letter he read it.

Normanby,

I have come into possession of information concerning your lack of resources and your betrothal to another woman. You are forbidden from approaching my ward Lady Alice Carpenter for any reason whatsoever.

Worthington

Normanby picked up the note and opened it. Lady Alice's words were like a sword being driven into this chest. Any hope he might have entertained about being able to coax her into eloping with him were ended. Still, there must be a way.

Another knock came on the door, it opened, and his valet entered again. "My lord, your solicitor is here to see you about the settlement agreements."

He did not want to deal with this now, but he had to keep up the fiction that he'd wed Miss Greenway. "Have him give you the documents and bring me a pen." He closed his eyes. "Never mind. I will get up."

"Yes, my lord." Bowing, his servant left the chamber.

He went to this desk and sharpened a pen. At least part would be done, and he could rest.

The footman returned and placed the papers on the desk. Normanby signed them and handed them back to the footman. "Give him my thanks for bringing them to me."

He had to come up with a plan to marry Lady Alice and soon. The only way to rid himself of Greenway and his daughter was to wed another. Normanby's head ached. He had to think of a scheme, but right now he needed sleep. Something would come to him. It always did. Thinking about Celeste would help ease his mind. She might even have an idea.

Chapter Twenty-Three

Giff arrived at three o'clock and was led to the same room in which Alice had written the missive. The family was already gathered, including the Great Danes. He had not even been able to greet anyone before Posy came to him immediately asking for attention. "You are a beautiful girl, but I must say good day to the rest of your family."

"I am glad you are here," Alice said. "I believe you know everyone."

"Good afternoon." He bowed.

"Welcome," Lady Worthington said. "I hope you do not mind. This is a family occasion."

"Not at all. It is a pleasure to be in company who does not stand on precedent."

Worthington shook Giff's hand. "Welcome. I'm glad you've joined us."

The two youngest members of the family, Gideon and Elizabeth, looked at him almost suspiciously if he was not mistaken. Ladies Mary and Theo smiled encouragingly.

Giff felt both welcomed and inspected. Just like when he first went to Scotland. No one knew what he was about. He'd love to put everyone at ease, but he had no intention of misleading any of them regarding his desire to marry

Alice. And she was not ready to hear a proposal. "I am very glad to join you."

Alice led him to a sofa. He took a seat after she did. Posy sat next to him on the other side. "I must say, I have never seen a dog sit on a sofa like a human."

"They are people too," Elizabeth said protectively.

Interesting. "They are." There was no point in arguing with a member of the infantry. "I have always wanted to have a dog in the house, but not one of the small ones."

Mary nodded approvingly.

"Are you a member of the Lords?" Gideon asked.

"No. And thankfully so. That would mean my Papa had died."

The boy looked at his father. "I would not like that at all."

"You see what I mean."

Gideon nodded. "But what do you do? My uncle Phinn is not a peer, but he and my Aunt Augusta study languages and foreign architecture."

That was a very good question. What was Giff's role in life? "You make a good point. Other than preparing to be a duke, I must find another occupation. It has been suggested that I can be politically active before I am a peer. I will look into it."

"Very good," Gideon said approvingly.

"You could become involved in charities," Theo suggested. "Our family has some that help a great many people."

She sparked his curiosity. "Such as?"

"Taking in and training children who have no one to care for them. We hold classes here to teach them to read, write, and do sums. When they are old enough, they can select jobs for which they wish to train."

Was that who had delivered the messages to his house,

and taught Lady Mary to slip them into pockets? Lady Theo could no doubt pick them as well. "What else?"

"We hire former military men and train them as footmen or in other professions," Worthington said.

"As you know, we also take care of widows and their children," Alice added.

She had mentioned that. Giff hadn't known anyone who did more than give money to charities. He wished he had been pushed into a direction before now. Because Alice had such a large family, he'd gone to Debrett's to find out more about them. Title- and bloodline-wise, they had married well. But there was something more. A bond that knitted them all together. When he married her, he would have to fit in.

He stroked the dog. "I have heard you have family meetings. My mother's family in Scotland do the same thing."

"We do." Gideon's face lit up. "Every summer and every other Christmas we are together at Worthington Place. Do you meet at the same place?"

"We do, or rather I do. My mother comes in summer for a few weeks. I am there for New Year's. In Scotland, Christmas is not much of a celebration. That takes place on New Year's Eve. It's called Hogmanay. One of the important parts of the night is welcoming a dark-haired man. He's called the first foot." Giff pulled a face. "Unfortunately, anyone with red hair is considered bad luck. We have to stay well away from a front door until a dark-haired fellow shows up."

Gideon's grin split his face. "I would be welcomed."

"You would indeed. Perhaps sometime in the future you can come to Scotland and be a first foot."

"May I, Papa?"

"When you are older," Worthington said. "Alice told us you have inherited a property in Scotland."

"I have. Just recently." Giff told them about the estate and whisky production.

Alice seemed to listen intently. He wished he knew more about it. "I understand you have visited the farm in Norfolk."

"I have as have my brothers-in-law," Worthington said. "There are many very good practices. The only difficulty is sometimes convincing our tenants there are better methods than the old ones."

"Yes, but that is the way with most things," Lady Worthington said. "You remember the problems starting schools."

Schools on estates? Giff considered the challenges and the possibilities. "I must look into that."

"The husband of a friend came up with the perfect solution," Alice said. "If you are interested, we may discuss it."

"I am extremely interested." The time had gone so quickly. He was surprised to look at the clock when it struck the hour to see it was already five o'clock. "We should be going."

Standing, she drew on a pair of leather gloves. "My carriage will be waiting."

He helped her into the high-perched phaeton before climbing into his own side. At a nod from her, the groom let the horses go, and she expertly feathered the corner on to Hill Street. Giff folded his arms over his chest and leaned back against the comfortable squabs. He could get used to this. Not saying anything, she cast him a quick look, then turned her attention to her horses. He studied her profile. Her rosy lips turned up slightly at the ends, and her jaw was relaxed. She must have a good deal of experience driving a carriage to be so calm. "How long have you been driving?"

"Since I was quite young. My papa"—her voice broke when she mentioned her father—"started teaching me. Later Grace had her friend Phoebe Evesham instruct us."

That was impressive. Her ladyship was one of the best whips in the country as well as being an excellent judge of horseflesh. "No wonder you are so good."

Alice's smile broadened. "Thank you."

They passed through the gate and onto the carriage way. As expected, they stopped every few feet as they were greeted by friends and acquaintances. His mother was riding with Lady Bellamny. He'd known her since he was a child, but neither that nor his rank saved him from the sharp edge of her tongue when she chose to use it on him. She greeted Alice as if she was a granddaughter. More pieces about the lady he wanted to marry fell into place. She had been raised amongst the *haut ton*, giving her a poise beyond her years. And she had not been sheltered from the suffering of others. She did not stand on ceremony, but she could give one an excellent bear-garden jaw when she thought it was needed. If only he had not been so full of himself when he'd first met her. He caught her ladyship's knowing look and inclined his head slightly. It was time to be seen with Alice enough to cause speculation about his intentions. And for her to see him as a possible husband.

Alice saw the look her ladyship gave St. Albans but could not work out what it meant. She was a little concerned about greeting the duchess. After all, she had not allowed St. Albans to attend her come out ball. She took a breath. "It is very nice to see you again, your grace."

The duchess's face was wreathed in smiles. "I am delighted to see you. I trust you are enjoying your ride?"

"I am." Alice could not resist shooting St. Albans a grin. "His lordship has not attempted to hang on to the rail once."

"Never let it be said I'm pudding-hearted," St. Albans said.

"No, my dear," the duchess said. "That you never were. Much to my consternation at times."

Alice found herself wanting to hear about his mishaps as a child. Many times they told more about the person than their good behavior. Alice glanced behind her. "We must be moving on."

Her grace opened her mouth to say something and stopped. "We will see you later, I am sure."

"Will you be at the balloon ascension tomorrow?"

"I shall, indeed." Her grace smiled. "I would not miss something so exciting."

"Mamma, whose ball is it tomorrow evening?" St. Albans asked, sounding just like Matt.

Gentlemen never seemed to be able to keep track of a social calendar. "Lady Tuttle's."

"Ah, yes. I remember now." He turned to Alice. "Would you grant me the supper dance? I promise you I will not serve you lobster patties."

Alice struggled not to laugh out loud. "Yes, you may have the set."

"Just in time. Here come Hereford and Bury."

Each of them asked for a dance as well, and Lord Bolingbrook rode up. "Lady Alice, may I have a set for the ball tomorrow?"

"You may. The third dance." Soon her dances were filled. When they reached the gate, it occurred to her she had spent most of the day with St. Albans and was reluctant to leave his company. "Shall we go for ices?"

"That is a wonderful idea." He smiled at her, and

butterflies took up residence in her chest. That was in addition to the tingles. This was not good. "I'm looking forward to seeing what their special flavors are today."

It was a warm day, and Gunter's was already crowded. A harried waiter ran up to them. "Our flavors today are blueberry, melon, raspberry, and lavender."

St. Albans glanced at her. "You pick first. Perhaps we can share."

She was between two of the ices. "If you select the melon. I will have lavender."

"Excellent. Lavender and melon," he ordered. "This should be interesting."

"I hope they both taste good." Not that she thought they would not be. Gunter's had wonderful ices.

"It is Gunter's. I'm certain they will." Alice had never noticed how much they thought alike. "Although, I am not particularly fond of the cheese ices."

"I seem to remember Harry saying the same thing." Alice wondered how he and Madeline were enjoying their honeymoon. It was sad Alice's children would not be born around the same time as her sisters' but wanting that too much had caused her to make the mistake with Normanby.

"Here they are." St. Albans took the cups from the waiter, handed them to her, and paid the man. She gave him the melon and he ate a bite. "Very good. Try yours."

She did, and it was excellent. "You should try this."

He dipped his spoon into her ice and tasted it. "You're right. It is much better than I thought it would be. Try the melon."

She felt like a child again as they each ate some of the other's ice. She had not shared like this in years. "We should do this more often." Alice slapped her hand over her mouth. "I should not have said that."

He looked at her in surprise. "I don't know why not? I

enjoy your company a great deal and would be happy to accompany you to Gunter's anytime you desire."

That was nice of him to say. "Thank you."

She was not ready for the day to end. "Would you like to join us for dinner?"

"I would. What time should I present myself?"

"We dine at six-thirty. It used to be earlier, but it is hard to get back from the Park in time."

"I must send for my kit."

"There is no need. We do not dress when we are dining with the children."

St. Albans tilted his head and stared at her. Did he not like the idea of being so informal? And why was she so tense? "What an excellent idea. I have often wondered why one must dress to have the evening meal with one's family."

She immediately relaxed. The prickles started again. What on earth did they mean? "We should go."

They arrived at Worthington House and strolled into the hall. "Thorton, Lord St. Albans will be dining with us."

"Yes, my lady. I shall inform her ladyship and Cook." He glanced at St. Albans. "My lord, if you will follow me. I will show you where you can freshen yourself."

"Thank you."

Grace was with the toddlers and Matt when they received the message that Lord St. Albans was joining them for dinner. "I like him. What do you think?"

Matt bounced their youngest son on his knee. "He's a much better choice than Normanby. I blame myself for letting that happen. I should have followed my instincts."

"Sweetheart." She placed her hand on his arm. "Even you are not all-seeing. According to what the duchess said, he hid his financial difficulties extremely well along with his betrothal."

He grimaced. "At least St. Albans is an open book, so to speak."

Grace held Gaia up for a kiss. "What an interesting way to put it. I have never heard that saying before."

"One of the gentlemen at Brooks said it, and it seemed apt."

"I do hope something develops between Alice and St. Albans. She seems to think he is interested in another lady, but he has not been seen with anyone else. Do you think he might have said that because of the set-down she gave him?"

"I believe that is entirely possible. The story gives him a way of spending time with her without her knowing he is still interested. The night Normanby was carried out of the ball, I asked St. Albans if he was still wanted to marry her, and he told me he did."

That did not surprise Grace at all. "I have always thought there was something between them. A spark if you will."

Matt's gaze heated. "Like the one we have, my love?"

"Exactly like the one we have." She put her daughter down. "I only worry that Alice will turn to him because she was hurt."

"Before this morning, I would have agreed. But you saw the way he encouraged her to hit him as if he was Normanby. Sometimes that can be the perfect way to rid oneself of unwanted feelings."

It had seemed to help a great deal. "An unusual method for a lady, but you might be correct. I never liked how she was rushing it with Normanby. In a way it seemed desperate. We should have planned for what would happen when two of them married and one was left behind."

Matt nodded. "We have several years to come up with

a plan for the next two. I am concerned about Theo coming out. She and Mary are so close, but the three years between them makes it impossible for them to come out together."

Matt was right. Grace sighed. "Let us go down to dinner."

"Ah, yes." He grinned. "Another meal with St. Albans today."

"Hopefully, it will not be the last one. You remember Con coming to breakfast in his attempts to convince Charlotte to wed him."

"I do indeed. Like St. Albans, he started on the wrong foot." Matt tucked her hand into the crook of his arm. "All we can do is help guide. That is especially true with Alice."

"She never did take well to being pushed to do anything." The worst thing about being a mother to her sisters was seeing them hurt. Grace straightened her shoulders. "It will all turn out well."

Matt smiled. "It always has before."

Chapter Twenty-Four

The next afternoon Giff strolled to Worthington House so that he and Alice could take her high-perched phaeton to the balloon ascension. Alice's carriage was parked outside the house. It had been joined by Lady Evesham's landau as well as what he assumed to be Lady Worthington's landau. It was the largest one he'd ever seen. He strode up to the open door and was greeted by a crowd of ladies and children.

"St. Albans." Lady Evesham smiled and held out her hands. "It is good to see you again."

"My lady. I am delighted to see you."

She signaled to two children who were speaking with Gideon and Elizabeth and appeared to be the same ages. "Anna, I would like to introduce you to Lord St. Albans. St. Albans, my eldest daughter, Lady Anna Finley."

The girl made a credible curtsey. "I am pleased to meet you, my lord."

Giff bowed. "It is my pleasure, my lady."

"And this is my son Lord Finley."

Giff held out his hand. "My lord. I'm pleased to meet you."

The child took his hand. "I'm happy to make your acquaintance."

He greeted Ladies Mary and Theo, Gideon, and Elizabeth,

as well as Lady Worthington, and, finally, Alice. "Will we try to place the carriages all together?"

"Matt arranged to have our travel carriages taken to the Park to save the places for us." She glanced at the corridor on the left. "Here he comes." Alice scowled at him. "You are late."

"I am." He shook his head slightly. "I do apologize." Worthington cut Giff a wry glance. "You, however, are on time."

He took Alice's hand and tucked it in the crook of his arm. "I have noticed Lady Alice is always prompt. A trait I greatly appreciate."

"Wise of you." Worthington surveyed the rest of the group. "It is time to depart."

Maids and footmen who had been standing off to the side helped their charges into the carriages, then took their own places. Giff was slightly surprised at how orderly it all was. Then again, he was certain that having eleven children to move around made being orderly important. He helped Alice into the phaeton, then climbed up on the passenger side. "How is this going to work?"

She lifted one shoulder in a shrug. "I am not exactly sure. Matt has been receiving reports all morning. We have baskets of food because we are arriving early. I was told to follow the landaus."

Giff imagined the park full of carriages and people, and he was not disappointed. Rather than go through the crowd, landaus went around and were guided into place by grooms. As soon as they arrived, the large traveling coaches departed, leaving them more than enough space for their carriages. "That was a well-executed scheme."

"It was." Alice tilted her head as if thinking. "I assume our former military men came up with it."

"That would make sense." He wondered what else the former soldiers did.

A curricle driven by Lady Kenilworth joined them. She glanced at Alice. "I am glad we made it in time."

Kenilworth rode his hack with Hugh riding in front of him. He gave Giff a rueful look. "Nothing is a secret in this family."

Chuckling, Alice glanced around. "Where are Dotty and Merton?"

He shrugged. "They are supposed to be here." Kenilworth scanned the gathering and pointed. "Across the way."

The Mertons were walking toward them. Once they arrived, they took seats in Lady Worthington's carriage. "This is much better than attempting to bring our own," Lady Merton said as she settled into the landau. "I remember wondering what you were going to do with such a large carriage after everyone began to leave."

"It is true that I do not use it much these days," Lady Worthington said. "Oh, look. The balloon men are here."

"They are called balloonists, Mamma," Gideon said.

"Thank you, dear." She smiled. "I would not wish to be incorrect in my terminology."

Hugh frowned. "I thought they were called argonauts?"

"That too," Gideon agreed. "But balloonist is used more often."

"Gideon is correct," Arthur added. "I do like argonauts better."

Giff placed his lips next to Alice's ear and felt her react to him. "How often do they get together?"

"Often enough to be friends. Although, Gideon and Hugh are closer. They were all born within a few months of each other."

Giff glanced around again. "I thought we'd see Rothwell here."

Alice gave him a sad look. "Louisa sent a note. Poor Alexandria wasn't feeling well this morning. She tried to hide it."

"Of course, she did. She has as much pluck as the rest of her cousins." He was sorry for the little girl that she'd miss the event. "I hope they have another one soon so that she can see it."

The balloon began to fill. Hugh leaned forward, but his father caught him. Gideon climbed to the coachman's seat clearly intent on keeping his promise but wanting the best view. Elizabeth and the Evesham children joined him.

"Look, Papa, look!" Hugh pointed his finger at the balloon. "It's almost full."

"So it is. Thank you for telling me." Kenilworth kept a tight hold on his son.

Giff imagined the children Alice and he would have and events like this where they joined their cousins and the rest of the family. His hand inched over to cover hers. But he stopped. It was too soon. She required a little more time. He stifled a sigh. At least he was here with her and her family. That had to be enough for now.

Alice watched as the balloon filled and the balloonists climbed into the basket. What would it be like to rise up in the sky and fly? She put her hand down on the bench, touched St. Albans's hand then removed hers. She had to remember that even though he was spending time with her, it was just as a friend. He had another lady in mind to be his wife. "Is it not marvelous?"

"It is." He was staring up at the balloon as she was. "I wonder if someday they will take passengers up. Perhaps not to fly, but to just look at the view."

"I think I might like to fly. Think about being able to see everything from above."

"You have a point. It would be interesting."

The balloonists gave a signal, and the men on the ground started detaching the lines from the stakes in the ground.

"Blast it, Hugh!" Con bellowed.

"There he is." St. Albans caught the reins of her brother-in-law's horse. "Go straight ahead."

"Come back here!" Con shouted.

Alice's heart stopped. Hugh dodged his way through the shallow crowd. Her brother-in-law had been right. "They should have put a lead on him."

St. Albans held her hand. "You see people letting Kenilworth through. He'll get to Hugh in time."

Her nephew jumped for a loose line that was being pulled up into the basket. Con caught him mid leap. Hugh stared up at the balloon and started to cry. "I wanted to go, Papa. I wanted to fly."

"That lad's got a lot of pluck," a man said. "You'll get there boy. Give it a few years."

Con handed Hugh into Charlotte's landau and came over to St. Albans. "Thank you. He's going to give me gray hairs."

Gray hair? Hugh was going to do more than that. "He's going to give us all heart attacks." St. Albans released Alice's hand and she missed the comfort and warmth. "What did you make him promise? He would never break one."

Con racked his fingers through his hair. "I didn't. I told him he could ride with me. I thought I'd be able to keep hold of him. I'll never do that again."

Alice stared up at the balloon. "You know, you cannot really blame him. I would like to fly as well."

That was the second time she'd mentioned it. St. Albans

nodded as he looked up. "I would too." He took her hand again. "Maybe one day we'll be able to."

"Do it before you have children," Con growled. He mounted his gelding. "I'm going home to have a large brandy. That child has taken years off my life."

The balloon sailed toward Greenwich, and Alice hoped it did not accidentally go out to sea. That would be dangerous. Once it was out of sight, people started to leave. "We did not even have time to eat anything in our basket."

St. Albans glanced at her with a frown. "You're right." A gleam entered his eyes. "Let's drive the phaeton over toward the Serpentine and have an alfresco luncheon."

"That is an excellent idea. Do you want to invite the others?"

"Yes, let's do."

"Charlotte, we have a basket and are going to the Serpentine to have an al fresco luncheon. Pass the word down to everyone else."

"That is a lovely idea. We have a basket as well. It will also give the children a chance to run around."

Soon they were all gathered together. Blankets were laid out as well as food, wine, ale, and lemonade. Alice watched St. Albans speaking with her brothers-in-law. That, of course, was not surprising. He knew most of them.

Charlotte came up. "He really is very nice."

"He is." Alice had to agree. Yet, she needed to disabuse her sister of the notion that he was interested in her. "Unfortunately, he is planning to wed another lady."

Charlotte's eyes widened. "Who would that be?"

"I do not know." Alice linked her arm with her sister's. "Let us eat before the children leave us nothing but crumbs."

Her sister laughed. "They can be rather ravenous."

Grace called Charlotte away as St. Albans joined Alice. "You have an interesting family. I like them." He had fixed himself a plate and one for her then poured the crisp white wine into glasses before sitting next to her. "I'm glad they all take care of each other."

She had often thought the same. Alice took a sip of wine. "I am as well. I do not know what I would do without them."

"I have a feeling you will never have to find out." He made a sandwich out of slices of chicken and tomatoes. "You would like my family." He grimaced. "Not my father's side as much, but definitely my mother's side."

Alice grinned. "The Scots."

"Yes."

As if on cue, the duchess strode up to them. "You have had an exciting day. Who was the little boy who got away?"

St. Albans rose and helped his mother sit on the blanket. "That was Kenilworth's son Hugh. He becomes a bit excited about things."

"That is one way of putting it." Alice's tone was dryer than she wanted it to be. "Everyone thinks he is very much like his father."

"Kenilworth. Kenilworth." The duchess tapped her chin. "He would be much too young to be the Kenilworth I knew as a young lady. Although, I must say, if he does not take after his father, he takes after his grandfather."

Since none of them, with the possible exception of Matt, had ever meant Con's father, they had not considered how that kind of behavior could run in a family. "Good Lord. You must tell Charlotte."

The duchess's smile broadened. "I would greatly enjoy coming to know your family better, my dear." She waved off St. Albans's help as she rose. "In fact, I shall do so now."

His brows drew together slightly. "I wonder what she is up to?"

Alice did not understand. "Why would she be up to anything?"

He shook his head. "No reason. No reason at all. Do you think I could hire a balloonist to take us up as long as we were tethered to earth?"

Just the idea excited her. "I have no idea. You would have to find them and ask."

"I think I shall. It would be an interesting experience."

What would it be like to be married to someone who wanted to have adventures? Whoever he wed would be a lucky lady. The thought made her happy feelings dissolve. Whoever it was, it would not be her.

For the following week after the balloon ascension, Giff had danced every supper set with Alice. They met in the mornings to gallop and race their horses. He'd taken to breaking his fast at Worthington House afterward. They had gone riding in the Park several times, ate ices at Gunter's, met at Hatchards, and talked about every topic under the sun. It was time to propose. Giff decided he'd do it at Hatchards where they had their first meeting of the minds. He was to join her there this morning, but he decided they should go together. Giff feathered the corner into Berkeley Street. He hoped he was in time to offer her a ride. To ensure he didn't miss her, he drove the route she usually took to the bookstore from Worthington House. He was traveling from Piccadilly toward Berkeley Square when he saw her. As usual, she was accompanied by Williams, her footman. Just as she turned on to Berkeley Street strolling toward Giff, a small boy ran out into the road in front of a coach that was traveling rapidly toward the lad. Alice said something, and her footman dashed out to save the boy. Before Giff knew what was happening, the coach stopped. The door flew open, and a footman jumped off the back of the coach, grabbed Alice and threw her into the vehicle, slamming the door behind her. She must have quickly attained the bench because he could see her through the window as the coach passed by. Unfortunately, her bonnet had a brim that hid the side of her face, and he couldn't ascertain if she had been injured. Who the devil was in the coach?

Normanby.

The idiot hadn't even bothered to hide the crest on the side of the carriage. This time, Giff really would kill him when he got his hands on the man.

Turning his curricle around, he shouted to her footman, "Inform his lordship. I'll go after them."

Giff followed the coach, keeping as close as he could with the traffic. Finally, they reached the start of the Great North Road. Where the devil was the bounder taking her? Surely, not to Greta Green. The blackguard would never be able to keep her in the coach that long without her assent. He settled back for the ride. They had to stop to either rest the horses or change them. The weather was fine and dry. Giff would wait until then to rescue her. Once he got her back to Town, he'd propose.

When he reached the first toll, he paid and handed the man his card. "If anyone comes by looking for the coach that just passed, please tell them to continue onward."

"I will do so, my lord. Good luck."

"Thank you." He started his pair again and sprung them the short distance needed to catch up to the coach.

Chapter Twenty-Five

Alice had scrambled up onto the opposite bench from Lord Bounder the second he'd spoken, and now glanced out the window, which was more difficult than usual because of the brim of her bonnet. What she did not understand was why the shades were open. Didn't abductors normally close them? She wished she had thought to bring her sword parasol or her pistol. She would like to wipe the smug smile off Normanby's face. If wishes were horses and all that. Unfortunately, all she had was her hat pin. It was a substantial one but, under the circumstances, not enough to help her escape from him and the coach. Alice felt around in her reticule and found a pencil. She could take his eye out with it, but would that help her escape? With no further attempts being made on anyone since Eleanor's wedding, Alice had grown lax. She glared at his lordship. If looks could kill, he would have fallen dead by now. If only she had had an inkling the scoundrel would do something like this. Well, there was no point engaging in unhelpful thoughts. She must gather the information she had. Williams would notify Matt and Grace. Still, it would take a while for them to be able to catch up to her. It would be better if Alice found a way to escape on her own.

The blackguard leaned back against the squabs looking very pleased with himself. "Do not bother trying to escape. You would injure yourself, and I would simply catch you again."

Alice was not stupid. Jumping from a moving coach was not something she had been taught. She might have to remedy that lack.

"Aren't you curious as to what I'm planning to do?" he asked teasingly.

Dreadfully curious, but she was not going to give him the satisfaction of letting him know. Alice raised one brow, removed the book she had, for some reason, left in her reticule, settled back into the squabs where she could not be seen, and opened it, holding the book in front of her face, pretending to read.

"Very well," he drawled. "You will find out soon enough." Thankfully, he lapsed into silence and seemed to fall asleep.

She discovered sitting back gave her a better view out the window. She recognized signs that they were traveling in the direction of the Great North Road. This was confirmed when they halted briefly at the Islington toll. Before Alice could call out, his hand covered her mouth as he jerked her to his side of the coach.

"I like the feel of you next to me." He used the tone she used to think seductive. Now his touch made her feel as if bugs were crawling over her. It made her want to vomit all over him and his boots. It was a shame she could not throw up on command.

When the coach started again, he barked a mirthless laugh and let her go. She threw herself onto the other bench. Carefully ignoring him, Alice picked up the book again and opened it. Once they stopped, she would try to escape again. In the meantime, it might be helpful to see if there was anything in the coach she could use as a weapon. The holsters for the coach pistols were empty. He either could not afford a pair, or he thought she might try to shoot him. He would have been right about that. The carriage slowed. He must be sparing his horses. Alice gave herself a shake and went back to her task. The coach itself was clean, but rather shabby. The velvet was worn in places and needed to be replaced. She knew he needed money. That was the reason he wanted to wed her. Still, why abduct her? He had or thought he had the other poor girl to marry. Then again, he would think of it as sullying his bloodlines. Instead, new blood might improve his line. If he thought Alice would ever agree to wed him, he was sadly mistaken. No matter what happened, her family would stand behind her just as they had with Charlotte. Then again, she had ended up falling in love and marrying Con. But they had still protected her until he had apparently changed enough for her to want to wed him. No matter what happened, Alice would never wed Normanby.

Thorton dashed into Grace's study followed by Williams as if the devil was after them. "My lady." Thorton sketched a quick bow. "Lady Alice has been abducted. Williams said Lord St. Albans was following the coach."

Having someone reliable in pursuit was helpful. Grace tugged the bell-pull for her maid. "What happened, exactly?"

"Lady Alice was going to Hatchards. A boy ran into the street. She told Williams to save the child." Obviously, a boy who did not need saving. "While he was trying to help the lad, a footman grabbed Lady Alice and threw her into the coach. Lord St. Albans directed Williams to tell his lordship."

"I would have shot at the coach, but I didn't want to hurt her. Unfortunately, I was too late to hit anything but the back of the vehicle," Williams explained.

"Thank you for keeping your head about you." Grace rose. "Very well. I want the traveling coach and a coach for our personal servants. Bertram must make up a bag for Lady Alice and herself." Grace's dresser hurried into the room. "I shall need a portmanteau with clothing for two to three days. His lordship will require one as well."

"Yes, my lady." The maid dashed out of the parlor.

She turned back to Thorton. "A basket with enough food for at least one day." Other than to change the team, they would not stop. "Send to Cleveland House and have Lord St. Albans's valet pack clothing for his lordship. He will need garments for the same amount of time. His valet may accompany us. Her grace must be notified. I shall write a short note. I need four footmen to take messages. I expect to leave within the hour. If his lordship is not here by then, he can follow us."

"He is having luncheon with the other gentlemen at Lord Merton's house," Thornton said.

It might be an excellent idea to have everyone join them. A story would have to be put about. Having a family excursion might do it. She resumed her seat and wrote the first note to Charlotte.

Charlotte,

Problems with A. Leaving within 1h. Pack for 1-3d.

G

She sanded, folded, attached her seal to the letter, and handed it to a footman. "Take this to Kenilworth House and give it to no one but Lady Kenilworth."

She repeated the exercise and sent missives to Louisa, Dotty, and Augusta, before writing to the duchess.

My dear duchess,

There has been a serious incident with Lady Alice. Lord St. Albans is in pursuit. I have already sent a message to his valet to pack for a few days. I will follow shortly with servants.

Sincerely yours,
G. W.

Grace hoped that would put her grace at ease and was not too cryptic. She glanced at the footman. "Take this to Cleveland House, only to be given to her grace. Give a verbal message to St. Albans's valet."

"Yes, my lady." The man strode out of the room.

"What about me, my lady?" Williams asked.

"You will come with us."

"Thank you." The footman dashed out of the room.

Now to change into travel clothing. As Grace climbed the stairs, she gave thanks that St. Albans had been there. God only knew what would have happened if they had had to find Alice alone. Grace trusted that St. Albans would have the presence of mind to leave messages as he went.

"Your grace." Her maid entered the parlor holding a note. "This came for you from Worthington House. It is urgent. Gunn has been told to pack for Lord St. Albans."

Mairead took the missive and opened it. "We are leaving in an hour for two to three days. I want to be ready as soon as possible." If Alice had been abducted, the only place the scoundrel could go was north. And the only place

Giff would take her, after he rescued her of course, was Whippoorwill Manor. Knowing the Worthington family, Grace Worthington would not be the only one following. Mairead quickly wrote a letter advising the butler at Whippoorwill Mannor to be prepared to receive her son, his betrothed, herself, and several guests. She took it to the footman stationed outside her door. "Have this delivered to Whippoorwill Manor. The rider can make as many changes as necessary, but I want it delivered as soon as humanly possible."

"Yes, your grace."

"Your grace." Her butler appeared at the door. "I understand you are leaving for a few days. Do you want me to find his grace?"

Although she loved Archie, he would be of no help whatsoever in this matter. A much lighter hand was required. "Not at all. I will only be away for a few days, and I do not want him to ruin my fun."

Her poor butler appeared confused. "What should I tell him?"

"Tell him I have gone off on an adventure and will return soon."

Giff kept Normanby's coach in sight. Fortunately, it wasn't difficult. After the first toll, it was clear the coachman was nursing the horses. If he could work out where the cad was likely to stop, he'd drive ahead of Normanby. But Giff didn't and couldn't take the chance of losing them. Fortunately, it was clear the blackguard didn't even think to look if he was being followed. He hoped the message he'd left at the toll gate got to Worthington. When the bounder did finally stop, Giff would be there to help

Alice escape. He had no doubt she was working on a plan. The only problem would be if someone they knew or who knew them saw her with the blackguard. He almost dropped the ribbons to slap his forehead. That was it. The cur was attempting to compromise her. He'd see that didn't happen. The only gentleman Alice Carpenter was going to marry was him. He had been planning to propose to her in any event. He just hoped she would accept him. If necessary, he'd offer her a pretend betrothal until he could persuade her to make it real. The coach ahead was still traveling rather slowly. This was going to be a very long ride.

After three hours, the coach finally pulled into the yard of The Swan in Hatfield. The posting inn was well-known and patronized by members of Polite Society. Various carriages and coaches were off to the side of the yard having their teams replaced. Normanby would require a new pair as well. Fortunately, most of the *ton* would still be in Town, and the chances of anyone Alice knew seeing her were slim. Still, there was always that possibility. People had begun to leave for the country. She closed her book, slipped it into her reticule, and waited. If necessary, she could swing the reticule at his head. The book would make it heavy enough to hurt. His lordship would no doubt depend upon her not saying a word. Which was a shame for him and a serious miscalculation on his part. She would be as loud as necessary. The door opened and he jumped down. He held out his hand for her, but Alice ignored it. No one was going to even think she welcomed his attentions. Instead, she lifted her skirts slightly and jumped down as well.

"That is no way to treat your betrothed." He scowled.

"I do not know why you believe we are betrothed. I have no intention of ever marrying you. In fact, I can assure you that I will *never* wed you."

He leered at her. "You will have to. You have been in a closed coach with me for three hours."

"Do not look at me that way. It is disgusting. I know about your mistress." Alice widened her eyes. "I have an idea. Marry her."

"Lady Alice."

Lady Bellamny. Thank God!

Alice could have fainted with relief. "My lady, I have—"

"Not here, my girl. I have a parlor." Her ladyship linked her arm with Alice's. "Come along."

She allowed herself to be led to a comfortable private parlor. Once through the door, the sight of the other person in the room made her stop until her ladyship poked her in the back.

"St. Albans." But what was he doing here? "How?"

He stepped to her and took her hands, enveloping them in warmth. "I saw what happened. I sent Williams to your house to notify your family and followed you here." He glanced over his shoulder at Lady Bellamny. "I saw her ladyship and explained what happened. She convinced me it would be better for her to approach you and"—he glowered at Normanby who had apparently entered the parlor as well— "him."

The cad raised his chin. "It won't do any of you any good. I have been with her for enough time to thoroughly compromise her. She must marry me."

Rage coursed through Alice's veins. "You are obviously hard of hearing. I would not marry you if you were the last man on earth. I would rather spend the rest of my life as a spinster than another second in your company. You are a vile, rabid cur."

"Nevertheless." Lady Bellamny held up her hand, cutting him off. "My dear." The sympathy in her voice and look she gave Alice made her want to weep. "I am afraid a few people might have seen you alight from the coach. You must think of Theo and Mary. This decision does not affect you alone."

Alice bit down hard on her lip.

"Marry me."

She turned on her heel to face St. Albans already on one knee. "You want to wed another lady."

"No. I have always wanted to marry you. If you will recall, I said I had met the lady I wished to wed, and I thought I was making good progress."

He was right. He had never mentioned who the lady was. And he met all the requirements of the list, including being her friend. Still, she needed to know why her. "Why do you want to marry me?"

A smile dawned on his handsome face. "You are intelligent, caring of others, even ones who could be considered below you. You are the bravest lady, woman, I have ever met. You care nothing about my present or future rank. You love dogs and children. And I love you."

"Good God, how maudlin," Normanby drawled.

As she turned, St. Albans released her hands. "I have had more than enough of you." Stepping forward quickly, she punched Normanby on his jaw. To her absolute surprise, he dropped like a stone. "Did I kill him?"

"More is the pity, but no," her ladyship drawled. "Please allow St. Albans to continue his proposal before he is interrupted again."

Alice turned back to him. "Yes, please do continue."

St. Albans, who had risen, resumed his position on his

knee. "As I was saying. Alice, I love you. Will you do me the very great honor of being my wife and the mother of my children?"

Her heart wanted to burst from her chest. Tears choaked her throat. She loved him as well. "I will. I love you too."

"Excellent." Her ladyship smiled. "Now that that is settled, I suggest you repair to St. Albans's estate not far from here. I assume your family will arrive within the hour. I shall leave a note directing them to"—she frowned—"what is that strange name of the estate?"

Alice grinned. "Whippoorwill Manor."

Her ladyship nodded. "Yes. That is the one. I suggest you tell the staff to make enough rooms ready."

St. Albans pointed at Lord Normanby. "What about him?"

Her ladyship's lips flattened into a thin line, and she pushed his inert body with the tip of her shoe. "I will see to it."

Alice tugged on St. Albans's hand. "Let us depart."

"You're right. We are well rid of certain scum." They strolled out of the inn and to his curricle. "I cannot wait to show you the manor."

She could not wait to see it. "How far is it?"

As he lifted her into the curricle, Alice started to prickle all over. It was the feeling she had had before with him. How strange she had not recognized it for the sensations her sisters talked about. She had been attracted to him from the beginning and did not know it. "Around six miles." He climbed up and took the ribbons. "How many of your family do you think will arrive? I believe there is only a reduced staff."

What would the staff think of him bringing her with no notice? She straightened her shoulders. It was no matter. They were betrothed. Her family would be there soon.

Alice would simply have to start as she meant to go on. "We will make do. My family will understand."

We.

Giff loved how she already thought of them as a couple. "At some point, I would like to kiss you."

She flashed him a smile. "I think that is an excellent idea. Where shall we live first?"

"Right away?" He hadn't even considered it. Giff would like to take a jaunt to Scotland to see his estate.

"Yes. I thought we might want to go to Scotland."

Once again, he was glad they thought along the same lines, but . . . "Do you not wish to have a honeymoon?"

"Yes." She frowned. "Well, I suppose I do. Still, we have duties."

She was amazing. He didn't know another lady who would put her duty before such a normal pleasure. "I have an idea. My mother's father has a ship. I can ask him to send it to the London docks or somewhere nearby, and we can sail to Scotland. After that, we will take it to France and join your sisters."

Alice looked at him as if he was the most brilliant person in the world. "What a perfect solution!"

"Now that that's settled, when would you like to marry?" He hoped she'd say immediately. But he remembered Montagu and Stern having to wait. All very well for them. They'd had work in the Lords and Commons. Giff would have to find something to occupy himself. He wouldn't mind starting the changes at Whippoorwill Manor, but he didn't want to be that far from Town, and he wanted Alice with him.

He was watching the road, but the burning on his cheek made him glance at her. She couldn't have changed her mind. "What is it?"

"What do I call you? St. Albans?"

"I would like you to call me Giff. It is short for—"

"Gifford." She laughed. "Very well. Giff it is. We shall wed in two weeks. Grace will not agree to a shorter period of time."

"Two weeks." It wasn't *that* long he supposed. After all, he had to arrange the church, purchase the special license, write to his grandfather, and negotiate the settlement agreements. *Lord save me*. He could accomplish any contracts on his own property, but his father would have to negotiate the agreements regarding the dukedom. Knowing Papa, that could take more than two weeks. Giff would have to get his mother involved as soon as possible. He could feel Alice staring at him again. "Agreed."

Chapter Twenty-Six

Less than an hour later, Giff turned into the gate of Whippoorwill Manor. He was surprised to see the lawn had been scythed. The circular drive led to the front stairs had been groomed, and large urns with flowers flanked the entrance. The door opened before he stopped the carriage. A tall man in his middle years dressed in black, obviously the butler, walked down the steps. He was followed by the rest of the servants lining up in order of precedence. The butler bowed. "Welcome home, my lord."

"Thank you . . . er." Giff raised a brow.

"Cummings, my lord." He waited until Giff went around to Alice.

"It appears someone notified the staff," she whispered.

He lifted her down. "It had to have been my mother."

"Most likely." Alice shook out her skirts, turned to the servants and smiled.

Giff placed his palm on the small of her back. "Lady Alice Carpenter, my betrothed. Members of her family will be joining us in an hour or two."

"I am pleased to meet all of you." She glanced at Cummings. "Cummings, it is a pleasure to meet you. I trust we will work together well. Please carry on."

"Yes, my lady." He bowed. "I am honored to both introduce you to your staff and welcome you to your home. We wish you and his lordship happy."

"Thank you."

Giff followed behind her as she first met Mrs. Cummings the housekeeper, then the cook, footmen, and maids. Giff was intrigued there were so many servants. Once the housekeeper took Alice to her chamber, he turned to Cummings. "I was given to understand the manor had a reduced staff."

"Until a few weeks ago, we were short-staffed. His grace's steward visited us and instructed me to hire the rest of the servants we needed. Her grace sent a rider to inform us of your imminent arrival. I hope you and her ladyship will be satisfied with the results."

"I am certain we will." Giff inclined his head. "I am already impressed with the manner in which you have kept the front of the house."

"Thank you, my lord. Shall I have a light nuncheon served in an hour?"

Giff was glad his stomach hadn't growled at the mention of food. Alice would be hungry as well. Would it take her an hour to freshen up? "Please serve it as soon as her ladyship is ready. I suspect that will be considerably less than an hour."

"Yes, my lord." Cummings bowed. "Shall I first take you to your chambers?"

Considering Giff hadn't been here since he was a child and had stayed in the nursery then, that would be a good idea. "Yes, please. I remember the gardens better than I do the inside of the house."

* * *

Alice had rarely seen such an interesting house. It had obviously been built during the Elizabethan period, but an early Georgian façade had been stuck on the front. Albeit the mullioned windows had been kept, giving the house a rather whimsical appearance. As the housekeeper led her to the family wing, Alice could see that although the residence had been enlarged, it was not a hodgepodge of halls, corridors, and rooms. From the main staircase, Mrs. Cummings turned down a corridor that ended with a door. She went to the room next to the end room and opened the door. The chamber was large and decorated in blues and greens. Long windows overlooked a garden, and a French door opened onto a small half-circle balcony.

"I hope it meets with your approval, my lady."

"It is very nice." She wondered if the master's and mistress's apartments were at the end of this wing. She would have to ask Giff. A pleasurable thrill shot through her at the thought of sleeping so near him.

"My lady." Alice had the feeling Mrs. Cummings had said that more than once.

"Mrs. Cummings?"

"Here is May to help you freshen up."

Alice nodded at the young woman. "Thank you, May."

The maid bobbed a curtsey.

"I would also like something to eat."

"I will have it arranged." Mrs. Cummings curtseyed and left the room.

Alice gave herself a rueful look in the mirror. Being thrown into a coach did nothing for one's appearance. "I will wash my face and hands, then you may make my hair more presentable."

"Yes, my lady." May stood with her hands folded in front of her waist.

Alice had not expected to formally meet the servants today, but she had been trained well and knew how to behave. What she had not anticipated, nor wanted, was the complete subservience of the staff. Being well-mannered and competent in their duties was required, but somehow she had to let them know they could be—oh, how to put it?—show their personalities as well. Perhaps they would relax a little after they got to know her and Giff. Having some of their own servants here might help as well.

Alice dried her face and sat at the toilet table. "I think a simple knot will do."

With her hair neatly dressed, she felt much more the thing. She smiled at May hoping to put her at ease. "Where will I find nuncheon?"

"I will call a footman," she said.

That had not been the answer Alice had wanted. "Thank you."

As expected, a footman arrived shortly after the bell-pull had been tugged. As she stepped into the corridor, the door to the end apartment opened. Giff stepped out and grinned. "There you are. I wondered where they put you."

She leaned around him. "I thought that was where my future rooms would be."

He tucked her hand into the crook of his arm. "Come. I'll show you around." He glanced at the footman. "Wait here."

The servant bowed stiffly. Alice stifled a sigh. "Lead on."

The door opened into a parlor flanked on each end with another door. A fireplace stood in the middle of the outside wall. The rest of the wall was filled with long mullioned windows. The upper half of which were stained and patterned glass. Light shining through the windows made patterns on the large Aubusson carpet that was anchored by two sofas. All the soft furnishings were in good condition. She would not have to do much at all. “It is beautiful.”

Delight shone in Giff’s eyes. “I’ll show you your chambers first.”

Her bedroom was decorated in pale yellows and greens. Next to the bedchamber was a dressing room. Through a door off the dressing room was a small bathing chamber. A colorfully tiled German style fireplace stood in the corner. The bathtub had a faucet with piped-in water. “Do you have a bathing chamber as well?”

He pulled a face. “I have one, but the water must be carried from the main hot water pipe for the floor.”

Before she knew it, she was in his arms. “How did you do that?”

He gave her a heated look. “I will show you sometime.”

Her lips began to tingle, and she leaned against him. As she reached up to kiss him, his mouth slanted across hers. His lips were firm as they feathered across hers and down over her jaw. He held her closer with one hand while stroking her cheek with his thumb. Feelings she had never experienced before infused her.

This is what it is like to be kissed!

His tongue caressed the seam of her lips, and she opened her mouth. He touched his tongue to hers, and her legs trembled. He groaned as he slowly explored her mouth. Alice quickly copied is movements. He brushed his hand against her breasts, and they immediately felt swollen. This was why her sisters could never explain how it felt. It was indescribable. An ache started between her legs. As if he knew what she was feeling, his leg parted hers and he rubbed there. The tension and aching grew until she exploded like a Catherine Wheel.

Giff’s kisses slowed as he stroked her back. “I love you more than I thought I could love anyone.”

Alice had never had such an intense feeling of rightness before. "I love you. I cannot believe we found each other."

"I was terrified that I'd lost you for good." His stomach growled loudly. "Let us eat. I am hungry."

He helped her straighten her gown before they left the apartments.

"I wonder when dinner will be served."

"I do not know." It occurred to Alice that she must ask when the cook planned to serve dinner, She must also arrange to have tea prepared for everyone when they arrived. They entered a small dining room toward the back of the house. Breads, cheeses, cold meats, and salad had been laid out on the table as well as a bottle of claret and a carafe of water. Cummings poured them each a glass of wine and stood back against the wall.

She had always wanted to be the mistress of her own houses. It was now time to begin. "Cummings, I would like to know when Cook plans to have dinner ready."

"At six o'clock, my lady. However, she is making a beef dish that will not be harmed by pushing the time back." He cleared his throat. "I should tell you that she does not want to be the head cook."

"We will arrange to hire someone. Please have tea served after my family arrives." She opened her brooch watch. It was three o'clock. "I expect them shortly. I doubt they will have had luncheon. However, tea should be sufficient until dinner is served."

"Very good, my lady." He bowed. "How many guests should we expect?"

That was a very good question. "Honestly, I have very little idea. At least two to four." If Mary and Theo accompanied Grace and Matt. "At most, ten I should imagine." She lifted one shoulder in a shrug. "We will have to see."

"My lady?" The butler's eyes had widened slightly.

Good Lord. He looked panicked. Well, as panicked as a butler could look.

"It will be fine. My family will not expect perfection. After all, this trip was not planned."

"Yes, my lady." Cummings was not convinced.

"Cummings, trust me. All will be well. You may leave us now."

He and the footman bowed (again) and departed.

She glanced at Giff, who had piled meats and cheeses on to a piece of buttered bread and topped it with another piece of bread spread with mustard. If she ate that much she would not be able to eat dinner. She took some salad, added cheese and a piece of chicken. To think the most exciting thing she had planned today was to meet Giff at the bookstore. Instead, she discovered she was in love, been betrothed, and had her first kiss. Alice finished her food and was about to take more when the door opened.

"My lady," the butler said. "Your family has arrived. My lord, her grace is with them and demanding she be put in a regular guest chamber."

Giff's lips twitched. Alice shot him a quelling glance. "Honor her grace's wishes and have a chamber prepared." She rose. "How many have arrived?"

"I counted four adults and four children. More coaches were arriving."

Had they brought the whole family? Who other than Grace and Matt were here? "Have the nursery made ready. There will be at least two boys and four girls. I will greet our guests."

Alice placed her hand on Giff's arm. "Are you ready?"

"Umm. I wonder if the Danes are here as well."

She tried and failed to stifle a giggle. "We will know soon."

Her housekeeper was in the hall greeting Alice's dresser

and the other ladies maids. Footmen carried small trunks, bags, and portmanteaux up the stairs. Alice wondered why the children were here until she realized today was one of the days they all had classes together.

Grace smiled and drew Alice into her arms. "I am so happy you are safe and well."

She blinked back tears. "Better than well. St. Albans and I are going to be married."

"We know." Grace's smile was a little watery as well. "Lady Bellamny sent a messenger with a letter. He caught up to us just before Hatfield."

Her grace came up and bussed Alice on the cheek. "We are so very happy for you, my dear. I understand you knocked down that scoundrel."

"I did." She had almost forgotten about the cur. "He was interrupting your son's proposal."

Her grace laughed. Not a polite laugh, but one from the belly. "He deserved it then, for that and other reasons."

Matt slapped Giff on the back as they greeted each other. Con, Rothwell, and Merton were here as well. "Are Charlotte, Louisa, and Dotty coming?"

"I expect them soon," Grace said. "We have the children. Once I was told what had happened, I wrote to them asking them to come. I believed the circumstances warranted a show of force."

"That is the reason I am here as well," her grace said.

People were missing. "Where are Theo and Mary?"

"Looking at the garden I suspect," Grace said. "They will be in soon."

"After you have had time to refresh yourselves, tea will be served. Dinner is at six." Alice wondered if she should have asked where everyone was being housed. "I have not had an opportunity to see much of the house. Perhaps we can all take a tour after tea."

"I will be happy to show you around, my dear," the duchess said.

"What I have seen is beautiful." The hall had been cleared of the initial luggage. Yet there were sounds of another coach arriving. "You have not left me much to do."

The duchess blushed. "After seeing the colors you chose for your come out ball, I used them to redecorate. You see, I had a feeling. Aside from that, you will have plenty to do in your wing of the London house and in Scotland. Neither have been refurbished in decades."

Giff joined Alice, placing his hand at her waist. His touch caused tiny fires to race up and down her spine. "I think either your sisters or their servants have arrived."

Hugh strode up to them as fast as his legs would carry him without running. "Sir." He looked up at Giff with beseeching blue eyes. "You have a very nice banister."

Alice exchanged a mirthful glance with Grace and the duchess.

Giff hunkered down to be at eye level with the boy. "I do indeed. If your parents agree, you may try it out."

Hugh turned and ran to his father. "I may slide down the banister. Lord St. Albans said I could."

Con glanced at Giff with a raised brow. He held the palms of his hands out and shrugged.

Con looked at Hugh. "Very well. After everyone is settled."

In short order another coach of servants and baggage arrived followed by Alice's older sisters and Dotty.

Williams came up and bowed. "My lady. Bertram said a gown is ready if you wish to change."

Alice's gown was rather mussed. Being thrown into a

coach did nothing for one's clothing either. "Thank you. I will be up in a few minutes." She turned to greet her sisters who had not heard about her betrothal. "Welcome to Whippoorwill Manor."

Charlotte's jaw dropped for a slight second. "You are betrothed!"

"This is perfect!" Louisa exclaimed.

"Just as I thought," Dotty said.

First Giff's mother and now Alice's cousin. "How could you know when I had no idea at all?"

Dotty grinned. "You had too many . . . oh, I do not know, feelings I suppose. Although, that does not explain it well, for him. There was just something there. Especially during the past couple of weeks."

That was fair. After that first day in Hatchards, Alice had started being attracted to him. "I think I understand what you mean."

After Alice changed and everyone else washed the dust of the road off, the duchess suggested the morning room for tea, and Alice ordered it served there. After tea, she and her sisters followed the duchess around the house. The rest of it was as well decorated as the rooms she had already seen. There was also a substantial garden on three sides of the building that included a maze and a courtyard between the two wings. Once they finished sliding down the banister, the children would have fun there. The fourth side held the dairy, a kitchen garden, and the laundry. It was no wonder the house was Giff's favorite. Alice already loved the estate.

They flustered the servants by dining in afternoon gowns instead of evening gowns and by having the children join them. Alice hoped their dress and customs would give her staff a hint that her family, ergo she, was more relaxed than they were used to.

The talk was, naturally, about the wedding. Alice told the duchess about the garden wedding. "Harry and Madeline could not get the date they wanted at St. George's."

"You could marry in the garden," Mary suggested.

Seated next to Giff, his mother leaned closer to him and whispered. He nodded. "If we cannot get a date at St. George's, would you object to a wedding at Cleveland House? The gardens are extensive and there is a ballroom." He smiled. "Naturally, the children and dogs would attend as well."

Alice had never seen the house much less the gardens, but she knew it was free-standing with a good bit of land around it. "I like the idea. When could I see it?"

"Tomorrow or the next day depending on when we depart."

Matt glanced at Giff. "I'll give you a letter for your father. We must settle the contracts sooner rather than later."

Alice suspected at least one of her brothers-in-law had spoken with her betrothed about them while she was touring the house. What would the duke say about Matt's conditions? She wanted to be present when they spoke.

The children began to yawn when dessert was served. Shortly thereafter, their maids were called to put them to bed. Hugh grinned at Giff. "It is a truly splendid banister."

Once the children had gone, Con said, "I suspect you will be plagued by him for invitations. Shall I forbid it?"

"Not at all. I'm sure when we are on the way to someone's house or another this will be a convenient stop. It will be a pleasure to have him and the other children visit."

Alice raised one brow and directed it at her betrothed. Giff added, "Provided he is accompanied by his nursemaid."

Alice rose. "It is time to repair to the drawing room." She glanced at Giff. "Are you remaining here or joining us?"

"We will come with you." He went to the foot of the table to escort her. "Cummings, have the port and brandy brought to the drawing room you have set up. A footman will lead us there."

"Yes, my lord." The butler's bow was not quite as stiff as before.

Chapter Twenty-Seven

Once they were gathered in the parlor and everyone had a beverage, Alice dismissed the servants.

"There is an issue we have not discussed," Worthington said.

Giff noticed the other gentlemen's countenances were grim. "Normanby. Do you know what happened to him?"

Worthington shook his head. "Unless Lady Bellamny had him locked up, which is extremely unlikely, he is no longer at the inn or its vicinity."

"He'd better not go anywhere near Alice or Town for that matter." Giff scowled.

"You are not to challenge him to a duel." His beloved directed a hard look at Giff.

"Alice is correct," his mother said. "It would start tongues wagging."

"What shall we do?" Rothwell asked.

"We could kidnap him and send him overseas somewhere," Kenilworth suggested as he gently twirled his glass of brandy.

Giff had no doubt at all they would do just that if they found the scoundrel.

"He did not harm me." Alice's tone was thoughtful. "He wanted to force me into marriage by having people see us together. The only time he touched me was to keep me from calling out at a toll booth. We should quietly put it about that he is a fortune hunter who is already betrothed."

"And make sure he is not invited anywhere." Lady Kenilworth glanced at Mamma.

She took a sip of wine. "I have already been asking questions about him. I can easily say I have found he is insolvent and betrothed to a Cit's daughter. That will stop most ladies from inviting him to their entertainments."

It would. Although would that alone be enough to stop Normanby? And would the man try to punish Alice for punching him? Giff met Worthington's eyes. Alice needed more protection. Giff was certain her brother-in-law would assign more footmen and insist she take a carriage. He would have Normanby's house watched and the man trailed. Giff glanced at his betrothed. Meanwhile, he meant to spend as much time with her as possible.

After tea, everyone made their way to their rooms. Other than Alice, his mother was the only person in the family wing. He stared at the paneled canopy of his bed, wishing she was here with him. He couldn't go to her. That would be a breach of his duties. The clock struck ten. She was probably asleep. Worthington had announced they would all leave fairly early in the morning. He rolled over and gazed out at the dark room. A figure dressed in white moved slowly toward his bed, feeling for furniture as she went. He waited until she was close to the bed.

"My lord," Cummings said.

Giff closed his eyes and sighed. How had he missed

how tall the figure was? Why the devil was his butler in his room? "What is it?"

"One of Lord Worthington's men caught someone sneaking around the house. He's being held in the stables."

"Wait for me." Giff threw back the covers and grabbed his breeches. Fortunately, he was wearing a nightshirt. He shoved his feet into a pair of shoes.

When they got to the stables, the man was bound to a post. It was the groom from Normanby's stable. "Where is your master?"

"I ain't got no master." The man spat on the brick floor.

"Indeed?" Giff raised his brow. He wished he'd thought to ask his groom to come. "You did the last time I saw you."

"I don't know what yer talkin about."

"Very well." He glanced at his butler. "When is the next assize?"

"Not for another six months. We can keep him in the dungeon. They haven't been used for a while, but we keep them ready in the event they are needed."

Giff nodded sharply. "Take him there. I'll notify the magistrate in the morning."

"Hey, ye can't do that!" The groom struggled against his bounds.

"On the contrary. I am well within my rights. You were caught trespassing and close to my house." Giff stroked his jaw. "As a matter of fact, I could have you shipped out of England, and no one would ever see you again."

"I actually like that idea much better than holding him over," Worthington said from the door.

The servant's eyes bugged out. "No! Ye can't. I ain't even been paid."

"Then tell me what I want to know, and I will take that

into consideration." Giff crossed his arms against his chest. "Immediately."

"I was supposed to nose around and find out when that lady was leaving."

"By lady, I assume you mean Lady Alice."

"If she's the one with the yellow hair, that's her."

Giff forced his hands not to curl into fists. Hitting Normanby's tool would not be either worthwhile or satisfying. "Then what were you supposed to do?"

"Tell his lordship. He says she should be marrying him as he was the one alone with her."

Worthington ambled forward. "As the lady's guardian, I can assure you your master will never wed her. I have already agreed to Lord St. Albans suit."

The groom slumped. "We're done for."

"Not entirely." Alice's hard tone came from the door. "Has he not told you he already has a betrothed? He is welcome to wed her."

"But he don't want her," the servant said glumly. "We don't want her. She ain't the right sort to be our lady."

Giff's patience was running thin. "It is of no matter. Her ladyship will marry me. If you want to help your master pay you and his other servants, you will tell us where he is."

"He's at the Six Bells."

"Under what name?" Worthington asked.

"He used his own name."

The man was a damned fool. But it made what they had to do easier. "You will be kept here until morning." He signaled to Cummings. "Lock him up."

"Yes, my lord." Two large footmen held the groom's arms while another untied him. The three of them led the servant out of the stables. "When do we go to the Six Bells?"

"As soon as we're dressed," Worthington said. "I'll have the others wakened."

"I am going as well," Alice said.

"As you wish." Her guardian strode to the door and stopped. "We leave in fifteen minutes."

Alice muttered something under her breath. "I do not have a riding habit. Do you have a carriage I can use?"

Fortunately, the moon was up, giving her enough light to drive. "My curricle. I'll have it made ready."

"Thank you. I must hurry." He took her hand, and they ran back to the house.

Stopping in front of her door, he raised her fingers and kissed them. "I'll meet you here."

Alice strode into her chamber to find Bertram already there. "What do you need?"

"Absent a riding habit, a carriage gown. I only have a short time."

She took out a gown from the wardrobe. "Here you are."

Less than ten minutes later, Alice was dressed, her hair dressed in a knot, and a bonnet on her head. She pulled on her leather gloves. "Go back to sleep. I doubt we're departing in the morning." Giff was waiting for her when she entered the corridor. "Let us go. Matt will leave if we are late."

"That is good information to have." He took her hand again, and they dashed through the house to the stables. They arrived just after her brothers-in-law.

Charlotte was also there. She grinned. "It has been a long time since I have had an adventure. Aside from that, I brought my lock-picking tool."

Alice wanted to throw herself into her sister's arms. "There are a number of things I am going to start carrying in my reticule from now on."

Charlotte gave a rueful laugh. "I know the feeling. The carriage is ready. Do you want to drive?"

"Yes, thank you."

Giff lifted Alice onto the bench, while Con helped Charlotte. The gentlemen mounted their horses. For a second, Alice was struck at how masculine and graceful Giff looked in doing so. And now he was hers. She took the ribbons in her hands and followed him. Thankfully, the road was macadam and reflected the moonlight, making it easy to see.

"Some men do not give up easily," Charlotte said. "I was abducted twice."

"I never heard the whole story." Perhaps her sister would tell her.

"It is rather sordid. I was abducted for the same reason you were. An ineligible gentleman wanted to marry me. However, he thought complete ruin was in order. He hired someone to abduct me. Con happened to be driving by when Thorton stopped him and sent him after the carriage I was in. To make a long story short. I was saved, but another woman was taken, and I was abducted again in the process of trying to save her." The corners of her lips tilted up. "I suppose it was not all bad. Con and I fell in love and married."

"It was the most harrowing time of my life," Con said from the side of the gig. "I hope never to repeat it."

They slowed and turned into the inn's yard. A sleepy stable boy ran out to meet them. "Don't think we have room for all of ye."

"We are not looking to spend the night," Giff said. "I want to know which chamber has been given to Lord Normanby."

"Don't know the name, but I carried a bag for some lordship up to the last room on the first floor. It's on the right side of the corridor." Giff slipped the lad several coins.

The boy grinned. "Let me know if I can help you some more."

"You can do so now. How do we get in without waking everyone?"

"I'll show you the way." He waved his arm, and they followed him to the back of the inn. "This door's always open. Go through it and up the stairs. You'll be right in front of the room you want."

"Thank you." Charlotte smiled at the boy, and his jaw dropped. She led the way, stopped at the door, took out a small bird-shaped tin of oil, applied it, then used her tool to turn the lock, and stepped back. "Gentlemen, after you."

Giff shot Alice a grin. "I'm going to like being part of your family."

She started to enter the room, but her sister stayed her. "You do not know his state of dress. Wait here until we are needed."

Alice was not completely certain what part she would play, or if she would be allowed to do anything at all. "Very well."

Charlotte patted Alice's arm. "Matt will not keep you out of the discussion."

That made her feel better.

The sound of a slap and a groan emitted from the bedchamber.

"What in the bloody—ooof."

"Mind your language." Matt said. "There are ladies present."

"What are you doing in my room?" Normanby blustered.

"Making very sure you do not cause my sister any more harm." Alice had never heard Matt's tone so hard.

"You should be happy for her to wed me. I'm a marquis." She rolled her eyes. Why did peers always think their rank mattered? Aside from that, so was Giff, and he was going to be a duke. If that was the competition, Giff won.

"What did you not understand about never approaching her again or there would be consequences?" Matt's tone was menacing.

"By any rule of propriety, she should marry me. You don't know what happened in that coach. Only she and I do. She was not unwilling."

The next sound was one of bones crunching.

Alice sighed. "You were right. Some men do not know when to stop."

"It would save the world a great deal of trouble if they did." Charlotte matched Alice's whisper.

"You have made your point, now go," Normanby wheezed.

That was not going to happen. She stepped into the room. "Why on earth should we believe a single thing you say when you have lied to us? You must think we are all feather-brained wigeons."

Matt rubbed his forehead. "We could lock him up in your dungeon."

"We could," Giff agreed.

"I have a better idea." The gentlemen turned to look at Alice. "I think we should keep him locked up near Town. I would hate for his betrothed to be waiting for him at the church and he not appear. It would not be fair to her."

"Richmond," Merton said. "There are cellars, and no one will breathe a word."

"Excellent." She glanced at Normanby. "What is the surname of your betrothed?"

"Why should I tell you?" His words were slurred as if he was having a bit of trouble speaking.

She shrugged. "You do not have to, of course. I will find out another way."

Normanby glared at her. "You are unnatural. You and your entire family."

The nerve of the cad. How dare he cast slurs on her family. "Simply because we are progressive thinking does not make us at all unnatural."

Williams entered the room. "We're ready to take him, my lord."

Normanby opened his mouth, and Giff punched him. "Just to keep him quiet, you understand."

This was probably not an appropriate time to smile, but Alice did so in any event. "Well done, my love."

Two more of their servants entered the room and began binding Normanby. One tied a piece of cloth around his head and over his mouth.

"My sweet." Giff took her arm. "We should leave. Perhaps we can get a little sleep."

"We're not leaving tomorrow are we, Matt?"

"No. We'll remain another night."

"Oh, good." Charlotte took Con's arm. "I am sleeping late."

He snorted. "Have you ever slept late in your life?"

"Probably not, but there is always a first time."

They made it to the inn's yard without waking anyone. A wagon was there as well as some of their grooms and footmen.

She felt sorry they would not have any sleep tonight. "You are taking him to Richmond and locking him in the cellar now?"

"Don't worry about us, my lady," one of the men said. "We've been through worse."

"We'll take turns driving," another one said.

"Do not take any unnecessary risks."

Giff lifted her into the gig. "You were splendid."

"As were you." She leaned down and kissed him. Perhaps she could spend the rest of the night with him.

The rest of the gentlemen arrived. Con helped Charlotte onto the carriage bench, then mounted his horse. Alice started the gig. Once the horses were far enough away not to hear her, Alice decided to ask her sister a question. "How would I approach making love to Giff?"

"Giff?" Charlotte smiled slyly. "I decided to seduce Con, but he knew a great deal more so I let him take the lead."

"Are you saying I could simply go to him? In his bedchamber, I mean?" Most of her family were in the house.

"Of course. You are betrothed. You will be wed in two weeks." She shrugged. "None of us has waited." She placed her hand on Alice's arm. "Be very sure this is what you wish."

It was. She loved him, and he loved her. He was everything she wanted and had truly never thought to find. "Thank you."

"Make sure there are no hidden passageways to his chamber."

That was strange. "Why would there be?"

"Dotty's two youngest brothers and sister found one when she was in bed with Dom."

Alice should be surprised but was not. *Good Lord.* Looking for something like that was exactly what her nieces and nephews would do. "I will ask, and if there is one, I will have him secure it."

"A good idea." Charlotte gazed at her husband for a few moments. "It is wonderful and beautiful when you are with a gentleman you love."

"So I have been told." And tonight, Alice would experience it for herself.

Chapter Twenty-Eight

Despite knowing everything with Normanby was well in hand, Giff could not stop himself from worrying about Alice. All he wanted to do was keep her with him day and night. Unfortunately, he had two weeks to wait before that was possible. He reached his bedroom and removed his clothing. Not bothering with the nightshirt, he climbed into bed. At least he'd have one more day with her here to show her the estate before they returned to Town. He was about to blow out the bedside candle when he heard movement in the parlor. What now?

Alice opened the door. "Giff?"

She was here. He sent a prayer to the deity. "I'm here." He started to stand and realized he was naked. "I'm not wearing anything."

"That is all right." She was wearing a pale pink robe that floated around her. "I—I wanted to be with you."

His cock twitched and came to life. What had he once said about not being bold? "Come here, sweetheart."

She reached the bed, and he stood, wrapping his arms around her. "You are sure?"

"Yes." She nodded and a smile grew on her beautiful

face. "I am absolutely certain. I sincerely hope you know what to do."

He chuckled lightly. "Yes." Everything he'd ever learned would go into pleasing her. "I do." He took in the ties on her robe. His fingers itched to undo all of them. "May I?"

Alice nodded. "Yes. I am a little nervous."

That was understandable. "Tell me if I do anything you don't like, and I will stop. If you change your mind, I will stop."

She shook her head. "I do not want to change my mind. I want to be yours and for you to be mine forever."

Slowly. Go slowly.

He took a breath. She was strong and bold and beautiful and completely innocent. He untied the first bow, then the second and the third. By then he could see the tie of her nightgown and undid that before pressing his lips to hers as he cupped her face and stroked. Her breathing increased, and he deepened the kiss, delving into her mouth and exploring as he gauged her reaction. Her tongue tangled with his, and she reached her arms up around his neck. He made quick work of the rest of the bows and slowly pushed her nightgown and robe down over her creamy shoulders, taking time to feather kisses over her jaw and décolletage. The insistence of her kisses increased. He cupped her breasts. So firm, so lush. And all his to enjoy and worship.

"Come with me." Giff lifted Alice into his arms and brought her to bed. She was so perfect he could look at her all night.

She reached up and brought his head down to kiss him. "This feels so good. So right."

His erection strained toward her. Distracting her with kisses, he stroked his fingers over her softly rounded stomach until he reached the curls below. She moaned, and he dipped lower until he found the core of her pleasure. Lightly he rubbed. Her hips lifted, and she moaned again.

"I want something."

"I know. Be patient, my love." Giff entered her with one finger, and she bucked.

"That is good. There is more."

"Yes."

She was so tight. He inserted two fingers and rubbed her nub at the same time. Alice's breathing changed, and her body tensed. She was close to her climax. Suddenly she spasmed, and he positioned himself at her opening. "It is time."

"Yes."

He pushed forward, breaking through the thin barrier, entering her passage. She gasped and clenched him. "Are you all right?"

After a few moments, she nodded. "I will be fine."

Slowly moving inside her, he kissed her until she started moving with him. "Wrap your legs around me."

Alice clung to him as he pumped faster and faster until she came again, and he followed her into oblivion. This was what he had always wanted. To make love to a woman he loved. He cuddled her next to him. "How are you?"

A soft smile appeared on her face. "Perfect."

"Give me a moment. I'll be right back." He went to the wash basin and wet the piece of linen, then went back to her. "Let me wash you."

Her eyes widened in surprise. "What? Why?"

Giff grinned. "We have made a bit of a mess."

"Oh. No one told me about that." Alice lifted herself on her elbows and looked down. "Blood."

He hoped she wasn't frightened. "I'm afraid it's a necessary part of this. Only the first time."

She looked so disgruntled. "I have been told. But somehow I missed the cleaning-up part."

He tried to hide his laughter and couldn't. Thankfully, she laughed as well. He threw the cloth over the bed and cuddled her to him and kissed her again. "I think this might be the best night of my life."

Alice reached up and stroked his jaw. "I know it is mine."

She curled up next to him and slept. He hadn't given any credence to what Normanby had said. Giff knew it wasn't true. Still, he was glad she was his. Forever.

Alice was wrapped in a warm cocoon and fought opening her eyes. She almost gave in to the desire to remain where she was. Yet something told her she needed to move. Light barely rose over the horizon. Was it time to ride? No. There was a heavy, warm arm over her. She had to go to her bedchamber before the servants were up. From the other side of the room, she heard a maid setting the fire. Even in summer, mornings usually required heat. If the servants were preparing the house for the day, it was too late. She closed her eyes again and snuggled into Giff's arms. She would have to tell him she did not want separate chambers. How had they missed putting that on the list?

"My lady. You must rise." Bertram's insistent whisper roused Alice.

Alice did not want to get up. "I am comfortable."

"I'm sure you are, but you must come back to your bedchamber. It is time to dress for breakfast."

The dresser's words finally penetrated Alice's brain. "My robe."

"Here." Her maid held it out. "I have your nightgown.

She tried to rise, and Giff's arm tightened. That was a

problem. She hated to wake him but needs must. "I have to go."

"A little while longer."

She took his chin between her thumb and forefinger and shook it. "Now."

His eyes popped open. He must have seen her maid. He dragged a hand over his face. "Oh, right. I will see you in the breakfast room."

Alice hastily donned her robe and left the apartments. She did not know quite what to say to her dresser. Probably the less said the better. Bertram had a bath set up and ready behind a screen. The bed hangings were still closed. It was still her secret. Well, a secret if you counted her maid, and Giff's valet, and the laundress. Less than two weeks now and they would not have to worry about it. She sank into the bathtub. But did she really have anything to worry about? Discretion was necessary. They were not yet married, but they were betrothed, and no one would condemn them for anticipating their vows. Parts of her that she had not known existed were sore. That would fade. Otherwise, her sisters would have told her. There was absolutely nothing to mar her happiness.

She had donned her earrings when a knock came on the door. Bertram opened it. "My lord."

"Good morning, Bertram, is it not?"

"Yes, my lord." She curtseyed.

Giff poked his head into the room. "Is her ladyship ready?"

Alice almost laughed as he tried to look around her maid who moved to block him. "I am." She strolled to Giff. "Do we know if anyone else is awake?"

"The younger set is demolishing the offerings on the sideboard." He held out his arm.

She tucked her hand into the crook. "I suppose no one

mentioned that was one of the reasons we have footmen serving."

"Ah, I had wondered about that." He chuckled.

"We must save what we can on the sideboard. I shall inform Cummings of the new custom when the children are visiting."

They met her sisters and brothers-in-law as they descended the stairs. "The children are before us."

Her statement was met by heartfelt sighs.

"I hope they left something for us to eat," Rothwell said.

Giff exchanged a glance with her. "I am certain we are not out of food."

"They are heathens," Kenilworth said.

"Yet you keep wanting to have more of them," his wife responded.

"I never said I didn't like heathens," Kenilworth quipped.

Alice strolled into the breakfast room and stopped. The sideboard was indeed demolished. Pieces of egg were everywhere. How far could an egg go? She clapped her hands and the footmen straightened. "Clean this mess. From now on, breakfast will be served at the table. Find out what is left and bring trays around. I also want racks of toast and a pot of tea for each person. If we do not have enough racks or pots, I want to know about it."

"Yes, my lady," one of the footmen said as the rest scurried around.

She glanced at the children who were looking guilty. "If you have finished, please go to the nursery and clean up."

"I told them it was a bad idea," Elizabeth said as she walked by. "But everyone wanted to try."

Giff's shoulders shook as he covered his mouth.

Charlotte, Louisa, and Dotty raised their brows and shook their heads.

The gentlemen escorted their ladies to their seats.

Alice would have laughed, but it would not be appropriate in front of the poor servants. "A lesson learned is no bad thing."

The rest of the day was spent touring the estate. An alfresco luncheon was packed and enjoyed on a rise. Alice was falling in love with the property and the tenants who were more welcoming than she could have imagined.

That night she entered the apartments that would be hers the next time she came to this house. Giff was waiting for her with a carafe of wine.

"I hoped you would come." He drew her into his arms and kissed her. They made love slowly. It was even better than before. This time there was no pain at all.

Later, Alice nestled her head on his chest. "I wish we could stay here and continue to be together."

"As do I, but that would scandalize everyone." He used his bored drawl, and she pinched his hand.

He jerked the appendage back. "That hurt."

"Then do not be dense. You know I meant as a married couple."

"I do." His kissed her. "Speaking of being married. Have you given any thought to my mother's suggestion?"

She had the only problem was that one could not schedule the weather. "A garden wedding would be lovely if it did not rain."

He stroked her hair. "It is England. I can't promise you a sunny day."

"I cannot decide. I like all three ideas." She turned to be able to look at him. He was more handsome than ever with his hair ruffled and stubble on his face. His green eyes sparkled as he gazed at her. "I will let Grace decide. She and your mother will be planning the wedding."

His brows rose. "That is diplomatic of you."

"A wedding is but one day in our lives. I would rather concentrate on what truly matters. Our trip to Scotland and our honeymoon. How long can we be away? Where will we go first when we return, and where will we reside most of the year?"

"I do not want to live in Scotland during the winter. However, I would like to be there for Hogmanay."

"We could take my family with us. I am certain everyone will be interested in the celebration." She laid her head on his chest again. "Shall we spend most of the summer in Scotland?"

"I like that idea. We'll have the bairns speaking Scots in no time."

Alice stroked his chest, enjoying the texture of the soft curly hair covering it. "And wearing kilts as well."

He kissed her. "Will we attend the Season?"

"I think we must. That is when we will be able to meet with people regarding politics and consult on charities." She kissed his chest, running her tongue over his nipple as he had done to her. His body tightened in response. "We should probably be in Scotland for the harvest and can spend the rest of the year here." She licked him again.

"Keep that up and you won't get much sleep tonight." His low growl made her smile.

"*I* can sleep in the coach. But *you* will have to drive your carriage."

"Minx." He rolled her over so her back was to his front, holding her close to him. "Go to sleep. We can continue this discussion later."

"I love you." It was so good to be able to say that and know it was true.

"I love you too. Sleep."

Her maid woke Alice early in the morning. "My lady. We are departing within two hours."

"That is not much time at all." She grabbed her robe and rose. Giving one last look at her beloved, she left the room. She truly did wish they did not have to leave Whippoorwill Manor, but there was so much to do to prepare for the wedding.

Giff was waiting for her when she left her chamber. She took his hand. "No one is panicking about breakfast this morning."

"Which means they are doing what I told them to do."

Yesterday while she and Giff had visited tenants, her nieces and nephews had taken boats out onto the lake, ridden ponies, and played in the maze. They barely made it through dinner before they were falling asleep. This was the perfect place to raise children. She touched her stomach. She could already be pregnant. "When are they going to let the groom go?"

"An hour after we leave."

"Good." Considering Normanby only had a pair for a traveling coach, there was no way the groom could catch them on the road. "I wish I could ride with you."

"Your sister would not allow it. Once we reached the toll road, it wouldn't be possible."

They would be lucky if there was not talk from the inn Normanby had taken her to. Thank God Lady Bellamny had been there. And Giff. If he had not immediately followed, they would not be preparing to wed.

"There you two are," his mother exclaimed. "Have you decided where the wedding should take place?"

Alice took her place at the foot of the table. "I have. I will give the decision over to you and Grace."

"Intelligent girl," Con whispered from her left.

On her right, Rothwell nodded his agreement.

"Before I forget," the duchess said. "I remembered to bring a selection of family rings. Alice, you may choose the one you wish to have as your betrothal and wedding ring."

Matt took out his pocket watch and flattened his lips. "Make it fast. I wish to depart soon."

She gave him a look Alice doubted he had received in years and signaled to a footman. "Please have my maid bring the ring case down."

The servant left immediately.

Giff caught her eye. His sparkled with laughter. "Thank you, Mamma."

"You are welcome, my son. This must be done properly after all. We will put it about that the gathering was planned to celebrate your betrothal."

Alice had been wondering what the duchess had decided. And now she knew. Having her as well as Alice's family and Lady Bellamny would depress any talk. No one would want to be on the wrong side of those ladies. The duchess smiled at her and lifted a teacup. Alice saluted her in return.

When the box arrived, her sisters gathered around as she inspected the rings. One stood out. It was a square sapphire with small diamonds on the sides. "This one."

Giff came to her. "Allow me." He slid it onto her left ring finger. "Perfect. I believe there is a parure that goes with it. Mamma?"

"There is. I will give them to her as a wedding present."

Which meant they were Alice's to keep. "Thank you. For everything."

"Now that that is settled," Matt said, "it is time we

depart." He glanced at Grace. "When is the next large entertainment?"

She worried her bottom lip and glanced at the duchess. "Tonight."

His mother's eyes flew wide. "My ball! The plans were made so long ago I completely forgot." She pushed her chair back and rose. "We must go immediately. I would like all of you to dine with us." A sly expression donned on her face. "We will put it about very quietly that this is where we planned to announce the betrothal."

"What an excellent idea," Grace said rising as well. "Alice."

"Your grace?"

"You shall wear the sapphire parure this evening."

That would certainly make a statement.

Chapter Twenty-Nine

This was better than her come out ball. Alice twirled in front of the mirror. Her gown was so creamy it looked like butter. The parure consisted of a gold filigree necklace in which square sapphires dropped down like flowers from gold and diamond leaves. The earrings were of the same design. The sapphires in the bracelet and tiara were set into the leaves. The pins holding Alice's hair had light-green tips that matched the embroidery on her gown.

A knock came on the door, and her maid opened it. Eleanor and Madeline stood there smiling. Alice almost fell into their arms. "How did you arrive so soon?"

"Well." Eleanor had a sheepish look on her face. "After Madeline's wedding, we all decided to stay in Richmond at a house John and I have. We were certain you would wed soon, and we wanted to ensure we were close by."

Tears filled Alice's eyes. "I have missed you so very much."

"We have missed you too." Madeline hugged her again. "We are overjoyed for you. All along we knew there was something between you and St. Albans."

Eleanor stepped back. "You look so elegant. You will cast the rest of us into the shade."

That was hardly true. They both had ball gowns befitting young matrons and wore parures. "You both look beautiful." Alice glanced at the clock. "We should go. I do not want to be late."

Eleanor and Madeline laughed as they linked arms with Alice and strolled with her into the corridor. Grace joined them on the landing. "You all look lovely."

John Montagu, Harry Stern, and Matt waited in the hall.

"I hope St. Albans realizes how lucky he is," Matt commented.

Alice glanced up at the ceiling. "You have to say that. You are my brother."

"I agree. And I'm only newly your brother by marriage," Harry added.

"Thank you both. However, we need to depart if we are not to be late."

"Is St. Albans as prompt as you?" Madeline asked.

"Indeed, he is." That was one of the things Alice had appreciated even when she had not liked him.

The gentlemen took one coach, and the ladies rode in the other. Eleanor placed her hand on Alice's arm. "Are you nervous?"

"No. Why would I be? I have had a chance to come to know the duchess a bit. She is extremely nice. I have only met the duke at our come out ball. Giff said he can be difficult, but I do not expect him to show that side this evening."

Cleveland House was almost as fanciful as Whippoorwill Manor, but in a different way. The three half arches with their long windows and curved balconies looked like something out of a fairytale. After they were announced, she found Louisa and Rothwell. Charlotte and Kenilworth were already there as well.

Giff was immediately at Alice's side. "Your sister, Rothwell, decided to make a point to show my father he wouldn't be the only duke at dinner."

"That sounds like something she would do." Alice was glad Louisa had thought of the idea. Alice wished she knew Giff's father better.

"Mamma seated us together. She didn't want Papa quizzing you."

That was something Alice had not considered. "Would he have?"

"He very well could have done." Giff grimaced. "He might not have been able to resist the temptation. This way he will not have an opportunity."

She could not imagine being interrogated by his father before a ball announcing their betrothal. Her family was certain to have become involved. "I will have to thank her."

He tucked her hand in the crook of his arm, and they began strolling toward his parents. "She is very good at avoiding disasters. I think it comes from being Scottish."

Alice could hardly wait to meet the rest of his family. When they reached the duke and duchess, she curtseyed.

"Alice, I would like to make my father known to you. Papa, this is Lady Alice Carpenter, my betrothed."

He bowed elegantly over her hand. "It is a pleasure, my lady. I cannot express my joy that you have decided to wed my son. Welcome to the family."

Alice could have rolled her eyes. Instead, she smiled politely. "Thank you, your grace. I am happy to meet you again."

He looked at her again. "Oh, yes. I remember now. You're the—"

"Archie, that's quite enough." She gave Alice a brilliant smile. "How good to see you, my dear. I hope you like the parure. I believe it suits you well." The duchess linked her arm with Alice's. "Come and make me known to those of your family that were not at the manor."

Giff looked at his father and shook his head. "Yes, she is the one who would not allow me to attend her come out ball. I do not want you to mention it to her again. If you wish to know anything about that, I will be happy to answer all your questions."

"Your mother was right. You made a mull of it." His father grinned and slapped him on the back. "I'm glad to see you came about. I know how that goes. The same thing happened to me."

That was a story Giff hadn't heard. "Come, I'll introduce you to Alice's guardian and brother-in-law, Worthington. Her eldest brother Stanwood is here as well."

Papa frowned. "Why isn't her brother her guardian?"

That was too long a story to relate now. "I'll tell you about it later. Suffice it to say that he was too young at the time their parents died."

"I was surprised to find she was related to both Rothwell and Kenilworth. I'm glad to see the girl is well-connected."

"You have no idea," Giff muttered to himself as he steered his father to a group of gentlemen. "Ah, here are Worthington, Merton, Montagu, Stern, Carter-Woods, Rothwell, Kenilworth, and Stanwood."

"They're all related to her?" Papa asked in a whisper.

"Every single one of them." That would put his father on his heels.

"Papa, may I introduce you to Lord Worthington. He is Lady Alice's guardian."

Worthington bowed. "A pleasure to meet you again, your grace."

"The pleasure is mine." Papa inclined his head. "I suppose we should make arrangements to discuss the settlement agreements."

"Indeed, we should. Please have your solicitor send your information to mine. St. Albans can give you his direction. We shall meet at Worthington House in two day's time. I will have the contracts drawn up."

Papa frowned. "I am not certain that will give my solicitor enough time."

Worthington cocked a brow. "Your grace, the wedding is in two weeks. No plans will go forward until the agreements are signed." He motioned with his head around the drawing room. "I have a great deal of experience in these matters."

Giff's father assumed a resigned expression. "Very well. Is ten o'clock too early for you, my lord?"

"Not at all. That is the time most of these discussions are held." He motioned to the other gentlemen. "I suppose you must know some of my brothers-in-law, but allow me to provide an introduction . . ."

"Carter-Woods," Papa stated with a frown when they got to Phinn. "Are you related to Dorchester?"

Phinn bowed. "I am his brother and current heir. I do hope he will have a son."

"I wish him well."

Next was Harry Stern who bowed. "I believe you know my uncle Bristol."

"I do. Excellent man. I knew his father as well."

"In that case, you must also be acquainted with my grandmother."

Papa narrowed his eyes. "You have the look of her. Formidable woman."

"It runs in my family." Harry's lips tilted up. "You will eventually meet my wife, one of Worthington's sisters." He glanced around. "She is with your duchess."

With those introductions completed Giff began strolling with his father toward the ladies. Papa turned to him. "I can see her bloodlines are excellent. Merton is a cousin, is he not?"

"He is." Giff maintained a sober countenance as his father began to recognize the strength of Alice's family ties.

His father nodded slightly. "I know that Kenilworth's line goes back to the conquest."

"I believe Worthington's line does as well, and the title is quite old."

"Yes, yes. Lady Alice is extraordinarily well-connected."

That was one of Papa's requirements met. "Mamma has placed Lady Kenilworth and the Duchess of Rothwell next to you."

"Excellent. That will give me an opportunity to learn more about your betrothed."

Not that it would matter to Giff. He was going to marry Alice no matter what his father's view of her. "I think you will find both ladies interesting."

Ardley stepped into the room and announced dinner. Giff was interested to see that Mamma broke protocol by having Worthington instead of Rothwell escort her into the dining room.

He found Alice, and she placed her hand on his arm. "You look exquisite this evening."

She grinned at him. "It must be the parure. I thanked your mother for sending them. They are perfect."

"It is not the jewels. It is you. You make the sapphires glow." What he would really like is Alice in bed wearing nothing but the necklace. His cock came to life, and he almost groaned. They reached their seats, and he held hers. "I have something for you before the ball begins."

Her eyes widened. "What is it?"

"You'll have to wait to see."

Dinner went better than Giff thought it would. More than once, his father roared with laughter. Mamma was deep into discussions with both Worthington and Rothwell. On the other side of Giff was Alice's twin sister, Eleanor. He told her about their plan to sail to Scotland then to France after their wedding while Alice told Montagu. By the end of the meal, they had all decided to travel together.

It wasn't long before his parents took their places to receive their guests. He drew Alice aside and handed her a long slender box. "I hope you like this."

She stared down at it and glanced at him. "You did not."

"I did."

Alice unwrapped the gift. It was the fan she saw when they were shopping. "It is even more beautiful than I remembered."

He took her other fan from her and handed it to a footman. "But not as beautiful as you, my love."

She had never been happier, and she would be happier still. This was just the beginning of their life together. She reached up and kissed him. "Thank you, my love."

"Now." He tucked her hand into the crook of his arm. "We must discuss the matter of dances for the evening," he said as they strolled toward the ballroom. "I believe I am allowed to claim every one of them."

"You are." It might appear odd if no one knew they were betrothed. "Do you know when your parents plan to make the announcement?"

He took two glasses of champagne from a footman and

handed her one. "At the opening of the ball. My mother already spoke with your sister about which time would be best."

Under the circumstances, it was the best idea. Alice was very glad she had taken care not to be seen in the coach with Normanby. The only time anyone could have spotted her was at the inn. "In that case, every set is yours."

Eleanor, Madeline, and their husbands joined them. Madeline leaned over and whispered, "There is some talk that you might have been with Normanby in his coach."

Lady Bellamny had been correct. Someone had seen them. Alice hoped rumors would soon be put to rest. "The announcement should dispel any gossip."

The room was filling, and the rest of her family joined them. Matt glanced at the short set of stairs to the ballroom. "Here they come." He placed Grace's hand on his arm. "It's time. Alice, St. Albans, come with us."

A small dais had been set up in the middle of the room against the wall. They met the Duke and Duchess of Cleveland and took their places.

The duke raised his glass of champagne. "It has taken many years. Longer than I wanted it to." Light laughter greeted his remark. "But I am delighted to be able to welcome a new daughter into my family. My son St. Albans is betrothed to Lady Alice Carpenter."

The announcement was greeted by polite applause. Once they had stepped down from the platform, people came forward to wish them happy and congratulate Giff on his achievement. Alice could hear various snatches of conversation.

One older lady smirked. "I knew the rumors were not true."

"I know for a fact that both families met outside of

Town for the betrothal. You cannot hide that number of coaches," another lady added knowingly.

Still another lady tapped her cane on the floor. "Whoever tried to blacken her name should be ashamed of themselves."

"Have you heard that Normanby is bankrupt?" a gentleman commented.

"No surprise there. I was told that he's betrothed to the daughter of a Cit," his companion added.

A gentleman with several daughters sighed. "I wish I knew how Lady Worthington managed to make such excellent matches for all her sisters. Perhaps I should have my wife ask her."

Giff leaned down and his breath caressed her ear. "Fences cleared."

Lady Bellamny caught Alice's eye and gave an imperceptible nod that she returned. "Now for the wedding."

Giff groaned. "It would be so much easier if we could do it the Scots way and just have witnesses."

It would, but neither of their families, with the possible exception of his mother, would agree. "I will be interested to hear what the plan is."

"I have received my orders. The first thing tomorrow, I am to go to St. George's and try to get a date and time. If they have nothing left, I am to convince that vicar your family has used to come to a garden. I hope they make that decision this evening."

"In the meantime, I have appointments for gowns, shoes, hats, and other things."

Giff's mien brightened. "I can attend some of those with you. We must also see what needs to be done to our wing of the house."

The strains of the first set began. "A waltz?"

"I asked Mamma to include as many waltzes as possible. I love holding you in my arms."

They strolled onto the dance floor. "I love being in your arms."

Chapter Thirty

Two days after the betrothal ball, Giff was breaking his fast at Worthington House. Yesterday, he, Worthington, and Alice worked out the settlement agreements regarding Giff's property. Today his father was meeting with them. At first, he wondered why Papa had decided to allow the meeting to be here rather than at Cleveland House. But decided he was curious to meet with the earl who thought nothing of commanding a duke. Or a marquis for that matter. Giff's future brothers-in-law had taken him aside and explained exactly what would happen during his meeting with Worthington.

Giff, Alice, and Worthington met in his study a half an hour before his father was due to arrive. Worthington waved them to the seats in front of his desk. He glanced at Giff. "Although I have met your father, I still do not have a good idea of his character. What can you tell me?"

"He has no respect for weakness, and he will be difficult and try to make you give up as much as possible."

Worthington gave Giff an appraising look as he tapped a finger on the desk. "How far are you willing to go?"

He understood then that if he wanted to marry Alice, he would take her side and not his father's. This was the start of his own family. He glanced at her. "What do you suggest?"

She turned toward him. "Based on some things your mother and you have let drop, I have given this some thought. I will demand he do as Matt wishes. I think you should declare you will not wed anyone but me. And if he wants his heir to have an heir, he will do as Matt demands."

Giff prayed he never got on the wrong side of her. "Ruthless, but it just might work. He has been turned before by firm intransigence." He glanced back at Worthington. "Very well. We'll play our hand."

"I want you two on either side of me. He must know from the beginning that we are negotiating as a united front."

Giff and Alice rose while the footmen moved the chairs.

If he was a gambler, he'd put his wager on Worthington. "How often have you done this?"

"Six," Alice said. "No seven. I forgot Cousin Jane. One duke, three marquises, one heir to a marquis, the heir to a baronetcy, and a wealthy nabob."

Thorton appeared at the door, and Giff and Alice quickly took their places. "The Duke of Cleveland."

Worthington strode forward and bowed. "Your grace, welcome."

"We'll see about that." Papa walked into the study. "I received your proposal. It is preposterous."

"Please take a seat." The duke was in the process of doing just that when he saw Giff and Alice. He glared at her. "What are you doing here?"

She raised her chin and a brow. "It is my life that is being discussed. Why would I not be present?"

"I hadn't thought of it like that," Papa mumbled.

Giff resisted smirking. Thus far, things were proceeding as expected.

Papa glared at Worthington. "As I was saying, this agreement will not stand."

Worthington tapped a pencil on the desk. "Why is that, your grace?"

Tea was brought, interrupting the flow of the conversation. Quite on purpose, Giff surmised. Alice served. "How do you like your tea, sir?"

"Milk and sugar, please."

As she gracefully poured tea for them all, his father watched her and nodded approvingly. She returned to her chair.

"Your grace," Worthington said. "In what way is the proposal inadequate?"

"It is not inadequate. It is outrageous." Papa reminded Giff of a bantam cock used to having his own way.

Alice leaned forward slightly and narrowed her eyes. "You think it is outrageous that I be protected as befits my station not only as the sister and daughter of an earl, but as your heir's wife? If he dies before me, I will not be made a poor relation, sir."

His father had probably never considered that a lady would keep her own property, including the dowry, and have guardianship of her children. As well as a generous allowance and a dower house separate from the one in which his mother might reside.

Papa held his serviette to his mouth as he spluttered.

"She is correct, Papa. The purpose of this contract is to protect my wife and children in the event of my death. If she gives birth to an heir and if she does not."

His father stood. "I did not come here to be told what to do."

Alice rose as well. "That is unfortunate. I dearly love

Giff, but I cannot marry him without the protections of the agreements." She glanced at him. "I am sorry, my darling."

That was a good touch.

"My son will wed another lady," his father practically shouted.

Giff stood. "I shall not. I will marry Lady Alice or no one."

Papa looked at Giff, then at Alice. Finally, he glanced at Worthington who was regarding Papa with an interested expression. "You put them up to this. Turned my own son against me."

Giff coughed. "No. Lady Alice is quite serious about these agreements."

"Young lady?" Papa blustered.

She raised her brows. "Your grace?"

The room was silent as they locked gazes for almost a full minute. "By God." He slapped the top of the chair. "You'll make a deuced good duchess. I almost gave up hope of him finding a lady with a spine like yours." He took his seat again. "Well, Worthington, let's get to it. I agree."

Giff let out the breath he'd been holding. He'd been right. All they had to do was to stand up to his father. While he, Papa, and Worthington signed the agreements, Alice tugged the bell-pull. The butler appeared with champagne and glasses.

As the secretary took the documents, the butler poured. Papa held up his glass. "Welcome to the family, my dear.

Alice inclined her head and returned the toast.

Next Papa saluted Worthington. "You are as formidable as I had been told. I'm glad for our connection."

Once the wine had been drunk, Worthington escorted Papa out of the study.

"Is he always like that?" Alice asked.

Giff pulled her into his arms and kissed her. "Only when he decides to be obstinate."

His father left muttering to himself, " Eight. Two dukes, three marquises . . ."

The door closed and they were alone for at least a minute or two. Alice grinned. "I think he likes playing a bully to see if someone stands up to him."

Giff wondered. "A trickster?"

"Not so much a trickster as an instigator. I suppose I shall have to get used to crossing swords with him."

Giff shuddered at the thought. "Which is the very reason we are not living at Cleveland Castle."

"Thank Heaven for that." She pulled a face. "We will be in the same house during the Season."

He took her hand. "It's now time for you to see the Heir's Wing of Cleveland House."

They called for her phaeton and made the drive to his parents' house.

They were greeted by the Cleveland under-butler, a tall well-built man who looked to be in his thirties. Alice had thought to make Williams the butler, but the under-butler was clearly hoping for the position. She would have to speak to Giff about it.

The servant bowed. "Her grace said you would want to inspect the wing today."

Alice smiled. "Thank you. What is your name?

"Simmons, my lady. Mrs. Simmons, my wife, is the senior maid. She is waiting to show you around and assist you."

Mrs. Simmons would most likely become their housekeeper. It was a good thing to have senior staff already in place. "Let us begin."

Mrs. Simmons arrived with a notebook and pencil in

hand and curtseyed. “My lady, I have had an opportunity to inspect the linens.” She grimaced. “Most of them will need to be replaced.”

Alice sighed. Yet she was not surprised. Her grace had said that other than regular cleaning, nothing had been done for years. “I will leave that to you.”

“Yes, my lady.” They all studied the hall.

It was a half-circle, the niches already occupied by Italian statues. Light gray and cream marble covered the floor. The walls were painted an odd shade of purple that Alice had never seen before. Although it could be faded. A grand staircase of pink marble rose to the first floor landing. It was beautiful but needed a carpet. “We must paint or paper the walls and add a carpet. Aubusson, I think. Something that will bring out the marble.”

Mrs. Simmons took notes as Alice spoke.

Giff nodded. “I agree.”

Two corridors opened on either side of the hall, and a door to the servants’ quarters was at one end. The green baize was faded and torn in places. “Replace the door covering with something that will not clash with the rest of the hall.”

“If I may, my lady. A medium to light gray might be best.”

She imagined how the color would appear and agreed. “Excellent idea, Mrs. Simmons.”

Simmons led them to the first parlor off the hall. It was clearly decorated to hold people who were not particularly welcome. The furniture was early Georgian. “I like the furniture. Although, it must be recovered. And, again, the walls need to be painted.”

“I believe you will find that in all the rooms,” Giff said.

“I suppose you are right.

They toured the rest of the wing. It needed just as much

work as the duchess said it would. The furniture, all of which Alice quite liked, ranged from the early Georgian they had already seen to Queen Anne with the occasional French Renaissance piece. That was where the charm ended. Most of the walls were covered with dark red or green wallpaper in patterns that were hard to describe. It was as if someone had drawn chandeliers and had them printed onto the silk. In more than one case, she could not make out what the pattern was supposed to be at all. She had seen this type of décor before in Madeline's house before Henrietta and Alice had redecorated it. But the Duchess of Bristol had given them unlimited funds. On the other hand, they had knocked out walls and re-planned a number of rooms. Alice would have to discover what her budget for this house would be. The ballroom was a good size, with rococo paintings on the ceiling and ornamental plaster. She would leave it the way it was. "Now for the nursery and schoolroom."

They climbed to the top level. When the door was opened, Alice stood there in shock. "It is nothing more than an attic divided into rooms, and a dirty one at that."

"I can't believe they put any of us in here." Giff entered and started making his way into the rooms. "I do not remember this at all."

"It does not appear as if any children actually used the area." Perhaps they did not bring them to Town. "How long has it been since anyone lived here?"

Giff's brows drew together. "Close to thirty years? Yes, it must be that long. I remember my mother had been discouraged from redecorating it. My grandmother did not want it changed. Ergo, the furnishings and everything else must be at least fifty or more years old."

"That makes sense." Thankfully, her future mother-in-law had said Alice could redecorate.

He scanned the room. "If we have children and bring them to Town, they cannot live in this."

"No. They cannot." They would probably not need anything as large as in Worthington House, but it must be made livable. "We will go back to Worthington House, and I will show you the nursery and schoolroom there." That would actually make it easier. "I will contact the firm I used to refurbish my sister's house, pick the patterns, and leave them to it. If we are at Whippoorwill Manor, it will be a short trip to Town in the event we need to be here for some reason."

He was frowning. "As you wish."

"Are we planning to return to Town this year?"

Giff shook his head. "Not unless there's a reason to do so."

She turned to Mrs. Simmons. "Will you be able to work with the decorator?"

"Yes, my lady."

Alice needed to know her budget. "The kitchen will need to be renovated. I cannot imagine any cook we hire will be happy with just an open fireplace. How much can I spend?"

Giff shrugged. "We must ask my mother."

A knock came on the door below and Simmons answered it. "Your Grace, his lordship and ladyship are in the nursery."

"There is a nursery here?" Her steps sounded on the stairs. When she reached them, she glanced around. "I have never seen this before. On the other hand, we did not bring the children to Town until Archie's father died, and he was the duke."

Alice glanced at the duchess. "I will not leave our children behind. I believe this must be renovated."

The duchess looked at the area and pulled a face. "Of course, my dear. Do you have any ideas?"

"We are going to Worthington House so that Giff can look at the nursery there. Would you like to join us?"

"I would. I wondered how you made room for so many children." His mother grinned.

"It is a double house." That was one of the things Alice had learned recently.

"Mamma," Giff held out his arm to help her down the stairs. "We were just discussing what the renovations will cost."

She glanced at Alice. "Other than this attic, what do you want to do, my dear."

Alice followed them. "It is really a matter of the wall-coverings and other soft furnishings. I like most of the furniture."

"I think I would have thrown everything out and started all over. Do not worry about the cost. The dukedom will, of course, pay for it."

"Thank you." That took care of that.

When they reached the hall, Giff took Alice's hand. "I must go to St. George's; the vicar wasn't there when I stopped by the last time. I'll meet you at your house and leave from there." He glanced at his mother. "Do you wish to ride with me or with Alice?"

"Believe it or not, I have never been in a high-perched phaeton. I will ride with Alice."

"Shall I order your carriage, my lord?" Simmons asked.

"Please." Once he had left, Giff said, "What do you think of hiring them as our butler and housekeeper?"

"I want to consult with Williams first. If he does not wish to be the butler, I believe we will do well with Simmons and his wife. Once that decision is made, we must consult with them regarding other servants." Alice and

Giff were almost in the same position as Madeline and Harry having to hire all their servants. "Your grace, if you are ready, we should go."

The duchess linked arms with Alice. "I cannot tell you how excited I am to ride with you."

Giff escorted them out to where her phaeton was brought around as well as his curricle. He helped them both into the vehicle, then climbed into his. "Lead on, my dear."

Alice glanced at their part of the house, and it occurred to her that it was almost as wide as Worthington House. Perhaps that was the reason it had not appeared small to her.

When they arrived at her home, Grace went with them to the nursery and the schoolroom. Both Giff and his mother's eyes were wide as they took in the light and space.

"I have never seen anything like this before, Grace. You said you designed it?"

"I did. The architect I used was able to include everything I wanted. Of course, after Matt and I married, we had to make some adjustments."

"Giff, I do not see why we cannot do the same thing in your wing of Cleveland House. After all, I would like to feel comfortable when I visit my grandchildren."

"Mamma." Gaia toddled out closely followed by Edward and Nurse.

"She heard your voice, my lady," Nurse said.

Grace picked up her youngest daughter, then her son. "Your grace, I would like to introduce you to Lady Gaia and Master Edward Vivers."

All the yearning for a grandchild could be seen in the duchess's face. "Oh, they are adorable. That settles it. We must have the nursery done as soon as possible."

Giff breath brushed Alice's ear. "Because if the nursery is finished that means we'll have a child?"

She was not going to laugh. "Apparently."

"I'm off to the church." He took her hand and kissed it. "I will find you after I'm done speaking to the vicar."

Alice kissed his cheek. "I will talk to Williams, and we can make a decision as to our butler."

After Giff left, Alice went down to the kitchen and waited until Jacques was done stirring and tasting something.

"My lady. You require my aid in hiring a *chef de cuisine, non*?"

"I do. I am uncertain if he will remain in Town or go to the country with us."

"Bon." He gave a sharp nod. "I will have someone in no more than *deux jours*." Unsurprisingly, he tuned back to the stove.

"Merci." Well that had gone well. Now to speak with Williams.

Once in the hall, she had a footman tell Williams she wanted to see him in her parlor. As expected, he arrived practically on her heels. "My lady."

"I have a question to ask you. Do you wish to be my butler in my new home?"

"Is that the only position available, my lady?" He was so good at masking his expressions, she did not know what he was feeling, but he obviously did not want to be the butler.

"No. You can be my personal footman. That would mean traveling whenever I did."

He seemed to relax at her suggestion. "I would prefer that position."

Alice really had thought he would be delighted with the promotion. "Will you tell me the reason?"

He looked directly at her. "I like London for a few months, but I would rather be in the country during other times. If you require it, I could act as the butler until you find someone."

"There is an under-butler at Cleveland House. A Mr. Simmons. I believe he will be happy with the position."

Williams's eyes grew round. "I am honored that you would have given me the job over one who is already expecting it. I hope I have not disappointed you."

In fact, he had made her task easier. "Not at all. I had already decided to hire his wife as the housekeeper."

Her footman bowed. "I am glad everything will work out."

So was she. "Carry on. Sometime within the next few days you, Robertson, and Bertram will accompany me to Cleveland House. The wing in which his lordship and I will reside has a separate entrance, ballroom, garden, and stables."

"Yes, my lady."

"That is all for now." Alice went to the desk, pulled out a piece of pressed paper, and wrote a letter to the decorator asking her for an appointment at her earliest convenience. She also mentioned that she would require her husband's skills for a new nursery and schoolroom as well. Once that was set off, she began a list. Mrs. Thorton would need to be consulted about any maids she might have that could work for Alice. Thorton might have an extra footman or two. Perhaps more. She would ask Simmons if he knew any of the Cleveland house staff that would be willing to change households. Then there were the stables. Naturally, she would take her groom, but Giff should know if he could pilfer a coachman from his father.

A knock came on the door, and Williams stepped in. "My lady, her ladyship would like to see you."

"I will be there directly." She set her pen down and picked it up again and wrote down that she needed scullery maids and a laundress. What else? Oh, yes, find time to be alone with Giff.

Chapter Thirty-One

Giff arrived back at Worthington House and was led to a good-sized parlor anchored by a large lady's desk. His mother, Lady Worthington, and Alice were seated near the window. Outside, the Great Danes were playing with the older children.

The butler announced him. "Lord St. Albans, my lady."

Alice glanced up. "Oh, good. We can go no further until we know if we are being married in church or not."

He took a seat next to her on a small sofa. "If we want to have the ceremony in church, it can only be in ten days at nine in the morning."

She took one of his hands between her smaller ones. "That is only two days earlier than we had planned."

Lady Worthington poured him a cup of tea, and Alice added the milk and sugar. Her ladyship glanced at his mother then at him. "Very well. I shall write to Madam Lisette to notify her of the change. The only other decision is where to have the wedding breakfast."

He and his mother had both thought the Cleveland House gardens would be perfect, but it would be much more difficult to keep track of the children. "Here."

Mamma shot him a look, and he tilted his head to the

window. Understanding dawned on her countenance. "I agree. It will be easier to have it here with the children."

He thought Lady Worthington heaved a small sigh of relief, and Giff said, "There will be plenty of time for them to explore our gardens later."

She glanced at a paper in her hand. "Number of guests. We generally invite family members and close friends of the bride and groom."

"I would like my father to be there," Mamma said. "I wrote to him as soon as Alice and Giff were betrothed."

His mother probably didn't know about the ship. "I asked for his ship to travel to Scotland after the wedding."

"Wonderful." Mamma smiled broadly. "He will no doubt sail down here." She gave Lady Worthington a chagrinned look. "We will not know how many of my family will be onboard until they have arrived."

"As long as you can house them, we will manage." She glanced down at the list and back up. "Are there any customs your family would like to see that we do not have here in England?"

"There are so many. I have an idea of some we could do here." His mother held up her hand and started ticking them off. "White heather for the groom and in the bride's bouquet, a sixpence in the bride's shoe, a piper to lead them to the table, the loving cup with whisky, they'll dance the first reel, and the sword dance at the end. The cake is usually a fruit cake. I had my cook start it already."

Alice looked at him. "Piping?"

He grinned. "Yes. If we were in Scotland, we'd be piped from the house to the kirk and to dinner."

"You mean bagpipes?" Alice's eyes were wider than he'd ever seen them. She'd obviously never heard of the tradition before.

His mother laughed. "Yes. Bagpipes. They don't sound

bad at all when played properly. Although, I do not know how easy it would be to find a good piper in Town."

"We generally do not dance at our wedding breakfasts," Grace said. "But there is a first time for everything, and the children will like it."

"It seems as if we have finalized the plans," Mamma said. "I will send my list of family and friends to you no later than tomorrow morning. My secretary is at your disposal if you need her." She turned to Giff. "What are your plans?"

He looked at Alice. "We must speak with Simmons and his wife about the positions of butler and housekeeper."

"Excellent," his mother said. "What else?"

"I am taking my personal servants to see the heir's wing. I hope to hear from the decorator and her husband soon. Her husband is an architect. And I want to be able to gather some maids and footmen from our housekeeper and butler here. Do you have anyone who would like to work for us?"

"I will speak with my housekeeper. She will not be at all happy about losing Simmons, but it is time for her to be responsible for her own house. What about a cook?"

"I have already spoken with our cook. He will find someone for us." Alice rose. "Whose carriage shall we take?"

"Mine is outside." Giff held out his arm. "Shall we?"

"In a few minutes. I must tell my servants to meet us there."

Once that was done, he escorted Alice out while Mamma waited for her coach to be brought around. "What are you going to do tomorrow?"

Alice settled herself on to the bench. "Shopping. A great deal of shopping."

"I will be happy to accompany you." He picked up the ribbons.

"That will be fun. I do trust I will hear from the decorator soon."

He did as well. The sooner the house was finished the better. Giff wondered if their bedchamber was in good-enough condition to make love to Alice. He needed to be with her.

He called for the Simmonses to join them in the library. He and Alice were seated behind an old walnut desk when they arrived. Giff indicated the chairs in front of the desk. "Please." He wished there was tea, but this would have to do. "Her ladyship and I would like to offer you the positions of butler and housekeeper."

The couple smiled at one another. "Thank you, my lord," Simmons said. "We will be happy to accept."

Alice folded her hands and placed them on the desk. "It occurred to me that it might be better if we had additional servants that already serve our families. I will ask the Worthington housekeeper if she has any maids who might like to come to us. Do you know any maids who would like to change houses?"

"Footmen too, my lady?" Simmons asked.

"Indeed." Alice inclined her head.

Mrs. Simmons pursed her lips. "I do know a few of the younger maids who have learned their duties well but have no opportunity of advancement at the present. I would be happy to ask them."

"There are one or two footmen as well," Simmons added.

A knock sounded on the open door, and Alice glanced over. Williams, her maid, and her groom stood waiting. "Come. I would like to make you known to Simmons and Mrs. Simmons, our new butler and housekeeper." Her personal servants entered the room. Williams found chairs for them and set them in front of the table. "Mrs. Simmons, Simmons, this is my dresser, Bertram, my personal footman, Williams, and my groom, Robertson. They will be joining our household."

While they greeted each other, she glanced at Giff. "Coachman and stablemaster."

"I believe I can steal a coachman from my father. I'm not certain about the stablemaster."

"We don't have an extra one at Worthington House, my lady," Robertson said. "Lady Madeline took him."

"My lady, my lord," Simmons said. "There is a second stablemaster here. He's been waiting for the old one to retire."

Giff rubbed his jaw. "That might be our answer."

"My lady," Bertram said. "May Williams and I look around?"

"Yes, certainly. Mrs. Simmons can accompany you if she would like."

The housekeeper rose. "Thank you, my lady. I would be happy to show them the house."

The three of them left the room chatting quietly.

"If you do not mind, my lord, my lady," Simmons said. "I found the inventory for this house and would like to compare it to what we have for silver and porcelain."

"Yes, of course," Giff said. "Please let me know of any discrepancies." He stood and held out his hand to Alice. "Let's go to the stables and see if we can pilfer a few servants."

Robertson accompanied them as they strolled through the garden door to the mews. The key hung to the side of the gate. "Mr. Thorton would have someone's head if he saw that."

He was right. They had learned their lesson several years ago. "We will have to have it moved."

"I'll find out who to talk to about it." Giff glanced up at the wall. "Anyone could climb that wall."

Alice took a look at the foliage and almost laughed. "Only if they wanted to have a very painful time of it. "Those are climbing roses. Under them are rugosa roses and hawthorn. It would not be at all pleasant."

Giff touched the bushes as if he was trying to grab onto them and jerked his hand back. "That hurt. I'm glad to see someone showed some sense."

"Just so you know, my lady," Robertson said. "Williams said as how Mr. Thorton has been training footmen since before the Season to go to your houses. You and Lady Madeline and Lady Alice. He wanted to make sure they were trustworthy."

Alice thought there had been more than usual. "Thank you for telling me. You do not happen to know if Mrs. Thorton has been doing the same thing with maids, do you?"

Robertson shook his head. "You'd think she would."

"I hope she did." That would make this process much easier.

Giff took the key and put it in the lock. It took a few moments before he was able to turn it. Then it stuck when he got it unlocked. "This needs to be repaired."

They crossed to the stable and it was locked as well. "Fergus!" Giff bellowed.

His groom ran out of the stable next to theirs. "Me laird?"

"Find the key. We need to make this standing suitable."

Fergus cracked a grin. "Aye, me laird."

He dashed off and came back with an older man following behind.

"No one told me we were to open this stable," the older man complained belligerently.

Giff lowered his brows. "Did no one tell you I'm getting married?"

The man scratched his nose. "Heard somethin' about it."

"If I am marrying and moving into the heir's wing, why would I not open my own standing?"

The servant took his hat off and scratched his head. "You got a point there, my lord."

Giff glanced at the cloudless sky and closed his eyes. "Exactly. Now open the door."

"Got to get the key, don't I?" The man walked off to the other stable.

Alice barely stopped herself from laughing. "Is he always like this?"

"I don't know." He scowled after the servant. "The last time I was here he ran me off by telling me my father didn't want me out here. I was to send for what I needed."

Robertson turned his back, but his shoulders shook briefly.

Fergus shook his head. "Right old codger he is, me laird."

Giff looked at him. "A laird now, am I?"

"Aye, me laird. Ye got yer own house and property in two places."

Alice couldn't hold in her mirth any longer. Giff glared at her. "What are you laughing about?"

In an attempt to stop, she waved her hand in front of her face. "It is funny. If you are a laird, what am I?"

"Still a lady." He barked a laugh when she pouted.

She was glad his mood had improved. "I assume he is the stablemaster. What is his name?"

"Smith." Giff stared across the short area separating the

door. "I swear he's been here since before my father. Here he comes brandishing a key."

He took the key and opened the door. The smell of rotten hay and offal almost knocked her back. "This must be cleaned at once."

"Ain't my stable." Smith said. "Not my job." And walked away.

"Fergus." Alice smiled at the Scotsman. "Just how many grooms might like to work for his lordship?"

An evil grin appeared on his freckled face. "Including the young stablemaster, me lady?"

"Naturally."

He glanced at Giff. "What'll ye pay, me laird?"

"I'll pay twelve pence more per quarter than they are earning now." Fergus looked at Robertson as if he'd just noticed him. "An who are ye?"

"Robertson." He stood his ground at the clear attempt at intimidation.

Fergus's eyes narrowed. "Got any Scots in ye?"

"My father's side of the family is still in Scotland. He got work for an English lord and left. My mother's English."

Fergus stuck out his hand. "Glad to meet ye." He pointed his chin toward Alice. "Working for her ladyship?"

"I am her groom."

"Make sure Bromley knows. Unless I'm mistaken, he'll be the new stablemaster." Fergus turned to Giff. "Do ye need yer curricle? It's best if ye come back later this afternoon to see about the stable. There's likely to be a lot of shoutin' and swearin' going on here."

Giff offered her his arm, and she took it but did not move. "Fergus, I would much rather have the stable staff hired before we depart. After that, you can swear and shout all you would like."

Fergus glanced at Giff who nodded and took off toward the other stable. A few minutes later, he came back with their new stable-master and a sufficient number of grooms for their needs.

Smith followed them back as well, but she expected that. "Mr. Smith, I understand that you are not happy about losing some of your staff. However, I must point out that you have abrogated any duty toward this standing. Therefore, we have taken matters into our own hands. As you are not needed here, you may return to your duties."

The old man opened and closed his mouth, reminding her of a fish, then turned around and stomped off.

"She always talk like that?" Fergus asked Robertson.

He smirked. "When she needs to."

"I think me laird got hisself a fine lady. She'll do well when we visit home."

"We'll be back later. Make a list of what we'll need." Giff led her off through the garden gate. "Well done, my love."

"I have experience with men having more fun arguing than getting their work accomplished. Let us find out what is going on in the house."

Chapter Thirty-Two

Giff didn't tell Alice, but when his grandfather arrived, Grandad's staff would be told by Giff's Scots servants that Alice was a right one. That made him proud. He took her hand as they walked through the garden to the house. "May we go to your house for luncheon and come back here later?"

"Yes. We can visit Hatchards before we return. We will need books to take with us."

He didn't plan to have time to read books, but one never knew. He supposed they couldn't spend all their time in bed. After all, they'd be in company on the ship and while traveling in France. "That's a good idea."

"We also require contracts for all of our servants. Do you happen do know how much your father is paying the grooms?"

No. But he would make a point to find out. Fergus would know. "Not at the moment."

"I will write to our solicitor and ask him to make up the contracts. We can add the amounts later."

"Wait a minute." He stopped and stared at Alice. "Do you mean to tell me you know how much they are making at Worthington House?"

"Of course I do." She seemed surprised that he wouldn't know that. "Ten pounds a year for a stable boy. The personal grooms earn fifteen pounds a year and the stablemaster twenty pounds."

Why had he even doubted her? He'd been told she learned everything needed to run not only a household, but an estate as well.

When they arrived back several hours later, he drove directly to the mews. A wagon stood outside of the stables loaded with stinking hay. It was enough to make one cast his accounts. The wagon moved off and another one arrived with new bales of straw.

Fergus and Robertson strode up to them. Robertson bowed, and Fergus said, "Almost done. We're waiting for oats and a few other things."

"How's the tack?"

He shook his head. "Some of it can be fixed. The rest will have to go. Mice and rats."

"It is unbelievable how the saddles were let to fall into ruin," Robertson said. "I have never seen anything like it, and I hope I never do again."

A man who looked to be in his late thirties with brown hair and eyes joined them. "Are you Bromley?"

"I am, my lord." The man bowed.

"Will you accept the position as my stablemaster?"

"I will. The second coachman wants to know if there's a place for him. He's the one that drove you down to London with the fourth coachman."

"I'll be pleased to have them both." Giff thought that other than a cook, that completed their staff. While they were with Alice's family for luncheon, she spoke with the housekeeper and was able to make arrangements for three housemaids. "I expect the stable to be run in an orderly manner without the abuse Smith was known for. You should know that Robertson and Fergus will assist when they are able, but they are our personal grooms and are expected to be ready to serve us when we require them."

"Yes, my lord. They both mentioned as much."

"My curricle can be moved in as soon as space is ready. Her ladyship's phaeton will come over just before the wedding. You are all invited to Worthington House for the celebration."

"Thank you, my lord." Bromley gave a small smile. "I'll see to the garden key as well."

"Good man. Carry on." Giff lifted Alice down from the carriage and escorted her into the garden. "That went well."

Glancing at him she tilted her head. "Do you not think someone should be held accountable for the ruined tack?"

"We have no idea how long they've been there. It probably wouldn't do any good at this point." He did plan to tell his mother what they would require.

"That is true. It is still a shame. "At least I'll be able to bring my saddle and the tack for my mare and the pair with me."

"That will help." Giff would have Fergus bring his as well.

"Let's look at our house again." In particular their bedroom.

He opened the back door and almost ran into Williams. What was he still doing here?

"My lady." He handed her a letter. "This came for you right after you left."

She opened it and shook it out. "It is from Mrs. Rollins. She and her husband can attend us tomorrow morning at nine-thirty. That is the only appointment they have for a longish meeting for the next two weeks."

That was fast. "Tomorrow it is. I hope we can find some paper and ink."

"Mrs. Simmons brought some over, my lady." Robertson led the way to a heavy French desk in the morning room. "It's here. I will take it to Mrs. Rollins when you are ready."

Giff hoped that meant they'd have the house to themselves after the footman left. Alice made short work of the letter, and they were finally alone. Now to make love to her without ruining her hair and gown. He untied the ribbons to her bonnet. "Is that all I need to do before I remove it?"

She rolled her eyes at him and pulled out a lethal looking hat pin with a bird on one end of it. "Now it comes off." She put the bonnet on the small square table next to her and wrapped her arms around his neck. "What do you have in mind, my lord?"

"This." He bent his head and teased her lips open. Soon their tongues were doing a sensuous dance together. He backed her up to a sturdy-looking table, picked her up and set her on top of it. "I feel as if it has been forever."

"Sometimes three days can be forever." She shivered as he lifted her skirt, and gasped when he touched her inner thighs.

He tried to go slowly, but when she wrapped her legs around him he almost lost himself. "I love you."

She grabbed his head and brought it down to her. "I love you too. Make love to me."

Later they slumped against each other. Giff noticed that although the sun was still high in the sky, it had shifted. How long had they been here? He took his handkerchief out and cleaned them both, then set about putting them to rights again. He helped her down from the table. "It's probably time to start getting ready for dinner."

Alice yawned. "I suppose you are right. This reminded me of bed and beds. I believe all the bedding for the stable staff must be replaced."

Giff blew out a frustrated breath. "That dratted stable is going to cost us more than the rest of the house."

A thrill of bell-like laughter emanated from her. "We will simply have our new stablemaster order everything. If Smith gives them trouble about sleeping where they have been, we can put them in the servants' quarters here for a few days." She yawned again. "I need to tell—"

"Mrs. Simmons." Giff kissed Alice. "Come, my bride. Hopefully, our housekeeper is here somewhere."

"They have apartments downstairs." Alice donned her bonnet. "It would not surprise me if they are taking the opportunity to move into them."

He was just glad no one disturbed them making love. "And I thought the next two weeks would be boring. How wrong I was."

"Nine days now." She kissed him. "We have a great deal to accomplish."

They found the Simmonses in the servant's quarters having tea. Both of them stood up with guilty looks on their faces. "I beg your pardon, my lady. I should have . . ." Mrs. Simmons glanced around. "I should have been doing something."

Alice's lips trembled. "There is not much for you to do at present. However, tomorrow you will receive some maids from Worthington House who have agreed to work here. Have you been able to convince anyone from next door to come work for us as well?"

The housekeeper nodded. "They will start tomorrow. We brought over our belongings and rearranged the furniture in our apartment. I suppose we were taking a rest before everyone else got here."

Giff glanced at Simmons who, intelligent man that he was, let his wife do the talking. "We have footmen coming as well. They've been trained by the butler at Lady Alice's home. They are all former soldiers."

"I will arrange for the tailor who makes the livery to take their measurements." Simmons glanced at Giff and frowned. "I don't think I have ever seen the St. Albans livery."

Good Lord. Neither had he. He only knew the crest. "I am as ignorant as you."

"Green and gold," Alice and Mrs. Simmons said at the same time and laughed.

"There you are, green and gold." Giff tugged Alice a little closer. "Leave it to our wives. Or in my case, almost wife."

"How did you know?" Simmons asked.

"There are some old suits in the attic. They will not be suitable for any of the new footmen, but they can be a guide." Mrs. Simmons looked at Giff and Alice. "There is a lot of gold on them."

"I'll wager you found periwigs as well," Alice said.

"I did, my lady."

"None of our footmen wear periwigs." Alice wrinkled her nose. "They are hot in the summer and become dirty easily. I think we can do without them."

"I agree," Mrs. Simmons said. We'll just order the livery." She glanced up at the ceiling. "If you will give me a few minutes I'll bring one down."

"I will accompany you," Alice said. "Other than when they are being used as a nursery, I am very fond of attics."

Naturally, Giff and Simmons followed them up. The housekeeper had not exaggerated when she said there was a lot of gold. "Good Lord." Giff held up the uniform. One could barely see the colors for the gilt. "We could melt this down."

Alice pulled a face. "Our footmen will bring over a set

of Worthington livery for a guide on the amount of gold to use. I do not remember anyone having this problem before."

"There is a lot to do and reorganize, my lady," Mrs. Simmons said softly. "But we'll get it all done, and you'll see how nice everything will be."

Alice patted her shoulder and smiled. "I know. I've been through construction and decorating before. This is just another part of it."

The housekeeper appeared concerned. "I hope you will be happy to hear I've ordered all the linens."

"Thank you for telling me." Alice sighed. "I am glad to know it. We will need new bedding for the stable staff as well. Perhaps you can coordinate with the new stablemaster."

"Yes, my lady. I would be happy to do so." Mrs. Simmons nodded.

As they passed the corridor leading to their apartment, Giff hoped that the next time, he and Alice could make love in their bed. After all the bedding had been replaced. He flipped his pocket watch open. "Shall we go, my love? We have just enough time to arrive and wash up before dinner."

More quickly than Giff thought possible, their house and stables were put in order. Every time he and Alice went to the house, something new had been done. Carpets and hangings changed, new paint and wallpaper. The kitchen took the longest, but with their new cook, Eugène, a relative of Jacques, in charge even that went smoothly. Relatively speaking. He and Alice shopped for everything from gloves to trunks. His mother even set about making sure the garden was in perfect condition. Which reminded

Giff and Alice to hire gardeners. The only place Giff was not allowed to go with her was to the fittings for her wedding dress. Instead, he went jewelry shopping. Alice deserved jewels that she owned aside from the sapphires and the ornaments required for a young lady's come out.

He selected a double strand of pearls with earrings to match and coaxed her into a set of pearl hair pins before he gave her the necklace. "Wear these at our wedding if they will go with your gown."

Alice grinned. "I shall." She wrapped her arms around his neck. "Thank you." After kissing him, she took a box out of her reticule. "I have something for you as well."

The box contained a square sapphire pin that matched her necklace. Giff had never expected such a gift from her. "This is marvelous."

"I am glad you like it." This, naturally, led to more kissing, which was broken up by Mary wandering into the morning room.

"Oh, I did not mean to interrupt you," she said. Suddenly, she glanced at the window. "You have more company than me."

Gideon and Elizabeth were at the windows peering in. One day, hopefully soon, Alice and Giff would have privacy. Until they had children.

Miss Susanna Greenway noticed a letter addressed to her on the dish in the hall. She picked it up and went to her room. Normally, her mother would read all the correspondence sent to her, but the careful and childishly elegant handwriting intrigued Susanna. She opened the letter.

My dear Miss Greenway,

It is with regret and heavy hearts that we must inform you that Lord Normanby has been courting Lady Alice Carpenter with a view toward marriage—he would scarcely be contemplating anything thing else with a lady. Lady Alice discovered he is betrothed to you and will no longer accept his overtures. I wished to warn you of his <u>*true nature*</u> *in order to give you an opportunity to save yourself from this blackguard.*

Yr. friends,
T.V. and M.C.

Susanna was not surprised. She had been both stunned and suspicious when he had started to court her and then asked for her hand in marriage. There was always something about him she hadn't trusted. His lordship probably used the betrothal to her as a way to stave off his creditors. She and her father knew about his debts almost immediately. After all, everyone in the City knew which members of the aristocracy were under the hatches. Although she doubted his lordship was aware that they had knowledge of his financial difficulties. He probably believed that he was fooling them. She glanced at the initials again. M.C. could be someone from the Carpenter family, but who was T.V.? It did not really matter. Lord Normanby had signed the settlement agreement exactly as she had wanted. He apparently did not care that he had ceded almost all control to her, or he had not read it. Susanna wondered if he was really as intelligent as he thought he was. She went to the library, took out a copy of Debrett's, and found the Earl of Stanwood. His sisters included a Lady Mary Carpenter,

Lady Alice and Lady Grace Carpenter who wed the Earl of Worthington whose sisters included a Theodora Vivers. Susanna called for her family's town coach. Perhaps it was time to put Lady Mary's and Lady Theodora's minds at ease. Susanna was also interested in meeting the ladies who would warn her about Normanby.

When she reached Worthington House, she was informed that Ladies Mary and Theo were out with their governess, but that Lady Alice was available. Susanna was then led to a parlor by the very correct butler. "Would you like tea, miss?"

"Yes. Please."

A few minutes after tea had been brought in, a blond lady entered the room. Her gait was so smooth it was as if she was floating. Susanna had been trained well at school, but she always thought that type of elegance must be natural or taught from early childhood. She rose. "Good morning. I am Miss Susanna Greenway."

"Good morning." The lady held out her hand and shook Susanna's. The action had the effect of putting her immediately at ease. "I am Lady Alice Carpenter."

"Thank you for taking time to speak to me, my lady."

Lady Alice appeared curious. "Please have a seat and tell me what I may do for you."

Susanna took the letter from her reticule. "Earlier, I received this missive. I wanted to ease the authors' concerns."

Lady Alice's brows rose. "Authors?"

Susanna nodded. "Yes."

Her ladyship took the note and laughed lightly. "They have been very busy lately."

The front door opened, followed by the parlor door opening. Two schoolroom ladies, one younger than the other with blond hair, the other older with dark chestnut hair, stood in the door.

"Come in," Lady Alice said. "This is Miss Greenway. She has come to address your letter."

The girls glanced at one another, entered the room, and took seats on the sofa.

"I am Lady Mary," the blond girl said.

"And I am Lady Theo," the older girl said. "We are happy you have come."

"How will you deal with his lordship?" Lady Mary asked.

"I intend to wed him. Faults and all." Lady Theo opened her mouth, and Lady Alice shook her head. "Firstly, I want you to know that we, my father and I, know about his debts." She glanced at Lady Alice. "I did not know about you. However, I am not surprised. No doubt he thought to jilt me as soon as he wed you. I take it you do not plan to marry him?"

"Not at all." A smile curved her lips. "I am betrothed to the Marquis of St. Albans. The Duke of Cleveland's heir. We will marry in three days."

Susanna was glad for the explanation of the relationships. She really would have to start memorizing Debrett's. "I wish you happy, my lady. In his arrogance or haste, Lord Normanby signed the settlement agreement drafted by my father and myself. He will find that all the servants will be mine and loyal to me. He will have an allowance, but nothing more. And as soon as he gives me two sons he may do as he wishes, but not in England. There was one other complication." All three ladies nodded, which surprised Susanna. "It has been dealt with in a manner of which I believe you will approve."

"She will be treated well." Lady Mary stated flatly.

"Extremely well." After speaking with the woman,

Susanna had arranged for "Celeste" to be sent to her family who had been searching for her. "She is going home."

Lady Theo stared at Susanna for several seconds. "Do you want to marry him?"

"I do not dislike the idea. I am marrying for the rank. So that my father will have a peer for a grandson. It is my mother's dearest wish, and I shall not disappoint her. I might have a few duties I will dislike, but knowing I am in control of all aspects of the marriage will compensate me." Lady Theo was still not convinced. "He will not harm me either physically or with words. If he does, I have a remedy. More than that I cannot say."

Lady Alice rose. "Thank you for visiting us. After everything is settled, do you mind if I invite you to one of our charitable meetings? We will all be back in Town in autumn."

"I would be delighted." Susanna had never expected to be approved of so quickly.

"Wonderful." Her ladyship held out her hand again. "I look forward to knowing you better."

CHAPTER THIRTY-THREE

Giff's grandfather, uncles, aunts, and whatever older cousins had been around when Grandad decided to depart arrived from Scotland two days before the wedding and tried to enact the ritual of taking the bride and groom out separately to drink a great amount of whisky that they just happened to have brought with them. Giff took them to Worthington House to meet Alice and her family and to see how quickly his grandfather's idea was shot down.

They were in a large drawing room drinking tea.

"Ye can no have a proper wedding without whisky," his grandfather said fully expecting Grace to cede to his wishes.

But Grace, as Giff had been told to call her, squared off with his grandfather and put her dainty foot down. "No one is going to get drunk before this wedding. I leave it to you to do as you wish afterward."

Brows raised, they stared at each other until his other family members began to fidget. "Are ye sure ye do nay have a tiny bit of Scots in ye? Ye're mighty fierce fer a wee Englishwoman."

She folded her lips together. "I have a great, great, great grandmother from Scotland. Are you satisfied?"

"Ach, aye. I can see my lad is marrying into a good family. Unlike his mother ye understand."

Grace inclined her head. "It was a pleasure meeting you, your grace."

He narrowed his eyes at her. "And just how did ye know about that? I do nay recognize the English king's title."

"In that event, you should contact Debrett's and convince them to stop including you in their publication."

Mamma patted Grace's shoulder as she followed her family out of the room. "Well done, my dear."

Once the door had closed, she resumed her seat. "I would like a glass of wine."

Alice quickly poured three glasses of claret and handed her sister one.

"Thank you." Grace glanced at Giff. "Other than your mother, do you have any relatives that are not intent on getting their own way?"

He shrugged. "A few of my father's brothers. You will meet them tomorrow evening."

She drank her wine. "This is the most interesting wedding we have had thus far."

Giff was simply glad he had talked his grandfather out of having them piped from Park Lane to Berkeley Square and over to St. George's church. He had agreed to wear the plaid sash they'd brought for him to honor his Scots side, but not the kilt. His father would have been apoplectic.

The night before the wedding Alice's family, his Scots family, and all the family members from his father's side who came to Town for the wedding dined at Cleveland House. Grandpa brought a few bottles of whisky as well. "Fer after dinner, ye understand."

His mother shared a look with Grace and sighed. "All I can say is that you had better not be late for the ceremony tomorrow. It is at nine-thirty in the morning."

His grandfather's, uncles', and male cousins' eyes shot open.

"That's a bit earlier than I thought it would be. No wonder ye didn't want us to pipe ye to church."

The ladies rose and left the gentlemen to whichever libation they chose to imbibe. After his second glass of very fine whisky, Giff signaled to Charlie Stanwood, at whose house Giff would be spending the night. If he'd have tried to slip away on his own, he'd have been brought back. Since Mamma would not allow a chamber pot in the dining room, they made their excuses under the guise of needing to relieve themselves and left the house.

"Was it my imagination, or was one of your aunts trying to matchmake me to a lady?" Stanwood asked.

"They're all prodigious matchmakers. Fortunately, you're too far away for much to come of their plans. However, you might not want to set foot in Scotland until you're safely wed."

They turned the corner on to Mount Street. "There doesn't seem to be much love lost between your father and grandfather."

There wasn't. He never actually understood how Grandpa had been convinced to allow his mother to wed his father. "They do seem to spend a great deal of time aggravating each other." They strolled silently for a while before turning into Berkeley Square. "Why didn't Phinn and Augusta join us?"

"Augusta would not have enjoyed herself and, consequently, would have begun speaking to people in a language no one understood."

Giff liked Augusta a great deal, but there was no doubting that she sometimes had strange ways. "But she can speak the Gaelic. She could voice her objections."

"She doesn't like arguing as much as your family does.

And if she had heard anyone say anything critical about Alice or your marriage, she would have given them a piece of her mind in Gaelic."

Back to his father and grandfather again. Between the two of them the meal had been rather loud. "Perhaps she can meet them when my father's not around."

"I hope so. I'm quite sure she would like your aunts and some of your cousins."

The next morning Alice woke and smiled at the sun shining into the room from the window. It was her wedding day. Her hair had been washed yesterday before they went to dinner. The most time-consuming thing she had to do was bathe and dress. She threw her legs over the bed, shoved her feet into the slippers, and padded to the basin. Bertram entered carrying a day dress. Alice would have to change into her wedding gown directly after breakfast.

She missed having Giff to join her at the breakfast table, but there was a tradition in her family that the groom could not see the bride before the wedding. After she broke her fast, Alice dressed in a Pomona green gown with an embroidered net overdress. Her hair was put up with the pearl tipped pins Giff had convinced her to buy before he'd given her the necklace and earrings. The only thing left to don was the small hat she would wear when a knock came on the door. This was also tradition, but a much better one than not being able to see her future husband. Elizabeth entered, first followed by Madeline, Eleanor, Grace, and Joan, one of Giff's aunts.

Elizabeth handed Alice a handkerchief embroidered with forget-me-nots. It was not nearly as lumpy as the last one she did. "I am getting much better."

Alice kissed her niece's cheek. "You are a sweetheart. This is beautiful."

Eleanor gave her the combs she had loaned to Madeline as something borrowed. "Do not forget to give them back. Although, we will be together for the next month or more."

"We will. But you may have them directly after the wedding breakfast."

Madeline carefully hugged Alice so as not to muss her. "I am so very happy for you. I have a new pearl bracelet for you."

She clasped it on Alice's wrist. "Thank you. It is just what I needed today."

Joan glanced at Grace before going to Alice. "It is a tradition in Scotland for a mother to give the eldest daughter a Luckenbooth Brooch. I was the only one blessed with all sons and no daughters. At least, they keep telling me I'm lucky. I'm no so sure about that. When I saw you, I knew this would be perfect." She held out her hand. As her fingers uncurled, they revealed a gold brooch in the shape of two hearts intertwined. In the middle was a sapphire. "It's been passed down from mother to daughter for well over two hundred years. I want you to have it to wear and give to your oldest daughter on her wedding day."

Tears sprung to Alice's eyes. "Thank you so much. I will cherish this always."

"Aunt Alice, use the handkerchief." Elizabeth tugged on Alice's skirt.

"Yes, of course." She dabbed her eyes.

Matt came to the door. "It's time to go. I do not want to give your future grandfather-in-law an excuse to pipe his part of the family from the church to here."

Joan laughed. "He'd do it too." She glanced at Alice. "He's really a sweet man. There's just something about Mairead's husband that sets him off."

Alice had noticed that the two of them could not seem to be in the same room together without coming to loggerheads. "I look forward to coming to know him when the duke is not around."

Matt held out his arm to Alice. "Come along. Your groom is going to think you're late no matter when you arrive, so you, of all people, should be on time."

Matt escorted her up the stairs to the front door and they paused. Theo took her place as the maid of honor, and they started down the aisle. Giff had never looked more handsome. He wore a blue jacket and breeches. His waistcoat was embroidered in gold. A plaid sash was across his chest, and the sapphire she had given him was in his intricately tied cravat. He caught her eye, and she could not look away. Thankfully, Matt was guiding her. Charlie joined them halfway to the altar. Like Eleanor, she wanted to honor both the man who had raised her and her brother, the head of her house. John Montagu stood next to Giff as his best man.

The vicar stepped forward. "I hear this is the last wedding I will perform for you for a few years. Let us begin. Dearly beloved . . ."

Alice was not surprised at the depth of feeling with which Giff said his vows. Nor the strength of her voice when she answered.

"I now pronounce you man and wife."

"Kiss her now, lad. Oof," one of the male cousins said.

"Not in England, ye great buffoon," another admonished.

Giff took her arm. "Let's sign the register and get out of here before there's a fight about Scots and English customs."

They signed quickly and headed up the aisle to the

waiting coach at the bottom of the stairs. She stopped and stared at the carriage. "Boots?"

"My cousins. They must have found the coach." Giff cringed.

"Remind me to ask your mother what they were like at her wedding."

"She got married in Scotland. But it's a grand story."

He helped her into the coach and just looked at her. "We are really married."

"We are." She kissed him.

Reaching over, he touched the brooch. "Where did you get this?"

"Your Aunt Joan. She does not have any daughters and wanted me to have it."

"She likes you a lot. To give you that." He sat back. "She has a granddaughter."

"I am going to cry." Alice took out her new handkerchief. "I had no idea."

Giff placed his arm around her shoulders. "I arranged to leave after we cut the cake if that is all right with you."

Alice dabbed her eyes. "It is. Where are we going?"

"I thought about a hotel, but except for the nursery, our home is ready. And everyone thinks we are going to a hotel, so we'll be all alone, with the exception of the servants."

"Our servants who will not bother us on our wedding night or tell anyone we are there." They might have even thought to leave food for them to eat, and wine to drink. If they knew. "Do they know?"

Giff was dragging one finger in circles on her back and up her neck. "Yes. I told my valet to inform everyone."

They reached Worthington House before everyone else. Once Grace, Matt, and the duke and duchess arrived, they took their places in the receiving line to greet their guests and receive their good wishes. The tables for food were set up inside, but there were small tables scattered around the garden where people could eat.

Giff led her out for the reel she had been practicing. It was very much like some of the country dances, but it seemed much faster. Afterward, they were piped to their table by the piper his grandfather had brought. The duchess was right, the music sounded much better than Alice thought it would. The duchess also insisted that the sword dance be held before the dancers became too "relaxed" as she put it. Alice was surprised at the skill it took to perform the dance. After the men were done, the children all insisted on being allowed to try.

This was a nice party, but she would rather be alone with her new husband. "When are we cutting the cake?"

He glanced at something. "Right now." He led her over to where the cake stood on the table and took a wicked-looking short sword from his grandfather. Giff and Alice gripped the sword together and cut the cake. He gave her a small piece, and he took a larger one. Their *chef du cuisine* finished cutting the cake. "It's time to make our escape. You go first. I'll meet you in hall."

Considering everyone was in the garden, that made sense. Alice signaled to her twin and Madeline, and they slipped into the house. "I will see you tomorrow at the docks. Someone will advise you when the ship plans to sail."

They nodded and hugged her.

"Happy night," Eleanor said.

Giff joined them. "Until tomorrow."

Alice waived as they escaped through the door to the waiting coach, cleaned of ribbons, boots, and other items.

The carriage drove up to the front door of the heir's wing—*They should really think of something else to call it*—and Giff jumped out lifted her down then turned to the coachman. "I will send word when we need you tomorrow."

"Yes, my lord." The coachman drove the horses away.

"Is he our new coachman?"

"He is, and he'll have a nice vacation while we're in Scotland. He and the second coachman are meeting us in France."

The door opened, and Giff swooped Alice into his arms and carried her into the house. "Welcome home, my lady."

She hung onto his neck. "Welcome home, my lord."

Simmons bowed. "The staff would like to offer their congratulations, my lord, my lady. We have arranged some delicacies we hope you will enjoy. If you require anything at all, please tug the bell-pull."

"Thank you all." She glanced at Giff. "Onward."

They spend a quiet afternoon alternately making love, eating, and drinking. Close to seven o'clock, a knock came on the door. "My lady.

"What is it, Bertram?" Alice asked.

"We just received news that the ship will sail at five in the morning."

It was a good thing she was tired. "Please have Williams send word to Lady Madeline's and Lady Montagu's houses. They already know to meet us at the docks. And tell the coachman."

"Already done, my lady. Good night."

Alice went to the basin and washed. Giff did the same. They crawled back into bed cuddled in each other's arms.

His valet and her dresser woke them the next morning.

Betram brought tea and toast. "I was told you will be able to break your fast on the ship."

Alice brushed her teeth and washed her face. She was glad she had given herself a through washing the previous evening.

She liked the design of their apartments. A parlor was the first room one entered. That led to the bedroom, which was flanked by dressing rooms and bath chambers. It made a great deal of sense. A bright yellow carriage gown was laid out in her dressing room for the morning.

She finished her tea. "Are the trunks downstairs?"

"They are already on the ship," her dresser said. "They were taken there yesterday."

Another thing that made sense. Now to brace herself for a full ship of family.

The main part of the house was quiet when they drove away. Giff's grandfather and the rest of his family must be at the docks already. Alice hoped she and Giff were not running late. "What time is it?" Why was she asking? She had her own watch.

"We have more than enough time to arrive."

She supposed the ship would not leave without them. They saw Harry's coach just ahead of them on Piccadilly. Giff glanced back. "Montagu is behind us."

"Does Harry know which dock?"

Giff shook his head. "We'll take the lead when we get closer to the area."

A half an hour saw them to Wapping where the New London Docks were located. Harry's coach slowed and moved over to allow she and Giff to pass. The ship was much larger than she thought it would be. "What type of ship is it?"

Giff helped her from the coach. "A four-masted barque."

"Even though it's been fitted as a yacht, it also carries guns and cargo." There were a few men on ship, but she did not see any of Giff's family. "I wonder where everyone is?"

He wrapped his arms around her and nuzzled her hair. "I have no better idea than you do. Let's enjoy the quiet while we can."

Chapter Thirty-Four

A man in a pristine blue uniform approached them. "Giff, it's good to see you again. All the luggage is on board, stowed in your cabins. Your servants arrived not long ago."

They had to have left when her maid carried out her bag with the last things in it.

Giff turned to her. "My love, may I introduce Captain Ewan Dewar, a cousin."

"It is a pleasure to meet you, Captain." She held out her hand, and he bowed.

"Ewan, please, my lady. It's a pleasure." He glanced at Giff. "I will meet the rest of the passengers once we are underway."

"Yes, of course." Giff waved to her sisters and brothers-in-law. "Come along. We need to cast off."

The captain accompanied them up a long wooden board. "Thank you for sending the luggage yesterday. It was helpful."

Alice scanned the ship. "Where is everyone else?"

Captain Dewar grinned. "They are traveling back to Scotland by coach. The laird sent the vehicles down. He thought you might want some time to yourselves before you are beset by the family again." He helped her aboard then glanced at the dock. Her sisters and their husbands were waiting to board. "Who are your guests?"

"My sisters and their husbands. We are all recently wed. You can hear the whole story when you have more time."

He welcomed the others onboard and gave the command to cast off. Alice as well as her sisters and brothers-in-law waited on deck until they were near Greenwich.

Giff's stomach growled. "Ewan, is there anything to eat?"

He grinned. "I thought you'd never ask." He took them to a steep staircase. "Go right down there. Your nose should lead you to the dining room."

Alice wondered where they would sleep. "Are our rooms down here as well?"

"No, my lady. They are down the other set of stairs." He pointed to the middle of the ship.

"Thank you."

They found porridge, eggs, bacon, some sort of grilled bread, and a smoked fish."

"Mornin' to ye," a man said. "Got tea. If yer wantin' coffee, it's in Inverness."

"Tea for me, please." Alice looked at her sisters and new brothers. "Tea for everyone."

They all nodded.

"Tea it is."

The dishes were placed in holders on a sideboard with raised edges. "I suppose this is so the plates do not fall or slide around."

Madeline seemed to have a hard time keeping her eyes open. "Eat and sleep."

"That sounds like an excellent idea." Alice took a bit of everything and poured tea. She took a sip. It was excellent but different than what she was used to. She would ask what type it was later.

On the fourth day, they landed at Inverness. After spending ten days touring the area, visiting Giff's family, and learning more about their estate, they were back on-board for the passage to France and a continuation of their joint honeymoons.

Paris, France

One night the ladies retired early, and Giff and his brothers-in-law were sipping fine French brandy.

Stern twirled his glass, watching the amber liquid coat the sides of the glass. "I am sure Madeline is breeding."

Giff did not understand. "You mean she told you."

"No." Stern took a sip then shook his head. "She has not had her courses since we . . . since we were betrothed."

Montagu set his glass down. "What do you mean, her courses?"

Stern glanced at Giff, but he had no idea what his brother-in-law meant.

Stern blew out a breath. "Let me start from the beginning. All female mammals have courses. Cows, sheep, goats, cats, dogs, women."

"What are courses?" Giff asked, feeling like an idiot.

"A woman bleeds. It is a sign she is not pregnant." He took a large drink of brandy. "Now, other mammals have their courses two or possibly more, in the case of cats, times a year. Women have them every month."

Giff stared at Stern. "If they are not pregnant."

"Yes." He frowned at Giff. "How do you not know this? Didn't you have a mistress?"

"No. I couldn't afford one." Damn his father and the skimpy allowance he was on.

Montagu choked on his wine. "I never had the opportunity." He motioned with his hand. "Go on. This is becoming interesting."

"As I said, women, our wives, have their courses every month if they are not pregnant. My wife has not. It has been two months."

Montagu leaned forward. "How would we know?"

"I cannot believe neither of you are acquainted with this." Stern dragged a hand down his face. "Because she would bleed. A lot. You would notice. It lasts roughly five to seven days."

Giff shook his head. "Alice has not. We have been together almost every day since our betrothal."

"No." Montagu fell back against his chair. "Neither has Eleanor. Do you think they know?"

"They must. Or they have a good idea." Harry took another drink. "It is very possible that the ladies are waiting until they miss their courses for a second time to make sure."

"Did you have a mistress that fell pregnant?" Montagu asked.

Stern stared at the man in shock. "I did not. I know how to keep that from happening. My father told me."

Giff wished his father would have told him. It didn't matter. The important thing was that Alice was probably going to have a baby. "What do we do? Wait until they tell us?"

Stern set down his glass. "That is one way. I prefer to ask her."

Giff followed suit. "I will ask Alice as well."

"Yes." Montagu tossed off the rest of his drink. "I shall approach Eleanor."

Giff's and Stern's eyes met, and they looked at Montagu. He'd never get it done. Giff rose. "I suggest we meet with our wives at one time. I am going up to see if they are still awake."

"I'll go with you." Stern stood. "If they aren't. Breakfast tomorrow seems like a good time."

"I am coming as well." Montagu followed.

The ladies were in their nightgowns and robes in the parlor they had all rented. Their countenances appeared anything but light. Had they been discussing the same thing the gentleman had? Giff went over to Alice. She sat on a chair, and he pulled another one over. "I'm glad you're still awake."

She held out her hand to him. "I am as well."

Stern went to Madeline who appeared rather wane. "My love, is anything wrong?"

Tears filled her eyes. "Not really, but a little."

Montagu sat next to Eleanor on the sofa. Before he could ask after her health, she said, "Ginger tea will help."

Giff leaned forward to catch Alice's eye and mouthed, "What?"

"Ginger tea." Stern pulled his wife into his arms. "Are you having what is inappropriately called morning sickness?"

One tear slipped down her cheek as she nodded. "At first I did not think I was, but now I am."

He stroked her dark hair. "Why would you think you are not?"

"I bled a little last month."

Giff reached for Alice's hand and squeezed. "We told you that a little bleeding can be normal," she said. "It only lasted a day."

"So little I didn't even notice," Stern said. "My love, I think we are going to have a baby."

Alice jumped up and grabbed a large bowl, sticking it under her sister's face just as she cast up her accounts. She left the bowl to Stern and sat down.

Giff kissed and caressed her hand. "Could it be that you are with child as well, my love?"

"Yes. I am certain of it now." She smiled at him. "It never seems to take long in our family."

Eleanor gazed at Montagu. "I am as well. We all just wanted to make sure. It is still a bit risky for another month."

"Harry," Alice said. "First thing in the morning, send to the apothecary for ginger root."

"I will. Thank you."

Giff worried Alice would suffer. "Are you all right?"

"Eleanor and I are healthy as horses. Neither our mother nor any of our sisters had more than a day of morning sickness if that."

"Naturally, you will tell your family, but please ask them not to tell mine. I will send a message to my mother." His beloved stared at him as if he were mad. "My grandfather Dewar wants our first child born in Scotland. My father wants our child born in Cleveland Castle. I will not have months of fighting between them."

Alice raised an imperious brow. "I will tell you right now where we will have this baby. Whippoorwill Manor. Grace will travel to Eleanor first; that is a long day from Worthington Place. Madeline will have hers at Stern Manor, near Stanwood Place. Whippoorwill Manor is only about a five hour drive from there. I shall not have my sister traveling to either Scotland or near Scotland, and I *will* have my sister with me."

"It shall be as you wish, my love. And it is the reason neither my father nor grandfather need know about the baby until just before it's due."

"The servants?" Montagu asked Giff.

"If any one of them contact either gentleman before I give them leave, they will be dismissed."

"As much as I love it here," Madeline said. "I think I want to go home."

"I will arrange it immediately," Stern assured her.

They arrived back in London in August. Madeline and Harry traveled to Stern Manor while Eleanor and Montagu journeyed to his main estate. Giff and Alice went first to what they had decided to call St. Albans in Cleveland House to see the changes wrought while they were away.

Once they had refreshed themselves, they climbed the stairs to the nursery. Light filled the rooms from every direction. She touched her stomach. "I knew it would be beautiful."

March 1823, Whippoorwill Manor

Grace knew before the rest of them that Alice and Eleanor were having twins. Alice was thankful her sister had arrived when she did. "How are you doing?"

"I want these babies to be out of me and into the world." She rubbed her stomach. "They have been fighting over position for the past week. One goes down and comes back up then the other goes down. They cannot decide who will be first."

Her sister laughed. "Tell them that story when they are fighting over who should have been first."

"I want to walk." Grace helped Alice to her feet. "My back is hurting like it never has before."

Grace's lips formed a thin line, and she glanced at

Bertram. "Send for the midwife. It's back labor. I just went through this with Eleanor."

"Yes, my lady."

Giff came in. "I heard you were here. How is she?"

"*She* is here." Alice hated it when people talked about her as if she was deaf and dumb.

"Please forgive me." He caressed her hair and took her arm from her sister. "I'm rapidly losing my mind."

"Alice is experiencing back labor. It is not enjoyable, but it is not dangerous. I received a letter from the duchess. She will be here as soon as possible."

Alice's back suddenly vellicated. Grace looked at her. "We need to keep track of the time between contractions. Where is your watch?"

"Right here, my lady." Bertram handed it to Alice.

"Tell Cook to prepare small light food for her to eat. We do not know how long or short the time will be. She needs to remain on her feet until it's time for her to use the birthing chair."

"What birthing chair?" Poor Giff's eyes were wide with concern.

"I brought it with me. It should be in her chamber momentarily."

Alice and Giff had decided she should use her chamber instead of theirs for the birth.

She patted his arm. "I will be fine. Stroll with me."

"You are the strongest lady I know."

They were making their way down the corridor when Charlotte strode to them. "I heard it is time. We arrived none too soon."

Kenilworth came up after her. "Well, at least you're not drinking brandy in the study."

Alice wanted to chuckle but could not. "That is a story I haven't heard yet."

He took her other arm. "Allow me to assist as well. I have some knowledge of twins. They can be a bit heavy before they make an appearance."

Giff wished he could be as glib right now. "Ah, here is the first footman with something for you to taste." He picked up one of the offerings on the tray. "Cheese on toasted bread."

He held it to her lips, and she bit into it. "That is heavenly. Is there another?"

"There is." She managed to eat four of them. Giff and Kenilworth finished off the rest. "Shall we see what is around the corner?" They turned into the other corridor and a footman held a plate with apple slices and grapes from the hot house. "What shall you have, my love?"

"The grapes, please." Once again, Giff fed them to her. She stopped once, and he wished he could take the pain from her.

"Open my watch and tell me the time."

"It is one-fifteen."

"That one was only seven minutes from the last."

His brother-in-law caught his eye and motioned his head back toward their rooms. "Let us wander this way."

Giff wished he had more experience with births. Any kind of birth. They continued to walk.

The midwife came up to them. How had she arrived so soon? An appointment. Giff had forgotten. "How are you doing, my lady?"

"It was seven minutes from the last contraction to the most recent one." She stopped again, and the pain was obvious.

He opened the watch. "Five minutes."

"Not long now, my lady," the midwife said "Keep walking for a while longer while I set up."

Alice was leaning on them more heavily than before.

He was glad Kenilworth was here to help. "Another footman stood waiting. Shall we see what he has?"

The servant held tiny strawberry tarts in puff pastry. Giff gave one to Alice, and she moaned.

"Was that the babies?"

"No, the tart."

Kenilworth barked a laugh. "Good girl. Take joy where you find it."

Alice scowled at him. "That is why I am in so much pain."

"Please forgive me," he said. "But trust me when I tell you that it will be over soon."

The pain struck again, and Giff pulled out the watch. "Three minutes."

"Time to take me to my birthing room."

Alice had no sooner been seated in the strange-looking thing they called a birthing chair then she screamed. Giff took her hand, and pain radiated through his as she squeezed. "You have an excellent grip."

The midwife was on the floor. "I see the first head. Push, my lady."

His wife gathered herself and groaned.

"Once more."

This time a baby dropped out. One of the maids rushed forward to take it, and Alice groaned again.

"Almost there with the second one. Push again."

Alice panted and groaned, and their second child was born. Her head dropped back. "Did you mark the first one?"

"Yes," Grace said. "He has been marked."

"My lady," the midwife said. "Once more."

Alice groaned a third time and something, Giff wasn't sure what, came out.

"Excellent. It looks to be whole," the midwife said.

"Giff, get her up. We need to clean her," Charlotte said.

He lifted Alice in his arms, and she smiled at him. "What do we have?"

"Two apparently healthy children."

"Boys," Grace informed him. "Two boys."

"We are in for it now." He grinned at his wife.

Mamma rushed into the room and stopped. "Boys?"

Alice chuckled lightly. "Two."

He took her into the bathing chamber where her dresser and a maid waited and set her down on the stool they pointed to. Why couldn't she have a bath? He'd have to find out later.

When he walked out, Kenilworth handed him a glass of brandy. "Congratulations. This group is outnumbering ours when it comes to boys. They'll be happy about that."

"I need to see my sons."

Grace held one and his mother the other. "Which is which?"

"This is your first born," Mamma said.

"Here is your second," Grace added. "Do you have names?"

They were both bald and stared up at him. He couldn't distinguish what color, other than light, their eyes would be. "We do. After Eleanor failed to plan for all contingencies, we have names for everyone. Our first is Mathias Archibald, Earl of St. Albans. Our second son is Lord Timothy Brian Palmer."

Alice entered the bedchamber, walking much better than Giff would have if he'd just pushed out two babies. "Let me help you."

As if they knew where they were to be fed, Mathias cried. Alice got into bed and held her arms out. "Is the wet nurse here?"

Giff had no idea. "I'll find out." Then second one cried. Good God. Now what? Alice held out one arm. "Help me put him to my breast. That will do until she arrives."

Mamma took him aside. "Your father and grandfather will be here soon. I suggest you let them see the babies before speaking to them."

"It will be up to Alice. She is the one who has just given birth." He pulled up a chair next to the bed where both his sons were nursing hungrily.

Her smile blinded him. "They are beautiful."

"They are."

AUTHOR'S NOTES

I hope you enjoyed Alice and Giff's story.

Although the Regency was technically at an end when George the IV took the crown, the long Regency lasted until Victoria was crowned queen. It is true that George did not lose his taste for the extravagant and did, indeed, require all the peers to dress in Elizabethan costumes for his coronation. It's also a fact that Queen Caroline showed up to the coronation and was denied entrance. George refused to allow her to be crowned queen.

When I started researching the infamous enclosure laws, I was shocked to discover there were over two thousand of them. The reason for that is because they were private laws dealing with discrete pieces of land. They were greatly misused and ended up turning a lot of people out of their homes. This was especially true in Scotland.

If you haven't read the other books in the Worthingtons series, Charlotte and Kenilworth's book is *The Marquis and I*. Grace and Matt's is *Three Weeks to Wed*. Dotty and Merton's book is *When a Marquis Chooses a Bride*. Eleanor and Madeline's books are in the Marriage List trilogy. All my books are on my website.

As always, please feel free to contact me if you have any questions. All my social media links are on my website www.ellaquinnauthor.com. I look forward to hearing from you.

Ella